WILLIAM W. JOHNSTONE

DREAMS OF EAGLES

ZEBRA/0-8217-6086-6 (CANADA $7.50) U.S.$5.99

Before the legend, there was a man. Before the man, there was a dream...

THE MACCALLISTER METHOD
FOR DEALING WITH BULLIES

"I think I'll tear your damn head off, boy." Buford Sanders stood up; he was nearly as tall and wide as Jamie but had a huge belly. "I've killed men with my bare hands."

Jamie smiled. "So have I, you puss-gutted, loudmouthed son of a bitch."

The two men closed on each other.

Buford took a wild swing that would have taken Jamie's head off if it had connected. But Jamie had sidestepped quickly and popped the man on the mouth with a solid left and followed that with a hard right to the jaw. Sanders stood flatfooted for a moment—no one had ever hit him so hard in his entire miserable life. Jamie was pleased to see his opponent's confusion he'd hated bullies since he was a child.

Buford rushed him, trying to get Jamie in a bear hug. Suddenly, Jamie jumped into the air and kicked out, the sole of his moccasin smashing into Buford's face. The force of the kick sent the loudmouthed bully-boy to the floor, blood dripping from nose and mouth. Men had come rushing into the bar to see the fight and stood smiling as Jamie MacCallister kicked the crap out of the man who had beaten and terrorized so many of them.

Jamie battered the man with terrible punishing blows to the face and belly. Finally, he finished him off with a right-handed blow that broke bones. Buford Sanders toppled over, landing on the floor with a mighty crash. He did not move.

Jamie MacCallister had hardly worked up a decent sweat.

BOOK YOUR PLACE ON OUR WEBSITE AND MAKE THE READING CONNECTION!

We've created a customized website just for our very special readers, where you can get the inside scoop on everything that's going on with Zebra, Pinnacle and Kensington books.

When you come online, you'll have the exciting opportunity to:

- View covers of upcoming books
- Read sample chapters
- Learn about our future publishing schedule (listed by publication month *and author*)
- Find out when your favorite authors will be visiting a city near you
- Search for and order backlist books from our online catalog
- Check out author bios and background information
- Send e-mail to your favorite authors
- Meet the Kensington staff online
- Join us in weekly chats with authors, readers and other guests
- Get writing guidelines
- AND MUCH MORE!

**Visit our website at
http://www.zebrabooks.com**

WILLIAM W. JOHNSTONE

DREAMS OF EAGLES

Zebra Books
Kensington Publishing Corp.

http://www.zebrabooks.com

Somebody said that it couldn't be done.
But he with a chuckle replied
That maybe it couldn't, but he would be one
Who wouldn't say so till he'd tried.
—Edgar Albert Guest

I slept and dreamed that life was beauty.
I woke—and found that life was duty.
—Ellen Sturgis Hooper

Prologue

In the late summer of 1837, Jamie Ian MacCallister, one of only two survivors from the battle at the Alamo, his wife Kate, and a small group of friends had pushed deep into uncharted country that would someday be called Colorado. They kept on pushing until Jamie, who was scouting far ahead of the wagons, came to a long wide valley, a respectable creek running right down the middle of it; the valley nestled amid towering mountains. Jamie dismounted and jammed his hands into the earth. The earth was dark and rich. The pass he had used to enter the valley was wide and not likely to be blocked, at least for very long, by snow. The valley was lush with timber. Jamie rose, still holding the handfuls of rich earth and looked all around him. His long shoulder-length blonde hair fanned under the breath of wind. He nodded his head and put the earth into a cloth sack. Then he mounted and rode back to the wagons. He tossed the sack to the big man called the Swede.

"How about that, Swede?"

The man smelled the earth, then fingered it. He grinned. "It will grow good crops, Jamie."

Jamie rode back to his wagon, driven by Kate. "We're almost home, Kate. Just a few more miles. It's beautiful, it's lovely, and it's lonely, but I think you'll like it."

She smiled at him. "If you like it, I like it."

A few miles further on, Jamie halted the small wagon train and pointed to the long valley. "Yonder she lies, people."

The children piled out of the wagons and ran forward, the tall grass waist high on the youngest.

"Jamie, it's the most beautiful place I have ever seen!" Kate whispered.

"It's our home, Kate. We've come home at last."

Book One

One

The journey of Jamie Ian MacCallister had been a torturous one even before he met and fell in love with Kate Olmstead when they were both just children back in Kentucky.

Born in the wilderness of western Ohio, Jamie had watched his parents and baby sister killed by rampaging Shawnee. The chief had taken Jamie prisoner and kept the boy until he was twelve, when Jamie and a young white woman named Hannah had escaped the village. Jamie's early years had been brutally hard, forcing the lad to grow up very quickly. He had been adopted by Tall Bull and Deer Woman and raised a Shawnee, learning the warrior's way while most white boys his age were learning their ABCs and playing marbles and mumbly-peg and hide and seek. At thirteen, Jamie was a grown man. His childhood had been virtually nonexistent. He was tall and broad-shouldered, tremendously powerful. He was lean of hip and strong of arm, his wrists larger than most men's forearms. He did not know his own strength. His eyes were blue and his hair was blonde, worn shoulder length. His face was tanned and rugged, the jaw square and slightly dimpled. Women considered Jamie handsome. Jamie never gave a thought to it one way or the other.

Jamie and Kate fell in love the moment their eyes

touched. From that instant forward there would be no other woman for Jamie and no other man for Kate.

After Jamie's escape from the Shawnee town, a young childless couple, Sam and Sarah Montgomery, took Jamie in to raise as their own. But again, a chance for some vestiges of adolescence were denied Jamie, for there were those in the Kentucky village who considered Jamie more savage than civilized. Kate's father, Hart Olmstead, forbade his daughter to see Jamie and beat her savagely whenever he learned of their clandestine meetings.

At fourteen, Jamie was forced into a killing and had to flee into the wilderness, branded an outlaw and brigand. Shortly after that, Jamie returned to the Kentucky village for Kate and together they rode westward to start a new life. They were married in the town of New Madrid, Missouri, and pushed on. They settled in the wilds of east Texas, in an area known as the Big Thicket, and immediately started a family. And what a family it was! Before Jamie became involved in the Texas drive for independence from Mexico, he had fathered eight children, for twins and triplets ran strong on both sides of the family tree.

Moses Washington, an ex-slave who, with his wife, Liza, had escaped from slavery in Virginia and settled in the Big Thicket before Jamie and Kate arrived, summed it up this way: "Good God, boy! Are You and Kate tryin' to populate east Texas all by yourselves? Am I gonna have to put a bundlin' board between you two? Slow down!"

The Alamo slowed them down.

Sam and Sarah Montgomery and Swede and Hannah showed up in the Big Thicket country a couple of years before Jamie left to fight at the Alamo, and a small community was carved out of the wilderness.

Then Jamie was called to fight. Jamie Ian MacCallister was the last man to leave the Alamo, ordered out at the last possible moment by Colonels Travis and Bowie with a pouch of messages from the gallant defenders of that old church. He was ambushed along the way, first by Tall Bull, who had been looking for Man Who Is Not Afraid, Jamie's Shawnee name, and then shot out of the saddle by a Mexican patrol. He was left for dead in a ditch beside a rutted road. The last farewells from that proud garrison, that bastion of Texas freedom, lost for all time. He was found and taken in by a Mexican family.

When he finally recovered from his near-fatal wounds, Jamie felt the vastness of the west silently calling him. His grandfather was out there somewhere in the shining mountains, a mountain man. Jamie asked Kate if she would like to move west.

"I go where you go, love," she replied.

Moses and Liza and their children, Sam and Sarah Montgomery, Swede and Hannah and their children, and Juan and Maria Nuñez and their children packed up and headed west with Jamie and Kate and their children. They would be settling a wild and often savage land, untamed, uncharted, free, and open. Soaring on the wings of eagles. Dreaming the eagles' dreams.

Two

The settlers had it all worked out. Sam was going to raise horses, Swede and Moses would be the farmers, Juan had brought sheep, and Jamie would hunt and trap and explore and in his spare time, look for gold.

"There is no gold west of the Mississippi, Jamie," Sam said. "Everybody says that."

But Jamie would only smile at that and reply, "Whatever you say, Sam." Preacher had told him there was gold. But the few mountain men who knew of it were keeping it to themselves. They didn't want a whole bunch of people to come a-traipsin' in and messin' up everything.

The additional men Jamie had hired in San Antonio left to return to civilization. Now the little group felt they were truly alone in the vastness of the high country.

But not for long, for there were cabins to build and horses and cows and sheep to look after and the men must hunt to provide food for the long winter ahead of them. There was meat to jerk and smoke, and Jamie and Hannah had taught them all how to make pemmican, a mixture of melted fat and ground and dried wild berries.

And Hannah was heavy with child. The women said she would birth in a few days. So the cabin of Swede and Hannah would be the first one up. With all the men working, that did not take long, then it was on to the other cabins. The men had wanted to build them behind log walls, like a fort, but both Jamie and Hannah had said no to that.

"The Indians know we're here," Jamie told the group. "One tribe or the other has tracked us the entire way. We're building right in the middle of Ute and Arapaho country. The Cheyenne are around us as well. We must not show any signs that we are unfriendly or hostile to the Indians. We can live together, but it's going to take some time to build trust. Many of these Indians have never seen a white woman before. Probably most have not. They'll be curious about you. Don't show fear when they do make an appearance. An Indian despises fear more than anything. Stand up to them without being belligerent about it. They'll demand a lot more than they truly expect to get. This winter will be important, for then when we hunt we can share what we hunt with them. Tomorrow I'm going to find a village and talk with them. I'll be gone for several days, maybe a week. Maintain a sharp lookout and don't stray far from the settlement. And keep a good eye on the kids."

Jamie was aware he was being followed after only a few miles from the settlement in the valley. A mile further, he crested a hill and suddenly wheeled his big horse, facing to the rear. He lifted his index finger and made the sign that he was alone. Then he placed both fists together, the fingertips of his right hand touching the center knuckles of his left hand, signaling that he wanted to council, or talk.

The Utes came out of the timber in a rush, galloping their horses toward him. There were six of them. Two carried old rifles, three had bows and arrows, and the sixth, the leader of the group, carried a huge lance. The leader touched the sharp point of the lance against Jamie's chest. Jamie did not flinch, just stared into the unreadable eyes.

"Is this the way you treat someone who comes in peace?" Jamie asked.

The leader grunted and slowly pulled the lance back, lowering it. "I talk your talk some good," he said. "Whites talk peace and mean war. How you different?"

"How are you called?"

"Black Thunder."

Jamie hid his surprise, for Black Thunder was a great war chief of the Utes. "I have heard much of Black Thunder. It is said that he is a fair man and a brave man. The same is said of me. I am called Man Who Is Not Afraid."

Black Thunder did not conceal his surprise. When he spoke, his tone was somewhat more respectful. "Also called Man Who Plays With Wolves and Panthers."

"That is true."

"See scar."

Jamie opened his buckskin shirt and the Indians all crowded forward, peering closely at the long scar on his chest.

Black Thunder grunted and pointed to a brave who was about five feet two inches tall but very powerfully built. "Small Man have no-good brother who was with foolish Shawnee when they attack you in spring. Small Man's stupid brother said you are much brave and mighty warrior. But Small Man's brother lie a lot, too. Not know when to believe. I believe him now. He said that Little Wolf was wrong to attack you. I guess so. You here, Little Wolf dead. You settle here for live?"

"We do. And we will cause no trouble. We will be a

friend to all who are friends with us. Come the cold winds and the snows, we will share what we have. That is a promise and I do not give promises lightly."

"Not take promise lightly. All those children with white hair and eyes of color of skies, they yours?"

"Yes."

"All of them?"

"Yes."

"How many wives you have in your wooden lodge?"

"Just one."

Black Thunder shook his head solemnly. "She must be tired. You come visit us someday. You will be welcome. We go now. You go in peace." They wheeled their horses and were gone.

Jamie did not hear Black Thunder mutter, "Man Who Is Not Afraid start own tribe."

Jamie quickly cast a sobering pall over the jubilation of those back at the settlement. "Black Thunder will keep his word—probably. But he is the war chief of only one band of Utes. Not the entire nation. And Indians often raid in another tribe's territory. There are a half-dozen tribes who hunt and raid in this area. You must never let your guard down, never go unarmed. Know where the kids are at all times. Horses will be the main attraction, for we have some of the finest stock west of the Mississippi. We've got to build a fine corral and not some rawhide affair."

Jamie didn't say it, but of them all, Juan Nuñez and his sons would be in the most danger from rampaging Indians. For although his flock of sheep was small, it would not remain that way for long. And grazing sheep had to be kept on the move in order to preserve range. That meant that Juan would, most of the time, be several miles from the cabins tending his sheep. Alone and vulnerable.

But fate dealt the pioneers a good hand that first fall and winter in the long valley in the high country. They saw no Indians and were trouble-free. The winter was bitterly cold and long, but the settlers were snug in their cabins. And much to the disgust of the children, there was plenty of time for schooling. For that was something that Jamie insisted upon.

The livestock survived the harsh winter, and come the spring, it was not just the stock who gave birth when the warm winds began to blow. Sarah Montgomery's cycle of barrenness was broken with the birth of twins. Maria Nuñez gave birth. Hannah had delivered a boy early the past fall. And for once, Kate did not birth. And Jamie took a lot of good-natured kidding about that.

It was 1838.

Back in the States, the Iowa Territory, consisting of what would someday be the states of Iowa, Minnesota, and most of North and South Dakota, was formed. The territorial capital was placed at Burlington. It would later be changed to Iowa City.

Joseph Smith and his followers fled Ohio and settled, for a time, in the Missouri frontier.

Samuel Parker had published a book called *Journal of an Exploring Tour Beyond the Rocky Mountains*. In it, he wrote about the west, the Indians, the animals, the mountain men, and the trails and rivers. Many people didn't believe it although the book would later be considered very accurate.

The U.S. government had ordered the Army, under the command of General Winfield Scott, to begin rounding up many Indians who lived east of the Mississippi River and start herding them westward. The journey, from Georgia through Kentucky, Illinois, and Missouri to Oklahoma, would be on foot, without adequate food and clothing. Thousands would die and the infamous trek would be called The Trail Of Tears.

But those in the long and lovely and secluded valley in the Rocky Mountains knew none of this. They had not seen a white man in months, had not read a newspaper nor heard any gossip from the outside world.

Moses and Swede had a bumper crop of vegetables, and the women stayed busy storing what they could. True to his word, Jamie took sacks and sacks of vegetables to Black Thunder's band and was received cordially, the Indians trading venison, buffalo meat, skins, and pelts for the gifts of vegetables.

"How your woman?" Black Thunder inquired.

"She's fine," Jamie told him.

"No more children?"

"Not this year. So far."

"Good. I tell my woman, Shining Bright, about your many family. Bad mistake. She not let me near her for long time. No talk about your family to my woman. You through fathering children?"

"One more," Jamie said with a smile. "Next year, maybe."

Black Thunder grunted and walked off, shaking his

head and muttering under his breath. "Stay away from Shining Bright, Ja-mie," he called over his shoulder. "Not want to go through that again."

"Mac?" the question came at a gathering of mountain men.

"Aye," a man said, turning his head and looking at the man who'd called his name. The mountain man stood up. He was well over six feet, his silver hair hanging down to his shoulders. His eyes were a startling blue. He was an old man, but he stood erect, tall, and proud, a man who would bow to no one. He was all wang-leather and muscle and gristle. Even at his advanced age, not a man to take lightly.

"I think you got kin down near the Arkansas, Mac. You recall that long wide valley where that crick cuts off from the Arkansas and runs all the way through it?"

"I do."

"I was jawin' with Preacher some months back. He told me 'bout a MacCallister he helped out down in Texas some years back. Big tall lad with yeller hair and blue eyes and a little bitty button of a girl with yeller hair and blue eyes. They come from Kentucky, on the run. Preacher was gonna tell you hisself but he never could catch up with you. I was talkin' to Black Hand 'bout a month back, and he says a whole passel of white folks done moved into that valley. One of them be a lad named Jamie Ian MacCallister. I heared you say one time that was yore Christian name."

"Aye. For a fact, it is." The old man smiled. "I'll be sayin' my farewells to you good lads and takin' to the wind. That there's my grandson, sure as I'm standin' here.

I'll be seein' you boys. Keep your powder dry and your arses covered." The elder Jamie Ian MacCallister packed up his kit, saddled his horse, and rode out of the camp, a smile on his lips. "I got me a grizzly bear for a grandson," he muttered proudly. "Takes after me, I reckon."

Three

Mac prowled the high country around the valley, watching the comings and goings of those in the tiny settlement below. The Utes knew he was there but left Silver Wolf alone, for the old man was a legend in the mountains. Practically every tribe of any consequence west of the Mississippi had fought with Silver Wolf at one time or another, and at no time had they been victorious. The Indians finally made peace with the man and let him wander, for he was not a man who started trouble . . . just finished it.

And the Utes who watched the old man were amused, for as good as Silver Wolf was, his grandson was better. Man Who Is Not Afraid was silently tracking Silver Wolf, and the old man was not aware of it. The conclusion to this game came one morning.

The elder MacCallister awakened with a start. Moving only his eyes, he carefully looked all around him. He knew something was wrong but could not figure out what it was. Then he smelled fresh coffee brewing and meat cooking. His senses working hard, he realized that someone, or some*thing,* was behind him, out of his field of vision.

"You going to lay warm abed all day, Grandpa, or get

up and join the land of the living?" the question came from behind Silver Wolf.

Chuckling, the old man threw off his blankets and stretched. Without turning around, he asked, "How long have you known I was here, boy?"

"From the very first day."

"Them Shawnee they done you right, boy." He turned around and stared for a moment at a young mountain squatting behind him. Great God but his grandson was one hell of a man. "Your pa, did he die well?"

"I suppose. I was in the house with Ma when the Shawnee struck. It was the day before my seventh birthday."

"Five year with the Injuns, hey, lad?"

"Yes." Jamie stood up and poured them both coffee. Then he speared pieces of meat from the pan with a stick and handed the food to his grandfather. "Don't feel bad about my slipping up on you, Grandpa. I've slipped up on just about every woods animal you could name."

"You the spittin' image of my pa, Jamie. You know you come from a long line of warriors?"

"No, sir. Pa never talked about that."

"Well, you do. MacCallisters' a been fightin' and dyin' for some damn fool cause for a thousand years. I hear tell you 'bout lost it all in some old church."

"I came close. A lot of good men died there, Grandpa."

The old man called Silver Wolf grunted and slurped at his coffee. "I just told you, MacCallisters have been fightin' other folks' wars for years. Not me. I fight my own wars. After your grandma died—you never knowed her—I went west. Only been back east a couple of times since then. Sell my pelts through an agent. Young Preacher says this country is gonna fill up with settlers. That'll be a sad day."

"Preacher helped us on the trail. I'd like to see him. Where is he?"

The old man laughed. "Boy, I doubt the Good Lord Hisself knows the answer to that one. Preacher is like the wind a-blowin." He looked at Jamie. "All them yeller-haired kids yours, Jamie?"

"No." The old man looked startled. Jamie laughed and added, "Kate had something to do with it."

The group gathered on the common ground in front of their cabins and watched as Jamie and his grandfather rode in. The family resemblance was startling. "Come and meet your great-grandfather kids!" Jamie called. "He's come to pay us a visit."

"My word!" Swede muttered, gazing at the tall, fierce-looking old man. He noticed that the old man dismounted with a spryness that belied his age, a rifle in hand.

"That, señor," Juan whispered, "is a man not to be taken lightly."

"I concur," Sam Montgomery returned the whisper. "Jamie comes by it honestly, doesn't he?"

"Hush up and come on," Sarah said, tugging at his sleeve.

The kids, all of them, were, naturally, in awe of the wild-looking man with the mane of shoulder-length silver hair. But Ian, as he told Jamie he preferred to be called, smiled and that broke the ice, for the smile changed his whole appearance.

Within minutes, Ian was rough-housing with the boys and tickling the ribs of the girls.

"Don't play so rough, boys!" Kate called. "You'll hurt your great-grandfather."

Jamie laughed at that and Ian roared like a grizzly. "Hurt *him?*" Jamie asked of Kate. "That old man is as hard as an oak tree. I'll tell you what, Kate. I wouldn't want to fight him."

Kate looked at her husband to see if he was really serious. He was.

The kids had been put to bed and were asleep. The men and the women sat in the dogtrot of Jamie and Kate's cabin and talked into the pleasant night.

"It's a fine and fair place you have here, laddie," Ian said to Jamie, after lighting his pipe. He was never quite able to get the burr out of his words. "A fine family and good friends. There is no more a man could ask for." He looked at Moses and Liza. "You two ran from slavery, you say?"

"Yes, sir," Moses replied. "Back in Virginia."

"I dinna hold with slavery. It's wrong. No man should be held in chains and beaten like some poor draft animal or be indentured to another man."

"I agree," Moses said with a smile.

"I 'spect you do," Ian returned the smile. He looked at Sam and Sarah. "You two, now, that's another story. I know quality when I see it, and it's written all over the both of you."

"We like adventure," Sam said quickly.

Ian chuckled. "Do you, now? Well, you'll find out here that names don't matter for much." He smiled in the darkness. "Or what a man leaves behind him back in civilization."

Sam arched an eyebrow at that but said nothing. Both Sam and Sarah were from rather well-to-do families back east. But Sam had a little trouble with a loudmouth and killed the man. Shortly after that, he and Sarah moved to Kentucky where they took Jamie in and then followed him westward a few years later. For the time, Sam and Sarah were moderately wealthy people and could be living in a grand house in St. Louis or New Orleans. But Sam had been speaking the truth when he said both he and Sarah liked adventure, for they did.

Ian cut his eyes to Hannah. "And you'd be the lady who escaped from the Shawnee village with Jamie."

"That's right. Had it not been for Jamie's cunning and skill, I think I would have killed myself rather than spend my life married to Big Head."

Ian nodded. "And you, shepherd," he said to Juan. "Why did you come along to the Big Lonesome?"

Juan lifted his hands in the gesture that only the Latins can do so well and so meaningfully. "Because these are my friends, señor."

Ian grunted. Pretty good answer, he thought. He looked at Moses and Liza's girl, Sally, who was married to Robert. They had taken in Robert's half brother and sister, twins, who had been fathered by a white plantation owner and were as white-appearing as any there. The white-looking twins were born to trouble, Ian thought. He was as sure of that as he was that a wheel is made to roll. The girl, budding into womanhood quickly, was going to be a beautiful woman, albeit a sneaky one. Ian wasn't sure about the boy, but he was going to be a handsome man, that much was for sure. With not a trace of negroid features in either of them. But it damn sure might show up in their kids.

His grandson had done well, Ian concluded. He liked everyone here at the settlement. If he could be sure every man and woman who had an urge to come settle the west were of the quality of these folks, Ian would volunteer to guide the wagons.

Might as well wish he could soar on the wings of eagles, the old man thought sourly.

When the settlers awakened the next morning, the old man was gone.

"He might be back tomorrow, next month, next year, or never," Jamie told them, unconcerned about his grandfather's sudden leave-taking. "He's seen that we're all right, everybody is well and happy, and there is nothing he could do. So he left."

Kate and Hannah understood; the rest were dumbfounded. But they'd get over it, Jamie reckoned.

In the fall of that year, Kate told Jamie she was pregnant. "Nine to live," she said. "That's what we agreed upon."

The baby was born during the hard winter of early '39 and was named Falcon. Neither Jamie nor Kate ever spoke of Baby Karen, killed by bounty hunters at the age of five months and buried in the tiny cemetery in the Big Thicket country of east Texas, but they each thought of her. She would have been ten this year.

Jamie Ian and Ellen Kathleen turned twelve that year. Andrew and Rosanna were eleven. Matthew, Megan, and Morgan were seven. Joleen was five. The family was complete.

"Is it over now, Jamie?" a thoroughly exasperated Moses asked him after the birth of Falcon.

Jamie laughed and patted the older man on one muscular arm. "It's over, Moses. We planned for nine and we now have nine living."

"Own tribe," Black Thunder muttered when he heard

the news. He did not tell Shining Bright about the new baby.

During the summer of '39, a few wagons began rolling out of the east, heading toward California. Their route would take them either north or south of the long peaceful valley in the mountains. But their coming would touch Jamie and the others, for it signaled the beginning of the end for one group of people and the start of a new way of life for the other.

The elder MacCallister rode up late one afternoon during the waning days of summer in the high country. The nights were beginning to turn cooler and fall was just around the corner. Silver Wolf swung down and began talking as if he had been gone for only hours instead of months.

"First little wagon train made it through," he said, accepting a cup of coffee from Kate. He eyeballed the new baby and shook his head at Jamie.

"What about the wagon train?" Jamie said, ignoring his grandfather's comments.

"Preacher led it through, or at least part of the way. And it's got the Indians so riled up they're talkin' war. Especially the Arapaho. There's blood on the moon, boy." He looked down at the baby asleep in the cradle. "What's the lad's name?"

"Falcon."

"Good, strong family name. My great-grandfather was named Falcon. He was a Highlander. Some called him a mystic. I dinna know about that, but he was a warrior supreme."

"What about the Indians?" Sam asked, walking over from his cabin.

The elder MacCallister waited until the entire settlement

had gathered around—which now numbered thirty people, including the babies—then told them about the wagon train. "They opened the gate, people. Now they'll be no stoppin' the pioneers, as some has taken to callin' the fools."

"Why do you call them fools, Grandpa," Kate asked. "Were we fools?"

" 'Cause that's what they are. Not like you folks. You all lived in the wilderness; many of you born in the wilds. You understand it. You know not to fight it but to live with it. These folks are townpeople. They think this is a grand adventure. They never learned that a wagon train was wiped out last year—wiped out to the last person. I didn't even know it myself until a Pawnee told me a few months back. From the glint in his eyes, I'd say he had a part in it, too. Wait a minute. I got something for you people." He went to his pack horse and retrieved a small bundle. "Newspapers," he said, dropping the bundle on the ground. "I got them down at Bent's Fort. Newspapers from all over. Course they's months old. But it's still readin.' "

The news-hungry men and women began mentally devouring the papers while Ian saw to his horses.

"Missouri has a university," Sarah said. "Amazing."

"People have begun settling on the west coast," Hannah said. "Someplace called the Willamette Valley in Oregon Territory. Wherever that is."

"The Trail of Tears," Sam Montgomery said softly. "Jamie, nearly four thousand Indians died while being relocated to Indian Territory just north of Texas."

"What tribes?" Jamie asked.

"Cherokee, Choctaw, Creek, and Seminole."

"The population of the United States is sixteen million people," Swede read. "That's incredible."

"Sixteen million and thirty," Jamie said with a smile. "They missed us."

"How could they count the Indians, Pa?" Jamie Ian asked.

"They didn't, son. And probably didn't count the negroes either."

"That don't hardly seem fair," the boy replied.

"Doesn't," his mother corrected.

"That, too," Jamie Ian said with a grin and easily ducked the open-handed swat Kate swung at him for sassing her. But he settled down immediately after his father cut his eyes to him, for when Jamie laid a branch across one's rear-end, it was an affair to remember.

Jamie did not believe in much physical punishment, usually leaving all that to the gentler hand of Kate. But when he did order one of his kids to go cut a branch, that punishable act was never committed again.

This was a time when discipline was necessary for life itself, for the wilderness was fraught with danger. There were grizzly bear and puma and rattlesnakes all about. Even Indians, usually friendly, had been known to steal children. And for the very young, it was easy to get lost.

The elder MacCallister returned and sat down. "Army wants to talk to you, Jamie," he said quietly.

"What about?" Jamie asked.

"Somebody named Fremont is plannin' some sort of explorin' trip, way I hear it. To find the best way to git to Oregon. Gonna leave St. Louis in about a year. He wants to meet you and see if you'd like to go along."

"I wouldn't," Jamie said shortly.

"That ain't all. They's talk of invadin' Mexico. You gonna be asked to take part in that, too."

"I'm not interested," Jamie replied, just as shortly as was his reply to the first notion. "Why me, Grandpa? I've only been about fifty or so miles west of where we are. I don't know the country west of here. Why not you or Preacher or Kit Carson or some other mountain man?"

The old man looked at his grandson. How to tell the boy that Jamie Ian MacCallister was a living legend and he was not yet thirty years old. Silver Wolf said, "How come you taught your kids not to be afraid of wolves, boy?"

"Because there is no reason to be afraid of a wolf. Stop changing the subject, Grandpa."

"Wolves are dangerous," the old man said with a smile.

"That's bunk and balderdash and you know it. I have never heard nor seen of any healthy, full grown wolf attacking a human being without some provocation."

The old man chuckled.

"You give a wolf just half a chance, and they'll run from a person."

"Hee, hee, hee!" Jamie's grandfather giggled, covering his mouth with one huge gnarled hand. "You do get a mite riled up about wolves, don't you, lad? How about a panther?"

"I've never had any trouble with them. But they're not very smart. Not near as smart as wolves. I faced a big cat down in the Thicket one time."

"You got lucky, boy. You faced a swamp cat down. The panthers you find out here, pumas, painters, catamounts, we call 'em, is a whole different story. Some of them get huge, boy. And they're dangerous because they are so notional. I faced one down one day on a ledge. Then about a year later damned if the same big cat didn't haul off and jump me for no damn reason that I can think of. I know it was the same one 'cause of the long scar on its snout. That was a fight, for sure it was. We had us a time, we did, bitin' and scratchin' and snarlin' and me with an empty rifle."

"What happened, Grandpa?" Kate asked, eyes shining.

"Why, Kate," the old man said, his face solemn. "That cat killed me!"

Four

As he had done before, the elder MacCallister was gone when the settlers awakened the next morning. Only Jamie had been up early enough to see the old man leave.

"How old is he, Jamie?" Sam asked, standing out in the coolness of early morning, a mug of coffee in his hand.

"I don't know. In his seventies, at least. Perhaps older. But Indians from Arkansas westward know him, or know of him." Jamie looked at his own mug of coffee. "Sam? We're going to have to head down to Bent's Fort for supplies. And we've got to do it before the snow flies."

"When do you want to leave?"

"Today."

That came as absolutely no surprise to Sam, for when Jamie made up his mind to do something, he did it. Right then. "All right, Jamie. The women have prepared a list of articles they need. When do we leave?"

Jamie smiled. "We?"

"That's right. I'm driving one of the wagons."

"We're not taking the wagons. It would slow us down too much. We'll use the mules to pack them back."

"When do we leave?"

"In about an hour."

After living with Jamie much of her childhood and all

of her adult life, nothing surprised Kate. She had known for some time that Jamie was going to the fort for supplies, for she had learned to read him like a good book. "I want you to order some books for our school," she told him. "We can pick them up next spring. Sarah says to get any of McGuffey's primers and readers."

"Who's McGuffey?"

"I have no idea. But Sarah says his textbooks are very innovative."

"Whatever the hell that means," Jamie muttered.

If the mules had wings and could fly, the journey would be about one hundred and seventy five miles. But in the wilderness, one seldom could travel in a straight line for very long. Jamie knew they'd be very lucky to be back in a month. His grandpa had warned him that the Indians were angry about the number of whites moving into their territory and to take caution when traveling.

Bent's Fort was at the crossroads for a number of tribes: Cheyenne, Arapaho, Comanche, Kiowa, Utes, and others. Jamie did not particularly worry about the Arapaho and the Cheyenne and the Utes, for he had traded with them and stayed in their lodges many times. The Comanche and Kiowa were quite another story. They were extremely warlike and disliked the whites with something that was close to wild unreasonable hatred. In the coming years, the settlers in Texas would rapidly grow weary of the savagery and blood lust of those two tribes and just about wipe out the Comanche and Kiowa. What remained would be herded up into Oklahoma Territory and put on reservations. But for now, the two nations were strong in numbers and many were determined to kill any white they saw . . .

although there was seldom any trouble in or close to
Bent's Fort.

Jamie fashioned a rifle boot for each mule's pack and
made certain the weapons were loaded. He wanted the two
of them to have as much fire-power as possible in case
of attack, and he felt there would be trouble, coming or
going or both.

The two men kissed their wives and kids, shook hands
with friends, and were gone within the hour. Five miles
later, it seemed the settlement was no closer than the
moon, for the men became mere specks in the vastness
of the wilderness. They made camp early and chose it
carefully, for mules were great prizes among the Indians.

"Could be any Indians who spot us will know that
we're heading for supplies and will wait until we return
before they strike," Sam said.

"Maybe. Unless they're Comanche or Kiowa. They'll
attack us simply because they hate us."

"With any good reason, Jamie?"

"Oh, sure. We're coming in and taking land they claim
is theirs. The mood among many whites is that the only
good Indian is a dead one. You saw what the various tribes
did when they went on the warpath back east, Sam."

Sam nodded his head in agreement and turned the venison in the frying pan. "It wasn't a pretty sight."

"It's worse than that out here. You heard the stories
Grandpa told."

"You believe them, Jamie?"

"Yes. Every word."

"Will the two cultures ever be able to live side by side,
you think?"

"Not in our lifetime. Not until the whites so thoroughly
defeat the Indians they break the backs of the tribes. It's

going to be a bloody next thirty or forty years, Sam. Our kids will be fighting the Indians long after we're gone, I'm thinking."

"What a depressing thought."

"Keep talking to me, Sam, and don't look around. We've got company."

"Indians?"

"Yes. They're creeping up on us. I think they might be Kiowa who want the fight over before dark. Grandpa said the Kiowa don't like to fight at night."

Jamie had chosen a good defensive position. The horses and mules were behind them and the Indians, tucked away in a cul de sac created by centuries of the creek over-flowing its banks. They had plenty of water but only slight graze.

Sam quickly cut his eyes. "I see them. Can you tell the tribe?"

"I'm sure they're Kiowa now that I've gotten a good look at them. They've painted their legs black and are wearing red shirts; that means we're in for a hell of a fight. They're the elite of the Kiowa warriors. So I'm told."

After pulling all their loaded weapons close to them, Sam looked up at the sky. "Plenty of daylight left."

Jamie watched a blur of black and red race from rock to rock. The Kiowa carried a lance and on the lance were scalps. Several scalps. One was light brown, the other from a blonde woman. "They're on the warpath, Sam. And damn sure of themselves, too. That's going to work against them. They're over-confident. When you see a tar-get, shoot."

Sam's reply was to jerk his rifle to his shoulder and fire. The muzzle spat fire and smoke and the ball flew true. A Kiowa jumped to his moccasins and then fell forward, his chest bloody.

They came in a rush, screaming war cries. Jamie fired, saw one go down, jerked up another rifle, and put one more Kiowa on the rocky earth. Sam's rifle roared and a fourth Kiowa went down. The others went to the ground and scrambled away. Four warriors down in a heartbeat was not good. Something was wrong with their medicine.

Jamie quickly reloaded and stole a glance at Sam. The man's face was pale under the tan, but his hands were steady. "They'll have to think about this now, Sam. They might camp just out of range and pray and sing and play flutes. And they'll play those damn things all night long. When they stop playing, they're coming at us. But no white man ever knows for sure what an Indian is going to do."

Sam smiled and asked, "How do you know all that about the Kiowa, Jamie?"

"By listening to others talk. I owe a lot to Preacher, that time he traveled with us for weeks. Even young as he was, he was very knowledgeable about the west. And Black Thunder is also a good talker, and I'm a real good listener." Jamie grunted as he caught a glimpse of red slipping toward them. "So much for my wonderful observations concerning Indians, Sam. Here they come again."

Sam cocked his rifle.

"I am Man Who Is Not Afraid!" Jamie suddenly shouted, startling the hell out of Sam Montgomery, who just about fired his rifle at the unexpected shout in a strange tongue. "I am a friend to all. Why do you make war against me?"

The Kiowa stopped their forward movement and fell to the ground.

"I am Little Otter!" the shout came to the two white men. "I do not care who you are. You will die."

"No, Little Otter," Jamie called. "It is you who will die. I have faced ten times your number. Alone. And I have emerged victorious. I have left the bodies of my enemies cold on the ground for hundreds of miles behind me. You know I speak the truth. I am friends with Black Thunder. You do not want Black Thunder for an enemy, Little Otter. Think about that."

"I am not afraid of Black Thunder!"

"I didn't say you were. Just that he would make a very bad enemy. And you are very deep in his territory."

Sam smiled as Jamie continued putting doubt into the minds of the Kiowa; at least he thought that's what Jamie was doing. Since he didn't speak a word of any Indian tongue, he could only guess. But it seemed a good guess.

Little Otter's blood lust was running high, and he was in no mood to listen to words of caution. But the Black Legs with him had also heard Jamie's words, and they all had heard of the great warrior Man Who Is Not Afraid, also known as Man Who Plays With Wolves and Panthers. Some of them exchanged glances in the late afternoon sun. Their eyes seemed to be saying: Man Who Is Not Afraid speaks the truth.

The Kiowa had also been careless in attacking the camp; they had not thoroughly checked it out. It was a good camp and would be very hard for them to overwhelm the two defenders. These were not cowardly thoughts. Just prudent ones.

"Take your dead and wounded and ride away!" Jamie called. "They died bravely and were fine warriors. I will talk of their bravery for years to come."

Most of the Kiowa Black Legs nodded their heads in

agreement with that. Man Who Is Not Afraid was a true warrior. He was paying them all respect.

But Little Otter's hate for the white man ran deep. And it was not unjustified, for his father and brother had been ambushed and killed by renegade white men. They had been scalped and their bodies mutilated. Little Otter hated all white men. He shouted insults at Jamie's words.

"I can't convince Little Otter," Jamie whispered to Sam. "I think most of the others would rather pull out. But Little Otter is not going to give that order."

"So where does that leave us?"

"We're all right. We couldn't have chosen a better spot to defend. They don't have enough men to storm this position. If we can kill two or three more of this band, the others will leave with or without Little Otter. Taking heavy losses is not acceptable to the Indian."

"It isn't acceptable to me, either," Sam said, his humor desert dry.

Jamie smiled. Sam was a good man to have when trouble called.

"What is he saying, Jamie?"

Jamie chuckled. "A lot of things that I'm glad you can't understand." He shouted something back to Little Otter and the leader of the band of Kiowa screamed his outrage at the words.

"What'd you say, Jamie?"

"Let's just say I questioned his manhood. That's the best I can do. It loses something in the translation."

Little Otter gradually began losing his warrior's way as Jamie continued to heap insult after insult on the sub-chief's head. The Kiowa with him saw this and were saddened, for it meant that Little Otter had failed as a Black Leg. The Kiowa sensed that Man Who Is Not Afraid was going to kill Little Otter, for the sub-chief was so angry he was trembling with rage. That was not good.

"We go," a Black Leg said to Little Otter.

"No." Little Otter knew his leadership days were over. He would be kicked out of the Black Legs Society.

"Our medicine is bad," another said. "We are too far away from our lodges and we are too few in number. Man Who Is Not Afraid has offered us our dead. Besides, if Black Thunder finds us, we will have no chance of staying alive. We must go."

"You are all cowards!" Little Otter spat the words at the Black Legs.

"And you are a fool!" Little Otter was told. "Man Who Is Not Afraid?"

"I'm right here," Jamie called.

"I cannot speak for Little Otter. But I say this for the rest of us: we will collect our dead and leave."

"I will not fire on you."

The Kiowa laid their weapons on the ground and quickly gathered up three dead and one badly wounded warrior. "We go now, Man Who Is Not Afraid."

"Have a safe journey back to your lodges. Go in peace."

"Thank you."

The Kiowa rode out. All but one.

"Now what?" Sam asked, when the sounds of the hooves had faded away.

"Little Otter can't return to his village. I've humiliated him in the eyes of his men. He's through as a leader. The only way he can in part redeem himself is to kill me."

"That's not acceptable either," Sam said quickly.

"He won't kill me, Sam. I was trained by the best knife

fighter in the entire Shawnee nation. Ride out, Little Otter!" Jamie called. "I give you your life."

Little Otter very bluntly told Jamie what he could do with that suggestion.

"I think I understood that," Sam said.

"Yeah, that's plain enough in any language."

Jamie and Little Otter exchanged insults for several minutes, with Jamie clearly the winner in the verbal war. Little Otter was so angry he was not making any sense toward the end. He threw his old rifle out in the clearing.

"What the hell?" Sam said.

"It's time." Jamie tossed his rifle out and stood up, pulling his Bowie knife from leather. He stepped out into the clearing. Little Otter leaped out from behind cover and the two men faced each other.

"Now you die!" Little Otter screamed at him.

"I don't think so," Jamie said calmly.

The two men closed.

Five

Little Otter threw himself at Jamie and that move almost ended the fight for one of the combatants before it even began. Just as Jamie braced for a cut and slash, the heel of his moccasin slipped in the dirt and threw him off balance. With a premature cry of victory, Little Otter lunged forward and the steel of their knives clanged in the late afternoon air. Jamie backheeled Little Otter, and the Kiowa stumbled, giving Jamie time to recover and get set.

Little Otter recovered, and some of his fury seemed to leave him. He realized he was in a fight to the death with a warrior who was known to every tribe in the west and whose prowess was highly respected.

Jamie faked a thrust and Little Otter ignored it. The Kiowa swung a vicious slash and Jamie moved a few inches to one side, the blade flashing harmlessly in the rays of the sun.

Jamie suddenly screamed like an angry panther and startled Little Otter. He lost his concentration and dropped his guard. Jamie quickly stepped in and cut the Kiowa on the chest, the big blade whipping up from side to shoulder. The wound was not a serious one, but Jamie had drawn first blood and it was a painful cut.

Little Otter became wary now, backing up a few feet

as the blood from the chest wound dripped to the churned-up earth. His eyes still burned with hate and pain, but caution had now tempered the fury. He shook his head to shake the sudden sweat away and the two men circled.

Sam stood and silently watched. Little Otter knew that even if he won this fight, the other white man would shoot him dead. He didn't care. He feinted with his left hand and lunged at Jamie. The big man's knife flashed like deadly lightning. Little Otter felt the shock of the blade as it cut through flesh and bone. He screamed and looked down at his left hand. But the hand wasn't there. It was on the ground. He screamed again and looked up in horror just as Jamie thrust. Little Otter dropped his knife as Jamie's meticulously hand-made Bowie buried to the hilt in his stomach, the cutting edge up. Little Otter had only a few seconds to live as Jamie jammed the blade upward, the heavy blade ripping through vital organs. The eyes of the two men met for just a moment.

"They did not lie about you," Little Otter gasped.

"I reckon not," Jamie said. "But you were warned."

Jamie jerked the knife out and Little Otter sank to his knees, both hands holding his belly and chest. He fell over, dead.

Sam stepped over and stood looking down at the fallen warrior. "Do we bury him, Jamie?"

"No. His friends have not gone far. They'll be back to get him. What we'll do is move on another couple of miles and make camp. Let's go while we still have light."

The mules brayed and were not happy about moving on, but the men finally got them trail-ready and moved out. Jamie cut his eyes just as they were leaving. The Kiowa who had left Little Otter were sitting their horses about a thousand yards away, watching. Jamie lifted a hand and they did the same.

"Does that mean they won't bother us tonight?" Sam asked.

"No. It just means they saw us and we saw them. Let's get out of here."

"I will never understand the thinking of an Indian," Sam said.

Jamie smiled. "We'll take turns standing guard tonight."

"That goes without saying, my friend."

But the Kiowa did not attack the camp that night. Jamie and Sam saw not another human being until they were about an easy day's ride from the huge fort-like trading post. And the lone rider was coming at them from the north. Jamie halted the mules and squinted his eyes.

"I'll be damned!" he said. "It's Preacher."

The two men swung down from their horses and shook hands, and then Jamie introduced Sam.

"I just seen your Grandpa, Jamie. He spoke highly of Sam, here. Spoke highly of the whole bunch with you. And that's a rare compliment from Silver Wolf."

"Where is Grandpa going to winter, Preacher?"

The mountain man shook his head. "Don't know, Jamie. He gets on real good with the Blackfeet. He might winter with them. But then, he gets on with most Injuns. He'll be all right, Jamie. That old man seen a doctor when he was in St. Louis a couple of years back. That doctor said he had the heart of a man half his age. He was plumb amazed, that doctor was. Come on. Let's ride down to a spot I know and make camp. We'll ride into the Fort come tomorrow."

At first Sam had not been impressed by the mountain man called Preacher. Preacher, at first sight, was not an imposing-looking man. But for a year, Jamie had been teaching those in his group how to visually size up a man. Sam began to notice the little things about Preacher. The man moved with no wasted motion—like Jamie. He moved without making a sound—like Jamie. His eyes missed nothing around him—like Jamie. He kept rifle and pistol within arms reach at all times—like Jamie. He was never without his big-bladed knife—like Jamie. He also carried a smaller hideout knife stuck down in one legging—like Jamie. And on Preacher's horse was a strong-looking bow and a quiver of arrows. Just like Jamie.

Watching Preacher, Sam soon learned that the man was tremendously strong and very, very quick. Sam concluded his observations by deciding that Preacher would be a very good man to have around in case of trouble—and a very bad enemy. Sam had pegged Preacher very accurately.

Bent's Fort, planned by Charles and William Bent and constructed by Mexican workers, located near the junction of the Arkansas and Purgatory Rivers, was in operation from late 1832 to the late 1840s. Within its walled, fort-like confines several hundred men could relax and drink and eat and hundreds of animals could be corralled, all of it designed for maximum safety. Men of all creeds and colors passed through the huge, fortified gates: mountain men and pioneers, Indians of the Cheyenne, Arapaho, Comanche, Kiowa, Ute, and Gros Ventre nations. Within the walls there was seldom any trouble. Outside the four-foot thick and fourteen-foot tall adobe walls of the fort, nothing was guaranteed.

As the trio of men and their long string of mules rode in, even the most grizzled and hardened of mountain men paused to look at the man with the long blond hair. Those who knew Silver Wolf, and nearly everyone did, knew at first glance this was his grandson, the living legend from the Alamo down in Texas. The man raised by Shawnees and called Man Who Is Not Afraid.

And Preacher immediately began enhancing that legend by quickly spreading the news of the Kiowa attack and of the knife fight with Little Otter.

A friendly—at least for the moment—Kiowa nodded his head at the news. "Knew Little Otter," he told Preacher. "He was a good warrior. But quick to lose his temper. There will not be many songs sung for him."

Lounging in the rough bar, six men sat, passing the jug back and forth. They'd ridden in from the States a few days back and, for the most part, kept to themselves. That did not bring them to anyone's attention, for many mountain men were notorious for demanding solitude. Fights had started over merely speaking to some mountain men.

"I'd not like to tangle with that one alone," a man who sported a full beard remarked in a whisper, his eyes on Jamie, standing just outside the watering hole.

"A ball will bring him down just like any other man," a dirty companion replied.

"Just make damn shore you place it well," another said. "He's big as a bear."

"An' from what I've been told, 'bout three times as dangerous," the fourth man observed. "An' now that I've put eyes on him, I agree."

"Bah!" the smelly, dirty man softly scoffed. "He's just a man. All them tales is hogwash and bunkum. I dasn't believe none of them."

"We was paid to do a job," the first man said. "And we don't get the bulk of the money 'til it's done and Mac-Callister's head is pickled. We'll talk no more of it 'til we're safe of unfriendly ears." He got up and walked out into the huge open area, roughly a hundred and fifty feet by two hundred feet.

Jamie and Sam socialized for a time with some of Preacher's friends, had a bite to eat in a relaxed atmosphere, and then set about ordering supplies. Their plans were not to tarry at the fort but to supply up and head back as quickly as possible.

Flour, sugar, coffee, dress and shirt material, and other staples were purchased, marked with their names, and stored until time to load the packs for the return trip. Candy for the kids was an important item not to be overlooked; ribbons for the girls' hair and some foofaws and geegaws for the smaller kids. Sam saw to the buying of seed for gardens and Jamie saw to the purchasing of lead and powder and percussion caps. Jamie bought a fine knife for his oldest son, Jamie Ian, and a locket for Kate.

"You better buy something nice for Sarah," he told Sam with a smile, just as Jamie saw a small man walking toward him.

"Mister MacCallister?" the slight man said in a very soft voice.

"Yes," Jamie said, turning and towering over the man.

"I'm Kit Carson." The man offered his hand and Jamie took it. The hand was small but calloused and hard as oak; Jamie could feel the gentle strength in the man's grip.

Sam, sensing that the noted scout and frontiersman had something he wanted to discuss in private with Jamie, excused himself and left the two men alone.

The six men who had traveled from the States to kill Jamie and bring back his head also took note of the verbal exchange between Carson and MacCallister, unaware that

Preacher was standing across the clearing, taking note of them.

"Bounty hunters if ever I saw any," Preacher muttered. "So they's still some back in the States filled with hate for Jamie MacCallister." Preacher decided he'd keep an eye on the bounty hunters.

Kit Carson and Jamie stood for several moments, conversing in low tones. Then they both laughed, shook hands amiably, and Carson walked away.

Sam strode over to Jamie's side. "That expedition matter again?"

"Yes. I told Kit I'd have to discuss it with my wife. I'd give him a reply come the spring."

"You want to go, don't you, Jamie?"

"Well . . . it does sound like it might be a right interesting trip."

Jamie and Sam, the mules loaded with supplies, pulled out at dawn the next morning. The six bounty hunters left about an hour later. Preacher saddled up and rode out an hour after the bounty hunters. He felt certain the guns-for-hire would not attack until they were several days away from Bent's Fort.

Preacher trailed the bounty hunters for two days.. During both nights he slipped up on their camp and listened to their foul talk of murder for hire. The mountain man could have killed them all right then and there and ended it, but this was a personal matter between them and Jamie, and he felt sure that Jamie would want to handle it his way. On the afternoon of the third day, Preacher skirted the bounty hunters wide and rode up to Jamie and Sam's camp. He saw to his horses and then squatted down by the fire and poured a cup of coffee from the blackened pot.

Preacher was not at all surprised when Jamie said, "You come to warn me about those six men on my trail, Preacher?"

The mountain man smiled and nodded his head. "I figured you'd have picked up on them by now."

"What six men?" Sam asked, clearly startled.

"I noticed them back at the fort," Jamie said. "Surly looking bunch of scalawags. I pegged them as bounty hunters, hired by Olmstead or his kin, or by the Saxons or the Newbys or the Jacksons. I thought that blood feud had ended years back. I guess I was wrong."

"I heard all them names and more mentioned over two nights of listenin' to their evil talk," Preacher said. "They aim to kill you, cut off your head, and tote it in a pickle jug back to the States."

"What are you two talking about?" Sam demanded. He stared at Preacher for a moment. "Cut off his *head?* Pickle it? My God, man!"

"Relax," Jamie told his friend. "I'm sort of attached to my head, not to mention rather fond of it. And Kate would certainly be irritated if I returned home without my head." He laughed at the serious expression on the older man's face. "Sam . . . when we get a couple of more days behind us, I'll take care of those following us and then we'll be done with it."

"You want some help?" Preacher asked, knowing full well what Jamie's reply would be.

"No. I'll stomp on my own snakes, Preacher."

"Figured you'd say that." Ignoring Sam Montgomery's open-mouthed expression of exasperation and concern, Preacher said, "When do we eat? I'm hungry."

Six

Wesley Parsons, leader of the bounty hunters, was ranging out about a mile ahead of the others. Wesley was known as a fearless and experienced man-hunter back east. But this was not the east and Jamie Ian MacCallister was no ordinary man. Wesley abruptly reined up and stared down at the ground. He began cussing, loud and long. On the ground was an arrow made of stones, pointing northwest, a slip of paper under the last stone of the arrow's shaft. He jumped off his horse and snatched up the paper.

WATER JUST UP AHEAD. GOOD PLACE TO CAMP. YOU BEST REST AND THEN HEAD ON BACK HOME. IF YOU KEEP ON FOLLOWING ME, I'LL KILL YOU.

It was signed Jamie Ian MacCallister.

The others rode up and dismounted, staring at the paper. "What do them words say?" Burl Dixson asked.

Wesley told him.

"You mean MacCallister *knows* what we're up to?" a man called Leo blurted.

"I reckon," Wesley replied.

"That makes me plumb uncomfortable," Delbert Newby said. Delbert was a distant cousin of the Newby brothers that Jamie had tangled with years back when he and Kate were heading for Texas, just days before they were married in the tiny village of New Madrid, Missouri.

"This here's a trick!" Delbert's brother Amos said, pointing to the slip of paper. "MacCallister's done pisened the water up ahead."

Wesley shook his head. "No. MacCallister wouldn't do that. That would be a danger to animals who might come to drink there. MacCallister loves animals."

"Why would anybody in they right mind love a goddamn animal?" the last of the group, John Mack, asked.

Wesley shrugged his heavy shoulders. "You'll have to ask MacCallister that."

"I don't aim to ax him nothin'," John Mack said. "I aim to kill him and cut off his head."

Wesley ignored that and pointed to the ground. "There's them other hoofprints. That third party is stayin' with them. One man and a pack horse. Has to be somebody from the Fort who overheard us talkin' back yonder."

"I don't believe that," Burl said with a shake of his head. "After that first day when MacCallister and the gentry rode in, we never said no more about it. Leastways me and Leo never."

"Nor us," Delbert said, jerking a thumb toward his brother.

"Not me," John Mack said.

"Well, I damn shore didn't," Wesley said. He frowned in thought. "It was a guess on his part, I reckon. But MacCallister shore knows 'bout us."

"He's a slick one for a fact," Delbert said, stroking his dirty beard. "We might have to ponder on this some more."

"Ponder, hell!" Wesley said. "They's six of us and three of them. We can take 'em. We'll do the deed just as soon as we catch up with them. Let's ride. Sooner we can get his head pickled and get back, the sooner we can get our money."

Everything had been explained to Sam. But he was mystified as to how Jamie had picked out the bounty hunters from all the men milling about back at Bent's Fort. Jamie would only smile and shake his head. When Sam and Preacher were alone that first night after Preacher joined them, Preacher explained.

"When you got men on your backtrail for as long as Jamie has, and me, too, I reckon, it comes natural to a man. A body gets all his God-given senses workin' hard to stay alive. You got to bear in mind that Jamie's been fightin' to stay alive since he was about six or seven years old."

"I wonder when they'll strike us."

"Soon. They know that Jamie knows 'bout 'em 'cause of that stone arrey and that note he left back yonder."

"That was bravado on Jamie's part."

"I know what that word means. Tain't neither. That was a warnin' to 'em. If they ignore it, then Jamie feels free to do his damnest." He smiled a grim curving of the lips. "And when Jamie decides to do that, 'way I hear tell it, that's sorta like openin' wide the gates to Hell!"

"And that is putting it mildly," Sam said.

On the fifth night on the trail, only Preacher watched as Jamie silently rose from his blankets and left the camp. It was not that Sam was a heavy sleeper, for he was not. It was just that Jamie could move as silently as a ghost.

Jamie disappeared into the gloom and Preacher closed his eyes to return to sleep. Those bounty hunters were in for a rough night of it, Preacher suspected.

The guard shift had just changed at the bounty hunters' camp, and John Mack was rubbing sleep from his eyes with one hand and holding a cup of very strong black coffee in the other. There was no moon and the night skies were filled with clouds, heavy with moisture. The wind was sharp, holding more than a hint of the hard winter that was not that many weeks away. John Mack set the tin cup down on the ground and stretched. One second he was standing, listening to the creaking of his joints, the next second he was flat on his back on the ground, a hard hand clamped like a vise over his mouth. The bounty hunter was dragged a few hundred feet from the dim finger of flame of the small campfire. Dragged by someone, or some*thing,* he thought in fright, with enormous strength. John Mack started drumming his booted feet on the ground in hopes of awakening his cohorts in evil. That got him a clout on the side of his head that watered his eyes and caused his ears to ring like church bells on a Sunday morning. John Mack was thrown into a shallow ravine with no more effort than a child hurling a rag doll. He landed on his belly, the air whooshing out of him, the sharp stones in the ravine cutting his hands.

John Mack finally sucked enough air into his lungs to roll over on his back just in time to see something very large and menacing looming over him. Jamie MacCallister with a knife in his hand. John Mack had not prayed since childhood. In just about one minute he made up for all his backsliding, whispering prayers that, at the moment, he meant very sincerely.

"Who is paying you to dog my trail?" Jamie asked, his

voice as hard as flint. When John Mack hesitated, Jamie laid the sharp edge of his Bowie knife against the man's throat.

"Kin of Olmstead, Jackson, and the Saxon and Newby brothers," John Mack blurted out the words. "They all men of substance and quality now."

"Those men and their kin will never be anything close to quality," Jamie corrected the man. "They're white trash, they came from white trash, and they will always be white trash. Just like you."

"Yessir. If'n you say so, sir."

"You have anything else to say before I cut your throat and leave you for the buzzards and the scavengers?"

John Mack immediately started praying. He peed his dirty underwear and began weeping. He could not remember ever being this frightened. He managed to gasp out: "Let me live, MacCallister. I ain't done you no harm. If'n you let me live, I'll be shut of them others come first light. I swear on my dear sainted mother's eyes."

Jamie removed the knife from John Mack's throat and the brigand almost passed out from relief. "You'll leave now or you'll never see another sunrise," he told the man.

"Yessir! I can do that. I can slip in and get my hoss and be gone 'fore them others know it. I promise I will."

Jamie didn't believe the man for a second. John Mack was an outlaw through and through and would die an outlaw. But Jamie did not want to kill the man. Not yet. "If you're with those after me in the morning, you'll be the first one shot out of the saddle," he warned him. "And don't doubt my words. This is the only break you'll get from me."

"Yessir. Thank you kindly, Mister MacCallister. You're a kind man and a man of quality. I knowed that right off.

Tried to tell the others that. Bless your heart, Mister Mac-Callister. I didn't want to come along on this hunt. I really didn't. But . . ." John Mack ceased his stupid babbling. Jamie was gone, melting into the night. John Mack laid on the gravel for a few moments, then jumped to his feet and ran screaming back to camp, jarring the others out of their sleep. They threw blankets in all directions and leaped to their feet, wild-eyed, staring into the night.

"He's out yonder, boys!" John Mack shouted, pointing into the darkness. "Arm yourselves. MacCallister slipped up into camp like a ghost. Hurled me to the ground like I was a baby and dragged me off into a ditch like a bear with a dead doe. I never been so skirred in all my borned days. Git your rifles."

The bounty hunters scrambled for their weapons as Jamie lay not fifty yards away and watched and listened. He had pegged John Mack accurately.

"I want him furst," John Mack shouted, standing up and waving his grabbed-up rifle. "I want him alive so's I can burn his feet and cut out his tongue. I want to skin him and listen to him holler and beg." John Mack babbled out all that he was going to do to Jamie.

Jamie notched an arrow, lifted his bow, and put an arrow into John Mack's stomach. The bounty hunter screamed and sat down hard on the ground, both hands gripping the shaft of the arrow. The others stared in horror at the gut-shot man for a few seconds, then all of them hit the ground, scrambling behind whatever cover they could find. John Mack sat on the ground and screamed.

Jamie did not move.

"Somebody douse that far," Wesley ordered.

"You douse it," Burl said. "I ain't movin'."

"Oh, Lard, Lard, hep me!" John Mack hollered as the shock wore off and the first hard waves of pain hit him.

"I seen men arrey shot in the guts," Delbert said. "Hit'll take him hours, maybe days, to die. Somebody shoot him and put him out of his misery."

"You black-hearted son of a bitch!" John Mack shouted. "Damn your eyes."

"Oh, shut up!" Wesley told him. "We's just tryin' to save you some pain."

The campfire popped as the wind picked up and fanned the flames into new intensity. John Mack began squalling as the pain in his belly grew.

"Hell, I'll shoot him," Amos said, cocking his pistol. "I dasn't want to put up with that all night through."

John Mack pulled out a pistol and shot Amos in the leg.

"You bastard!" Amos yelled. "My leg's broke."

"Serves you right, you savage," John Mack said.

Amos lifted his pistol and shot John Mack in the head, the ball striking John Mack right between the eyes and blowing out the back of his head. John Mack fell over into the fire, his greasy hair quickly blazing in the cool night. The fire spread to his clothing and for a brief time, John Mack illuminated the darkness.

"Toss some water on him," Wesley shouted. "I can't stand the smell no more."

No one moved.

Jamie lay in the darkness and watched and waited. Only his eyes moved. The Shawnee Warrior's Way now consumed his being. He had warned them. Now it was warfare of the cruelest kind—guerrilla warfare—and Jamie was a master at it. Tall Bull had started his training at age seven, and Jamie had taken to it like candy to a child.

"Just hold what we got," Delbert said. "Come the mornin', we'll git him."

"Shit!" Amos groaned. "My leg's broke for fair, brother. Hit's swellin' up somethin' awful. He shot me in the knee. I'm crippled for life. I hope he burns in Hellfire forever. Damn you, John Mack."

Jamie took that time to move, knowing the loud words and the popping and sizzling of John Mack cooking would cover any slight noise he might make.

Leo, who was closest to the fire, began throwing handfuls of dirt into the flames, finally extinguishing the blaze. The dirt did nothing to dispel the terrible odor of flesh cooking. It gagged them all.

"Come on, MacCallister!" Burl shouted into the night. "Fight like a man."

Jamie smiled. He knew there were no rules to fighting. Only a fool thought otherwise. There was only a winner and a loser. No more and no less than that. And that was just one of the reasons why Jamie could never again live in any type of structured society. The men and women who settled and tamed the west could not call the sheriff or wave for a uniformed constable to come solve their problems. For many, many years west of the Mississippi the only law was the gun and the knife and the tomahawk and the lance, even though many, if not most, of the people who were called pioneers held the law they had left behind in high regard.

"You're a coward, MacCallister!" Wesley yelled. "You hide in the dark."

Fool! Jamie thought. He shouts to hide his own fear. Jamie tossed a fist sized rock far to his left and the now dark camp roared with rifle fire. Jamie used that to cover another move. As on the hands of a clock, Jamie had started at six, and was now at twelve, located not more than fifty feet from the camp. His eyes could pick out the dark shapes of the men. Jamie rose up on one knee and notched an arrow, drawing back and letting it fly. It flew true and buried deep into a man's shoulder. Burl screamed in pain as the arrow drove clear through and the head ripped out his upper back.

The instant Jamie let the arrow fly, he shifted positions, now coming up behind the camp from the east, or at three o'clock. A man jumped to help the wounded man and Jamie let fly another arrow. This one was a clean miss, the arrow clanging off the hanging cook pot. Jamie again shifted positions.

"I felt the breeze from that arrey," Leo said.

"They's more than one of 'em!" Wesley shouted. "I figure all three of 'em is out there."

"Got to be more than just MacCallister," Leo called. "Who'd have thought that hoity-toity fancy-pants Montgomery would larn how to use a bow and arrey."

They know something about Sam, Jamie thought with a frown. Who are these men? Did I meet them while living with Sam and Sarah as a boy? He didn't think so. John Mack had told him they were being paid by the kin of Jamie's old enemies. So the hate still ran deep. Would it ever end? Would he and Kate and the kids ever be allowed to live in peace? Jamie didn't think so.

"We got to go out there after him, Wes," Delbert said, the words carrying easily to Jamie, along with the stink of John Mack's charred body. "Hit's the only way. We stay here, and he'll pick us off one at a time."

"No," Wesley nixed that suggestion. "MacCallister would love that. Just hold what we have and no movin' around. We can't see him, but he can't see us neither.

Come the dawnin', we'll pull out and head on back to the fort."

Jamie laid his head on the ground and closed his eyes for a moment. If that meant you would never be back, I'd certainly let you go in peace, he thought. But I don't believe that. My God but I am so tired of the killing!

Jamie opened his eyes, aware that the loud talking had diminished into whispering. Something was up.

"MacCallister?" came the shout. "I know you ain't gonna answer me, so just listen. I'm Wesley Parsons. Kin of the Saxons. They's big money on your head back in the States. But it looks like we ain't gonna be the ones to collect it. I don't feel like dyin' for no small sack of gold coins. Somebody's gonna have to come up with a lot more money for me to ever ride out into this goddamn wilderness again. I hate this damn place. If'n you'll let us, come the dawnin', we'll ride back east and odds are you'll never see us no more. Now I ain't makin' no promises on that. But right now I'd say you've seen the last of us."

Jamie thought about that. The man was leveling with him, he finally concluded. No doubt about one thing: Wesley Parsons had his share of courage and damn little backup in him to speak so frankly.

Jamie scooted back until sliding into a small depression in the earth where he would be safe from rifle and pistol fire. "Parsons?"

"Right here, MacCallister."

"Build up your fire, tend to your wounded, and get the hell gone from here. I'll send no more arrows at you. When you've gone, I'll bury John Mack as decently as possible. But hear this well: If I ever see any of you again, I'll kill you where you stand. Is that understood?"

"Understood and taken. I'm gonna build a fire and tend

to the wounded. We'll lay our weapons on the ground whilst we move about saddlin' up and packin' up. Then we'll ride. Deal?"

"Done."

Jamie shifted positions and watched the men break camp. There were no more verbal exchanges between them. Long after the sounds of their horses' hooves had faded, Jamie stretched out on the cold ground and slept. At dawn, he'd see to John Mack. He had a hunch that Preacher and Sam would be along about that time.

He was right.

Seven

The bounty hunters had left him a piece of a shovel and Jamie had just started digging the hole for John Mack when Sam and Preacher rode up, the string of mules stretched out behind them, Preacher leading Jamie's horse. Sam took the shovel and relieved Jamie while Preacher looked around him.

"Blood here and here and here," he remarked. "Just one dead?"

"Yes. One of the others was shot by this man," he pointed to John Mack, "and I got an arrow into another before they decided to give it up."

"Who were they, Jamie?" Sam asked.

"Bounty hunters. Two of them, maybe all of them, were related to the Newbys or the Jacksons or some other family that felt I wronged them years back."

Sam paused in his digging. "Kate's father or brothers, you think?"

"Could be. Probably so. I'll see them again. I'm sure of that."

"We're gonna see something else 'fore that happens," Preacher said, looking to the south. He pointed. "Co-manche."

It was a hunting party, not a war party. And some of them had been only a few hundred yards from the fight the night before, lying in the darkness, watching and listening.

Big Eagle, the leader of this band, although no lover of whites, did not want to tangle with Man Who Is Not Afraid and Preacher. He knew nothing of Sam Montgomery, but if he rode with Man Who Is Not Afraid, he was a good warrior. There was no doubt in his mind but what they could kill the three whites, but their losses would be heavy. It was just not worth it. "Good fight last night," he said, his eyes hard on Jamie.

Jamie spoke some Comanche and he replied, "They were not worthy opponents." He pointed to the blackened remains of John Mack. "This one did not die well."

Big Eagle grunted. "Few whites do." He turned his horse's head and the hunting party rode off.

"Unpredictable bastards," Preacher said. "I get on with most Injuns. But Pawnees and Comanches ain't among them. And Kiowas ain't no prize, neither."

Jamie shoved the body of John Mack into the shallow hole and took the shovel from Sam. Preacher began gathering up rocks. When the lonely grave was covered, the three men stood around the mound for a moment. Finally, Preacher took off his hat and said, "Lord, here lies the remains of some white trash called John Mack that made the mistake of tanglin' with Jamie MacCallister. I don't know nothin' good to say about him. Probably wasn't nothin' good about him to speak. But it ain't up to me to judge him. That's up to You. So have at it. Amen." Preacher plopped his hat back on his head. "Let's fix breakfast. I'm hungry."

Sam stood for a moment, staring in disbelief at the mountain man. Never in his life had he heard such a disrespectful offering for the dead.

Sam had a lot to learn about mountain men.

* * *

Preacher left the pack train several days before Jamie and Sam reached the long lovely valley they called home, saying he had some business to tend to before he settled in for the winter. With a wave of his hand, he was gone.

"Strange breed of men, those mountain men," Sam said, lifting the reins.

"They opened up the west," Jamie said. "They rode trails that no white man had ever before seen and blazed that many more." There was a wistful note to his voice that Sam picked up on.

"You're going with this expedition, aren't you, Jamie?"

"I reckon so. But there's more. Carson wants me to spend all next spring and summer and as much of the fall as possible scouting out the Wind River Range. That's up north of our place. Indians call it Maughwau Wama. Whites shortened it to Wyoming."

Kate received Jamie's decision with a shrug of her shoulders. She had long ago accepted the fact that she had married a wanderer, a man who had the blood of adventurers coursing through his veins. She had never tried to use womanly wiles to keep her man at home and she never would. That was just not her way.

"You'll be gone for how long, Jamie?" Kate asked.

"Several months."

She looked at the bolts of cloth and flour and sugar and the dozens of other articles stacked around the large cabin. She pointed at them. "Get busy, love. I'm not going to be falling all over these things."

And one of the heroes of the Texas fight for independence, one of the very few men that Jim Bowie ever admired and looked up to, the adventurer known to Indians all over the west as Man Who Is Not Afraid, the mountain of a man who had killed men with one single blow from his fist, said the words that married men have been saying for centuries, "Yes, dear."

Winter locked the high country in with an icy white fist. But even with temperatures dropping at times to forty or fifty below zero, the winds blowing the snow so hard the settlers had to string ropes between cabins and barns and outhouses, the men had to stay busy. They tended to the livestock, chopped open water holes, kept young calves and lambs alive, and did a hundred other things just to survive. But spring would come as it had from time immemorial and one day the morning broke in sapphire hues, the sun bubbling in the sky, the temperature climbing, and the ice and snow began melting. Of course it was a false spring, and it snowed again several times, but spring finally came with a spectacular burst of color from meadow flowers, and humans and critters alike gloried in the warmth.

"We need fresh meat," Kate told Jamie early one warm spring morning. "If you're going to be gone all summer, we need lots of meat to jerk and lots of fish to smoke." She pointed toward his rifle and then to the open door.

Jamie smiled and said, "Yes, ma'am." He saddled up, took a pack horse, and headed out to get fresh meat, with no way of knowing that he was riding straight toward an encounter with a huge old grizzly who had long despised the scent of man.

* * *

The Indians called him Big Paw, for this grizzly was indeed king of all his surroundings. Big Paw stood almost ten feet tall and weighed over a thousand pounds. A normal sized grizzly has no natural enemies, for there was no other animal in the wilderness that could take him down. And a grizzly will attack without any provocation. Big Paw had been wounded several times over the years, and still carried the arrowheads in his hide. He also carried in his brain a wild hatred of man. It is a myth that all grizzly bears cannot climb trees. They generally don't because of their long straight claws and huge bulk, but when angered a grizzly can do just about anything he or she wants to do. If they can't climb the tree, they can, and have, torn the damn tree down to get at their prey.

And Big Paw and Jamie Ian MacCallister were on a direct collision course.

Jamie reined up and sat his saddle, staring wide-eyed at the marks on the tree. He shook his head in disbelief. The claw marks denoting the grizzly's territory were a good fourteen feet off the ground and they were fresh.

"Big Paw," Jamie muttered, recalling what Black Thunder and some of the others in his tribe had told him about the legendary grizzly who roamed these mountains with impunity. Big Paw had killed several Utes who had foolishly come hunting for him. Jamie looked carefully all around him and then wisely decided to leave the bear's territory. Jamie had no desire to come nose to snout with any just-out-of-hibernation grizzly, and even less of a desire to face Big Paw.

Jamie's horse snorted and suddenly became skittish; it was all Jamie could do to control the animal. Jamie could feel the fear in the animal. His horse was a huge stallion, afraid of very few things in the animal kingdom. But even the bravest of animals has a natural fear of grizzlies.

"Easy, Buck, easy," Jamie said, patting the animal's neck. His words did nothing to calm the now very nervous animal.

Jamie managed to turn Buck's head just as a roar that caused the leaves to tremble came out of the thick brush. Jamie could actually feel the thunder of the bear's charge. Buck screamed and reared up unexpectedly. Jamie grabbed for the saddle horn. But with his rifle in his right hand and the reins in the other, it was a tentative hold and Jamie left the saddle, hitting the ground hard.

He managed to hold onto his rifle just as Buck wheeled to face the charging grizzly. Big Paw hit the stallion and knocked Buck screaming to one side. The only thing that saved Jamie was one of Buck's hooves striking the bear on the side of the head and addling the huge animal for a few seconds. That was all the time Jamie needed to leap to his feet and run into the brush, picking them up and putting them down with all deliberate haste. Buck was wisely heading the other way, reins trailing.

Jamie was under no illusions. He knew he could not outrun the grizzly. Grizzlies have been known to outrun a horse for short distances; they can certainly outrun most humans, and for their size, grizzlies are very agile.

But Jamie had his mind made up: Big Paw was going to have a race on his hands, or his paws, as it were, and one hell of a fight if he caught up with Jamie.

But Jamie was losing the race. Big Paw was snorting and roaring, pounding the ground behind him, and gaining. Jamie cocked his rifle on the run, rounded a tree in a fast half circle, and turned and fired. The heavy ball hit the huge bear in the shoulder and stopped him momentarily. Big Paw roared in pain as Jamie was once more on the run, trying to reload while zigging and zagging through the underbrush and around trees. Big Paw had resumed the chase, this time with real blood in his eyes.

Jamie tried the same tactics again, but Big Paw was a smart bear and somehow anticipated the move. He angled to meet Jamie's move and Jamie lost precious yardage. Jamie pulled his double-shotted pistol from behind his belt and fired. Both balls struck the grizzly and Big Paw again paused as the pain hit him. Jamie took off running as fast as he could. He had spotted a large tree, too large for any bear to bring down, and thought he just might have a chance to make it. He barely did. With Big Paw snorting and grunting just a few feet behind him, lashing out with those terrible claws, Jamie had just enough time to sling his rifle and leap for the lower branch. He swung his legs up as Big Paw reared up and lashed out. Jamie went up the tree with a speed that would put a squirrel to shame.

While Big Paw pounded the trunk of the tree and slobbered and roared, Jamie got his ragged breath under control and reloaded rifle and pistol. Big Paw grabbed the tree in a massive hug and attempted to tear it down. While the bear could not bring down the tree, he did manage to strip off a lot of bark and give Jamie some very anxious moments.

Jamie sat on a sturdy limb and studied the old silver-tip. Even after all that Big Paw had put him through, he really didn't want to kill the old bear.

"Go on, old man," Jamie called. "Leave me alone and I'll let you live."

Big Paw slammed his paws against the tree and roared, slobber flying. Jamie cut his eyes at movement. Buck had trailed his master and was a few hundred yards off, trembling with fear but nostrils flared wide and ready for a fight. Big Paw whirled around at the horse scent.

"Oh, no, bear," Jamie yelled. "You don't kill my horse." Big Paw looked up at Jamie just as Jamie felt a warm stickiness on his face. He put his hand to his face and was surprised to find blood there. He had cut his face in a dozen places on thorns and low branches during the wild chase. He'd been so busy concentrating on the wild, rushing, life and death foot-race and on staying alive he had not noticed the slight cuts. The blood was dripping from his face down onto his buckskins. So it was the blood scent that was enraging Big Paw.

Buck took several steps toward the bear, and Big Paw roared and whirled around, facing the big stallion. Big Paw lifted his massive arms and Jamie took aim and placed his shot true. The ball pierced the grizzly's heart. Big Paw screamed and staggered, then fell to the rocky earth.

Jamie waited several minutes, making certain the huge grizzly was indeed dead before climbing down. He leaned his reloaded rifle against a tree just as his pack horse found Buck. Jamie secured both still skittish animals, petting them and calming them. Then he pulled his knife from leather and began the slow job of skinning the bear. It would be a prize rug. He straightened up at the sound of hooves to stand over the bear, his Bowie knife held at what seemed to be a defensive position.

Black Thunder and several of his tribe burst out of the timber and sat their mounts, staring in disbelief at the sight before them. It was a fearsome scene and would be told and retold, thoroughly embellished with each repeated telling, all over the west. Jamie's face was streaked with blood. Blood had dripped down to darken his buckskin shirt. There was blood on the big mans hands.

Black Thunder was speechless, his mouth gaped open. But his eyes did not lie—at least as he saw it. Man Who Is Not Afraid stood over Big Paw, a knife in his hand. Man Who Is Not Afraid had killed the mighty grizzly with only his knife.

"Iliyee!" Black Thunder screamed, and the others screamed their approval. Man Who Is Not Afraid was indeed the mightiest of all warriors. For in all the annals of Indian history—or white history for that matter—very few men had ever been victorious over a grizzly armed with only a knife. Jamie started to correct the story then paused. Maybe it was best this way.

Black Thunder jumped off his horse and walked to Jamie's side, putting one arm around Jamie's shoulders and one foot on the dead Big Paw. "He is my brother!" Black Thunder called. "My brother, Bear Killer. Man Who Is Not Afraid will be known to all Utes as Bear Killer."

The warriors with him hollered and cried out, shouting out the name over and over.

Jamie decided to let Black Thunder keep his own version of what had happened. He said, "I give the skin to you, my brother. It will keep you warm for many years."

Black Thunder could not conceal his delight. "There will be many songs sung about this, Bear Killer. Yes. It is good that we are brothers. I could not sleep well knowing such a warrior as you is my enemy. We will have mixing of the blood soon and all will know we are brothers. Shining Bright will make you a fine necklace from the teeth. You will wear?"

"I will wear with pride."

"We will feast tonight on the meat of Big Paw. You will come?"

"I will come."

Black Thunder frowned in thought, then added, "Leave yellow-haired tribe at home. Not want to frighten Shining Bright."

Eight

Jamie received word that the Fremont party would not leave for another eighteen months but that Fremont wanted him to leave as soon as possible to scout out the way. Fremont wanted maps and lots of them.

Jamie smiled at that. He would give Fremont maps, but somebody else would have to draw them, for Jamie would carry them in his head.

The horse he chose from his stock, and they were all superb animals, was a huge stallion that only he could ride. He had traded for the horse from a very disgusted Indian who simply could not tame the animal. It had taken Jamie less than two weeks. The Ute had called him Horse, and Jamie saw no reason to change his name now. Horse was the color of sand, with dangerous eyes and enormous strength. But around Jamie, Horse was gentle as a kitten. But Horse was also fiercely protective of Jamie and both loyal and watchful.

Jamie packed carefully and chose wisely. He took ample powder, shot, caps, and a mold. He would hunt and fish for most of his food, but he had to take flour and beans and sugar. He hadn't wanted to do it, but he was forced to take a pack horse. The pack horse he chose was tough, strong, and trail-wise. Even without a lead rope Jamie had trained it to follow.

The spring flowers had started to fade and lose their brilliance when Jamie kissed Kate and the kids, shook hands all around, and mounted up. He had no way of knowing he was again about to take a ride into history.

From both mountain men and Indians, Jamie learned where he needed to go and what he needed to avoid. Needed to avoid but probably wouldn't, for he wanted to see it all. When he reported to Fremont, or Fremont's man, as the case may be, Jamie's report would be comprehensive.

Jamie followed the Arkansas, heading straight into the heart of the Rockies. He had been perhaps fifty miles north, west, and south of the valley, so for the first several days out, he was in familiar country. But he soon found himself in country that was unknown . . . and he loved it. It was wild and lonely and beautiful. Jamie deliberately climbed high, as high as he could take the horses. When it became too steep and rocky for them, he dismounted and continued on foot.

Jamie stopped often during his slow ride north, memorizing every trail, every blind canyon, every creek, every river, every spring. As was nearly always the case with the early pathfinders, Jamie would carry those trails and rivers and springs in his brain until death. He could return forty years later, and know exactly where he was.

As he rode and etched the countryside in his mind, always riding with rifle ready, he recalled what Kit Carson had told him about Fremont. Kit had been quite taken with the man. And Carson was not a man to give his friendship lightly. He only had one reservation about Fremont.

Jamie had pressed him on that point. Carson had smiled

and said, "Drinks his coffee with his little finger stickin' way out like this here."

And that was all he had to say about it.

Jamie had tried drinking his coffee with his little finger sticking out. It was uncomfortable.

Fremont may or may not have held his coffee cup with his pinkie finger sticking out (history doesn't divulge that) but John Charles Fremont was a very ambitious man. He was born in Georgia, some say Savannah, around 1813. He was a woods colt, something that he fiercely resented. But that resentment only served to fuel his driving ambition to succeed. Fremont decided, at an early age, that he could get ahead by associating himself with successful men, and before he was out of his teens, he did—with a man named Joel Poinsett.

Poinsett was very rich, a world traveler, and a highly sought-after statesman and diplomat. Poinsett had traveled extensively in Mexico and brought back a flower that eventually was named for him—the Poinsettia. He took an immediate liking to young Fremont and soon had him appointed as a government surveyor, working with the army in the southern mountains of the United States.

Poinsett was appointed Secretary of War during the Van Buren administration and since he was an avid explorer, he organized the Army's Corps of Topographical Engineers. Then he appointed Fremont as a civilian with that group. The Corps' first expedition was an outing into the largely unexplored country between the Upper Mississippi and Missouri Rivers. This was in 1838, just about the time that Jamie and those who chose to follow him were really getting a foothold in the long valley in Colorado. The team spent nearly two years in the field, and when they returned, Fremont felt he was ready for bigger and better things. Poinsett agreed.

Jamie was not aware of any of this political wrangling. Had he been aware of it, he more than likely would have refused to take any part in the mission, for Jamie despised politics. He admittedly knew very little about politics, but what he did know, he disliked. Jamie Ian MacCallister was no deal-maker. He was no diplomat. He knew that right was always right and wrong was always wrong. And one did not make deals to skirt or avoid the two. He placed politicians in the same low esteem he felt for lawyers and bankers. The former would lie and the latter would cheat. Period. One might conclude that Jamie was a tad on the narrow-minded side of some issues.

Jamie spotted several bands of Indians, and he was sure they had spotted him. But he made no contact with them, nor they with him. He never got close enough to determine what tribe they belonged to.

He was camped along the banks of the North Platte, about twenty-five miles south of what would someday be Wyoming, when he saw Horse's head come up, the big stallion's ears pricked and his eyes alert. Jamie leaned forward to pour another cup of coffee with his left hand while his right hand closed around the forestock of his rifle and pulled it toward him. Horse snorted and pawed at the earth and Jamie heard the slight brushing of boots against the ground.

"Mighty careful man," the voice spoke from behind

him. "But I got you cold, mister. Now you just turn a-loose of that rifle and keep your hands in plain sight."

"And if I don't?" Jamie said.

"Then I reckon I'd just have to blow a hole in you. I ain't aimin' to kill you, mister. But I need your hoss and supplies. And I aim to have them. One way or the other."

Jamie smiled. If this fool thought he could ride Horse, this might turn out to be fun. "Come on in," he called cordially. "I have coffee and food. Help yourself."

"That's smart on your part." The voice moved into the camp and Jamie got his first look at the man. He was not impressed. The man was dirty and smelled like a goat in rut. When he opened his mouth, he exposed stained and rotted teeth. His eyes looked much like the eyes of a cornered rat. Jamie had no doubt but what he could easily take the man, but decided to play along for a time. He wanted to see the man attempt to ride Horse.

"You have a name?" Jamie asked.

"Biggers," the man said, picking up a piece of pan bread with extremely dirty fingers and sopping it through the grease left in the frying pan. He stuffed his mouth full and said, "Jack Biggers." He stared at Jamie for a moment while he chewed. "You a big'un, ain't you?"

"I've been told that a time or two."

"But I got the rifle, so big don't mean shit, do it?"

Jamie shrugged at that. "Indians get you?"

"Naw. Trappers. Caught me stealin' some of their supplies and set upon me fierce. It was uncalled for. They had a-plenty and I had nothin.' They seen that plain. They could have shared with me."

Give me something for nothing, Jamie thought. The trappers would probably have willingly shared what they had with Biggers had he asked. But he chose to steal.

Jamie felt nothing but contempt for the man. And he wasn't sure he believed the man's story.

"You 'member that name, mister," Biggers said. "Jack Biggers. I got kin to meet me down to Bent's Fort. They's waitin'. I'm a-fixin' to take your hoss and git back to them. Then we'll come back here and I'll settle up with them goddamn trappers, and you, too, if'n you get antsy with me."

"Take what you want," Jamie said.

Jack sneered at him. "You a big'un, all right, but you ain't got no sand to your bottom. If'n I had the time, I'd give you a whuppin' just for the fun of it."

Jamie was amused at that. But he managed to hide his smile. Several times in his life he had killed men with just one single blow from his fist. Jim Bowie had seen him do that in south Texas one day. Besides, Biggers was almighty careless in his movements. Jamie had let several opportunities slide where he could have taken the rifle from the man.

He watched as Biggers stuffed food and other supplies into a sack and then moved toward Horse. When he bent down to pick up the saddle, Horse kicked the snot out of him. Jack Biggers went flying and tumbling and rolling ass over elbows and came to a hard halt on his belly about twenty-five feet from point of impact.

Jamie rose from the ground—he'd been sitting with his back to a log—and walked over to retrieve Biggers' rifle. Biggers was moaning and writhing on the ground. Jamie felt the man was at least badly bruised in the ass area but had no way of knowing if his injuries were any more than that—and didn't care.

He put out his small fire and saddled up, after stowing his supplies. He swung up into the saddle. He had unloaded Jack's rifle and now contemptuously threw the rifle on the ground beside the man.

"Hep me," Biggers moaned. "I'm hurt fearsome."

"Help yourself," Jamie told him. "I would have given you supplies had you but asked for them. But men like you never learn. Hell with you."

"I'll kill you someday," Biggers threatened. "You got a name?"

"MacCallister. Jamie Ian MacCallister."

Biggers paled under the dirt on his face. "Heared of you. But that don't make no difference. I'll git my brothers and kin and we'll be back."

"I'll be around," Jamie said, then rode off, leaving Jack Biggers shouting wild curses and threats to his back.

Jamie made camp about five miles north of where he'd left Jack Biggers. Two days later, he crossed over into Wyoming. He had put Jack Biggers out of his conscious mind, tucking the man into the far reaches of his brain. But Jamie had certainly not forgotten him. He never forgot a threat. Jack Biggers might have just been running off at the mouth, and he might not have been. It was best to take a threat seriously.

Jamie camped early in the shadow of what would someday be named Bridger Peak, after the legendary Jim Bridger. He was being watched and he knew it, he had known it since early that afternoon. And he was sure it was Indians looking him over. And it certainly was one of the four predominant tribes in this area: the Shoshoni, the Arapaho, the Crow, or the Cheyenne. He was still some south of the usual Blackfoot stomping grounds, but they sallied down this far occasionally. And the Blackfoot Indians were great warriors.

Jamie's grandpa had told him the Crow were friends of

the Americans, with many bands boasting that they had never harmed a white man. But the elder MacCallister had smiled when he said that.

Jamie had not unpacked, just pausing long enough to fry some bacon, make some coffee, and let the Indians think he was camped for the night. He left his small fire burning in a pit, surrounded by a circle of stones, and quietly pulled out, deliberately choosing the rockiest route he could find to better hide his trail. It wouldn't fool the Indians for long, but it would buy him some time. He hoped. For Jamie had a gut hunch these Indians were hunting scalps.

Jamie found a very rocky trail and took it, not knowing where it might take him. It took him straight into a cul-de-sac.

"Damn!" he whispered, looking at the sheer rock walls that surrounded him. Then he smiled. He knew where he was! Preacher had described this place to him. Preacher had used it to hide from a war party one time. Yes. There were the skinny trees and scrub bushes. If he was right . . .

Jamie carefully slipped into the small stand of trees and found the opening. There was the lightning bolt mark Preacher had scratched out near the narrow entrance. Then Jamie heard the faint sound of hooves striking rocks. He quickly led his horses down the dark and narrow passageway and turned them loose in the two acre clearing, with a small spring and plenty of graze. He quickly stripped the gear from the horses and they immediately began to graze on the lush grass. Jamie ran back up the passageway and carefully brushed out all sign of his ever being in the rocky cul-de-sac. Then he slipped back into the brush, rifle and pistols at hand, and waited.

He'd been lucky. These were Blackfeet. But what the

hell of were they doing so far south of their usual territory? Then he saw the paintings on their mounts. The dark square meant the war party leader. Beside that square, there was a hand painted. A recent kill in hand to hand combat. There were scalps tied to the pony's mane and also on the leader's lance—fresh scalps.

Jamie did not speak the Blackfoot language, so he had no way of knowing what they were saying, only that they were definitely arguing, and some of them were getting hot about it. They seemed pretty sure that Jamie had come this way, and now he had disappeared. That just was not possible.

Jamie had a couple of anxious moments when the war party leader slipped off his horse and inspected the rocky ground. Several times he looked directly at the trees and the brush. Then he walked over and stepped into the small stand of timber. He stood for a moment, then muttered something and walked out to join his party.

But Jamie had seen something in the war chief's eyes and had read it right: the man wasn't convinced. He *knew* Jamie was near. But he was not about to venture deeper into that stand of timber. He did not get to be a war chief by being stupid.

Jamie watched him make a big deal out of commanding his men to leave. They wouldn't go far. Only back to the mouth of the blind canyon. That was fine with Jamie. He was in no hurry to pull out. He had plenty of food, there was graze for the horses and water for horse and human. If the Blackfeet found the entrance, Jamie could pile bodies up head high, for he had two rifles and six pistols, all fully loaded and ready to bang. He had his bow and arrows and his big Bowie knife. It would be one hell of a fight, that was for sure.

But Jamie didn't think the Blackfeet would stay long, for they were a long way from home and he knew they were not on the best of terms, at this time, with the Cheyenne and the Arapaho. He would wait them out.

The passageway behind him was probably a hundred yards long and twisting, the stone walls around the hidden little valley hundreds of feet high. Even if the horses whinnied, they would not be heard.

Jamie returned briefly to the horses. They had grazed some, drank their fill of the cold, pure spring water, and rolled. They were fine. Jamie returned to the mouth of the opening. He would remain there until the danger was past.

Several times during the night, the Blackfoot war chief returned silently to the small copse of timber. He would stand for a few moments, listening, his eyes busy. Jamie could feel his anger and frustration. The Blackfoot war chief knew his prey was near. But if he could not find the opening in the daylight, he certainly was not going to find it at night. He returned once more just after dawn and prowled the timber, actually coming within a few yards of the opening. Still, he failed to spot it. Finally, he threw up his hands, and with a snort of disgust, he walked out into the clearing and yelled. His horse was brought to him and he swung up and rode away. This time, Jamie felt he really was leaving.

Jamie stayed in the tiny clearing for another twenty-four hours, resting and eating. Come the dawning, he packed up and saddled up, leading the horses to the entrance of the passageway. Jamie stood in the timber for several minutes, listening and watching. Birds pecked the rocky ground for food and squirrels were chattering in the timber above the cul-de-sac. But he knew that really meant nothing. For if the war chief had returned to lie in wait for him, the animals would have grown used to his presence.

Jamie could wait no more. He walked back to his horses and rode out. At the mouth of the cul-de-sac, he rode smack into the Blackfeet.

Nine

The war chief had sent most of his men on ahead, staying behind with three of probably his best warriors. With a scream of triumph, the Blackfoot rushed Jamie. Jamie leveled his rifle one-handed and shot the war chief in the chest, the heavy ball knocking the Indian off his horse and creating panic among the three warriors with him, as Jamie had hoped it would. For without their chief, the three others, in all likelihood, would not continue the fight. They would have to make medicine.

Amid angry shouts, Jamie put the scene behind him and rode hard to the west, hoping to throw off any pursuers. Several miles later he stopped to rest his horses. He could spot no signs of being followed. He had guessed correctly; the Blackfoot warriors were confused and not likely to pick up the chase now.

But one thing had caught Jamie's eyes: two of the scalps tied to the war chief's lance had come from whites. And they were fresh scalps. One of them appeared to be that of a woman.

Jamie decided to backtrack the war party. He waited an hour, then rode cautiously back to the entrance of the blind canyon. The Blackfeet were gone, riding north, taking the body of the war chief with them. Jamie found the trail of the war party and began tracking it south and slightly east. After two days' ride, he found wagon ruts and concluded that this must be what some people were now calling the Oregon Trail. He was undecided as to what direction to go, east or west. He finally chose west. A few miles later, he found what he had been hoping he would not find. The remains of a small wagon train. The wagons had been turned over, looted, but not burned.

The buzzards and ground scavengers had made a mess out of the bodies, but Jamie could tell that some of the women and girls had been raped. He squatted down amid the carnage and thought back. None of those Blackfeet had been wearing any articles of white man's clothing. They had been traveling light, and carrying no booty. Jamie inspected the wagons. He could not find even one arrow.

"Indians didn't do this," he muttered to the wind, which thankfully carried off the stench of the bloated dead. "White men did this. Renegades." He wondered if Jack Biggers had been a part of it and later had a falling out with the others in the gang. "More than likely," he concluded. That story about the trappers had seemed a little thin to him.

Jamie found a shovel and began the task of burying the bodies. There was no way of knowing who was man and wife, or what child belonged to what parent. He could find no identification and didn't feel right searching the stiffened and bloated dead. He buried them all in a shallow and common grave, then piled rocks and small logs over the grave.

After a short rest, Jamie began the task of more carefully going through the wagons. He knew that movers cached valuables in hidden places. He had just risen from the log when he heard the sound of hooves. Horse and the pack animal were hidden in the timber out of sight. Jamie picked up his rifle and slipped into some brush.

It was a half-dozen mountain men, coming from the south, heading north. Their pack animals were loaded, so Jamie guessed they'd been down to Bent's Fort or some other trading post he had yet to learn of for supplies.

"Someone come along an burred 'em," a big mountain man rumbled.

"This wasn't the work of no Injuns," a second man declared.

"No, it wasn't," Jamie said, stepping from the brush.

A half dozen rifles were trained on him.

"Who you be, lad?" the big mountain man asked.

"Jamie MacCallister. You might know my Grandpa."

The rifles were instantly lowered, for all could see the strong family resemblance. Jamie gathered up the reins to Horse and the lead rope on the pack animal and walked over as the men dismounted. They shook hands all around.

"You got any idee who done this deed, lad?" Jamie was asked.

"Only a guess. But I strongly suspect that a man called Jack Biggers had some part in it." He told them about Jack.

They all had a good laugh when he told them about Horse kicking Biggers in the butt. The huge mountain man looked at Horse, who was looking at him. "I'd not like to tangle with that brute. He's got killer eyes."

Jamie stroked Horse's nose and the animal nuzzled him gently. "Harmless as a baby," Jamie said with a smile.

Another mountain man said, "I heard tell of Jack Biggers." He frowned. "Give me a second. Yeah. Now I recall. They was some shady-lookin' men down at the Fort talking about some kin of theirs they'd come west to hook up with. Jack Biggers was the name, all right. They all looked like highwaymen to me, they did."

Then Jamie told him about the Blackfeet he'd had a run-in with.

"You mean that damn hole in the wall is really there?" the big mountain man hollered. "Why, I been thinkin' Preacher was lyin' all these years."

"It's there, all right. And saved my bacon, too, it did," Jamie replied. "You watch out for those Blackfeet. I imagine they're some irritated about my killing that war chief."

" 'Some irritated' is talkin' light, lad," yet another mountain man said. "Was you 'bout ready to leave this place?"

"I was going to go through the wagons and see if I missed anything the first time around. But if I found cash money, I wouldn't know who to send it to, and I wouldn't keep it for myself."

"I would," the fifth man finally spoke.

"Well, the rest of us wouldn't, Barney," the big man said, a note of finality in his words. "They's the blood of innocent folk on that money. Babies and the like. Let it rest like the dead it rightly belongs to."

Barney held up a hand. "All right, Gabe. All right. But how do we know that MacCallister here ain't already found the money and is just talkin' for our benefit? He's probably got it in his pocket right now. Who says he's some angel?"

Jamie took one step and popped Barney on the mouth with a huge left fist. Barney went down as surely as if he'd been pole-axed. He was not unconscious, but he was hovering very close to it. "No man casts aspersions upon my character," Jamie said. "No one."

Barney groaned and put fingers to his mouth. They came away bloody. He spat out a piece of broken tooth and struggled up to one elbow. He shook his head. "I'll kill you for that, MacCallister," he said.

"If you do, it'll be from ambush," Jamie told him. "You don't have the courage to face me hand to hand."

The other mountain men stood back, taking no part in this. Their code stated that every man saddled his own horse and stomped on his own snakes.

Finally, after Gabe silently looked at the other four mountain men and received a slight nod from each of them, said, "Here is where we part trails, Barney. I'll not ride no more with a fool. You know this here lad's reputation as good as the rest of us. And when Silver Wolf hears of what you just said 'bout his grandson robbin' from the dead, that ol' he-coon will be comin' after you, and anyone who rides with you. And I'd sooner have the devil hisself after me than Ian MacCallister. You git to your feet and git gone, Barney."

"Yeah," another mountain man said. "I never did like you no way. I always shook off and didn't believe all them stories I heard 'bout you robbin' from the dead back east. But now I see they was all true. I dasn't trust you no more, Barney. So git movin'!"

Barney slowly got to his feet, being careful to keep his hands away from the brace of pistols stuck behind his belt. "Damn your eyes! All of you! You've not seen the last of me." He cut mean eyes to Jamie and wiped his bloody mouth with the back of his hand. "And you, MacCallister, me and you, we'll meet up some day. Bet on it."

"I'm not hard to find, Barney. But why wait? Why not settle it right now? Guns, knives, or fists. It doesn't make a bit of difference to me."

But Barney would have nothing to do with that suggestion—certainly not with fists, and he was no knife fighter. His was the way of a back-shooter.

As Barney was vanishing into the wilderness, leading his pack horse, Gabe said, "Look down your back trail often, Jamie MacCallister. Barney ain't been ridin' with us very long. I don't want you to think that we partner-up with skunks and weasels. But out here we like to give every man a chance to prove his worth. I think all of us has been knowin' for several months that Barney was no good."

"What's Barney's Christian name?" Jamie asked.

"Why . . ." Gabe frowned. "Let me think. I heared it oncet, I know. Yeah! Saxon. That's it. Saxon."

Long after the mountain men had said their farewells, Jamie sat away from the burial site and thought it over. Saxon. Another of the clan who had sworn to kill him. Another family who had sworn blood oaths to bury Jamie Ian MacCallister. But was Barney Saxon a part of that family? Jamie felt sure he was. Come to think of it, now that he had time to think it through, the family resemblance was there.

Jamie sighed. Would it never end? Was he to be faced with personal vendettas the rest of his life? "Probably," he muttered. "Perhaps I was born to that."

With a shrug of his massive shoulders, Jamie tucked the name of Barney Saxon in the back of his mind and stood up. He had work to do. No time to be lollygagging about, wondering about what might or might not occur in the future. Jamie stepped into the saddle and pointed Horse's head north.

* * *

Jamie prowled the country all that summer, from the Red Desert north to Togwotee Pass and back again. He saw a few white men and a lot of Indians—mostly Cheyenne, Sioux, and Crow. When they learned who he was and knew his intentions were honorable, he was welcomed into their villages. But he never went in without fresh meat from a recent kill. A Cheyenne woman made him new moccasins, a Crow warrior gave him a fine quiver, and a Sioux chief carved him a pipe. They were three of the most peaceful, lovely, and eye-opening months Jamie had ever spent. In the middle of August, Jamie pointed Horse's head south and began the long journey back to the Colorado valley and Kate and the kids.

If there was a spring, Jamie knew where it was. If there was a fine meadow with good graze, Jamie had it stored in his head. He had a wealth of information to share with Fremont. If and when he ever got to meet the man, he thought with a smile.

Jamie crossed the Sweetwater and stayed to the east of the Red Desert—called that because of its red clay—and made camp along the banks of the North Platte. His camp was very near the exact spot where, some twenty-five years in the future, the Army would build Fort Steele to help protect the Union Pacific and the Overland Trail. It would remain an active post until 1886.

Jamie had long run out of flour and sugar and salt and coffee, and as he gazed wistfully at the skinny rabbit impaled on a spit over a low fire, he made up his mind to cut east and stock up at a trading post over on the Laramie River. Once provisioned, he would head straight south to the valley . . . and Kate.

* * *

The trading post was a busy one, both for trappers and Indians, and on the day that Jamie rode in it was unusually busy. Or at least it seemed that way, with about a dozen men lounging outside and eight or ten inside the low-ceilinged, dark interior. Jamie had to bend down to enter the place, and the men inside stopped their buzz of conversation to take in Jamie's size. Jamie stood six-four and had the bulk to go with that height.

"Damn!" one man muttered.

Jamie was not a drinking man, only occasionally enjoying a whiskey, and after three months alone in the wilderness, this was one of those occasions.

Jamie walked to the rough bar and ordered. He towered above the men on either side of him. One of the men stared—not an unfriendly stare, just curious.

"You resemble a feller I been knowin' for years, lad. Mayhaps you're related. Ian MacCallister?"

"My Grandpa," Jamie said, then took a sip of the whiskey. He opined it was at least a week old.

"You'd be Jamie MacCallister, late of Texas."

"That's right." Jamie had been warned not to say anything about what he was doing up in the Wind River country.

"Folks shore didn't lie none about the size of you," the man's companion remarked quite pleasantly. "I've seen full growed grizzly's that t'wern't up to you."

"The bigger they are the harder they fall, I always say," a man spoke in low tones from a darkened corner. " 'Sides, I ain't never seen none of that pup's graveyards."

Jamie smiled and ignored the man. Take any room filled with men, whether they be rough outdoorsmen or soft-handed dandies, and there will always be at least one who is disagreeable and thinks he has something to prove.

"That's Buford Sanders," the man on Jamie's right whispered. "He's a bad one, lad. He's killed men with his bar hands."

"So have I," Jamie replied, and took another small sip of his whiskey.

"Even drinks like a little girl," Buford kept it up. "I reckon he slips out of his dress when he has to associate with men."

Jamie didn't know why Buford had chosen him to needle. But he had taken all of this nonsense he was going to take. He set the cup on the bar and the crowd around him parted, swiftly moving to one side or the other. The barman moved quickly to gather up the jugs of whiskey and stow them in a safe place.

Jamie turned around and looked at the thoroughly obnoxious individual. "I have a suggestion for you," he said. "And it would behoove you to pay close attention. For I am only going to say it once."

"Speak your piece, you silly fop!" Buford said with a dirty laugh.

"Very well. My suggestion is this: it would be very wise on your part if you were to immediately shut that goddamn flapping mouth of yours, you ignorant son of a bitch!"

Buford's mouth dropped open. No one had ever spoken to him in such a manner. Well . . . Preacher had one time. But everybody knew Preacher would as soon shoot you as look at you. And, to be truthful, the old Silver Wolf, Ian MacCallister, had backed him down more than once. But that crazy Scotsman would whip out a knife and cut a man from neck to crotch in a flash. He'd done it more than once. Buford Sanders hated all MacCallisters because of the Silver Wolf. And he was going to kill this one.

"I think I'll tear your goddamn head off, boy," Buford

said, standing up. He was about the same height as Jamie, and a powerful man, but one with a big belly.

"You've got a man-sized job ahead of you then," Jamie said. "And I don't think you're a big enough man to do the job, you puss-gutted, loudmouthed, bully-boy."

The two men closed on each other.

Ten

Buford took a wild swing at Jamie, and Jamie side-stepped and popped the man on the mouth with a solid left and followed that with a right to the side of his jaw.

Jamie felt good about this, for he was a man who hated bullies. As a child, he had been bullied in the Shawnee village and had vowed then that he'd take a lifetime stance against those types.

Buford rushed him, trying to get Jamie in a bear-hug. Jamie stuck out a foot and tripped him, sending the man to the floor with a crash that shook the room. Buford cursed Jamie soundly as he leaped to his feet. Jamie would bear in mind that the man was very quick and light-footed for his size.

Buford raised his big fists and assumed the proper stance for fisticuffs: left arm extended out and right fist tucked close to the body and almost under the chin. To Jamie's way of thinking, it was a very stupid stance.

He kicked Buford on the knee.

The big man started hollering and cussing as he backed up, favoring his injured knee. Jamie pressed him, landing powerful body blows to the man's arms and belly. Buford got one through and slammed Jamie hard on the side of his jaw. The man could punch, for Jamie saw little birdies and heard them chirping and experienced bells ringing for a few seconds. He recovered and blasted a right through Buford's defensive posture. The hard fist landed flush on Buford's mouth and smashed his lips. The blood splattered. Jamie followed that with a clubbing left to the side of Buford's head, the fist landing solidly on the man's ear. Buford screamed like a puma and quickly stepped to one side, shaking his head.

Jamie suddenly leaped into the air and kicked out, the sole of his moccasin smashing into Buford's face and breaking the man's nose. Buford was thrown back against the bar and almost toppled it over. Jamie whirled and kicked again, the sole of his moccasin slamming against Buford's jaw. The force of the kick put the loudmouthed bully-boy on the floor, blood dripping from nose and mouth.

This time, Buford was not nearly so nimble in getting to his feet. The men from the outside had come rushing into the huge room to see the fight, and almost to a man, they stood smiling as Jamie MacCallister kicked the crap out of Buford Sanders. Buford was not a well-liked man.

"Yield and it's over," Jamie told the man.

"You go to hell!" Buford said, and picked up a rough-hewn chair. He hurled the chair at Jamie, and Jamie stepped to one side, the chair crashing against a wall. Buford roared and rushed across the room, both big fists whipping the air.

Jamie set himself and hit Buford a right and a left, both powerful blows landing on the man's jaw, right and left side. While Buford was stopped cold, trying to clear his head of the pain, Jamie set himself again and started his punch down around his ankles. He landed a solid right to Buford's mouth and the blood and several teeth flew.

Buford's feet flew out from under him and he landed on his back on the floor.

Jamie stepped back and waited. He wasn't even breathing hard and had yet to work up a sweat—a fact not unnoticed by the men in the room.

"Give this up, Buford," one of his few friends in the room called. "Afore the lad kills you with his fists."

"I'll yield to no goddamn dirty Scotsman," Buford pushed the words past pulped and bloody lips. "I'll see you dead this day, MacCallister."

"No, you won't, Sanders," Jamie said easily. "I don't know why you carry such black hate in your heart for me, but it's going to get you killed if you continue this."

Buford heaved himself off the floor and advanced toward Jamie, his face a mask of wild hatred, his boots thumping heavily on the plank floor.

Jamie didn't wait. He took the offensive and began battering Buford with terrible, punishing blows to the face and belly. Buford could do naught but attempt to cover up. After two full minutes of taking blows that would have killed a lesser man, Buford's face was mottled with bruises and slick with blood. But still he would not go down.

Jamie stepped back and looked at the swaying man. "It's over," he said. "I'll not continue this."

"Good lad," the man who ran the post said.

"No!" Buford screamed. "No, by God, it ain't over. Fight me, you dirty bastard out of a spread-legged whore."

No man present would have taken that slur, and Jamie was no exception. His eyes narrowed as he stepped forward, one big right hand balled into a huge fist. He laid that fist against Buford's jaw and all present could hear the breaking of bone. Buford's eyes rolled back into his head, and he toppled over, landing on the floor with a mighty crash. He did not move.

His few friends came to his aid and dragged the man outside and placed him beside a horse trough.

"That was as good a tussle as I've ever seen," a mountain man remarked. "And I have seen some kick, gouge, and cuts in my time."

"Aye," another said. "Twust a good 'un, all right."

"Step up to the bar, Jamie MacCallister," the barman said. "And have a drink on me. Buford Sanders has had that comin' to him for a long time."

"Aye," a trapper said. "And Jamie MacCallister shore give it to him."

"You made a powerful enemy there, Jamie," yet another said. "He'll not forget or forgive. He's a hater, he is."

Jamie began to relax his muscles as the tenseness gradually left him. He had not come out of the fight unscathed, for his head and jaw hurt and there was blood on his lips where Buford had smacked him a pretty good lick. Had Buford not lost his temper, he could have done some real damage to Jamie. But the Shawnee chief had taught Jamie well in the art of hand-to-hand combat. Jamie tried to never enter into a fight with his blood hot and to always keep a cool head.

Jamie did not want the cup of whiskey the barman had set before him, but neither did he want to insult the man. He took a couple of small sips, and then when the man went to serve another customer, Jamie moved away from the bar and started picking out items for the long ride home.

The crowd thinned as men went outside to take another look at the battered Buford Sanders, who was now on his feet and wobbling around, muttering dark threats, all directed at Jamie. He was muttering because his jaw was clearly broken and badly swollen. His friends got the man into the saddle and they rode off, with Jamie taking note of the direction they took. He liked the look of none of Buford's friends, figuring them all for brigands and back-shooters.

Jamie paid for his supplies and was gone a half hour after the fight. He offered to pay for his share of damages done to tables and chairs, but the man who ran the post would have none of that.

"Watch your back, lad," a burly trapper told Jamie. "Them that rides with Buford is no-count."

Jamie certainly agreed with that. He headed south.

There was much to do in the long and lovely valley before winter's cold fist closed over the countryside. But for the first couple of days after Jamie's arrival, he and Kate did nothing except get reacquainted . . . several times.

Although all the men who settled in the valley with Jamie were skilled hunters, none were in Jamie's class; indeed, few men anywhere were. Jamie spent the first week back hunting for game, meat to jerk and smoke and to make pemmican. He put the older children fishing and the women began smoking the fish. The younger children gathered what berries were left, under the supervision of adults.

Black Thunder had taken his people to new winter camping grounds, and those in the valley were now truly alone. Had there been word from Carson or Fremont, it was to have been dropped off by the first trapper or mountain man leaving Bent's Fort traveling east. There was no message from either.

But the cabins were snug and the winter that season was mild, if one calls temperatures occasionally dropping down to ten or twenty degrees below zero mild. No one got sick, and even though the food was very bland toward the end of the winter, no one went hungry. In the spring of 1841, Jamie and Sam once more made ready their mules and headed for Bent's Fort, with Sam complaining that the shopping list was longer than his arm.

"More mouths to feed," Sarah told him.

That was sure a fact, for when Sarah's barren streak ended, it didn't just break, it shattered to the four winds. Sarah gave birth to another set of twins that winter. As before, a boy and a girl.

"You trying to catch up with Kate and me?" Jamie kidded his friend.

"God forbid!" Sam said.

Jamie looked at his oldest son, Jamie Ian, who was now thirteen and very nearly a grown man. He was not yet as tall or heavy as his father, but he would be someday. "Look after your ma and your bothers and sisters, Jamie Ian. It's in your hands now."

"Yes, Pa. I will."

"Next year, I'll more than likely be gone by this time. I'll speak to Sam about you going along with him and probably Swede for supplies. Would you like that?"

The boy's smile would have lighted up a dark room. "Yes, sir!"

Sam and Swede and all the rest had toughened both physically and mentally during the years out in the vastness of the west. During Jamie's absence, a crew of brigands had happened along and tried to have their way with the women while the men were in the field. Ellen Kathleen had rung the warning bell and the men had come at a run. There had been eight brigands. Five of them now lay in the ground some ways out from the plot of ground designated for the community cemetery—when the time came—and all knew it would. Sam would not have them buried among decent folks. Sam had killed two, Swede had killed two, and twelve-year-old Jamie Ian had used his handmade Bowie on the fifth, cutting him open from neck to crotch.

Three had gotten away. Lewis, Watkins, and Smith. Jamie had been given their descriptions and silently vowed to find them. For they had been the ones who had manhandled Ellen Kathleen, almost stripping her naked before Juan and the others had shown up causing the brigands to take flight.

"You have a talk with that son of yours, Jamie," Kate told her husband. "He is entirely too quick to use that knife of his."

Jamie had stared down at her. "He used it protecting his mother and family and the others."

"Jamie!" she stamped her foot. "He wanted to *scalp* the man!"

"So?" the rugged frontiersman said coldly.

"I fear for him, Jamie. He's too much like you."

"That's bad, Kate? Who stopped him from scalping the bastard?"

Kate stared up at him. "Sam."

"I'll have to speak to Sam about that."

Kate's blue eyes turned cold and she swung around and walked out of the home, before she said something that both of them would later regret. Kate and Jamie quarreled little, but when they did, the kids scattered to nearby cabins to wait it out and the others in the community left them alone until they had patched it up.

But try as hard as she could, Kate could not stay mad at Jamie for very long, and Jamie could not stay mad at Kate. Kate knew that she had to always bear in mind that Jamie had spent his formative years living with Indians, where scalping was not only acceptable, but a sign of bravery and honor. But she darn sure didn't have to like it when father told son it was acceptable white behavior.

But she also knew that Jamie Ian was so much like his father that the best thing she could do was keep her mouth shut and learn to live with it. Like it or not.

Andrew now, the twin of Rosanna, their second born, was not at all like his father. Andrew was serious and sensitive, tending to be a bit of a dreamer and to lean toward books and the classics. Rosanna was just like him.

"Put in an order for a piano," Kate told Jamie, just before he and Sam pulled out.

"A *what?*" Jamie blurted.

"You heard me. I want Andrew and Rosanna to learn to play."

Jamie very nearly lost his temper. "How in the name of God am I going to get a piano out here?"

"You'll think of a way. Just do it."

"Do you have any idea how much that is going to cost?"

She smiled sweetly at him. Very sweetly. Jamie took a step backward. He'd seen her back down an angry Ute with that smile.

"We can afford it."

"If you say so." He bent down and kissed her. "We're gone."

Jamie muttered under his breath for several hours on

the trail. Sam was amused but said nothing. He knew Jamie would get to whatever was bothering him in time.

"A piano," Jamie said aloud.

"Beg pardon?" Sam asked, doing his best to hide his smile.

"A piano. Kate wants me to order a piano."

"Oh, that would be grand! Oh, my, yes. The girls should learn how to play."

"She wants Andrew to learn how to play the piano," Jamie said sullenly.

"Nothing wrong with that, Jamie. The greatest composers in the world are men, you know?"

"No. I didn't. Andrew is a boy. Damn near grown. Sits around and dreams all the time. Invents things—when he doesn't have his nose in a book. Makes up little tunes in his head and hums them. Good Lord, Sam. The boy can't hunt worth a damn, can't fish worth a damn, couldn't track a wounded bear across an open meadow. Can't shoot a rifle, can't shoot a pistol, can't shoot a bow and arrow. Sam, if he stays out here, he's going to get killed. He's as different from Jamie Ian as day from night. I keep hoping he'll grow out of it. But now I don't think he ever will. I just don't know where I failed the boy."

Sam smiled. "He is what he is, Jamie. If you try to make him something he's not, he'll resent it for all his life. And probably hate you for it."

Jamie looked at his long-time friend. Sam was graying now, his hair all salt and pepper. And his wife Sarah was no longer a young woman. Her last birthing had been a very difficult one. After the hard birthing, Sam had said they would have no more children.

They rode in silence for a few more miles. Finally, Jamie heaved a great sigh and nodded his head. "If Kate wants a piano, then a piano she shall have." He smiled and lifted his head up. "Oh well. Perhaps a musician or two in the family will be a good thing."

"Of course, it will. We'll have a good time gathered around the piano." Excitement grew in his voice. He twisted in the saddle. "Jamie. Let's build a combination school and church building. We're growing and soon there will be others coming in. Won't it be grand to gather on a Sunday and sing praises to the Lord while Andrew or Rosanna plays the piano?"

Jamie smiled and agreed with his friend. Jamie was more inclined to worship in the Indian way—to Man Above, the Great Father, Wakan Tanka. It just made more sense to him. But Kate had been firm about that. The children would be raised in a Christian home with white European concepts of God. "You're right, Sam. It would be a good thing."

"Wonderful, lad! Wonderful."

"But right now, let's pull in them rocks up yonder and see who it is that's trailing us. There's a spring in there and I have a bad feeling about them who's been slipping up behind us."

Eleven

As soon as Jamie and Sam and the mules vanished into the rocks those behind sought cover.

"No decent man would do that," Sam remarked. "They must be scalawags."

Jamie did not reply. His mind had already shifted to what the Shawnee called the Warrior's Way. His eyes had taken in all his surroundings, picking out the best defensive positions and any place he and Sam might be vulnerable. He concluded that they were in a very good spot.

"Secure the mules, Sam. And bring the rifles up here when you return."

"Are they Indians, Jamie?"

"No. White men. But I don't have a clue as to who they might be. And that troubles me."

After Sam had picketed the mules and gathered up the rifles, he said, "You told us about the man you had trouble with last summer, Jamie. Could this be him and his kin?"

"Maybe. But it could be anybody. To have lived no longer than I have, I certainly managed to gather more than my share of enemies."

Sam nodded his head in agreement with that. Jamie had just passed his thirtieth birthday, and Sam had never known nor could think of anyone in recent memory who had more enemies than Jamie MacCallister.

The puzzle was suddenly solved when a shout rang out. "You give us them fine-lookin' mules and you boys can ride on. There ain't no mules worth dyin' for. Think about that."

"Highwaymen," Sam said with a snort.

Jamie smiled. "How can they be highwaymen when there are no highways out here, Sam?"

Sam shook his head. Jamie's sense of humor could surface at the strangest of times. "Then we'll just call them thieves."

"Among other things."

"How 'bout it, boys?" the shout came from the west of their location.

"Why don't you come and take them," Jamie yelled defiantly.

"That ain't very smart on your part," the unknown man yelled. "You bes' think 'bout that some."

Jamie leveled his rifle and put a big ball whining and bouncing among the rocks where the thieves were hiding. He did not expect to hit anyone, and he didn't, but judging from the yelling, he sure caused some anxious moments among the brigands.

"Fire into those rocks, Sam. Let's give them something to think about."

Sam and Jamie emptied eight rifles into the rocks as fast as they could pull their triggers, and this time they drew blood. A man gave out a terrible shout of pain, which was followed by horrible choking sounds, then silence.

"You sorry sons!" the voice shouted again. "You've kilt my partner."

"Good!" Sam yelled.

Jamie looked at him and grinned. It had taken Sam

awhile to learn about law and order in the wilderness, but once he caught on, the lesson stayed with him.

"That ball took half his head off!" the indignant brigand yelled.

Jamie and Sam remained silent. They had a small spring behind them in the rock. Not enough water for a sustained standoff but enough to get them by for a day or two. However, Jamie had no intention of letting this continue for a day or two. Sam, looking at the set of Jamie's jaw, could read that in his face. Jamie's eyes were bleak and cold, the pale blue softness replaced by a terrible hard light. Jamie would befriend anyone who needed help, but cross him, and he would become a deadly foe.

Suddenly, there came a shout from the rocks. "We'll meet again, boys! No man crosses Pete Thompson and lives long to boast about it."

"Who is Pete Thompson?" Sam asked.

"I don't know," Jamie replied. "But he's a fool, telling us his name after threatening to steal our mules."

Seconds after the sound of the brigands' leaving reached them, Jamie was out of the rocks and moving toward the rocks just below them. He stood for a moment over the body of the dead man. Thompson had been right: the ball had made a mess of the man's head.

"You know him?" Sam asked.

Jamie shook his head. "No. Ground's too hard to dig here. Let's gather up some rocks and cover him best we can. Then we'll move on."

Sam had long grown accustomed to Jamie's coldness when it came to dealing with outlaws, so the suggestion did not shock him as it would have years back. Sam went through the man's pockets and found only a few coins; no clue as to who he might have been. After covering the outlaw with rocks, Jamie went to retrieve the mules, and Sam Montgomery stood for a moment over the mound of rocks, battered hat in hand. He knew he should say something over the remains, but the words just would not come to him. He finally shook his head and walked back to Jamie and the mules. Jamie just looked at him and said nothing. Five minutes later, they were on the trail, heading east toward Bent's Fort.

Jamie asked around at the fort, but no one there had ever heard of anyone called Pete Thompson.

"Country's fillin' up," a trapper said. "A body can't ride a whole week without seein' some settlers tryin' to scratch out a crop somewheres. But with the good comes the bad. I'll shore pass the word 'bout Thompson. I get him in gunsights, that'll be the end of Pete Thompson. We don't need his kind out here."

"I got a harpsichord in the back," Jamie was told when he placed his order for a piano. "Been here nigh on five years. Man ordered it and never come back to get it. I guess his horse throwed him or a bear grabbed him or a rattlesnake struck him or the Injuns got him. I can make you a real deal on it."

"I'll take it," Jamie said quickly, without even inquiring as to the price.

A trapper standing nearby said, "You cain't tote no harpsichord acrost country on a mule, son. Thar wouldn't be nothin' left of it time you got where you was goin'."

"Who owns that piece of a wagon out back?" Sam asked.

"Why . . . nobody," the counterman said. "You want it, take it."

And thus began the legend of the harpsichord. Years later, long after Andrew became one of the young country's best loved concert pianists, he still delighted in telling how his father and Sam Montgomery transported a harpsichord across several hundred miles of wilderness . . . and managed to get it to the valley in one piece.

It was quite a sight as Jamie and Sam—with Sam driving the wagon—pulled out at dawn from Bent's Fort.

"I want to hear some pretty music from the high country!" a trapper called out. Jamie waved.

"Hell," another mountain man said. "Let's ride with them. I want to be shore that music machine gits to where somebody can make pretty sounds come out of it."

"Damn good idee," another said. "Let's do it."

And so it was that a dozen heavily-armed, grizzled, buckskin-clad, bearded, and uncurried trappers and mountain men escorted the harpsichord from Bent's Fort to the valley. They encountered several bands of Indians, some of whom were decidedly unfriendly. But none of the war-painted Indians wanted to tangle with that tough-looking bunch. Several times, after supper, the men unloaded the harpsichord and Sam played the few tunes that he knew. It didn't matter that he played the same songs over and over, for to the mountain men, long separated from kith and kin, it brought back memories of parents, brothers and sisters, sweethearts, and a way of life they had long abandoned. Many times, Sam played long into the quiet night. Indians listened in amazement to the sounds in the darkness, looking at one another and shaking their heads. Truly, all white men were crazy.

Twelve

Andrew took to the harpsichord like a duck to water, while Rosanna's interests had shifted and she began to write. Sarah and Sam said she was gifted and should be encouraged.

Jamie listened and did not have to be hit on the head to know what was coming next. As usual, he was correct in his thinking.

"I've been talking with Sam and Sarah," Kate said one evening, as she and Jamie sat in the dogtrot of the large cabin.

"Uh-huh," Jamie said and waited for her to drop the other shoe.

"I think that Andrew and Rosanna should go back east to school."

Jamie smiled in the darkness and waited.

"Well, what do you think, Jamie Ian MacCallister?" Kate asked.

Jamie stifled a chuckle. When she called him Jamie Ian MacCallister, the game was over and it was time to go home. For Kate would brook no further argument. "Oh, I think it's a grand idea, Kate."

"You do?"

"Oh, yes. I have to go to St. Louis to hook up with Fremont and his party, and then proceed to someplace called Fort Levenworth to jump off. I can take the kids to the city and see them on their way east."

"Really?" Kate was astounded. It wasn't like Jamie to give in so easily. She narrowed her eyes and stared at him through the darkness of evening. "Do you feel well, Jamie?"

"I feel fine." The times Jamie had been sick in his entire life could be counted on the fingers of one hand.

She leaned over and put a small hand on his broad forehead. "No fever."

He laughed and took her hand in his. "Kate, I want what is best for the children. It just took some time for me to get used to Andrew's not wanting to be like his dad, that's all. But I can't live their lives for them. Do any of the other kids want to go back east?"

She shook her head. "No. And I asked them separately so one wouldn't influence the other. When will you leave?"

"As soon as this Fremont person gets word to me. Do you want them to go now, Kate?"

She was silent for a moment. "Yes," she said softly. "Sam and Sarah's families will see to it that they get into the best schools."

Jamie nodded his head then, realizing that Kate could not see the silent agreement, said, "I'll get Black Thunder and his people looking for Grandpa and for Preacher; tell them to come at once. I can't take Sam away from the fields. They'll ride with me to St. Louis. We'll probably hook up with a few others at the fort, so we'll have lots of protection along the way. You want go back for a visit, Kate?"

"No," she said quickly. "This is my home. Here I stay." Her reply came as no surprise to Jamie, for Kate had cut all ties with what family she had remaining back in the States.

"It's going to be expensive," Kate said. "The kids can't have homespuns in some fancy school. Their clothes will have to be store-bought."

"We'll manage. I'll buy them both proper clothes in St. Louis." Jamie would be carrying a small leather sack of gold nuggets. He had found a thin vein in the mountains and took only what they needed to buy supplies. So-called government experts had declared that there was no gold anywhere west of the Mississippi River. Jamie and Preacher and Jamie's grandfather and a few other mountain men knew better. But they were keeping that knowledge to themselves. In a few more years, gold would be discovered in California, and that would start a rush of people moving west to seek their fortunes. Most would lose everything they had in a futile search for the yellow metal; still others would become rich beyond their wildest dreams. The vein that Jamie found would see to the needs of his family for decades, long after Jamie and Kate had made their mark on the settlement of the west and were laid to rest on a lonely plateau in the high country.

The women in the small settlement went to work, pulling dresses out of trunks and cutting and redesigning the fabric, making new patterns from the material for Rosanna. They used pictures from newspapers and magazines brought back from Bent's Fort by Jamie and Sam.

Fields of education were wide open for Andrew, but opportunities for women were slim in those days, and it was decided that if need be, Rosanna would be sent overseas for a proper education. With a sigh, Jamie went to his vein in the high country and started work with shovel and pick. That stopped when the elder MacCallister rode in and tossed a sack of gold nuggets on the table.

"That will see to the lad and lassie's education," Silver Wolf declared. "I dinna know what I was goin' to do with the gold anyway. Now I know it will be put to a good use."

"The girl's gonna have to ride sidesaddle when we get to St. Louis," Preacher said.

"Sidesaddle!" Rosanna shouted.

Kate and Sarah took Rosanna aside and began explaining to the young woman about the responsibilities of being a proper young lady. But surprisingly, it was her great-grandfather who calmed her down and worked with her on horsemanship, for riding sidesaddle was not nearly so easy as riding astride.

When the day came for the twins to pull out, it was a sad one for Kate, for she knew it would be years before she again saw her children. Jamie busied himself with the pack horses while Kate walked through the meadows with her kids.

For this trip, Jamie would ride a horse he had swapped for up north, from the Nez Perce, a big rump-spotted stallion the Nez Perce called "appaloosa." The animal was much larger than the average appaloosa and had the same disposition as Horse, which is to say it was a killer. But around Jamie, the animal, whom Jamie had named Thunder, was gentle as a lamb.

Jamie's grandfather took one look at the big stallion and remarked, "You do like them mean, don't you, boy?"

Jamie smiled as he fed Thunder a tiny bit of sugar. The animal took the treat as gently as a baby. "He's not mean around me, Grandpa."

Then the goodbyes were over and it was time to go. Kate stood dry-eyed (she had done her weeping the night before, lying in Jamie's arms) and watched them go. Then without another sign of emotion, she walked back into the large cabin, closed the door behind her, sat down at the harpsichord, and began playing.

Preacher joined them on the first day out, and on the second day out of the valley, another mountain man joined the party—Preacher introduced him as Sparks. Sparks didn't have a whole lot to say, but Jamie liked him immediately and pegged him as a man to ride the river with.

"I been puttin' off goin' to St. Louie for five years," Sparks said. "I got kin over in Ohio I need to see. Might as well tag along."

Two other mountain men, a dwarf called Audie, and his partner, a huge bear of a man named Lobo, joined up halfway to the fort. Audie had been a schoolteacher back east until the west had beckoned him and he left all that behind. No one knew where Lobo came from or what his Christian name was, and nobody asked. It was not a polite thing to do. Audie talked like a walking dictionary, and before the first day had passed he and Rosanna and Andrew were the best of friends and the former headmaster was coaching the twins on grammar and what to expect once in school.

With the twins safe, Jamie began ranging out far ahead. He was well aware that trouble could rear up at any time: from Jack Biggers or the renegade mountain man Barney or Buford Sanders or Pete Thompson and his gang. Jamie was not particularly worried about the Indians, for even though the party was small in number, the Indians were well aware that with six mountain men, there would be at least forty guns between them, all fully loaded and ready to bang.

The journey to Bent's Fort was made without incident and the mountain men there immediately went on their best behavior around the lovely young Rosanna. There were probably a few who would have taken advantage of her, but to a man, they did not want to risk the terrible retribution of Silver Wolf, Preacher, Sparks, Audie, Lobo, and especially Jamie Ian MacCallister. In the raw west, men had been killed for merely accidentally jostling a good woman. Do a harm or a slight to a good woman and one risked the wrath of the entire community.

A train of wagons was about to leave for the trip back to the States, and Jamie hooked up with them. There had been some Indian trouble over on the Plains (in what would one day become the state of Kansas), and the wagon master was glad to have the added rifles. But the trip back east was uneventful. Perhaps it was the size of the wagon train and all the mounted and heavily armed men. Perhaps the Indians just did not feel like attacking. It was difficult, if not impossible, to tell.

Jamie and the others saw to the boarding and the safe passage of Andrew and Rosanna, and then Jamie's Grandpa and the others headed back to the High Lonesome. Jamie decided to prowl about St. Louis for a time. Stepping into a smoky tavern one evening, he spied Carson, holding court with a group of St. Louis dandies. Carson spotted Jamie and waved him over with a shout and a grand flourish.

"Now here, folks, you have a living legend. Jamie Ian MacCallister. Scout, Injun fighter, one of the heroes of the Alamo, and a man to ride the river with."

The men took one look at the bulk of Jamie and wisely made a path for him. Amid much shouting and hurrahing, Kit pulled Jamie over to one side and whispered, "What's been happening west of here, lad?"

"The first large wagon train pushed through over the Oregon Trail," Jamie said. "Fifty wagons, so I was told."

"Damn!" Carson said. "The gates is open now, Jamie. And they'll be hell to pay amongst the Injuns."

"They're not happy about it," Jamie agreed, taking a mug of ale someone thrust into his hand. He took a sip and asked, "When do we leave?"

"Next spring. We'll meet on the Missouri River at an army post called Levenworth."

Jamie nodded his head. "Then I'll see you there." He drained his mug of ale and left, ignoring the shouts from those who wanted him to stay and relate some of his adventures. But Jamie would leave the bragging to someone else. Boasting about his exploits was not his forte.

Jamie took the northern route back because he wanted to see some of the country he'd be helping to explore. He found the entire mission to be mildly amusing. If Fremont wanted information about any particular area, all he had to do was ask the mountain men or trappers. They'd been roaming all over the west for more than fifty years. The more Jamie dealt with the federal government the more he realized they wasted money, duplicated efforts, and in general, didn't know what they were doing much of the time.

Jamie had a hunch that in a hundred and fifty years it would be just as bad.

Maybe worse.

* * *

Jamie rode into the valley in late summer. He topped a long rise and sat his horse for a time, looking down at the peaceful scene. During his two and a half months of wandering he had ridden through some lovely and lonely country, seen some sights, and encountered no problems with any Indians. He had stayed in their villages, eaten their food, sat around the fires and talked, and been welcomed. Both his grandfather and Preacher had warned him about the Pawnee, however, and he took their warnings to heart, giving that tribe a wide berth.

Jamie spotted a new building and figured rightly it was the new church and schoolhouse. Then his eyes narrowed and his jaw tightened as he spotted two new graves in the outlaw cemetery. He quickly shifted his gaze to the spot picked out for the community's burying ground. No graves there. Yet.

Jamie noticed something else, too: the new graves were fresh, the mounds of earth still raw. He spoke to Thunder and the big stallion moved down the slope toward the settlement. He'd been spotted now, and the folks had gathered outside their cabins, watching him ride in.

Jamie swung down and handed the reins to Jamie Ian, one of the few people other than Jamie that Thunder would allow to handle him. He embraced Kate and shook hands with the others.

He cut his eyes to the graveyard and said, "What happened?"

"Renegades," Sam said. "They came in a rush late one Sunday afternoon."

"The graves are very fresh," Jamie remarked.

"Yes. Last week, as a matter of fact. There were ten of them. The man who appeared to be the leader shouted that they'd be back, and soon. With more men."

"Which way did they ride out?"

Sam pointed to the west. "That way." He stared at Jamie. "What are you going to do, Jamie?"

Jamie did not reply directly to the question. Instead, he called to Jamie Ian. "Saddle Horse for me, son." He turned to Kate, putting his big hands on her slender shoulders. "The children got off safely and I waited in St. Louis until I received word that they were met by Sam and Sarah's people. Now, Kate, pack food for me. I will not tolerate attacks upon this community. Not now, not ever."

Kate did not argue. Their long awaited homecoming in each other's arms would have to wait for a little longer. She turned and walked into the large cabin. Jamie called to his son. "Jamie Ian! Saddle a horse for yourself and then provision yourself and take up arms. You're coming with me."

Kate paused at the doorway and slowly turned around to stare at her husband. There was a terrible expression on her face and her blue eyes were cold. Jamie met her icy stare and said, "He's a man growed, Kate. And he's already been bloodied. Besides, where were we at his age?"

Kate forced a smile and her eyes warmed a bit. To the temperature of a fjord in January. "On the run, as I recall. Or very close to it. I'll pack food for the both of you. It's time for Ian to flee the nest, I suppose."

"He won't be flying far," her husband told her. "And he'll return to hearth and home."

"He damn well better!" Kate said, then turned and entered the cabin. Kate almost never cussed. But the kids had long ago learned that when she stamped her little foot and said, "Shit!" it was time to make tracks for safe ground. It usually took the kids about five seconds to exit the scene.

"Do you want any of us to go with you, Jamie?" the Swede asked.

Jamie shook his head. "No. Stay and guard the settlement. We'll be back when you see us."

He entered the cabin and emerged with fresh clothing. At the creek, he carefully bathed and then stood barechested and shaved at a broken piece of mirror wedged into a tree. Jamie carried terrible knife and bullet scars on his upper torso—mute testimony to the hard life he had endured since early childhood. He heard Kate coming up the path.

Kate stood and watched him for a moment. "Jamie, it's not easy for a mother to see her children ride off into danger."

"You think it's easy for a father?" Jamie wiped his face on a bit of cloth and faced his wife. "Every time I ride away there is a real possibility I won't return. Jamie Ian has to learn to be the man. He's a warrior, Kate. Now it's time for him to go into battle and count coup." He leaned down and kissed her lips. "We'll be back."

"Let's go, Pa!" Ian shouted from the flats above. "We're burnin' daylight!"

Jamie laughed softly and slipped into a buckskin shirt. He kissed Kate again. "Keep the coffee hot, honey."

"Among other things," she told him.

Thirteen

"Why is Ma so dead set on havin' me hang onto her dresstails, Pa?" Jamie Ian asked.

"Because she loves you," his father told him, his eyes on the ground, easily picking out the day's old tracks of the brigands.

"She loves Andrew and Rosanna, too. But she turned them a-loose, didn't she?"

Jamie ducked his head and smiled. "That's different. And there ain't no such word as a-loose, boy."

"Ain't no such word as ain't either, Pa."

Jamie slowly straightened up and stared at his oldest son for several very long heartbeats. Ian hushed up quickly. He knew full well just how far to push his father. And he had pushed him right to the line.

"Tell me what happened when the outlaws attacked the settlement," Jamie said.

Ian hesitated and Jamie knew then that his suspicions were correct: those back yonder in the settlement had not been totally truthful with him about the outlaw attack.

"All of it, boy!"

"They handled Ma pretty rough, Pa. She made me swear never to tell you. And I swore, too. Now I done broke my word."

"Handled your mother how?"

The boy's face was crimson. "Felt her all over. Run their hands up her dress. Ellen Kathleen told me."

"And how did she know all this?"

" 'Cause them men was doing the same to her. You see, Pa, they caught Ma and sister down by the creek. Swede, he heard them yellin' something fierce and grabbed up his rifle and give out a holler. By the time he got there, they had purt near stripped Ma and sister down to the buff. One man, the leader, was tryin' to . . . well, he was . . ."

"I know what he was trying to do. Did he?"

"Oh, no, sir. The Swede said that Ma kicked him right in the parts, she did. And Ma can kick. I know. She's kicked me in the butt a time or two."

"You deserved it, didn't you?"

"Oh, yes, sir!"

"Go on."

"While the leader of the gang was rollin' around on the ground pukin', Swede he shot one of the gang and just about that time Juan run up and killed the second one. Sam, he got a ball in another one and then they took off, yellin' about how they was goin' to come back and finish what they started that day. Now you want to tell me why Ma is so anxious to keep me hid under the bed for the rest of my life?"

"Keep your scalpin' knife in its sheath, boy. Your ma don't think that is civilized behavior for a white man. When you get older and get out on your own, then do what you think is right. But not until then. Is that clear?"

"Yes, sir. Pa?"

"What?"

"How old was you when you took your first scalp?"

"Older than you. Now hush up and read signs."

Jamie and Ian followed the hoof marks, looking more

like brothers than father and son. Ian was beginning to fill out but still had a long way to go to match his father's legendary strength.

The outlaws were brazen in their contempt for those who lived in the settlement in the long, lovely valley. They had made camp not ten miles from the small community and were being very obvious about it. As so many men did in the wilderness in that time, they fairly bristled with guns—many of them carrying as many as six pistols. They had rifles stacked all over the camp, within easy reach. And Jamie knew it was done for a reason. Most Indians of that period did not have guns, still relying on arrow, lance, and war axe. But they knew what guns could do and the sight of so many guns would be a deterrent to most Indians, and an open invitation to a few.

"Those the men who attacked our settlement, Ian?" Jamie asked his son.

"Yes, sir."

"You're sure?"

"Positive, Pa. Right there is the man who tried to have his way with Ma. The man with the stovepipe hat. Stupid lookin' thing, ain't it?"

"Isn't it."

"Whatever. Do we attack?"

"When you are absolutely certain in your mind that this is the right bunch. Death is final, boy. And it don't help a damn bit to say you're sorry while standing over a grave."

Jamie Ian carefully eyeballed the motley bunch from their position on the ridge. Slowly, he nodded his head. "I'm sure, Pa. There ain't, *isn't,* a doubt in my mind."

"Stay right here," Jamie told his son. "And I mean stay

right here, boy. If you move I'll wallop you proper. You understand?"

"Yes, sir."

"You better. I don't want to tote you home hurt and have to face your ma."

"What if you get in trouble down yonder, Pa?"

"I won't. You stay put."

Jamie took his rifle and his bow and quiver of arrows. His two pistols were stuck down in hardened leather holsters. He worked his way slowly down the ridge, circling the fairly well chosen camp of the outlaws. He was ninety-nine percent certain this was the right bunch, but he wanted to get in close to listen to them talk. Then he would be sure.

It was said among the Indians that Jamie Ian MacCallister could slip up on a snake . . . and the talk was not that far from the truth. Jamie crept in close and listened. The talk was sometimes crude and most of the time filthy. Jamie had been known to curse from time to time, but he had never used the words this pack of rabid skunks were using.

Then the man with the stovepipe hat mentioned Kate. In extremely vulgar terms. Jamie felt his blood run cold and his eyes narrowed in anger.

"What a set of tits that yeller-haired gal had on her, boys!" he shouted, marching around the camp. "I tell you for a fact, now, for a little-bitty thang, I shore had my hands full of them titties." He pulled at his crotch. "I got to go back and bed her down, boys." Then he proceeded to tell all that he would do to Kate, and Kate to him.

Jamie lifted his rifle and shot the vulgar brigand. The ball struck the butt of one of the man's guns stuck down into his waistband and it discharged, blowing a hole in the crotch of his dirty britches and setting them on fire.

"Oh, good God, boys!" the man screamed. "I been ru-int!" He started running for the creek, and Jamie lifted a pistol and knocked a leg out from under the man, sending him sprawling and howling to the rocky ground. He lay on the ground, screaming as his crotch burned.

Jamie lifted his second pistol and shot a brigand in the belly, just as his son opened up from the ridge, his first shot taking a man right between the eyes and dropping him dead on the ground.

The men in the camp had frozen for a moment and then reacted, diving for their guns and spreading out in a half circle. Jamie backed into the brush and quickly reloaded. Then, on his belly, he began making his way toward the north, where he had seen a man jump into the brush. And it was a man he had seen before, over at Bent's Fort. Jamie had recognized him by the long scar on the side of his face.

Stovepipe hat was squalling and cursing and shouting orders, most of which had to do with his burning private parts and some of which dealt with the question of whether he had shot off his own manhood.

"I want that bassard alive!" stovepipe yelled. "I want to gouge out his eyes and put hot coals in his mouth. You hear me? I want him alive."

Nice people, Jamie thought.

One of the gang made the mistake of exposing the lower part of a leg. Up on the ridge, Ian took careful aim and put a ball through it, splintering the shin. His yelling joined that of stovepipe, who had now made the creek and was sitting in the cold rushing waters, soothing his burned private parts.

"Hey!" the shout came from behind a jumble of boulders on the far side of the camp. "Who you be, mister?"

Jamie said nothing. Only his eyes moved.

"How come it is you attacked us?" the man hollered. "We ain't done you no harm."

Jamie remained silent.

"I don't thank they's but two of 'em," another voice was added. "Luddy, you start circlin'. Frank, you go the other way."

"Which way, is Luddy a-goin'?" Frank asked.

"Idiot!" the second voice said. "Move to your left."

"Winslow?" another voice said. "Be you all right?"

"I'm in the creek," stovepipe called.

Winslow, Jamie thought. I will remember that name.

"Is your privates all right, Winslow?"

"Burned some. But they's still hooked on to me. Now y'all listen to me. They's one up yonder on the ridge above us. And another a-creepin' around in the brush. I thank they's from the settlement. They just got the jump on us, that's all. We got to settle down and thank this out. Everybody hold your positions."

"Do that mean me and Luddy don't start circlin'?" Frank called.

"Yes, it do," Winslow called. "Just hold still."

I am dealing with some near idiots, Jamie thought. Coming from the ridge he could hear his oldest son's laughter at Frank's question and Jamie had to smile.

"They's laughin' at us," Luddy said. "I don't like that, Winslow. I don't like bein' made light of."

"Y'all stop that there laughin'!" Frank shouted. "You hear me. I won't stand for it."

But Ian's funny bone had been tickled by the stupid remarks from the outlaws and he only started laughing all the harder and louder. Even Jamie, very close to one of the brigands, had to struggle to contain his own laughter.

"They's just tryin' to goad us into doin' somethin' stupid!" Winslow yelled. "Don't fall for it. We got 'em outnumbered, boys. Just hang on. I'll thank of somethin'."

"Think?" Young Ian yelled from the ridge. "None of you are smart enough to think!"

"That's a damn kid!" Frank hollered. "You little whelp son of a bitch!" he yelled and jumped to his feet.

Ian's ball took him in the center of his chest and knocked him dead to the ground.

The boy is devious and dangerous, Jamie thought, with no small amount of pride in the thought.

"Frank!" Winslow yelled. "Frank? Answer me, ol' son."

"Frank's dead," another voice was added. "That may be a kid up yonder on the ridge, but if'n that's so, he's a damn fine shot, he is."

"Oh, hell, Winslow!" yet another voice shouted. "I know who them attackers is. I 'member now. I know who settled in that valley. I heared talk 'bout it. That Jamie MacCallister!"

"Shit!" the man with the busted shin said. "If'n that's so, we bes' start prayin' to the Lord for help."

"Shut up!" Winslow screamed. "MacCallister is just a man. And if'n that's his son up yonder on the ridge, the boy cain't be no more than thirteen or fourteen at the mos'."

"You know how old Jamie Ian MacCallister was when he kilt his first man?" Luddy called.

"How old?" Busted-shin asked.

" 'Bout ten year old way I heared tell it."

"Shut up, goddamnit, shut up!" Winslow screamed. "I don't wanna hear no more of this clap-trap."

"MacCallister!" Luddy shouted. "Can we talk?"

Jamie said nothing, he was close enough to a brigand to touch him. He had been moving no more than two or three inches at a time, and the smelly man was completely unaware that he was only moments from death. Jamie figured the man had not bathed in weeks, maybe months.

"Talk about what?" Ian called from the ridge, knowing that his father was stalking and would not break silence.

"Where is your pa, boy?" Luddy asked.

"Over to Bent's Fort."

"Bent's Fort! Wal, who the hell is with you?"

"My younger brother. He's eleven."

Jamie smiled. He and his oldest son were so much alike it was scary.

"He's lyin'!" Winslow screamed the words. "There ain't no eleven-yar-old got the nerve or the moves to slip up on experienced men like us'n. Don't listen to him."

"Jim!" Ian called. "Don't take no scalps, now, you hear. Ma don't hold with us scalpin'. You know what she said. She swore she'd tan our hides if we brung back any more scalps. Just kill a couple more of these sorry wretches and we'll go on back home and wait for Pa."

"I'm out of here," Busted Shin said. "I'm gone, boys. You'll not see hide nor hair of me no more. And that there's a solid promise, boys. You let me go?"

"Dave, goddamn your eyes!" Winslow squalled. "Don't you turn tail and run off, you hear me?"

"Hell with you, Winslow," Dave called. "If'n I'd a knowed that was Jamie MacCallister's woman I'd a not come within a hundred miles of her. I'm gone. I'm leavin', MacCallisters. You gonna let me go?"

"Go on," Ian called from the ridge. "But if I was you, I'd be more afraid of my friends shootin' me in the back."

"I hadn't thought of that," Dave admitted. "How about it, boys?"

"Go on," another man shouted from his position. "I'll personal shoot the first one who blows a hole in you, Dave."

"That is some small comfort, Harold," Dave called after a few seconds pause.

"Best I can do," Harold said.

"Go on, Dave," the shout came from the creek. "I never liked you no way. Never did trust you, neither. I knowed all along you was a coward. Don't let me see your ugly face no more. You hear me, Dave?"

"I hear you, Winslow. The hell with you, too. I'll see you boys," Dave hollered, then he limped to the horses, saddled up, and was gone.

The man who was hiding about two feet from Jamie said, "I ain't had me a boy since I was in jail back east, Winslow. I like to hear 'em holler. What do you say?"

"My equipment ain't up to it at the moment, Ned," Winslow yelled. "But you and the boys go right on. You capture them kids, y'all can corn-hole to your heart's delight."

"I'm gettin' all excited just thinkin' about it," Ned yelled.

Jamie put an end to the brigand's excitement by silently reaching out and cutting Ned's throat with his big Bowie knife.

Fourteen

Now Jamie had two loaded rifles and six loaded pistols, counting the rifle and four pistols taken from Ned, who would no longer have any use for them.

One of the no-counts suddenly jumped up and made a run for better cover. He should have stayed where he was. Ian and Jamie fired as one, both balls striking the outlaw. He was flung forward and was dead before he hit the ground.

"They might be kids, but they can damn shore shoot," Harold remarked. "What do you think about it, Ned?"

"I'm no kid," Jamie spoke in low tones. "And Ned can't hear you. I just cut his throat."

"Damn," a man said. "It's Jamie MacCallister."

"Back out!" Winslow shouted. "Stay to cover and back out slow and easy. Over to the crick."

There were at least five outlaws left able to ride, Jamie figured. Maybe one more than that. Either Winslow had hooked up with more brigands, or those at the settlement had been wrong in their count. No matter. They still had to be dealt with.

But not at this time. The outlaws made their horses and were gone in a frantic pounding of hooves and wild cussing and shouted threats.

"Let them go!" Jamie shouted to his son.

"But, Pa—"

"Let them go!" Jamie repeated. "Come on down here. And bring the horses."

While Ian was working his way down the ridge, Jamie collected the weapons of the dead, gathered up the three pack horses they had left behind, and then began dragging the bodies to a ravine and unceremoniously dumping them into the natural pit. "Stand watch," Jamie told his son.

"You going to say words over them, Pa?" Ian asked.

"I'll say something."

"Something" was very brief and to the point, for Jamie had absolutely no use for outlaws and even less for rapists and child molesters. He caved a wall of the ravine over the dead and told the Lord to do what He felt was best with them. And if He didn't know what to do, Jamie had a few suggestions. Amen.

"Do we go after the others, Pa?"

Jamie hesitated for a moment. "We probably should, but that bunch will be laying up in ambush for us. Don't run after a scared man, son. A scared man will hurt you."

"So what do we do now?"

"Go home."

By lamplight, Jamie tallied up the names of those men who had sworn revenge against him and his family since moving west. The list was getting longer. Jack Biggers and kin, Barney and kin, Buford Sanders, Pete Thompson, Winslow and gang. With a sigh, Jamie put down his pen and closed the ink well.

Cold winds blew against the cabin, but the logs were close-fitted and chinked well. The large cabin was snug against the winter's fury. In the months since Jamie and

Ian had confronted Winslow, the brigand had not been seen. Black Thunder had told Jamie his men had reported the outlaws had headed east.

In a few weeks, it would start to warm, and Jamie would have to leave to join Fremont and Carson. The winter had been unusually mild, and hunting had been good; not that a lot of hunting was necessary now. Cows and bulls and a few pigs that had broken loose from wagons on the way west had made their way into the valley and the settlers had a fairly respectable herd going. During the early fall, two weary families, whose wagons had broken down and who had been abandoned by an unscrupulous wagon master had been found by Black Thunder's men and after getting over their fright (which Black Thunder's men had found highly amusing), were led to the long and lush valley and welcomed by the settlers there. Sam and Swede returned to the broken wagons—not that many miles to the north—repaired them, and drove them back. As luck would have it, one of the men was a minister and the other a skilled blacksmith and farmer. Both men had families and all were welcomed into the settlement— William and Lydia Haywood, Eb and Mary French, and a total of eight children. The settlement was growing.

But that summer of '41 was the summer that Roscoe and Anne, the twins, now fully grown and with absolutely no negroid features, left the valley. And as was their way, they stole supplies and horses and pulled out in the dead of night.

Wells, who had married Moses and Liza's daughter Sally, was beating on the door to the cabin before dawn. "Get up, Jamie. Get up. They're gone."

Jamie, clad only in a long nightshirt, rifle in hand, unbarred the door and flung it open. "What's wrong, Wells? Who's gone?"

"Roscoe and Anne. They've stolen supplies and horses and slipped away."

"Give me a minute to dress."

Kate had gotten up with Jamie and was putting on water for coffee, stoking up the coals in the fireplace. During the summer months, she cooked outside, under the dog-trot, on and in a stone and metal stove that Jamie had made for her (many, many years later much the same apparatus would come into vogue as a grill and smoker and people would marvel at how good the food tasted). During the fall and winter months, the cooking was done inside to help heat the cabin.

"Get Moses and Liza," Jamie told Wells. "And the rest of the people. No point in having to repeat the same story over and over."

Sally came over, carrying half a side of bacon and Sarah came with a plate heaping with hot biscuits and Hannah brought over several dozen eggs. Maria Nuñez brought sliced potatoes and peppers to fry with them, and Lydia and Mary came with bowls of hot gravy and several jars of jams and jellies. Breakfast was a very important meal. The women started cooking breakfast while the men gathered with mugs of steaming hot coffee.

"They won't be hard to track," Juan opened the conversation.

"Do we want to track them?" Moses said bitterly.

"They are both grown," Sam offered. "We don't have the right to force them to stay."

"Neither will turn out well," Wells said. "They're both sneaks and thieves."

Jamie stood silently, listening to the exchange. He agreed

with Wells, although he felt sorry for both Roscoe and Anne. They were torn between two worlds, never feeling they truly belonged in either one. Their father had been a white plantation owner and their mother, Ophelia, a very beautiful, albeit a rather foolish and shallow, woman of high color. After her husband, a no-count named Titus, had deserted the family back in the Big Thicket country of Texas, Ophelia had hanged herself.

Titus and his son Robert were somewhere in the west. Jamie hoped he would not run into them.

"Let them go," Jamie finally said, putting an end to the quiet bickering. "The horses they stole were not much, and the supplies can be replaced. Let's just wish them well and get on with our lives."

"And eat," Swede said, his stomach rumbling at the good smells wafting through the cool morning air.

Fifteen

Jamie camped by the banks of the Missouri River, just north of the jumping-off place, and waited for them to show. He'd told Carson where he'd link up with the party. The winter past had been an uneventful one in the valley, with no births or deaths among the settlers and no more outlaw attacks. The Indians in the area had accepted them and were friendly, due in no small part to Jamie, who told the new preacher not to attempt to convert the Indians. They worshipped their own gods and were happy. The minister didn't like that, but he wasn't going to argue with Jamie about it.

Jamie knew that trouble with the Indians came when the white man tried to change the Indian into a mirror image of the whites. It wasn't going to work, now or ever.

An Indian was an Indian and the best way to get along with the red man was to leave him to his own ways. But Jamie knew the white man had to try to change everything and everybody into what he felt was best for them—in reality, he was changing others into what he felt was best for himself.

Jamie knew he would never change the white man's ideas about Indians, so for the most part, he kept his mouth shut about his views and managed to get along with most Indians.

Fremont was impressed with Jamie (most men were)

and began talking at once about manifest destiny. Jamie didn't have the foggiest idea what in the hell Fremont was talking about, but he managed to nod his head in all the right places. Jamie liked Fremont but considered the man to be a bit on the windy side. Fremont's second in command, a tall German named Charles Preuss, was excellent at his job, but a tad on the stuffy side. Jamie saw immediately that Pruess and Fremont did not really get along.

Jamie had to smile in somewhat of a bitter remembrance, for Colonels Bowie and Travis had not gotten along well either, but when it came right down to the nut-cuttin', they got in double harness and gee-hawed with the best of them.

The rest of the party were men that Jamie got on well with, eager types who knew their business and were chomping at the bit, ready to go to work.

It was May 1842.

Kit Carson was the group's official guide and Jamie the scout, which suited Jamie fine. That meant that he could range out far ahead of the others and therefore stay pretty much to himself.

Fremont's expedition went off without a single incident with the Indians in the area, although the party was well armed and expecting trouble. Fremont's only obvious mistake was in declaring that a mountain of his choosing was the highest peak in the Rockies. It wasn't. There were about sixty other mountains in the area that were higher. But in August of that year, as the expedition was winding down, Fremont and a few others climbed the peak and planted the American flag on the summit. The mountain was later named for Fremont.

Jamie considered the entire expedition the most boring few months of his life. Fremont and Pruess squabbled much of the time, usually over minor matters. Pruess became outraged when Fremont insisted upon shooting the rapids on a part of the Platte in a collapsible rubber raft. The raft capsized and many valuable records of the trip were lost in the white water. Jamie left the party shortly after that and headed west. The findings of Fremont were presented to Congress the next year, and Fremont was the hero of the time. No mention of Jamie Ian MacCallister's part in the expedition was noted in the report.

Jamie drifted northwest. He had told Kate he would be gone for the better part of a year so he was not expected back for many more months. There was a natural restlessness in Jamie; the urge to see new country, to stand on windswept mountains, and to camp and relax in lush valleys that few, if any, white men had ever before witnessed. He pointed Horse's nose to the northwest.

Preacher had told him about a place where scalding hot water shot out of the ground and into the air for hundreds of feet. Knowing that Preacher sometimes tended to stretch the truth just a bit, Jamie decided to see for himself. He headed deeper into the wilderness, even though winter was only a few weeks away from lashing out with its first cold fury.

Jamie ran into Sparks, Lobo, and Audie in Jackson Hole and told them what he'd been doing and where he was planning on going.

"For once Preacher didn't embellish the truth," Audie said. "I have personally witnessed the astonishing sight of those geysers of which he speaks."

"Say what?" Lobo questioned.

"I've seen the hot water come out of the ground, you ninny," Audie said.

"I wish to hell you'd speak plain words just once in a while" Lobo groused.

"Osborne Russell seen the things," Sparks said. "He said they was good in helping to fix food. Gets the kettle hot real quick. He said they was thousands and thousands of the squirtin' things scattered all over the place. I personal ain't never seen none of them."

"Want to ride along with me?" Jamie asked.

Sparks thought about that for a moment. He nodded his head. "Might as well. But I'll tell you this: we get caught by winter in that country, we're stuck for a time."

"For a fact, it's a hard country," Lobo said. "But I'm game."

"We shall all go," Audie said. "Why not? Demand for beaver is over. I fear our days are numbered. What else do we have to do?"

"I wish you'd quit talkin' like that," Lobo said. "I don't know what I'd do if trappin' plays out."

"Seek honest employment," Audie told him with a smile. "Work, for an example."

"Wagh!" the huge mountain man said. "I run away from a farm back east. Ain't never been back. Started to go back a few years ago. Then I run into a feller who come from the same part of the country. He told me my ma and pa was both dead. I never did get along with none of my brothers or sisters, so I decided there wasn't no point in makin' that long trip for naught."

"I do know the feeling," Jamie said.

"Let's pack up and ride," Sparks suggested.

"Magnificent!" Audie said, staring at the spouting geysers as the men stood in what one day would be known as Yellowstone National Park.

"Quite a sight," Sparks admitted.

"It's . . . awesome," Jamie said.

"Godamnest thing I ever seen, that's for shore," Lobo rumbled.

The men scouted the area and found one geyser that seemed to erupt at fairly regular intervals.

After a time, Sparks said, "A faithful ol' spouter, ain't she?"

In 1870, the surveyor general of Montana Territory, Henry Washburn, and a bank examiner, Nathaniel Langford, named the world's most famous geyser, "Old Faithful." Old Faithful erupts every thirty to one hundred twenty minutes, blowing hot water as high as one hundred and sixty feet into the air.

After a few days, Lobo and Audie decided to head back south and Jamie and Sparks decided to head west. Jamie had written Kate a letter and Audie promised that he would "personally deliver the love-filled missive to the dear lady."

"Quite a pair," Sparks said, as he and Jamie packed up and pulled out. "Ol' Lobo cain't hardly write his own name and Audie's got so much education he's fairly bustin' with it."

"I have a hunch that Audie, in his own way, would be just about as dangerous as Lobo," Jamie remarked.

"Worser. That little man will shoot you faster than a rattler can strike. Or cut you. I've seen him do both. He ain't no one to fool with."

"Preacher speaks highly of him."

Sparks chuckled. "Preacher's something, ain't he? I been knowin' him since he furst come out here. He was just a raggedy-assed kid, maybe twelve or thirteen at the most. Ridin' a wore-out old mule. Preacher's a good friend to have, and probably one of the worst enemies a man could ever have."

Jamie and Sparks rode straight west, past Targhee Pass and right into the Centennial Mountains. Nez Perce and Flathead country. They crossed the Bitterroot Range, forded the Lemhi River, and touched the northern part of the Lemhi Range. Days later, they found a place to cross the Salmon (the River of No Return) and were immediately swallowed up by one of the harshest wilderness areas Jamie had ever seen.

"Most men I know fight shy of this country, Jamie," Sparks said one evening, as the men were enjoying coffee and fresh caught trout. "She's wild and beautiful and dangerous. They's creatures roam this part of the country that's not human, but they ain't animal, neither."

"Are you having a joke on me, Sparks?"

The mountain man shook his head. "No. Injuns call 'em Sasquatch. Among other things. Now, I ain't never seen one, and I hope to God I never do. But I've knowed plenty of ol' boys out here who has. Brave men. And more'n one's left these parts swearin' to the Almighty that they'd never come back. One of the bravest warriors I ever seen was a Nez Perce name of Two Bears. He come face to face with a Sasquatch and when he returned to his village, his hair was snow white—and he was a right young man at the time. Sasquatch is real, Jamie—they prowl this land. And mighty creatures they is, too. All covered with hair . . . some of them nine feet tall and a good five hundred pounds."

Jamie knew that mountain men often took great liberties with the truth, but looking at Sparks's face in the flickering glow of the fire, Jamie sensed that the man was serious.

He drank his coffee and asked, "Any of them ever hurt a human being?"

"Not so far as I know. Injuns say they're shy creatures. Not much is known about them."

"Where do they live?"

Sparks shook his head. "No one knows. But I seen the bones one time of what the Blackfeet said was a Sasquatch. I can tell you this much: it weren't no human nor bear. Just looking at them bones give me a fright I ain't never forgot. This Blackfoot was investigatin' a cave he found and there was the bones, all laid out proper on some sort of crude-made bed."

Long after the fire had burned down to coals and Sparks was asleep, Jamie lay awake in his blankets. Wouldn't it be something if he could see one of those creatures? But not up too close, mind you. Jamie finally closed his eyes and slept. He dreamed about great hairy monsters, nine feet tall.

Jamie came awake with a start, reaching for his rifle. It was about two hours before dawn, he guessed. Cutting his eyes, he saw that Sparks was wide awake, both hands gripping his rifle.

"What was that noise, Sparks?" he whispered.

"Don't know. Tweren't no Injun though."

"Bear?" Jamie asked hopefully.

"Not unless he's a clumsy bastard."

Both men were thinking the same thing, but neither of them wanted to put it into words. Both of them reached out at the same time to toss wood onto the fire. Using a long stick, Jamie poked around until a small flame sprang up and touched the dry wood.

"Ain't it amazin' how fire gives such comfort to a man?" Sparks whispered.

Another crash came from the dark timber and both men nearly jumped out of their buckskin britches.

"Dead tree falling," Jamie said.

"You wish," was Sparks reply.

"Could be it's the Indians playing a joke on us," Jamie suggested.

"Not likely."

Not another sound came out of the forest and both men cautiously crawled out of their blankets and rolled them. Jamie put the battered pot on to boil water and then dumped in the coffee, adding cold water to settle the grounds. Sparks crawled around gathering up more wood to build two more fires.

"Is that wise?" Jamie asked.

"Woods creatures don't like fire. 'Sides, it comforts me."

"It'll be light in about another hour or so."

"Not soon enough for me."

A roar came out of the woods that sent chills racing up and down the spines of both men. Neither of them had ever heard anything like it in their lives. It was not human, but neither was it animal.

Long after the echoes of the roaring had died away, Sparks broke the silence with a whispered, "You a prayin' man, Jamie?"

"Occasionally. I did a sight of it at the Alamo."

"I 'spect you did. I just done me a little talkin' with the Lord."

"I hope He heard you."

"No more'n I do."

"Coffee's ready."

"Pass me a cup. I ain't takin' my eyes off them woods yonder. I seen something movin'."

Jamie poured and passed the mountain man a cup. "What did it look like?"

"You know what it looked like."

A crash came from behind the men and both men nearly spilled their coffee spinning around to face the sound.

"More'n one of 'em," Sparks said. "I think they're gettin' ready to attack."

"I thought you said they never bothered humans."

"I have been known to be wrong from time to time."

Then came the sound of something beating a stick against a tree, followed by grunts and howling and roaring.

"I think we done something to make them mad," Sparks said.

"If I knew how, I'd apologize."

"I just wish it would get light."

"How far is it across this range?"

"Don't know. Like I said, most white men avoid this area. They has been trappers who dared try it, though."

"How long did it take them?"

"I don't know. They never come out."

"Is there a way around it?"

"Couple of hundred miles out of our way."

"Hell with this!" Jamie said and stood up.

"What are you doing? Git back down to the ground, man. Them things can hurl a rock hundreds of feet."

"You ever seen one do it?"

"Well . . . no."

Jamie stood in the dancing light of the fires and roared and shook his rifle at the darkness that surrounded the tiny pocket of light in the wilderness.

"You gonna make them damn things mad, Jamie."

A roar came out of the woods, but it sort of choked off near the end.

"What'd that thing do?" Sparks asked. "Swaller a bug?"

Then they both heard the sounds of muffled giggling.

"I know that giggle," Sparks said, standing up. "Come on!"

Both men ran toward the timber. They pulled up short when they came upon Preacher. The mountain man was sitting on a log and laughing so hard tears were running out of his eyes.

Both men picked him up bodily, hauled him off, and threw him into the cold waters of a creek.

Sixteen

"I never seen two growed-up men so skirred," Preacher said, sitting by the fire with a blanket wrapped around him. He sipped coffee and giggled.

"I ought to shoot you, Preacher," Sparks said.

Preacher giggled.

"What are you doing up here, Preacher?" Jamie asked.

"Roamin' around. Skirrin' growed-up men by actin' like the boogy man."

"You been through this country a-fore, Preacher?" Sparks asked.

"I've skirted it a time or two. But I ain't never traveled east to west all the way through. Been aimin' to do it, though. You boys game?"

"That's why we're here," Jamie said.

Preacher was oddly silent for a few moments. So still and quiet that Sparks finally asked, "Something wrong, Preacher?"

Preacher slowly nodded his head. "Yeah. I ain't gonna say it ain't never been done, 'cause it has. But winter is nigh, boys. We get trapped in there, we're gonna be in a world of hurt."

Jamie smiled. "Then we'd better get going, hadn't we?"

The trio of men were days deep into mostly unexplored

wilderness (by white men) before Sparks started looking back over his shoulder and muttering to himself.

Finally Jamie asked, "Sparks, what are you mumbling about?"

"Something is followin' us, that's what."

Preacher looked behind them. "I ain't felt the short hairs on my neck standin' up, Sparks. 'Sides, this is Nez Perce and Flathead country, mostly. We all get on well with them."

"This ain't no Injun," Sparks grumbled.

Despite himself, and he was immediately irritated at himself for doing so, Jamie twisted in the saddle and looked behind him. He could see nothing out of the ordinary.

"Now, Sparks," Preacher said. "Don't you be tryin' to spook me and Jamie. We got to make camp shortly 'cause the night is fast upon us."

"I ain't tryin' to spook nobody," Sparks insisted. "But something is damn shore followin' us. I been feelin' it in my guts all day. Started last night. But I was loathe to say anything about it."

"It's your imagination, Sparks," Jamie said.

"Tain't no such of a thing, neither," Sparks said sullenly.

"Looks pretty good up ahead, Jamie," Preacher said. "I'll scout it out. I'm gettin' hungry around my mouth and that deer you kilt earlier today ain't gettin' no tenderer."

Camp made and the venison cooking, the men settled in for the night. But Sparks kept looking nervously around him. Preacher was amused by the man's antics and so was Jamie.

"Laugh," Sparks told them. "But I tell you both that something is out there."

"Shore there is," Preacher replied. "They's grizzlies by the hundreds, wolves and panthers by the thousands, and all sorts of other critters. Relax, Sparks. We got a warm fire, plenty to eat, and good company. Life can't get no better than this."

But while Jamie and Preacher slept soundly that night, Sparks was up every hour, walking around the camp, stopping to listen to the darkness. A little before dawn split the sky, Sparks managed to sleep a couple of hours. But he was the first one up and had coffee made and meat sizzling before the others opened their eyes.

"Sasquatch didn't come and tote you off, huh, Sparks?" Preacher questioned with a grin.

"Very funny," Sparks said sourly.

The camp had been set up in a tiny clearing, the lushness of deep timber all around them. Preacher was sitting with his back to a tree, Jamie sitting across the fire from him. Sparks had gotten up to walk once more around the camp as the men waited for full light before heading west. They were already saddled up and packed and ready to go.

Preacher was gnawing on a piece of meat and Jamie was enjoying a cup of coffee when Preacher felt someone tap him on the shoulder. "What do you want, Sparks?"

The tap came again. Heavier this time.

"Huh?" Sparks called from across the clearing.

"I said what do you want? You tapped me twicet on the shoulder."

"How the hell could I tap you on the shoulder when I'm twenty-five feet away lookin' at you?"

Preacher froze where he sat, the meat on a stick forgotten. Two seconds later, the camp erupted in activity and thirty seconds later the men were in the saddle, heading west.

Had they looked behind them, they would have seen a

Nez Perce named Night Stalker bent over in the clearing, convulsed with laughter. Preacher had played a trick on him several years back, and when Night Stalker picked up their trail the day before, he thought this would be a fine time to return the favor. Night Stalker sat down where Preacher had been sitting, for the spot was warm, and ate the venison. This was going to be a good story to tell around the fires back at his village. He would get a lot of laughs for pulling this trick.

Night Stalker stopped chuckling when something tapped him on the shoulder. One minute later, Night Stalker was a good quarter of a mile from the clearing and galloping his pony hard.

Maybe he wouldn't tell this story after all.

When the three men reached Oregon Territory, Preacher decided to cut south for a trading post and Sparks opted to head north up to the Whitman Mission. Jamie pushed on west. Weeks later, he sat his horse on the bluffs overlooking the Pacific Ocean and marveled at the sight. He turned Horse's head and rode south. He'd check out California—or at least part of it. Weeks later, after talking with a dozen or more trappers and fixing creeks and water holes firmly in his mind, he decided to head on back to the valley and Kate. This time, he vowed, he would stay put. Jamie had no way of knowing, but staying put was not in the cards for him.

Jamie resupplied and headed back, riding east, straight across the center of what would someday become Nevada, crossing mountain ranges and desert, memorizing everything he saw.

It was late spring when Jamie topped the ridge that led

to the valley. Everything was as he had left it, nearly a year ago, except for two new cabins. He sat his horse and watched as a tall young man rode up to meet him—Jamie Ian. Good Lord! but the boy had grown. Jamie quickly did a little figuring. His oldest son was nearabouts sixteen years old.

Father and son stayed in their saddles and stared at each other for a few moments. Jamie finally broke the silence. "Son. How's your mother?"

"Fine, Pa. She's been lookin' to the west most every day, waitin' on you."

"Well, I'm home now, boy. And home is where I intend to stay."

"Ma'll be pleased to hear that," Ian said drily.

Jamie ignored the sarcasm and asked, "Any word from Andrew and Rosanna?"

"Two letters. Grandpa brought one, and a trapper name of Nighthawk brought the other. Ma got your letter and was some thrilled about it."

"Two new cabins down yonder."

"Settlers come in and asked if they could stay. Mister Sam, he said he reckoned it would be all right, but the final word would have to come from you."

"Good people?"

"Real nice, Pa. Daniel and Marsha Noble and their kids. Wiley and Anne Harper and their children. They got a daughter name of Linda. Me and Linda been sort of sparkin' some. We think we'll get married this summer. We was waitin' on you to come back."

Jamie grunted. "Married, huh? What's your ma have to say about that?"

"She said she'd wait and talk to you about it."

"This girl, how old is she?"

"Fifteen."

"Both of you mighty damn young, don't you think?"

"Old as you and Ma was."

"For a fact, I reckon. But times are changing." Jamie's eyes twinkled. "This girl you're sweet on . . . she's pretty, huh?"

"Got hair the color of wheat, Pa. Blue eyes. 'Bout the size of Ma."

"Well, we'll talk about it."

"Me and Linda is betrothed, Pa. That's all there is to it."

"I didn't say I was against it, Ian. But we'll still talk about it. And that's all there is to that." Jamie lifted the reins and rode down the grade without looking back.

Ian came galloping up and grabbed hold of Horse's reins. Horse almost took his arm off and Ian jerked back just in time. "I'll fight you, Pa," the young man said hotly. "Don't you stand in my way."

Jamie kept his composure. He was still very much young enough to remember how hot the blood gets between a boy and a girl when they sparked. "Boy," Jamie said. "Don't you ever show temper to me. Not ever again. Your ma and I will talk about this and meet with you and the girl and her parents. I reckon you're a man all grown up now. And it's time you settled down and started a family. But don't you ever bow up to me again. I'll jerk you out of that saddle and kick your ass from here to Bent's Fort. Is that clear?"

"Yes, Pa," Ian said quickly and wisely.

"Fine." Jamie reined in close and put a massive arm around his son's shoulders. "Now, boy. You and this girl ain't been doin' no bundlin', have you?"

"Pa! No!" Then he grinned. "I tried once, and she like to have took my head off."

"She should have. Now, then, before we get to the settlement. Your sister was makin' goo-goo eyes at William and Lydia's oldest boy, Bill, when I left. What's going on there?"

"They sorta want to get married, too."

Jamie grinned. "Winter nights, they do get long, don't they, boy?"

"Pa!"

Jamie reached out and dug a thumb into the boy's ribs, and laughing, father and son rode down to the settlement side by side.

The Nobles and the Harpers had all heard of Jamie Ian MacCallister and his exploits, but none of them were prepared for the big man who swung down from the huge mean-eyed stallion and swept up Kate in his massive arms and kissed her lustily right in front of God and everybody. Then damned if he didn't kiss her again and pat her on the butt. Kate slapped his hand away, but not too hard. It was obvious to all that the two were very much in love and always would be.

Jamie shook hands with the men and kissed all the ladies and greeted all the kids, while the Harper and Noble families and their broods hung back, not really knowing what to expect from this mountain of a man.

But Jamie soon put them at ease. An eatin' on the grounds was planned for that evening, and Jamie and Kate disappeared into their cabin, while Jamie Ian and Ellen Kathleen made certain the kids stayed out.

"How come?" the younger ones demanded.

"I'll explain when you're older," Ellen Kathleen said.

Jamie and Kate's first born were all grown up.

* * *

It was quite a feast. There was fried chicken, venison, pork roast, mashed potatoes, gravy, hot fresh bread, and plenty of dried apple pie. It was quite a gathering for the settlement now had fifty-nine people in it, a very respectable number. Many established towns back east didn't have that many residents. Jamie and Kate had spoken with the girl's parents late that afternoon—after they had reacquainted themselves a couple of times first—and all had agreed that their children could marry. But not until cabins were raised and furniture was made—especially beds. Ian and Linda and Ellen Kathleen and Bill all blushed furiously at that.

Somebody brought out a jug and all the men had a drink. What the men didn't know was that the ladies had made several gallons of wine the past summer and were doing their own toasting back of the cabin. Ladies simply did not do much imbibing of hard liquor back in 1843.

That the men knew about.

Seventeen

The double wedding was planned for June, which would give the ladies time to sew up wedding dresses and Jamie time to melt and mold four gold wedding bands for the kids. Sam was astonished when Jamie finally took him into his confidence and showed him his vein.

"Jamie!" the older man exclaimed. "Do you know what this means?"

"It means that none of my family will ever want for anything they really need. And that's all it means. Sam, mountain men have known of gold in these mountains for years. We just don't want a bunch of pilgrims swarming in here, that's all."

"But Jamie, this country would grow and expand with businesses and people and churches if this was known."

"And the Indians aren't ready for that, Sam. Settlers will be along soon enough. Then the Indians will fight and they'll die and the survivors will be put on reservations to rot. Let's give them a little more time."

"I will never understand your love for the Indians, Jamie."

"They're free, Sam. But they won't be for long."

Jamie decided to ride to Bent's Fort for supplies and for once, Jamie Ian did not pester him to go along. The boy was so much in love he was walking into trees.

Swede, Wells, and Sam opted to go, and they pulled out one warm morning in late spring, trailing a long string of pack mules and horses, for the settlement had grown so that many more supplies were needed to sustain the group.

"You really crossed barren deserts, Jamie?" Wells asked.

"I'll say I did. Me and Horse."

Horse was out to pasture for a long rest and to breed with some selected mares. Jamie was riding the big appaloosa, Thunder, and the stallion was ready for the trail and showed it. When Jamie would let him, he pranced, head held high and mean eyes taking in all that lay before him.

"And the ocean is vast?" Wells asked.

"Like nothing I had seen before. Just rolled on endlessly. It sort of held you in its power. The longer you looked at it the stronger it held on to you."

"I'd like to see it," the black man said, then grinned. "But to tell the truth, I'm content to be livin' as a free man."

Stories about the valley where Jamie and the others had settled had spread back east; many folks had taken a notion to settle there, but it wasn't easy to do so. The difficulty was twofold: the valley was very hard to find, and those who were already there were being very selective about who settled in the valley. Half a dozen families had rolled in over the years and after looking them over and talking among themselves, the newcomers had been told to keep on traveling.

Some of those had professed a dislike for negroes; others had looked down their noses at Mexicans. In MacCallister's valley, as it was now called, the color of a man's skin went unnoticed; it was the man himself who counted. Some westward movers had been white trash, shiftless rawhiders who would forever be expecting something for nothing, constantly whining about one thing or the other. They were called rawhiders because when they patched something, they used rawhide to hold it together for the moment, instead of taking the time to repair it to last.

A few had taken umbrage at being told to move on. But one look into Jamie's cold eyes was usually all it took to get them going. Only one man had elected to fight. He had been buried among the others in what the kids had started calling "Outlaw Acres." The adults had attempted to stop that but to no avail. They had finally given up and Outlaw Acres remained the name of the final resting place for those who chose to live by the outlaw code.

Back in the States, 1843 saw other changes and events. The Oregon Bill passed the Senate, but the bill to encourage migration to the Northwest died in the House. A thousand pioneers left Elm Grove, Missouri, bound for Oregon. John Fremont and his friend and guide Kit Carson started their second expedition. Jamie was asked to go along and politely refused. A shaky truce was declared between Mexico and the Republic of Texas. A convention in Ohio adopted a resolution to make 54-40 the American line for the Oregon Territory, thereby pushing the boundaries to take in what would someday be Washington State. Washington, D.C. started to show interest in annexing Texas, but Sam Houston was opposed to it. James Bridger opened Fort Bridger on a fork of the Green River in southwest Wyoming.

* * *

But those in the long and lush and peaceful valley would know little of these events until long afterward. The newspapers and the few magazines they read were months old by the time they reached Bent's Fort; another few months old before they reached MacCallister's Valley. The settlers there were content; they enjoyed news of the outside, but it didn't really affect them. They felt insulated from outside events. The Indians in the area were their friends; they visited each other and traded back and forth. They learned from one another, with neither side making any effort to change the way of the other . . . no matter how strange they might have seemed.

On the trek to Bent's Fort, the men saw only a few Indians, and they were friendly—and not just because of the reputation of Man Who Is Not Afraid, also called lately, Bear Killer. The Indians in the area had seen, over the years, that those who settled in the valley respected the land. Unlike most whites, they hunted only for food and, again unlike most whites, used all of the animal that was useable. There were many other little things that did not go unnoticed by the Indians.

A day from the fort, Jamie was ranging far out ahead when he spotted a small band of Cheyenne. Jamie knew he spotted them only because they wanted him to spot them. He rode over to the band and made the sign of peace and friend.

"Bear Killer," the leader said, after signaling peace and friend. "All is well with you?"

"Life is good and all my family and friends are well. How are things in your village?"

"Very fine. Hunting is good and sickness has stayed

away. We are returning from the walled fort and we have news. No time to sit and smoke and that saddens me."

"As it also saddens me," Jamie replied. "For Dark Hand is a good friend. We must hunt together sometime."

"It would be an honor. Bear Killer, there are many men at the fort who ask quiet questions about you. They are not good men, I think. They smell very bad and seem to not like to bathe their bodies. They all have sneaky ways and shifty eyes."

Contrary to what has been written by a number of people, most Indian tribes maintained very strict hygienic practices, often times breaking the winter's ice daily to bathe. Only a few tribes chose to live in filth and they were looked down upon by the other tribes and associating with them was strictly taboo.

"I have heard the names Sax-on and Big-ers mentioned several times," Dark Hand concluded. "They are enemies of yours, Bear Killer?"

"Yes. Old enemies."

Dark Hand shrugged. "Then the answer is simple. We shall wait here with you and when the smelly white men come, we shall kill them."

Jamie knew that he had to answer that very wisely, for to refuse outright would be a great insult. "Your offer is much appreciated, but I think it would be unwise for you to involve yourself in this, Dark Hand. For if just one of the smelly white men got away, then the alarm would be sounded against all Indians in the area."

"Ummmm," Dark Hand said. "Yes. You are right. Bear Killer is wise beyond his years. And kind, too, for putting our safety over that of his own." He looked at the long string of mules and horses. "Your village is growing, yes?"

"Yes. And there is to be a wedding in two moons. My oldest son and the daughter of a friend."

"They have my blessing," the Cheyenne said. "May they have strong, brave sons and beautiful and obedient daughters. Ahhh," he sighed. "This younger generation now. No respect for their elders. I tell you, Bear Killer, I don't know what is going to become of them." He lifted his painted hand. "We go!"

Jamie rode back to the others. "Trouble?" Swede asked.

"Not from them. Come on. I'll tell you on the way."

When he had finished, Sam said, "There is always a certain type of person who wants to knock off the king of the hill, Jamie. You have quite a reputation, and it's growing, and I fear it will continue to grow as long as you live. For you do nothing to keep a low profile."

"That's not my style, Sam."

Sam grunted. "And naturally, you're going straight on into the fort."

"That's what I came for, Sam."

"And if I suggested that you camp outside the fort and let us go in and get supplies?"

Jamie smiled and it took years off his still young face. "I would think you had taken leave of your senses, Sam."

"I believe it was Alexander Pope who wrote that line concerning fools who rush in where angels fear to tread, Jamie."

Jamie laughed. "You think I'm a fool, Sam."

"No. I don't. But you are a family man who has tremendous responsibilities."

"I'm aware of my responsibilities, Sam. But look at it this way: would you rather have the fighting done at the settlement?"

Sam was silent for a moment. "I see your point," he finally conceded.

Several trappers that Jamie knew walked over to him as soon as he swung down from the saddle inside the fort. "They's some bad ones here, Jamie," one said. "They ain't come right out and made no direct threats toward you. But several whispers has been heard and they're up to no good."

"If you've a mind to, we can run them out now," another said.

"Is Jack Biggers here?" Jamie asked.

"Was. He pulled out a few days ago. But some of his brothers is among them whisperin'. Most of 'em is camped outside the fort. But they's a bad one still here calls hisself Rodman. Watch him. He's a sneaky one."

Rodman was pointed out and Jamie thanked the men and went on about his business. Wells found Jamie in the blanket section of the huge store; the black man was badly shaken.

"What's wrong, Wells?"

"Poppa's here, Jamie. And Robert is with him."

Jamie stood rock still for a moment, as the memories came flooding back. Titus Jefferson, the ex-slave who had pushed his wife Ophelia into whoring for the white plantation owner, and whose union had produced the white twins Roscoe and Anne. Robert, Moses's son, who had turned bad and run away with Titus and then joined up and begun plotting with Olmstead and Jackson and the others to kill Jamie.

"Did he see you, Wells?"

"Looked right at me but didn't recognize me. I reckon I have changed some."

Wells had filled out and matured in the years since his

father had deserted family and friends down in the Big Thicket country of Texas. He had grown a moustache and was now all dressed out in homespun britches and buckskin shirt. It was easy to understand why Titus had not recognized him.

While the country was not overflowing with negroes, there were many in the wilderness. A few were free men but most were runaway slaves.

"Well, he's heard by now that I'm here," Jamie said. "Let's see if he approaches me."

It would have been difficult for Titus and Robert to avoid Jamie within the walls of the fort, and within the hour, Titus and Robert hailed Jamie.

"Can I have a moment of your time, Jamie MacCallister?" Titus said.

Jamie turned and looked at the man. Titus's hair was now all salt and pepper, and Robert appeared to have matured. Neither man's eyes held the wild hatred for whites that had been there in Texas. Jamie smiled and stuck out his hand. "Sure, Titus. Good to see you. And you, Robert. Let's step over into the shade, shall we?"

Both men seemed to relax and the tension went out of them. In the coolness of shade, sitting on a bench, Titus said, "We knew this day would come, and we was both dreadin' it."

"No reason to," Jamie assured them. "I hold no rancor toward either of you. You went down some wrong paths years back, that's all. Have you found the right paths out here?"

Both men nodded their heads. "We got us a place in a small valley," Titus said, and then he smiled. "Really, not that many miles from where you and the others have your settlement. But we were afraid to come see you for fear you would kill us."

"No danger of that, Titus. All that is in the past."

Robert said, "We both are married, in the Indian way. I have two children."

"I figured I was too old to start a family," Titus said. "But Moon Woman thought different. We have two children also."

"Titus," Jamie asked, "have you heard news of Roscoe and Anne? They slipped away in the dead of night some time past."

"I heard they're in St. Louis, passing for white." He shook his head sadly. "They're both talented actors and singers—they've made quite a reputation for themselves. They go by the name, Le Beau. I fear they're in for a terrible time if they're discovered."

"How are my mother and father?" Robert asked.

"Healthy and happy. They would be glad to see you."

"You would not object if we came for a visit?" Titus asked.

"I wouldn't object if you came to live there. Both of you. It's a big valley."

There were tears in the eyes of both men. Jamie pointed to a tall and ruggedly built black man standing in front of the smithy's shop. "That's your son, Titus. Wells. He and Sally are married and have a family. You're a grandfather several times over."

Titus stared at Wells for a moment and then put his face in his hands and wept.

Jamie patted the man on the shoulder. He waved at Wells and the man hesitantly began the walk over to his father. "Robert, let's you and me make ourselves scarce for a time. There are some folks I want you to meet."

Before they had gone fifteen feet, a shout stopped Jamie in the courtyard of the fort. He shoved Robert away from him.

"MacCallister!" the burly man shouted again. "Stand and deliver. You choose to harbor a murderin' son of a bitch, then pay the price!"

Eighteen

Jamie turned to one side just as the man drew a pistol from his waistband and fired. The ball whistled past Jamie's head, just missing him by a couple of inches. Jamie was running toward the man as the ball whizzed past him. Before the man could jerk and cock his second pistol, Jamie had closed the distance and flattened the man with a crashing right fist. He reached down and pulled the man's pistol from him and threw it to one side. The man's knife followed the pistol two seconds later. Jamie jerked the man to his feet and popped him again and again with powerful lefts and rights to the jaw and face. The man fell to the hard-packed ground and lay still. His face and mouth were bloody from the savage blows.

Jamie stood over the man as the crowd gathered. This was not the man who had been pointed out to him as Rodman. Jamie had never seen this man before in his life.

The mood of the crowd gathering around was ugly, for violence inside the four-foot-thick walls of Bent's Fort was frowned upon. Outside was an entirely different thing, but inside everybody— white, black, and red—was treated the same and could feel safe.

"Anybody know him?" Jamie asked.

"Aye," a trapper said. "That's John Wilmot. He's a scalawag through and through. A killer. Somebody paid him to do you in, Jamie. John Wilmot only kills for money."

"Somebody fetch a rope and let's hang the bastard!" a trapper said.

"Wait!" one of the Bent brothers shouted, running out to the crowd. "They'll be no lynching here!" He bulled his way through the mass of trappers and Indians and free black men. He looked up at Jamie. "Do you want to have this man bound over for the Army?"

Jamie shook his head. "I want him awake and able to talk. I want to find out why he tried to kill me."

"Good man," the Bent brother said, patting Jamie's arm. He turned to the crowd. "All right, gentlemen. Let's break it up and see to our business."

Sam found a bucket of water and dumped it on John Wilmot. The man came awake sputtering and cursing. Jamie reached down, jerked the man to his boots, and literally threw him across the courtyard of the fort. John hit against the side of the men's quarters, and those trappers who witnessed the scene winced as John slammed into the wall and slumped to the ground.

Jamie strode over nonchalantly and picked up another bucket of water and tossed it onto the prostrate man. John Wilmot's left arm was bent at an impossible angle and was clearly shattered in several places. Jamie squatted down and spoke in low tones to the man for several minutes, with John seemingly eager to answer each and every question.

Jamie concluded his conversation with, "I'm going to give you a piece of advice, John. And it would behoove you to take it. Leave. Don't ever come west of the Mississippi River again. But I 'spect I'll see you again, John Wilmot. But when I do, bear this in mind: if it's west of the Mississippi, I'll kill you where you stand and not give a second thought about it. You've been warned fair. The rest is up to you."

Jamie walked away, with Sam and Swede on either side, over to where Wells and his father stood, shoulder to shoulder. Both men had been weeping, for their eyes were red-rimmed. But they had made up, and that was all important. Robert stood with father and son; he, too, had been crying.

"What was that all about, Jamie?" Wells asked.

"More trouble. But this time I had nothing to do with it. I'll explain later. Let's get our supplies as quickly as possible and get out of here."

"It'll be mid-day tomorrow, Jamie?" Wells said.

"That's fine. John Wilmot is in no condition to pull anything any time soon. But he has men coming up behind him. They're still several days out, but closing fast."

"This has nothing to do with you, Jamie?" Sam asked.

"No. Not directly. It seems one of our newest settlers has a rather dark past. Wiley Harper killed a constable back in Delaware."

As soon as the mules and horses were loaded, Jamie and party pulled out. That night, after pushing hard all that afternoon, Jamie explained.

"I had to sort of read between the lines, so to speak," Jamie said, as the men gathered around the fire. "But I gather that the killing was an accident. Wiley panicked and ran. He and his family were already planning on a move west and were packed and ready to go. They just came a little bit faster than they planned, that's all. Wiley was a very outspoken man back east and angered some monied people with his comments. I don't know what he said to anger them, and John Wilmot didn't know either, or wouldn't tell me. No matter. Our valley is well-known so we've got to be ready for the bounty hunters when they come. And they will come."

"Jamie," Swede asked. "This John Wilmot. What did he hope to gain by confronting you?"

"A reputation," Sam answered that. "There are still bounties on Jamie's head totaling many, many thousands of dollars. Years ago, just after he and Kate left our community back east, Jamie and Kate ran afoul of the Newby Brothers. They are a large family and they all believe in the blood feud. The kin of the Newbys will never rest until Jamie is dead. The same with the Olmstead family, the Saxons, and a dozen others." Sam shook his head. "Jamie has made a lot of enemies over the years."

Jamie said, "I can't change all that, so I don't worry about it."

Titus and Wells broke off from the pack train two days from the valley to go get their families and possessions. Back in the valley, Jamie informed the others about finding Titus and Robert and that the men and their families were coming to join them. Then he took Wiley Harper aside and told him what had happened back at the fort. Wiley was badly shaken but insisted upon calling for a community meeting. If they wanted him to leave, then he would. Jamie had smiled at that. He knew these people well, and correctly predicted the outcome of the meeting. It was unanimous—Wiley and his family would stay.

Within a few days, the people in the valley had put the incident behind them and welcomed Titus and Robert and their families. All began making preparations for the double wedding, the first in the valley. But double wedding or no, there was ground to be broken and crops to plant, for the summer's growing season was short and everybody had to work. There were calves and lambs to be born, sheep to sheer, berries to be picked for jams and jellies and homemade wine. There was much to be done during the warm summer months.

Titus and Robert and their families moved in, built their cabins, and immediately fit right in with the community. Moon Woman and She Who Watches, both of whom were Cheyenne, spoke very good English and were accepted without question.

Kate, looking at Jamie one evening as they sat in the dog trot of their cabin, wondered aloud about his quiet smile.

"We've done it, Kate. Right here in this valley. We have proven that people of all creeds and all colors can live and work together peacefully. Back in the States, people are buying and selling human beings like so many cattle, chaining them like wild animals and, in many cases, working them to death. Back in the States, entire tribes of Indians are being either moved or wiped out. With no one taking the time to try to understand the feelings of the other. But here in this valley, it seems that we have made the impossible easy. It's both amusing and sad."

Kate hid her own smile. How to tell her husband that the people in the valley knew that Jamie expected everyone to get along and would accept no less than that? How to tell him that while the people in the community held him in high respect, they were also a little afraid of him? He would never have believed any of that.

"Yes, dear," she said.

* * *

It was to be an outdoor wedding, and the day was warm and beautiful for the ceremony. Jamie had ordered a black suit for his oldest son, and it had arrived just in the nick of time, with Jamie's grandfather bringing it from Bent's Fort. Silver Wolf was dressed in white buckskins, all beaded and fringed. The old man looked as magnificent and fierce as an eagle.

Jamie Ian's starched high white collar was chafing his neck, and the stiff new shoes hurt his feet, but he knew better than to say anything about it. Jamie Ian was nearabout the size of his pa, but the young man knew full well his pa would still not hesitate to haul him off behind the house and wallop the hell out of him.

Jamie Ian had not seen Linda all day, and Bill had not seen Ellen Kathleen; something to do with tradition. The altar was adorned with fresh flowers, and little girls held baskets of petals, waiting to toss them on the path where the couples would walk. Falcon was the ring bearer, and he, too, was dressed in a new suit his pa had ordered for him, complete with high stockings and knee-length britches. Falcon had set up a howl when he saw the suit, but one look from his pa was all it took to convince the four-year-old boy he'd better calm down and act right.

Almost three months had passed since Jamie's confrontation with John Wilmot at Bent's Fort, and the incident had been all but forgotten by everybody except Jamie. Just before the ceremony was to begin, Jamie walked to his Grandpa's side.

"You armed, Grandpa?"

"I got two pistols under my shirt. Why?"

"I believe in staying ready, that's why."

"There ain't been hide nor hair seen of Wilmot, Parsons, Biggers, Sanders, Winslow, or Thompson in some time, boy." The old man was silent for a moment. "But today would be good time for them to hit here, wouldn't it?"

"A dandy time. How come Preacher couldn't make it?"

"He's doing some government work. Sparks is up in Canada, and Lobo and Audie both said they always cry at weddin's and that wouldn't seem manly. But they sent their best."

"I got a bad feelin' in my guts, Grandpa."

"That's 'cause your oldest is gettin' hitched up, boy. It's an important time for all concerned." He grinned. "We gonna give 'em a evenin' surprise, ain't we?"

Jamie smiled. "You bet. Just as soon as their cabin lights go out this evenin', we have some fun."

"Here comes the brides. My, my, ain't they pretty?"

And the girls *were* beautiful. Their dresses were sparkling white and there were flowers in their hair. Most of the women started crying softly, and some of the men started clearing their throats . . . a lot. All eyes, including those of Jamie, were on the two youthful couples standing in front of Reverend Haywood. The harpsichord had been carefully carried outside, and Sarah was softly playing.

For the occasion, Jamie was dressed in a suit made for him by Kate—since no store-bought suit would fit his massive shoulders and arms—and he was wearing handmade boots a cobbler over to the fort had done up for him. His grandfather was also wearing new boots, and that was the reason neither of them felt the earth start to gently pound under their feet.

The attackers had waited until the entire community had gathered outside, with everybody laughing and talking and having a good time before they had slipped in close, with cloth sacks over their horses' hooves to muffle the sound.

The attackers, led by John Wilmot and including some of the Biggers gang and some of the Winslow trash, were only a few hundred yards away when they burst out of the timber and started their wild charge toward the settlement. They had the reins in their teeth and both hands filled with pistols.

Jamie heard the pounding of hooves and spun around just as the minister had smiled, closed his Bible, and announced that the boys could kiss their wives.

Silver Wolf shouted, "To arms, men!" and jerked both pistols out from under his shirt.

Jamie cursed and pulled both pistols from his waistband and shouted, "Kids, see to your mother, quick now! Everybody to cover."

There was no more time for talk as the settlement was filled with galloping, wild-eyed, rearing horses and the smash and roar of guns.

Jamie blew two attackers from their horses just as his Grandpa did the same with two others. Out of the corner of his eye, Jamie saw Wiley Harper go down with a ball in the center of his forehead. Two of the attackers leaned out of the saddle and grabbed him before he could hit the earth and went galloping off, Wiley's feet dragging the ground.

Silver Wolf reached up and jerked an attacker out of the saddle and snapped his neck like a dry twig. Juan Nuñez grabbed up a hay fork and drove the tines all the way through a man before the galloping horse rode him down and left him unhurt but addled in the street.

Jamie heard Kate scream and the sound chilled him. Trying to charge his pistols, he searched wildly for her and found his wife kneeling over a woman all dressed in white.

Jamie Ian leaped onto the back of a galloping horse and ripped the attacker's knife from its sheath. He cut the man's throat, let the body fall, then reined in the horse, jerked the rifle from the boot and charged into the crowd of attackers, now trying to escape. Jamie Ian blew one out of the saddle and reversing the rifle, nearly took the head off of a second man, hitting him so hard the stock shattered.

Then there was only the crying of the young kids, the wailing of Anne Harper, and the fading of the horses' hooves.

Jamie walked over to where Kate was kneeling, holding Linda in her arms. The young woman's chest was covered with blood. Jamie did not have to look twice to see that she was dead.

Juan Nuñez was on his feet, shaky but otherwise unhurt.

Anne Harper's wailing abruptly ended. She had fainted.

"It'll take us hours to round up the horses," Sam said, appearing at Jamie's side. "I watched the bastards drive them off."

Jamie nodded his head, his eyes on Jamie Ian. The young man was standing over his mother and his dead wife.

"Who's hurt?" Jamie shouted. "Calm down and let's see to our people." He looked over at Ellen Kathleen. She was standing beside Bill, both of them pale-faced and shaken. "You two all right?" Jamie asked.

They nodded their heads.

"Bill, see to your parents. Ellen Kathleen, help your ma."

"Poppa!" Ellen Kathleen cried. "Linda, she's . . ."

"I know. Do what I told you."

Jamie looked at his oldest son. Jamie Ian had ripped off the high collar and let it fall to the ground. The tie followed that. The son looked at the father and the expression in the young man's eyes was a terrible thing to behold. The young man turned and walked into his parents' cabin, closing the door behind him. Jamie went to Kate and knelt down beside her, forcing her hands from Linda and pulling her to her feet. He held her for a moment while Kate wept, and then she pulled away and composed herself.

"I'll see to Anne," she said numbly, and Jamie nodded.

"I'll make a coffin," Swede said gently. "I'll just do that right now."

"I'll go fetch young Jamie's horse," Silver Wolf said. "He'll be ridin' the black he favors, won't he?"

"Yes," Jamie said.

"What the hell do you mean, 'he'll be riding the black'?" Kate screamed.

"Be quiet, Kate," the old Silver Wolf told her. "Just be quiet. He's a MacCallister. He's got the blood of mystics from the Highlands in his veins. He'll do what has to be done. And there is naught you nor anyone else can do to stop him. If you dinna know that now, you never will. Go on with what you're doin'. Do you help get the lassie ready for the earth."

The sounds of sawing and hammering reached the still-stunned gathering.

"I'll go help the Swede," Juan said.

"Me, too," Titus said.

Jamie Ian stepped out of the cabin. He was dressed in buckskins and carried two rifles, one in each hand. He had two pistols stuck down behind his belt.

"No!" his mother screamed.

Jamie Ian looked at her and said, "Leave me be, Ma. You know I've got to do it."

"After we've committed Linda to the ground," Jamie said softly, but with tempered steel behind his words.

"Of course, Pa," the young man replied, his eyes dry and his voice hard.

Before the coffin was completed, Silver Wolf returned, leading two horses, Jamie Ian's big black and a pack horse with the headless body of Wiley Harper draped over its back.

Anne took one look at the bloody remains of her husband and went into a screaming rage. It took William Haywood, Daniel Noble, and Eb French to hold the woman down until she had calmed.

Titus started on another coffin.

Jamie and Sam lifted the body of Linda and gently placed her in the narrow coffin, hands folded across her chest. Jamie Ian sat on the porch of the newly built cabin that he would never share with Linda and said nothing.

The holes dug in the summer earth and the caskets sealed and lowered, William Haywood conducted the short service. Jamie Ian had not moved from his place on the porch.

While the soft earth gently fell on the twin caskets, Jamie Ian walked by his mother's side and kissed her on the cheek. Kate's face seemed to be set in stone. He shook hands with his dad and then went to his horse and swung into the saddle. The young man rode off without looking back. He paused only briefly, to take the scalps of the raiders he had killed and to tie them onto the black's mane.

Kate looked at Jamie. "You not going with him?"

"He didn't ask me to."

"He wants no help," Jamie's Grandpa said. "This is something he has to do alone."

"Is that right?" Kate asked, her words like chipped ice. She walked to the cabin and entered, closing the door, momentarily shutting out the tragic events of the day.

BOOK TWO

Till hell freezes over.
—*Anonymous*

One

To say that Kate was highly irritated would be rather like saying boiling water is hot. But Jamie had seen her angry before and knew what to do: stay the hell out of her way until she cooled down.

He helped drag the bodies of the dead raiders to Outlaw Acres and bury them . . . without benefit of casket. Reverend Haywood flatly refused to read over their graves, so the dead attackers, several of them minus their scalps, were committed to the earth without any ceremony.

Jamie had seen his Grandpa leave the settlement, dressed in his trailworn buckskins. He would follow Ian from a safe distance, watching the boy's back. Young Ian was good but still had a lot to learn. The old Silver Wolf would be his unseen ghost until he did learn.

Jamie spent part of the rest of that day helping to round up the horses and repairing the corral. Then he closed up the cabin that had been built for his son and bride. Just as he was shuttering the windows, Kate appeared at his side with a sandwich and a glass of cool milk. Together, they sat down on the porch and Jamie ate.

"When do you suppose Ian will be back?" Kate asked.

"When he's tracked them all down and killed them."

"He's awfully young."

"Not as young as we were, Kate."

"The valley will never be the same."

"No. It won't."

"I've written what happened in the Bible, Jamie."

"Good."

"I spoke with the other women. Most of the food we had prepared for the wedding feast was saved. We'll all have an early supper on the grounds late this afternoon."

"I think that's a fine idea, Kate. We must not forget that Ellen Kathleen and Bill still have their honeymoon ahead of them."

"They'll be left alone," Kate said firmly. "Moon Woman and She Who Watches have gone into the hills to build a hogan for them so they can be alone. Titus and Robert went with them to help."

"That's good."

Both of them sat on the porch of Ian's cabin, their eyes on the fresh mounds of earth in the community cemetery.

Kate said, "Come next late March I would imagine that we'll be grandparents, Jamie."

"If Ellen Kathleen is anything like you we sure will be," Jamie said straight-faced.

Kate fixed him with a look that would melt ice. Then the hotness faded as she watched the smile he could not contain play around his lips. She poked him in the ribs so hard it brought a grunt from Jamie. "And I suppose you had nothing to do with it?"

"Oh, I contributed a mite, I reckon."

"Haw! One more comment like that, and I'll suggest that this would be a nice night for you to sleep outside."

"It might rain."

"Then you'd get wet, wouldn't you?" Kate said sweetly, and left the porch to join the other women.

* * *

The raid cast a pallor over the settlement for a time, but as the summer wore on, the bloody memories of that awful day began to gradually diminish and everyone resumed their normal routine.

"Life must go on," Reverend Haywood preached one Sunday morning. It was one of the rare Sundays that Jamie elected to attend church. Reverend Haywood was always very pleased when Jamie attended his services, even though he knew that Jamie was doing it merely to please Kate and also to help insure that the children had a good church foundation.

When the first cold winds began to blow through the valley, the settlers were ready for winter. The crops were in, the hay stacked for the cattle, and the barns full. And there had been no word from or about Jamie Ian. But all that was about to change.

The front door to the trading post was pushed open, and the tall stranger had to duck his head to enter. The trappers and drifters all stopped their talking and card playing to look up as the cold winds blew in behind the young man.

"Shut that damn door, you fool!" one said. "Was ye raised in a barn?"

"No," the tall young man said. "But since your voice bears a striking resemblance to a jackass braying, I would suspect you were."

The others in the trading post burst out in good-natured laughter as the lout's face reddened. One of the trappers narrowed his eyes as his gaze followed the young man to a corner table. It couldn't be, he thought. The lad is far too young. But my God, the resemblance is striking.

"Some food, please, sir," the tall blonde-haired stranger said. "And a pot of coffee."

"Oh, please, sir!" the loudmouthed lout mimicked sarcastically. "My, my, ain't he the po-lite one now. I bet he's got ruffles on his underwear."

"Shut up, Flooky," the trapper whose eyes had followed Ian said. "Afore your ass overloads your mouth."

Ian said nothing, just tore off a huge hunk of bread and fell to eating the good-smelling stew that was placed before him, along with a pot of strong coffee.

"I don't take that kind of talk from no pup!" the man called Flooky said. "Hey, you!" he shouted. "Kid! Look at me, boy!"

Ian continued to concentrate on his stew, for he was hungry, having run completely out of supplies almost a week before, and had been living on rabbits, and there is not much fat on a rabbit. A man needs fat to help survive in the dead of winter. He ignored the man called Flooky.

"Goddamn you, boy!" Flooky shouted, rising from his chair. "Is ye deaf as well as stupid?"

Ian looked up, those amazingly pale blue eyes as cold as death. "Shut up," was all he said. Then he returned to the business of eating.

Flooky sat back down hard in the leather-strapped chair, his mouth open in amazement. Nobody talked to him that way, especially some damn kid. He was momentarily speechless.

Several of the trappers in the room, and also the owner of the trading post, had put together who this young man was, and to a man, they were smiling. No decent man liked Flooky, for he was a borderline ruffian and a notorious bully. He was also suspected of being a thief, albeit a clever one, since he had never been caught at it.

Ian polished off that bowl of stew and the counterman was johnny-on-the-spot with the pot, ladling him another heaping bowl. "It's very good," Ian said.

"Thanks, young feller. I made it myself."

"I'd match it up with anyone's." He smiled. "Except my mother's cooking."

The cook smiled. "Can't no one beat mama's cookin', that's for shore."

"Ain't that sweet?" Flooky sneered. "He misses his mama."

"I miss my mama, too," a burly trapper said softly. "A whole bunch. You want to make something out of that, Flooky?"

Flooky had nothing to say to the trapper. He dropped his gaze and studied his cup of whiskey. Big Jim Williams was no man to play deadly games with.

Big Jim stood up and carried his jug and cup with him over to Ian's table. "You mind some company, son?"

"Not at all, sir. Please sit down."

"Thankee kindly." Big Jim sat and studied Ian for a moment. "You be a MacCallister, right?"

"Yes, sir. Jamie is my father and Silver Wolf my great-grandfather.

"Thought so. I been knowin' the old man for forty years. Ain't seen him in a spell."

"He's about a day behind me," Ian said with a smile. "Birddoggin' my backtrail. He thinks I don't know it. So if you see him, don't let on."

Big Jim chuckled. "You on the prod, boy?"

Briefly, Ian explained what had happened that dreadful day back in the valley. Big Jim grunted and shook his head. "I don't blame you. But is you plannin' on takin' on the whole damn gang all by your lonesome?"

"Why . . . yes," Ian replied. "It's just one gang, isn't it?"

Big Jim smiled. "Flooky's a bad one, boy."

"Yes, I 'spect he is."

"You been in many fights?"

"A few. My pa taught me how to fight."

"Flooky ain't your pa, boy."

"Thank God for small favors." Ian finished his stew and sopped out the bowl with the last bit of bread. He refilled his coffee cup and sat back in the chair.

Flooky sat at his table and grew madder by the moment.

Big Jim sat across from Jamie Ian and studied the young man. Real calm, Big Jim concluded. He's very sure of himself. Then it came to Big Jim Williams: Jamie Ian wasn't going to mix it up with Flooky. He was going to kill him.

"Be back," Big Jim said, pushing away from the rough hewn table and walking over to Flooky. He sat down and spoke in low tones. "Leave the lad alone, Flooky. He's a bad one. He's on the prod and he ain't gonna take a lot of crap from you. As a matter of fact, he ain't gonna take *any* crap from you or anybody else. Leave him be and let him go his own way."

"That kid sassed me," Flooky said. "I'll not take lip from no kid."

"You been warned," Big Jim said. "Where's your next of kin, Flooky."

"Huh?"

"You heard me."

Flooky cursed in a low voice. "All I aim to do is slap him around some, Jim."

Big Jim shook his head. "No, you ain't gonna do

nothin' of the kind. When you draw back agin this one, he's gonna kill you."

"When Hell freezes over," Flooky said, and stood up. He walked across the room and stopped about ten feet from Ian, who was standing with his back to the man, buying supplies and stacking them on the counter. "Turn around and take your whuppin', boy," Flooky said.

Ian turned his head and looked at the man. "Go to hell."

Flooky cursed and jumped at Ian. Ian sidestepped and hit the man in the face with a fifty-foot length of coiled rope. The rope was new and stiff and made a terrible weapon. Ian smashed the man in the face again and again with the new rope, the power behind the blows awesome. He beat Flooky to the floor and continued smashing his head with the rope until Flooky was unconscious, lying on the boards in his own blood.

Ian tossed the rope back on the counter and said, "Some beans and flour and salt, too, please."

The other men in the room made no move to assist Flooky.

Big Jim started the low whisper. "That's Jamie MacCallister's boy, Ian."

"Damn!" a trapper said. "I see the family in him now."

Before leaving the valley, Jamie had given his son a small leather sack of cash money, and another sack of gold dust and nuggets. Ian paid for his supplies with coins and picked up the canvas bag he had brought in and packed full. He looked once at Flooky, still unconscious on the floor. Ian lifted his eyes and met the silent gaze of every man in the room.

"I didn't come in here looking for trouble. If this man follows me, seeking vengeance, I'll give him a proper burial as best I can." Ian walked out into the cold of Oregon winter. He closed the door behind him.

For a moment, no one spoke. Finally, a bearded trapper said, "That boy'll do to ride the river with."

"Aye," another one said. "He's got a lot of Old Mac in him. 'Ceptin' Old Mac would have cut Flooky from eyeballs to belly-button."

Briefly, Big Jim explained why Ian was on the prod.

To a man, the crowd all shook their heads in disgust and understanding.

Flooky groaned and sat up on the floor, his face torn and bruised from the beating with the rope. He put his hands to his face and looked at the bloody palms and cursed, long and loud. He struggled to his boots and staggered to the counter, leaning heavily against it. "A pan of hot water," he ordered. "And some cloths to bathe my face." One eye was swollen shut and his lips were raw and puffy.

"I'll kill that kid!" Flooky swore.

"Leave him be," a trapper warned. "That's Jamie Mac-Callister's boy."

"That don't spell nothin' to me," Flooky said, bathing his badly beaten face with the hot, wet cloth. "I ain't never seen none of Jamie MacCallister's graveyards."

"I have," Big Jim Williams said. "I've seen them from Ohio to Colorado."

Flooky said nothing; he wasn't about to call Big Jim a liar.

A trapper who had followed Ian outside returned in time to catch the last few words. "The lad's got scalps tied to his horse's mane. Three of them that I seen. That there's a boy to leave alone."

"Injun scalps," Flooky said. "Big deal."

"White men's scalps," the trapper said.

"Shit!" Flooky said. "Give me some whiskey to dab on these cuts. And some beans and flour and coffee. I'm a fixin' to take me a scalp of my own—a blonde one."

"You'll not do it," yet another trapper warned. "Leave him be, Flooky. He's a bad one."

Flooky cursed the man and jerked up the bag of supplies. He staggered out of the trading post and stumbled toward the stable for his horse.

"If anybody's got anything they want to say to Flooky, they better do it now," Big Jim said. "'Cause you'll not see him no more after this day."

"Well, he wasn't much good no way," a grizzled old mountain man said. "Give me a bowl of that stew, Morris. I worked up a hunger watchin' MacCallister use that rope."

"There he goes," the cook said, peeping out through a crack in the shutters. "Flooky's gone after the lad."

"His hoss'll be back in a day or two. Pretty good hoss."

"Where's that stew?" the old mountain man said.

Two

Just as the warm winds of spring began to gently bathe the land, two trappers wandered into MacCallister's Valley and had a home-cooked meal at the large cabin of Jamie and Kate. They had news but were loathe to speak in front of Kate.

"Say it," Jamie said. "She's the boy's ma."

"A no-count name of Flooky braced your boy in a tradin' post over in the Deschutes. The lad purt near beat him to death with a length of new rope. Flooky, he got it in his mind to avenge the beatin' and rode out after the boy. The winter was a cold one and the ground too hard to dig. Big Jim Williams found Flooky's body about a week later. He'd been shot through the head and propped up agin a tree, his hands folded acrost his lap. Name carved in the tree. The lad come up on one of the men who kilt his bride over in the Willamette Valley. Shot him dead in a tradin' post and took his scalp right there in front of everybody. Then about two weeks later, he found another one up along Roarin' River—kilt him and scalped him. The boy is gettin' a real bad reputation amongst the folks who want eastern law to be applied out here."

"Any word about my Grandpa?" Jamie asked.

"He's never more than half a day behind the boy," the second man said. "Sometimes they ride together. He's teachin' the boy right good, I hear. You know your grandpa, Jamie. He ain't got no use for no law other than hissen."

Long after the men had left, heading for Bent's Fort, Jamie sat at the table drinking coffee. He finally lifted his eyes to meet those of Kate. "Do you want me to go after him, Kate?"

She frowned and then shook her head. "No. Ian is a man grown. He's got to find his own way. He'll never be able to rest and make a useful life for himself until the vengeance he feels in his heart is over and done with." She smiled at her husband. "Are you getting itchy feet, Jamie?"

"No," Jamie said truthfully. "I am not." He drained his cup and stood up. "Time to break the ground, Kate." He looked at his wife, still beautiful and with the shape of a woman half her age. "When is Ellen Kathleen going to deliver?"

"This month, I'm sure—Grandpa!" she said with a laugh.

"Grandpa!" Jamie snorted and walked out of the cabin. "Thirty-four years old and a Grandpa." He looked back at Kate. "It's your fault," he said, then ducked the chunk of stovewood she flung at him.

Ian pushed open the door to the trading post and stepped inside. His great-grandpa was seeing to the horses at the livery. Ian knew they were in Canada, he just didn't know how far into Canada they had pushed. What he did know was that four members of the gang who'd attacked the settlement were here, or close by, for he and the old Silver Wolf had tracked them all the way from the Yakima. And he knew their names: Joe Forrest, Blake Evans, and two men called Shaw and Zack. Neither Ian nor his great-grandpa had minded the distance, for if Joe and Blake and Shaw and Zack wanted to be buried in Canada, that was fine with the two of them.

Ian took a corner table and ordered food and a pot of coffee. Just as Ian was pouring a cup of coffee, the door burst open and a man rushed in.

"They's two men just rode in, Fred!" he said, not seeing Ian in the gloom of the far corner. "One of them's got scalps tied to his horse's mane. A lot of scalps."

Fred was frantically waggling his eyebrows and cutting his eyes to Ian. The messenger finally got the message and shut up and crowded close to the bar. He and the barkeep began conversing in low tones until Silver Wolf walked in, looking like an eagle about to sink talons into prey, and then they both shut up. The old man took a seat at Ian's table, and the barkeep quickly brought out the food. He sat the big steaming bowls down quickly and backed off.

Ian and his grandpa, as Ian called him, fell to eating.

Between mouthfuls, the old Wolf said, "After the shootin's over and the smoke clears, boy, we're gonna have to make fast tracks out of here. These Canucks don't hold with gunplay."

"Suits me," Ian said, washing down the stew with sips of strong coffee.

Ian had changed dramatically since he had left the valley nearly a year ago. He was no longer a boy. He had filled out and his face had hardened. And he was the spitting image of his father. He had grown a blond drooping moustache that added years to his face.

The elder MacCallister had not visibly changed in more than thirty years. He was still all wang-leather and gristle and dangerous as a grizzly. "In case we get separated, and it might be best if we lay down two trails, you 'member where I told you we'd meet."

"Yes."

The Wolf looked out through a crack in the shutters. "All right, son. You best eat quick, for here they come. All four of the bastards. They've been to the livery and seen the horses. Ian?"

The young man looked up.

"You going to take scalps?"

"What do you think?"

The old man smiled. "Thought so. Cut 'em quick and jerk 'em hard. We ain't gonna have much time."

"That's why you insisted we camp just a few miles from here last night, right, Grandpa? So's the horses would be rested when we make our run?"

"You're learnin', boy. You're learnin'. You got a ways to go, but you're gettin' there fast. Maybe too fast."

"You thinkin' about my ma, Grandpa?"

"Yeah, I am. You've matured fast. And you got the name of a man who is quick on the shoot."

"Like you, Grandpa?" Ian asked with a smile. Ian looked out through the crack in the shutter. The four men had stopped in the street, talking things over. It was obvious they didn't quite know how to handle this.

"I think you got more of a reputation than me, boy. But news travels a lot faster now than years back. Is them trash comin' on in or not?"

"They're talking."

The old Wolf shifted his chair so he had a full view of the front door. Both men picked up the pace of eating. The barkeep, the cook, and the messenger made ready to hit the floor when the shooting started, and they sensed it was just moments, perhaps seconds, away.

"Here they come," Ian said.

Silver Wolf looked. The men all had their hands filled with pistols. "They're goin' to come in shootin', Ian."

The barkeep, the cook, and the messenger all hit the floor behind the rough bar.

Ian and Silver Wolf filled their hands with pistols, all of them double-shotted.

Joe Forrest was the first one in the door. Ian and the Wolf waited while Joe got his eyes adjusted to the dimness of the interior of the trading post. Forrest found Ian and said, "You bastard! You've chased me long enough."

He lifted his pistol and Ian shot him, the heavy ball taking the man in the chest. Joe Forrest stumbled backward, his pistol discharging as death touched him, the ball blowing a hole in the floor.

Zack ran around to the rear of the post and kicked in the back door. He made the corner before Silver Wolf drilled him clean, right between the eyes. Zack's feet flew out from under him and bits of bone and brain splattered the wall.

Blake Evans and Shaw crowded into the trading post from the front, both of them cursing and hollering. Ian and Wolf fired as one. Two more lay dead on the floor. Ian and the Wolf reloaded and then Ian quickly scalped the men, conscious of but ignoring the eyes of the barkeep, the cook, and the messenger watching him in undisguised horror and disgust.

"That ain't decent!" the messenger said.

"It wasn't decent when these men come charging into the settlement, shootin' and killin', neither," Silver Wolf said. "And it damn sure wasn't decent when they killed Ian's new bride. Now shut your blow-hole."

The bloody souvenirs tucked behind Ian's belt, Ian and the Wolf walked out into the sunlight and calmly walked the short distance to the livery.

"I saddled your mounts, boys," the liveryman said. "You best ride hard."

"Thanks kindly," the Wolf said. A moment later the two men were galloping away, neither of them aware that young Ian was about to become a wanted man, with a bounty on his head.

Ian had been gone fourteen months when the news of the killings up in Canada reached Jamie and Kate. Big Jim Williams rode in from the fort and brought a stack of newspapers. A reporter from a New York City newspaper had gotten his silk and lace underwear in a wad and written a long column deploring the killings and wondering when this terrible violence would end. He called for an immediate ban on all pistols except those in the hands of the police and the military.

"This columnist must be a total fool," Kate remarked.

"It'll get worse as the years go by," Jamie said. Jamie read another newspaper while Big Jim sat on the porch and drank coffee and ate hot biscuits, spread with butter and jam. "Ian is wanted by Canadian authorities and he's got bounty hunters after him. That means they'll surely come here."

"And?" Kate asked.

"If they come here and start trouble, they'll be buried here" Jamie said. "I'll show them no mercy."

"Wesley Parsons and crew was at the Fort," Big Jim

called through the open window. "They're ridin' after Jamie. He was spotted up near Powder River Pass."

Kate looked at Jamie. "I would like to know that my oldest is all right," she said.

"I'll get my gear together," Jamie said.

"I'll ride with you part of the way," Big Jim said. "Then I got to angle off and meet up with some ol' boys. We're fixin' to winter in California. I would saddle up your hoss, but if you're gonna ride that monster you usually ride, I'll pass."

Jamie saddled up Horse and the two men were gone in less than an hour. Jamie was carrying a long letter for Ian, written by his mother while Jamie was packing. Big Jim said his farewells and cut west at Bridger Pass and Jamie continued on north. Except for hunting trips, Jamie had not left the valley in months, and both he and Horse were ready for the trail. When he could, he stayed in Indian villages, only entering after he had killed game to share with them.

A hunting party of Indians told Jamie where his son was camped, and Jamie rode close and helloed the camp. His grandpa was nowhere to be seen. But Jamie recognized the tall young man who stepped out from brush and rocks.

Jamie walked Horse down to him and sat his saddle for a moment, staring at the young man. "You've changed, son."

"That's what the Wolf tells me."

"Where is Grandpa?"

"Gone for supplies. Light and set, Pa."

"Thank you."

Ian shoved the coffeepot back on the fire and found two cups and shook them out. "You hungry, Pa?"

"I could eat. I've got a side of bacon in the left-hand pack and some of your ma's put-ups in jars on the other side. They're for you and Grandpa."

"Ma send you?"

"In a manner of speaking. I'll break out the fryin' pan while you get the grub, all right?"

"I'll put your horses up, too. I think Horse probably still remembers me."

"He's not the only one," Jamie said drily.

That got the father a cool look from the son, but Ian wisely curbed his tongue.

The animals put up and cared for, the bacon frying in the pan, Jamie handed Ian the letter from his mother. "I'll just step over here and fetch some wood while you read what your ma wrote."

But Ian was already lost in the letter from home and did not acknowledge his father's words.

Jamie returned after a few moments and put a few sticks on the fire, then poured himself coffee. He studied his son while Ian was totally engrossed in the letter, reading it for the second time. Jamie noticed that the young man's eyes were a bit red.

Ian carefully folded the letter and tucked it safely away. He snuffed a couple of times and wiped his nose on the sleeve of his shirt, a shirt that his ma had made for him, Jamie noted. "Guess I caught a bit of a cold," Ian said.

"Yeah. It's easy to do up here. Gonna be a hard winter, too, I reckon."

Ian poured him a cup of coffee and stared at his father for a moment. "I ain't goin' back 'til my mission is done, Pa."

"I didn't ride up here to talk about that. I come up here so's I could tell your ma how you was lookin' and how you was doin' and so she wouldn't take a notion to put a bundlin' board between us."

Ian grinned for a moment, then the grin faded. "Ma keepin' flowers on Linda's grave?"

"Everybody does, boy. She's never going to be forgotten."

"I still dream about her, Pa."

"I 'spect you will for a long time, son. But there'll be someone else come along in the years ahead. You've got your whole life ahead of you."

"That's what the Wolf tells me."

"He's comin' yonder," Jamie said.

Ian spun around, almost spilling his coffee, then settled back down. "Will I ever be as good as you, Pa?"

"In time. Me and your ma, Ian, we grew up on the run. You can remember how it was back in the Big Thicket."

"The younger generation has it easier than the one before?" Ian asked with a smile.

"That's the way it's always been. It's the way it should be."

Both of them got up to greet Silver Wolf and help him unload the pack horse. Then they all settled down around the fire to eat bacon and bread, drink the strong coffee, and talk.

"You asked about your ma, Ian," Jamie said. "I'll just flat out shoot straight with you. She doesn't like that price on your head."

"You've had one on your head nearabouts all your life, Pa," the son retorted.

Silver Wolf smiled and leaned back against his saddle, for the moment, at least, staying out of this. Besides, he was enjoying the exchange.

"You're gonna sit over there and grin like the cat who ate the cream, aren't you?" Jamie asked his grandpa.

"I just might take me a snooze," the old man replied. "Man my age needs his rest."

Jamie snorted at that.

"Because," the old man added, "I figure I'm gonna need all my strength when Wesley Parsons and his bunch get here." He again smiled.

"Say it all, Grandpa," Jamie urged, picking up a note of warning in the old man's smile and words. "Is that bunch of bounty hunters close?"

"'Bout five miles out and closing," the old man said with a satisfied smile.

Three

"Thanks for tellin' us right off," Jamie said.

"Them ol' boys is comin' on slow, son," the old man said. He looked up at the sky. "I figure they'll be here 'bout three o'clock. We got plenty of time to set us up an ambush." He leaned forward and refilled his coffee cup.

"How many?" Jamie asked.

"Twelve or fifteen, I reckon. It'll be an easy shoot. We'll put the animals in the center of them rocks where they's some graze and a tiny spring. But I reckon we best be gettin' set."

While they worked setting up defensive positions, Ian asked, "Didn't this Wesley Parsons you said was leadin' this party swear to you one time that he'd never come back west, Pa?"

"Sort of. But I didn't believe him. He won't have to worry about it after this day, howsomever. I 'spect we'll bury him right here. If he's got the courage to head this pack of filth."

"They'll be more after we do in this bunch," Silver Wolf said. "I learned over to the tradin' post that Blake Evans's father is a mighty rich man back east. Got more money than he knows what to do with. Powerful government connections, too. Blake was no-count from birth. In some sort of trouble all his life, but his daddy always bought him out of it. Finally, he raped and killed a young woman and had to hit the outlaw trail. Young Ian's future is gonna be like your life down in the Big Thicket country, Jamie. It ain't gonna be easy."

Jamie's eyes turned hard and mean as he looked at his grandfather. "Whereabouts back east?"

"New York City. Why?"

"I just might pay Mister Evans a visit if he wants to keep this up."

"Now that would be a right interestin' trip," the old man opined with a smile. "'Deed it would."

"I fight my own battles, Pa," Ian said.

"You hush up and take help from family when it's offered," his father told him. "If this was something you had started, I could understand a father's position. But it wasn't none of your doin' to begin with. Blake done a terrible thing and he paid the price for it. Far as I'm concerned it's tit for tat. If Mister Evans wants to drag this thing out, then he can face me. That's my say on the matter and it stands."

"Yes, Pa," Ian said.

The men settled in among the rocks.

"There they are," the old Wolf called from high up in the rocks. They each had two rifles, and the plan was that each man would take out two bounty hunters during the first few seconds of the fight and then get the hell out of the rocks before ricochets started screaming all around them and head for a creek that ran alongside the upthrusting of stones. They all felt that with half of the bounty hunters down in the first volley, a lot of the fight would go out of those remaining.

Jamie smiled as the men rode right up to the now

cleaned up campsite, and one said, his words clearly reaching those high up in the rock, "This here looks like a dandy place to make camp. Water and some graze. My back hurts from the day's ride."

"Yeah," another bounty hunter said. "That trapper we tortured yesterday said the bastard's daddy was headin' up this way. If we can kill and behead father and son, that'll be twicet the money for us."

"I want Jamie MacCallister alive," another one said, just as the men in the rocks were sighting in. "I owe that bastard. I want to burn him and see how brave he is."

The men in the rocks fired as one and three bounty hunters went down dead. Before the echo of the shots faded, three more balls ripped into the knotted up men and four of them hit the rocky ground, as the ball fired by Ian went right through the neck of one and slammed into the skull of the fourth man.

The remaining bounty hunters went into a panic, and the men in the rocks jerked out pistols and let them bang. The distance was really too great for any type of accuracy, but the lead flew true and two more man-hunters were knocked from the saddle.

Those bounty hunters left raced away from the death scene and Jamie's grandpa watched them go from his high-up position. "They ain't even thinkin' about stoppin'," he called, pausing to reload his weapons. "They've had enough for this trip."

The grandfather, father, and son made their way down to level ground and began rolling over the bodies to check for signs of life. Two of the man-hunters were alive, and one was not that badly hurt, with only a neat hole punched through one shoulder. The other one would not last long.

"Murderin' bastards!" the slightly wounded bounty hunter spat the words at the trio of men.

"You really ain't in no good position to be callin' folks names, laddie," the Wolf told him. "As a matter of fact, was I you, if I wasn't goin' to say kindly things, I do believe I'd shut my mouth."

The wounded man took the suggestion to heart and closed his fly trap.

Ian was busy retrieving weapons and stacking them. He made a second pile of shot and powder and caps.

"Go on and kill me and get it over with," the wounded man said, after watching the other man die. "I know you're goin' to murder me. Go on and do it."

Jamie knelt down beside the man, his big Bowie in hand, and the man paled and tensed. Jamie cut open the man's shirt and looked at the wound. "You'll live," he told the man. "I'll fix up a poultice and you can be on your way."

"Huh?"

"I didn't see Wesley Parsons in this bunch. Where is he?"

A sly look came into the man's eyes. "That's for me to know and you to find out."

"You're a fool!" Jamie told him, standing up. "Tend to your own damn wound."

"Is you just gonna leave me here alone and hurt to be butchered by the red savages?" the man cried.

Grandfather, father, and son made no reply to that. The Wolf had rounded up the horses and roped them together. Ian stashed the weapons in saddlebags and boots and Jamie got their own mounts from the rocks. The bounty hunters had left two pack horses behind, filled with supplies and equipment. Jamie tossed the wounded man a rifle and pistol, shot and powder and caps. He pointed to a lone horse.

"You have beans and bacon and coffee in those saddle-bags. Ride out of here and don't ever come looking for any of us again."

The three rode out, leading the saddled horses and the pack animals.

"Wait!" the wounded man yelled after them. "Ain't you gonna bury the dead. That ain't no Christian way to act. Wait! I be feared to stay here alone."

None of the three looked back.

The bounty hunters stopped several miles from the ambush scene before they killed their rapidly faltering animals. To a man they were almighty scared. "Damn Wesley Parsons' eyes!" one said, so badly frightened he could barely stand. "He said this hunt would be easy."

"Then that makes you a fool for believin' him," another said. "If Parsons wants the MacCallisters, he can damn well go after them his own self. I hate this damn western wilderness. Me and this hunt is done."

"Where you be headin', Leo?" another man asked.

"Back east. I'm done with this country. It's bilin' hot during the day and freezing cold at night. I don't see why no man in his right mind would choose to live out here. It ain't for me. Who's goin' with me?"

Everybody.

Jamie had given his grandfather and son the supplies taken from the bounty hunters and bid them both farewell. He had seen within the first few moments of talking with his son that Ian was not going to quit the hunt until all involved in his wife's killing were dead.

He rode south and picked up the trail of those bounty hunters who had survived the ambush and was amused by the haste in which they had seemingly elected to quit and go back home. There had not been much sand to this bunch.

Jamie headed back to the valley, for there was much to do before winter closed in the settlement. He carried in his pocket a letter from Ian to his mother. It would be of some comfort to her. Providing she could read Ian's hurriedly penciled scrawl.

On the fourth day from the rocks, riding easy and trailing what was left of the man-hunters, Jamie saw the smoke from the bounty hunters' camp. They had not chosen well, for none of them were experienced western men. Jamie, being the man he was, rode right up to the camp and walked Horse in. The bounty hunters looked up at him with a mixture of disbelief and open fear.

"Howdy, boys," Jamie said, sitting his saddle, his rifle across the saddle bows, the muzzle pointed directly at a big hulk of a man. "I saw your smoke. Figured you might have a cup of coffee for a man."

"You got a lot of nerve, MacCallister," the hulking oaf said.

"I suppose I have to take that as a refusal to share your camp with me."

"Sit down and have some food and coffee, MacCallister," yet another man said. "Don't pay no attention to Tiny yonder. He don't like nobody. We give up the hunt. I had me a bad feelin' about it all along."

"I ain't give up crap!" the huge oaf called Tiny said.

"You git off that horse and I'll pick up the hunt soon as your boots hit the ground."

"You'll do it alone, Tiny," another ex-bounty hunter said. "You're welcome to sit and drink and eat, Jamie MacCallister. But if you want your hoss tooken care of, you'll have to do that yourself. I ain't touchin' that mean-eyed stallion."

Jamie laughed and swung down. He tied Horse to the picket line and turned around. Tiny was standing about five feet from him, hate shining through his piggy eyes.

"I warned you, MacCallister. Now you're dead meat and all mine."

Jamie stepped forward and hit the man on the jaw with the butt of his rifle. Tiny's jaw cracked, his eyes rolled back in his head, and he stretched out on the cool ground for a long, involuntary rest.

"Nobody never could tell Tiny nothin'," a man said. "He always figured he knew it all."

"You made yourself a bad enemy, Jamie MacCallister. Tiny will carry the hate in his heart for as long as he lives."

Jamie poured himself a cup of coffee and took the offered pan of beans and bacon and bread and sat down and started eating. "I've got lots of people who hate me," he finally spoke. "For one reason or the other. That seems to be the cross I have to bear for the rest of my days."

"I'd say you was bearin' up mighty well under it," the first friendly man said . . . with a twinkle in his eyes.

The rest of the men laughed and Jamie joined in with them. Whatever tension there might have been vanished.

But not being a terribly trusting man, Jamie thanked the men for the food and company and pushed on for a few more miles before settling down in a cold camp for that evening. None of them knew Tiny's last name, at least they said they didn't. But since the man stood over six and a half feet tall and was as ugly as sin was bad, Jamie would have little trouble describing him to other trappers. Someone would know him, for though the west was vast, it was still sparsely populated.

The trip south was uneventful, and Jamie was grateful to once more top the ridge and look down into the valley. As always, his eyes drifted to the tiny cemetery to check for new graves. There were no new additions. But there was a new building going up, and parked beside the building, a half dozen big wagons.

"Well now," Jamie said and rode on down to the valley floor.

Kate ran out to meet him, and when Jamie handed her the letter from Ian, she went to the porch and sat down without another word or greeting kiss. "I will never understand women," Jamie muttered, as he led Horse off to the barn and a well-deserved rest.

"It's a store, Jamie," Sam said proudly. "We have a real store here now."

Jamie was introduced to the man who owned the store, one Abe Goldman, his wife Rebecca, and their three children, Rachel, Walter, and Tobias. Rebecca was very gracious and the kids well-behaved.

"We'll soon have everything anybody might ask for," Abe said proudly, obviously eager to please the man whom the valley was named after. "From buttons to bacon." He smiled nervously, took a deep breath, and added, "And there will be a wagon train in next spring with people to settle in the next valley over."

Sam took Jamie aside. "In the next valley over, Jamie," he repeated. "Not here."

Jamie shrugged his massive shoulders. "The days are gone when I have much say about who settles where, Sam. It'll be good to have a store close by."

And that was all he had to say about the new store.

That night, snuggled close together in their bed, Kate asked, "Ian is never coming back, is he, Jamie?"

Jamie was long in replying; so long Kate thought he might have drifted off to sleep. Finally he said, "I don't know, Kate. If he does it won't be anytime soon. This valley has bad memories for him. Losing Linda was a terrible blow."

"Is our son going to turn out to be a gun man?" she asked, using the newly coined western phrase which would soon become just one word. "Is he, Jamie?"

"A gun man, Kate?"

"That's what some reporters and columnists are beginning to call western desperadoes. I read it in the latest papers several times."

"Interesting phrase," Jamie muttered. "I don't know, Kate. I hope not. But I'm really not sure what it means. I do know that Ian is no desperado."

"Did he take scalps back at the ambush site?"

Jamie never tried to hide things from Kate. Like most married men, he had found out the hard way that it's better to come right up front with matters.

"Yes."

Kate sighed and turned on the feather tick, putting her back to Jamie.

"He'll come back someday, Kate. When the hate in his heart is gone, then he'll return."

"I wonder," Kate said. "I just wonder about that."

So did Jamie, but it seemed the right thing to say at the time.

Four

Those in the valley heard no word of Jamie Ian and Silver Wolf all that hard and long winter. When spring finally arrived, after several false starts, the wagons had already begun rolling out of Missouri and onto the Great Plains, and the Indians were getting angry about the influx of whites into country they had long claimed as their own. It was to be the beginning of a terrible and bloody time in the west, a time of sporadic wars that would last well into the 1880s.

In June of that year, Jamie received word that his oldest son had cornered John Wilmot's younger brother in California and killed the man with a knife. Jamie did not keep the news from Kate. She stood in the kitchen of their cabin and received the news with a coolness in her eyes that belied her true inner feelings. "Was John Wilmot's younger brother a member of the party that raided this settlement?"

"I . . . don't think so, Kate. But we don't know the whole story about the killing. Wilmot may have braced Ian, called him out. Let's not judge until we learn all the facts."

Kate stepped outside to stand on the porch for a time. After a few moments, she called, "Jamie. I think it's Grandpa riding over the ridge yonder."

The old man was still spry, but his color was bad and his face twisted in pain. Jamie really didn't know how old he was. In his late 70s at least, probably older than that. He walked up to the porch, kissed Kate, ruffled the hair of the kids, and shook Jamie's hand. Kate showed him to a porch chair and went inside to fix him something to eat.

"I'll eat first," the Wolf said. "Then share the news with the family so's I won't have to repeat it."

The Wolf didn't have much of an appetite. He ate a small bowl of beef stew, a few pieces of fresh-baked and buttered bread, and a pot of coffee before he spoke, and then only after the younger kids were at play or at chores, well out of earshot.

"Ian almost killed them all," the old man said. "Right down to the last man-jack of them. Sixteen men in all. But he never got John Wilmot, Biggers, or Winslow. And the lad ain't gonna quit until he does. Them's his sworn words. I brung you a letter from your boy, Kate. I watched him write the words and sometimes a-cryin' he was whilst he done it. He loves both of you. But he's got a devil ridin' his back. And the only way he's gonna get loose from it is by killin' them who kilt his bride. I seen it in him and said it and he agreed. He's a man growed now, and he don't need my help no more. He's stayin' out from here so's them kin of them he kilt won't attack the settlement. That's why he's stayin' away. Too many goddamn bounty hunters lookin' for him."

The old man pointed to a bluff about mid-way up a mountain. "See that spot up yonder? Jamie, you told me that's where you wanted to be buried when your time come. Well, my time ain't far off and that's where I want you to plant me. I got me a cancer growin' in my belly.

Feel it near'bouts all the time. I might have a year, six months, or two days. I don't know. But I know I'm goin'. I left my white buckskins here after the brigands struck, and I want to be buried in them. You plant me with my rifle, my pistols, and my good knife. When I'm gone, you put my horse out to pasture and see that he never wants for nothin'. I'm goin' up yonder and dig the hole myself, just the way I want it. You won't see much of me. I'll chisel out the stone and put the words I want on it. Jamie, you come check on me from time to time, 'cause I'm growin' weaker daily. Pisses me off, too, it does. Pardon my filthy language, Kate." He stood up and reached inside his jacket, handing Kate the letter from Ian. "Thank you most kindly for the fine grub, Kate. It hit the spot. I'll be goin' up yonder where the winds blow and the pumas prowl and snort. I'll see you in a few days, Jamie."

"I'll be along, Grandpa."

The old man stepped off the porch, tall and straight and proud. Kate and Jamie watched him ride off into the high-up country.

"A dying breed," Jamie said softly. "When he's gone, it'll be the last of a breed."

"No, it won't," Kate said softly. "You'll just step in to fill his moccasins."

A week later, Jamie rode up to the far-off bluff he had chosen for his own final resting place and checked on his Grandpa. The old man had lost weight and looked bad but was still moving around well and working on his headstone.

"Sit down, boy," the old Wolf said, pointing to a spot

by the fire, for it was cold this high up. "Pour us some coffee."

Coffee poured, the old man laid out a piece of deerskin, on which was a beautifully drawn map. "Done this myself, boy, over the years. See all these little Xs? That's where they's veins of gold. Some veins might not yield no more than ten pounds of gold. Others will give up maybe five hundred or a thousand pounds of it. They's enough there to see that your family and offspring for a hundred or more years will never want for naught."

The old Wolf laid back against his saddle and pulled a blanket over him. "Tired, boy. I'm almighty tired. You know how old I am, Jamie?"

"No, sir."

"I think I was born in 1757. What year is this, son?"

"1844, I think, Grandpa."

"How old would that make me?"

Jamie did some head ruminating. "Nearabout 87 years old, Grandpa."

"Damn!"

"What's the matter?"

"My daddy lived past ninety and his pa lived to be over a hundred. I thought shore I'd hit ninety at least. Well, I come close, didn't I?"

"You sure did, Grandpa."

"Maybe it was 1747," the old man said, his eyes still closed. "Oh, hell! It don't make no difference. When your string's run out, it's gone. You take that map, boy, and after I'm gone, you tell your woman that you'll be gone until the snow flies. You dig out that yeller metal and cache it where nobody but you knows where it is. Take a goodly mess of it back to home with you and cache it up here. I found a spot over yonder." He waved a hand that suddenly looked awfully frail. Jamie's eyes followed the movement and saw where the Wolf had marked a spot in the rock wall of the bluff.

"I see it, Grandpa."

"I lived me a full life, Jamie Ian MacCallister. So I don't want no weepin' and wailin' and blubberin', and a bunch of nonsensical carryin' on over my bones. You hear me?"

"Yes, sir."

"Fine. Now go on back to your woman and love her. Come back in a few days. Go on, boy. I've made my peace."

Jamie sat for a few minutes beside his grandpa. He could see that the old man was asleep and breathing, if a bit ragged. With a sigh, Jamie tucked the map inside his shirt and rode back to the valley.

On the third morning after leaving his grandfather in the high-up, Jamie stepped out onto the porch of his cabin just as dawn was splitting the skies. He looked up to the mountain and saw no smoke. He knew his grandpa was dead.

"Is Grandpa dead?" Kate called from the open shutters.

"Yes." Jamie finished his coffee and saddled up Thunder. No one in the settlement asked where he was going—they knew.

When Jamie reached the bluff, he found his Grandpa all dressed in his white buckskins, laying by the deep hole he'd dug. Jamie wrapped the body in the buffalo robe his grandpa had laid out and as gently as possible, for the old Wolf was no small man, placed the body in the ground. He turned at the sound of hooves on rock. Kate.

She hopped down and walked to her husband's side, taking his big hard hand in her small hand. "How old was he, Jamie?"

"Nearabout ninety, I think. He thought he was born about 1757. He wasn't real sure."

Kate knelt down and looked into the dark hole. "He dug until he hit bedrock."

"Yeah. We'll mound it good with rock and . . ." Jamie paused as his eyes touched the rock where his Grandpa had carved out his final eulogy. Jamie pointed and both he and Kate chuckled at the inscription.

> JAMIE IAN MACCALLISTER.
> B 1757 SCOTLAND
> D 1844 AMERICAN WILDERNESS.
> I NEVER BACKED UP FROM
> NO SON OF A BITCH IN MY LIFE.

"He must have wore out a dozen chisels doing that," Jamie said.

"I'll go get Swede and the others," Kate volunteered.

"I'll get busy filling in the grave."

The service was a short one, just as Silver Wolf had requested. A few of the women cried but demurely, and the Wolf would have liked that. Reverend Haywood read from the Bible and that was that. Jamie told Ellen Kathleen to take the rest of the kids home, and when he and Kate were once more alone at the gravesite, Jamie showed her the map his grandpa had given him.

"No one else must ever know of this, Kate. I thought long and hard about whether to tell you, for fear that if outlaws ever learned of the map, they would torture you to tell them. I'll be gone the rest of the summer, and when

I return, none of our kids or grandkids will ever have to want for anything. And it means that Andrew and Rosanna can travel abroad to continue their studies in music. And you and I can enjoy a few extras in our life."

"And also help others less fortunate than we are," Kate said.

"Right," Jamie smiled through the words. "I was just about to say that."

The first X on the map was less than twenty-five miles from the valley, and it was not a big vein. It played out after only a day's digging and gouging. But Jamie figured he had about forty pounds of gold after everything was knocked off and cleaned up. He cached it safely and rode on to the next X, about half a day's ride away.

After crawling through about fifteen yards of thick brush and chipping away at the stone, Jamie sat back with a gasp. It wasn't a mother lode, but it was going to take him a good week or better to dig it all out.

It took him longer than that, working from can to can't, to dig out and clean up the gold. He found a spot and, marking the exact location in his head, he carefully buried the gold and moved on to the next X.

This one was a tiny creek that played out after only a few hundred yards' run. And it was loaded with nuggets. Grandpa MacCallister always had a small sack full of nuggets, and now Jamie knew where he got them. What Jamie didn't know, and was not likely to ever know, was how his Grandpa managed to get rid of the gold without arousing suspicion, for government experts had already assured two presidents that there was no gold west of the Mississippi River.

The old Silver Wolf had told Jamie that a government expert was a man who couldn't get a job nowheres else.

Jamie cleaned out the creek and moved on.

He had not nearly covered even half of the Xs on the map before he knew it was time to head back to the valley. For humanity's sake, he could not load another pound on any of the pack animals he had brought with him. He didn't know what gold was going for then, but he figured he had thousands of dollars worth of gold in the packs lashed onto the frames.

Jamie returned to the valley and spent the night on the ledge where his grandpa was buried, hiding most of the gold before anyone knew he was back. Only Kate and a lawyer he trusted back in St. Louis would know about the gold, and only Kate would know where it was hidden. The next day, before the sun was up, Jamie rode down into the valley and put the weary pack animals out to pasture for a long and well-deserved rest. Jamie was sitting on the front porch when Kate arose and threw open the shutters to air out the cabin.

"I figured this was what you did while I was out working my hands to the bone," Jamie said, maintaining a straight face. "Just lay a-bed and lollygag about all morning."

Kate hadn't seen her husband in weeks, still she didn't bat an eye. "Go fetch some wood if you want breakfast. And wash your hands. They're filthy."

Jamie sighed. After almost twenty years of marriage, he was still hard-pressed to get one over on Kate.

Five

Folks from the valley to the east of the settlement began coming over to trade at Abe's store—warily at first, for they had all heard the many tales about Jamie Ian Mac-Callister, adventurer, pathfinder, hero of the Alamo, and so much more. The men walked light around him, the kids were big-eyed staring at the huge man, and a few of the women batted their eyes and openly flirted with him . . . until Kate stepped in and with one glance put an end to all that.

Jamie stayed back and surveyed the new settlers. He felt that most of them would do and had the wherewithal to make it out here in the wilderness. A couple of the men would not last; Jamie was certain of that. They were trashy and shifty-eyed and their women were loose. They would cause some trouble before it was all over, Jamie would bet on it.

"That Hankins woman is rather pretty, don't you think?" Kate asked Jamie one evening. Supper was over and the younger kids in bed.

Jamie knew a loaded question when he heard one and wasn't about to pull the trigger. Julie Hankins was one of the new women who had openly flirted with him. "I suppose so," he replied carefully. "If you like that type, which I don't." He hid a grimace—wrong choice of words.

Kate perked right up. "So you did notice her?"

"Be kind of hard not to, Kate. Way she was swishin' her butt around and battin' her eyes like a lost calf. A couple of those women and their daughters are going to cause trouble around here. And their husbands are trash, pure and simple. I wish they'd leave."

Kate relaxed and sat back in the rocker Jamie had made for her. She adjusted the shawl over her lap, for the nights were getting cold. "Matt and Morgan are nearabout thirteen years old, Jamie. A couple of those trashy girls—especially the Hankins girls—were making goo-goo eyes at the boys. Those girls are older and they've been to the hay loft a time or two. I want you to talk to them."

"The girls?" Jamie asked with a smile.

Kate didn't reply, just looked at him with those arctic blue eyes; they got colder by the second.

"Right," Jamie said. "I'll speak to the boys." But he didn't have the foggiest idea what he was going to say. The boys had matured fast for their age and were feeling their oats . . . among other things.

"You just be sure you do. They're far too young to be thinking about things like that."

Jamie looked at her to see if she was serious. "Are you forgetting when we were thirteen and fourteen years old, Kate?"

"That was different."

"The hell it was! I had to go jump in the crick ever' time I got around you. Kate, you could raise the temperature in a room ten degrees just by walking in!"

She suddenly had to put a hand to her mouth to stifle a giggle. "I wasn't *that* bad, Jamie."

"Five degrees, then."

She smiled and made a show of fanning herself. "Isn't it getting warm out here, Jamie?"

"Come to think of it, it is."

They rose as one and walked into the large cabin. Kate giggled a couple of seconds after Jamie blew out the lamp.

Jamie sat the boys down in the barn and gave them a talking-to about the birds and the bees. He was shocked to discover they knew more about the subject than he did.

"Where the hell did you two learn all this?" he demanded.

"Ian and Andrew mostly," Morgan said. "The rest just come natural, I reckon." He grinned.

"You think this is funny, boy?" Jamie asked.

Both boys started laughing at the expression on their father's face, and it was infectious, with Jamie hard-pressed to contain his own laughter. He understood how it was when the blood ran hot. But he quickly sobered.

"Boys, you stay away from those two girls. They just might give you something you can't get rid of."

"What do you mean, Pa?" Matt asked.

Jamie told them about diseases they might contract and the boys were visibly horrified. Of course, Jamie embellished the telling quite a bit and both boys turned a tad green around the mouth.

Matthew immediately declared his wishes to find a Catholic church and become a priest, and Morgan said he was through with women . . . forever!

Jamie figured those fervently offered declarations would last about a week at the most, but he thought he had gotten through to the boys.

But as it turned out, Jamie and Kate's worries were

groundless. It wasn't a young boy who was caught with one of the Hankins girls. It was Cyrus Hankins's best and most trusted friend, the man he had come west with, a married man and father of four, Bob Altman.

Abe Goldman came knocking on the door of the cabin just as Megan and Joleen were clearing off the supper dishes. Jamie opened the huge oversized door—built that way so Jamie wouldn't bump his head going in and out—and faced a very worried looking Abe Goldman.

"Come in, Abe," Jamie opened the door wider.

"You best come outside, Jamie," the storeowner said. "This is news that is not proper for ladies to hear."

Kate immediately stepped past Jamie and onto the porch.

"Very forceful woman," Jamie said.

"I'm told," Abe replied.

Jamie stepped out onto the porch and closed the door behind him.

"I've got Caroline Hankins over to my house," Abe said. "She's pretty badly beaten up and the wife says she's pregnant, too. How she managed to walk from one valley to the other is a mystery."

"Caroline is fourteen years old," Kate said. "Who beat her?"

"Her father, Cyrus. With a belt and with his fists. She won't say why."

Kate pushed open the cabin door. "Matthew, Morgan! You both look after Joleen and Falcon. And I mean look after them. Megan, get your cloak and fetch mine and come with me." She turned to Abe. "We'll be over to your cabin, Mr. Goldman."

"Thank you, Kate. The wife will appreciate the help. She's about beside herself with this thing."

When Kate and Megan had gone, Jamie said, "Who did Cyrus catch his daughter with, Abe?"

The storekeeper was speechless. "Why . . . I hadn't thought of that, Jamie."

"You can bet that's what this is all about." Jamie reached inside the cabin and strapped his pistol belt around him. He didn't have to check to see if the guns were loaded . . . guns were always loaded on the frontier. "You go back to your wife, Abe. I'll saddle up and ride over the ridge and find out what this is all about. Tell Kate where I've gone."

Before Jamie had put the lamplights of the settlement out of sight, he heard the sounds of a galloping horse coming hard. "Hold there!" Jamie shouted. "Before you kill that horse."

Cyrus Hankins reined up the exhausted and trembling animal and Jamie had a notion to slap the man out of the saddle for nearly ruining a good horse.

"Get out of my way, MacCallister!" Cyrus said.

"Watch your mouth, Hankins," Jamie warned him. "Before your ass overloads it. You'll not lay another fist or belt on that girl of yours in this valley."

"So she did come over here!"

"That's right, and to a safe place. Now you just calm down and tell me what all this is about."

"I'll tell you nothin'! You're not the law around here, MacCallister."

"You wanna bet?" Jamie said softly.

Like most men of his ilk, Cyrus was a bully, and most bullies are cowards at heart. Cyrus slumped in the saddle, not really wanting to tangle with Jamie. "Caroline ain't nothin' but a damned whoor, MacCallister. Takes after her ma, I reckon. I found her with Bob Altman in the barn this afternoon, both of them all caught up in the desires of the flesh. It was a terrible sight to behold, it was."

"Where is Altman?"

"Dead. I run him through and through with a hayfork. I reckon he's still there in the barn. Then I whupped that girl to a fare-thee-well. Now git out of my way, MacCallister, 'cause I'm a fixin' to whup her some more."

"No, you're not, Cyrus. She's had enough. Too much, really. Go on back home and calm down."

Cyrus tried to jump his tired horse to get some distance on Jamie, but the horse was just too weary to jump. Jamie lashed out with a hard left fist and smacked Cyrus flush on the jaw, knocking the man from the saddle and stretching him out on the narrow trail. Jamie took the man's pistol and knife and led the tired horse back to the settlement and put him in a stall to eat and rest. Morgan came out to see what was going on.

"Give him some water when he cools down, Morgan. I'll be over at Abe's."

Jamie was shocked at the girl's appearance. Both eyes were nearly swollen shut and her face was a mass of cuts and bruises.

"Is she pregnant, Kate?"

"Yes. About four months, I'd say. She's a strong, healthy girl, so she might not lose the baby. It's just too early to tell."

"Ya, it's a bad ting," the Swede said. "A bad ting, it is."

"Go wait outside," Hannah told him. "And you, too," she told Jamie.

"You go with them," Rebecca told Abe. "This is woman's work. You men just get in the way."

On the porch, the men lit their pipes and Jamie told them what had happened across the ridge.

"Killed him?" Abe said.

"I knew dem movers was trouble when I seen dem," Swede said. "I told Hannah they was, I did." He shook his big head. "But to kill someone . . . it takes two for a coupling, you know."

"That's true," Abe said. "And the girl is pregnant."

"But is it Altman's child?" Jamie questioned.

"What do you mean, Jamie?" Swede asked.

"Something is wrong here. I sensed it in Hankins's voice back yonder on the trail. I got a notion this is darker than any of us realize."

"You better believe it is," Kate spoke from the doorway. No one had heard her pull open the door. "Caroline is awake. She says Bob Altman raped her . . . but she's pregnant due to her father. Cyrus began forcing himself on her several years ago . . . threatened to kill her if she told anyone. I believe her, Jamie."

The men were shocked into silence. By now, most of the settlement had gathered around, their breath making steam in the cold night air.

"Murder and incest," Reverend Haywood said. "The murder might be justified, but the incest is certainly not."

"It might be a blessing if the child is aborted," Sarah said, stepping up on the porch to stand beside Kate. "It could well be a monster."

"That is in God's hands," Juan Nuñez said.

"Yes," Reverend Haywood said. "Quite right."

"What do we do, Jamie?" Moses asked.

Nearly every man there was older than Jamie, but still they looked to him for leadership. "It's her word against his. Even back east, no jury would convict Cyrus for killing a man who raped his daughter. Especially since he caught him in the act. Incest is another matter. But there is no law out here. No proper judge. I don't know what to do."

"Tar and feather the bastard!" Daniel Noble said.

"Yes," Eb French agreed. "And then send him on his way."

"No!" Jamie thundered, his voice stilling the crowd. "There will be none of that. I told you, it's his word against hers, even though I am inclined to believe Caroline. I think she's a good girl born into a rotten family. We'll send Cyrus and his brood on their way and Caroline can stay here. She can stay over in Ian's cabin. No point in it going to waste when there is need."

"I agree," Kate said.

"Me, too," Hannah said.

"And I," Sarah said.

"I tink dats a good idea," the Swede said. "Yes, I do."

"Hannah, Sarah, and I will stay over here tonight," Kate whispered to Jamie. "Mrs. Goldman is about done in. You go back home and—"

"No," Jamie said. "I'll stay over here just in case Cyrus decides to do something tonight. I'll sleep in the barn. I'll see Megan home and be right back."

"Yes. That's a good idea. I'll get Megan."

The crowd began to slowly break up, with Swede and Sam staying at the Goldman home until Jamie returned. If Cyrus was foolish enough to try something at Jamie and Kate's home, it would more than likely be the last time he ever tried anything, for Megan could outshoot the boys, and Jamie knew his daughter well. She would not hesitate in using a gun to defend hearth and home. The boys would probably shoot quicker, but not as straight as Megan, something that always irritated Matt and Morgan and never failed to amuse Jamie.

"Don't worry, Pa," she told him on the way home. "If Cyrus comes around our cabin, he'll regret it . . . for a real short period of time."

Six

Just after dawn, when Juan and Daniel Noble relieved him, Jamie saddled up and rode over the ridge to the other community. Cyrus's horse had come up lame; nothing serious but Jamie wanted to keep him away from Cyrus, so he left the animal in his barn.

The people in the settlement across the ridge were up and gathered all around the community building that served as a school and church. The blanket-wrapped body of Bob Altman was laying in the bed of a wagon.

"If you're lookin' for Cyrus, Mr. MacCallister," a man said as Jamie swung down from the saddle, "you're too late. He and his wife and kids pulled out before dawn. They was up all night, a-packin' and a-fightin' and a-fussin' amongst themselves. You never in your life heard such a commotion. I say it's good riddance."

"You're right. How about Mrs. Altman and family?"

"Damned if they didn't pull out with them." The man shook his head. "Somethin' mighty queer goin' on with them two families. Mighty queer."

Jamie told the gathering that Cyrus had beaten his daughter savagely. But he did not tell them about the incest or that the girl was pregnant. To a person, they received the news with shock.

"Caroline?" a woman asked.

"She's staying with us for a time."

"We know that Cyrus caught Bob assaulting his daughter," a woman spoke up. "And Cyrus killed the man for it. But he said that you would be coming after him for that."

"No," Jamie said. "I just wanted to tell him that his horse came up lame and I have it in my barn, that's all."

"Why did he beat the girl so?" another woman asked.

"I reckon that's something you'll have to ask Cyrus," Jamie said, lifting the reins. "See you folks."

Back in his own valley, dismounting at the Goldman place, Kate met him. "She lost the baby, Jamie. About an hour ago. But it was for the best. She was further along than I thought. The baby was . . . well, not normal."

"Burial?"

"Swede and Reverend Haywood took care of it. They buried the poor thing quickly . . . and unmarked."

Jamie told her about the Hankinses' pulling out, with Altman's widow and kids with them.

"That's mighty queer," Kate said.

"It's a closed book, Kate. We'll never see them again." I hope, Jamie thought.

"Poor Caroline."

"She's better off without them. How is she?"

"She's all right. I think she'll probably be able to have more children. If she ever wants more children."

"Let's go home."

For the next eighteen months the settlement on the western side of the ridge prospered and grew while the newly formed settlement on the eastern slopes faltered and finally died. One by one the families packed up and moved away, with most of them returning to the settled east. Four families, who were making a go of it across the ridge, asked if they could settle in MacCallister's Valley and were welcomed. There were now almost a hundred people living in the valley.

Andrew and Rosanna MacCallister were in Europe, studying music under the watchful eyes of the masters in their chosen field.

There had been no word from or about Ian. The young man called "desperado" and "gun man" had seemingly dropped out of sight.

"He's holed up somewhere in the high country," Jamie told Kate. "Staying low until all this blows over. He's all right." Jamie smiled mysteriously.

"You find this amusing?" Kate asked.

"Ian's probably planted him a garden, cussing all the while. You know how he hated the plow."

Outside the peaceful little valley, events were whirling furiously and change was rampant. The United States was preparing to go to war with Mexico. On December 29th, 1845, Texas became the 28th state of the union. In January of 1846, Captain John Fremont reached Monterey, in Mexican California—it is believed he was under secret orders to make that territory ready for acquisition by the United States. In February of 1846, thousands of Mormons left Nauvoo, Illinois, led by Brigham Young, heading west. Austin became the capital of Texas.

The settlers in MacCallister's Valley had not seen a newspaper or received any sort of news for several months—winter locked the valley up tight. The settlers had no way of knowing that the United States was busy moving army troops about, ready to fight the Mexican Army. General "Rough and Ready" Taylor commanded the American forces and moved his army to the left bank of the Rio Grande River. In early spring of 1846, American troops, under the command of General Worth, built Fort Texas. Just across the river, in Matamoros, six thousand Mexican troops fortified the town.

In early spring 1846, the Mexican commander sent nearly two thousand troops across the Rio Grande and tangled with some seventy American soldiers on a scouting mission. Those American troops who were not killed were captured and taken back across the river into Mexico. Rough and Ready Taylor proclaimed that, "The war may now be considered as commenced." But President Polk didn't learn of that until nearly two weeks later.

The governors of Texas and Louisiana sent volunteers to aid General Taylor just about the same time the Mexican Army once more crossed the Rio Grande to attack Fort Texas.

In early May of 1846, the battle of Palo Alto took place, with two thousand American troops soundly defeating six thousand Mexican troops.

On the eleventh of May, President Polk addressed Congress, "Mexico has passed the boundary of the United States, has invaded our territory and shed American blood on American soil."

On the thirteenth of May, Congress formally declared war on Mexico and authorized millions of dollars toward the war and the immediate recruitment of fifty thousand troops. General Taylor crossed the Rio Grande and occupied the town of Matamoros.

In June, the Army of the West, as it was called, seized

San Francisco Bay and with the help of naval gunboats, set up blockades of Mexican ports on the Gulf of Mexico.

Young Ian MacCallister became a scout for John Fremont, who was instrumental in the Big Bear Revolt in California. After taking the town of Sonoma, Fremont was chosen to lead the new republic.

In July, the U.S. Navy landed at Monterey and Commodore John Sloat raised the Stars and Stripes and declared California part of the United States.

The mountain man, Sparks, scouting for the U.S. Army up in Montana, was asked to take a message to Jamie Ian MacCallister. It was the middle of July before Sparks rode into MacCallister's Valley with the message from Washington. Fontaine, a man who had become friends with Jamie down in Texas and who was working for an organization that would someday be called the Secret Service, wanted Jamie to scout the best and quickest way to California, through the rough country of the southwest. The government was preparing to send several battalions of troops to California, if needed, and going there by ship would take too long.

Jamie was reluctant to go, but Kate made up his mind for him. "Find out how Ian is and come back to me."

"You want to come along?" Jamie asked Sparks.

"I wish I could. But I got orders to head on back to Montana. You ever wintered in Montana?"

"No."

"Don't."

In mid-July of 1846, Jamie saddled up and rode out, heading south for New Mexico. Grandpa MacCallister had been a good talker and Jamie a good listener. The old

Silver Wolf had prowled all over the southwest, and he had told Jamie the best way to cross to California. "Just watch them Injuns down yonder," the old man had cautioned. "Some of them desert Injuns is pure hell, boy. The Navaho is right nice folks, but them Apaches is mighty mean. And that's bein' kind."

Horse was an ideal desert animal, the color of sand and as tough an animal as Jamie had ever ridden. Horse loved the trail and was ready to travel. When Jamie rode into the raw and rugged town of Taos, feelings among the Mexicans were running high against the Anglos and the feeling was mutual. Jamie didn't tarry long. He supplied up and pulled out, unaware that Colonel Kearny already knew the way to California and had left New Mexico about two weeks ahead of Jamie, heading for the new territory of California. Fontaine had tricked Jamie. Fontaine thought that with two MacCallisters fighting for California independence the war could be won a lot quicker.

A few days out of Taos, Jamie came up on the camp of Kit Carson. The two men had a rousing welcome and then settled down for coffee and food.

"What are you doing way to hell an' gone down here, Jamie?" Kit asked.

Jamie explained.

Kit was puzzled. "Hell, Jamie, I just come from California. I run into Colonel Kearny not a week ago. He knows the way out there. They's a truce on between us and the Mexicans. There ain't no fightin' out there."

Carson, unaware that conditions in California had taken a terrible turn for the worse, the truce being violated a dozen times a day on both sides, had convinced Kearny to send more than half of his troops back to New Mexico.

"'Sides, I hear that the Mormon Battalion is blazin' a trail from Santa Fe to San Diego. I can't figure out what Fontaine has on his mind."

The Mormon Battalion, recruited from the men who were wintering at Council Bluffs under the command of Captain George Cooke, did indeed blaze a trail. But history has treated their epic journey very lightly. On several occasions, the men and horses went without water for days, and at least twice the wagons had to be completely dismantled to get through narrow passes along the way. Other than that, not much else is known about their backbreaking trek.

Jamie crossed the land much faster than the slow-moving Mormon Battalion and had no trouble with Indians. He reached Los Angeles a short time after the main Army garrison had pulled out, leaving only about fifty soldiers behind. The city itself was left under the rule of Archibald Gillespie, a man who held the Californios in contempt and did nothing to hide his feelings. He was little more than a tyrant.

Jamie rode right into a growing rebellion.

Ian, having no desire to head south with Stockton to fight in Mexico, had left the volunteers and was having dinner one evening in a cantina when he looked up and met his father's eyes. The men quietly embraced and sat down to wine and food and conversation.

Jamie explained to his son how he'd been tricked into coming out to California. "But," he added with a smile, "it was only a matter of time. Your ma would have made me come out to see you anyway."

"Things are bad here, Pa. There's a Mexican fellow named Serbulo Varela who's really stirring up trouble. This whole city could blow up at any moment. The Californios really hate Gillespie."

"What do you want to do, son?"

Ian smiled. "I think we ought to stick around and see the action."

"Uh-huh. And just maybe take a hand in it, too, right?"

"Since when have you ever backed away from a fight, Pa?"

Jamie smiled and studied his oldest son. He was a boy no longer. He was almost the mirror image of Jamie at that age. Indeed, the two could pass for brothers. Ian was the same height as his pa, with the same broad shoulders and massive arms and chest. He was now clean-shaven and wore his hair shoulder-length, like his pa.

"I'll back away from no fight that concerns me, Ian. Does this fight concern me?"

"You fought at the Alamo and have to ask that, Pa?"

"I reckon not, son. All right. You got any followers?"

"Nary a one. I kind of like to lone-wolf it. I reckon I picked that up from you."

"Well, let's scout around some and see which way the wind is going to blow. Then we'll plan."

Jamie prowled the town and liked none of what he saw or heard. Gillespie had so angered the Californios that one could almost smell trouble in the air. Before he had pulled out, Stockton had put a curfew into effect—rigidly enforced by Gillespie—even going so far as to forbid family reunions in private homes and arresting any Mexicans who walked abreast on public streets. The Californios had taken just about all that they were going to take. And to make matters worse, the Californios had no respect whatsoever for Gillespie's troops, who were, for the most part, rude and undisciplined.

Jamie looked over the small garrison of troops and shook his head. They were some of the most unsoldierly troops he had ever seen, sloppy in manner and dress and attitude.

Jamie really wanted to take no part in the upcoming fight, but he was an American, and duty sang him her song—not nearly as strong as she had in Texas, but he could nevertheless make out the melody.

Jamie sought out an audience with Gillespie. But the man rudely refused to see him. Jamie told the clearly startled guard what Gillespie could do with his refusal and how far he could stick it.

It was the afternoon of September 22, 1846.

"I tried, Ian," Jamie told his son back at the hotel. "But the man refused to see me."

"That's like him. What now, Pa?"

"We get a good supper and ride out for the valley at first light."

"I reckon. Maybe it's time I came back home. I have been missin' the place."

"Not nearabouts as much as your ma's been missin' you, I can tell you for sure."

Both Jamie and Ian noticed that the streets were devoid of horses, buggies, and foot traffic early that evening. They put it off merely as the Californios obeying the curfew and thought no more of it.

Jamie and Ian were jarred out of bed early the following morning by the sound of gunfire and shouting. They jumped into their clothes and grabbed their guns.

The excited night clerk stopped them in a dimly lit lobby. "Don't go outside, gentlemen," he urged. "You'll be killed. The revolution is underway."

Seven

Jamie and Ian ignored the warning and stepped out onto the street. A Mexican galloped up and, seeing the men were Anglos, snapped a pistol shot at them. The round missed them and broke a window in the hotel. Ian cleared the saddle with a ball and the man bounced in the street.

"My God, now we'll all be killed!" the panicked night clerk shouted from the floor behind his desk.

"They're attacking the garrison!" the faint shout came to the men. "To arms, to arms!"

"Let's get our horses, Pa."

"No," Jamie stopped his son. "We can be more effective on foot. This is going to be close-in work, son. Go back upstairs and get all our pistols. Make sure they're fully charged. We'll fight silently from the shadows."

It was three o'clock in the morning when the Californios revolted against the harsh rule of Archibald Gillespie.

Father and son ran through the alleys of the town until they reached the garrison. The scene amazed Jamie, for the American troops were more than holding their own and slowly beating the attackers back.

"There's Varela," Ian pointed out and lifted his pistol.

But the leader of the uprising had ducked into the shadows and Ian held his fire.

"There's only a handful of them," Jamie said. "The troops are holding. Let's get back to the hotel and pack up. This might not prove to be anything to worry about."

But Jamie was wrong. After the brief battle at his garrison, Gillespie immediately ordered all Anglos to arms and closed up the town tight; no one out and no one in. The Californios began digging up weapons they had buried when the Anglos took power and the revolution was really on.

Commander Gillespie sent a messenger to the hotel to tell Jamie that he would see him now.

"Tell him to go to hell," Jamie told the soldier.

"I can't tell him that!" the soldier protested.

"Then tell him you couldn't find me."

By that night, some five hundred armed Californios had gathered at an old Mexican military base about a mile from the American garrison. The Californios were under the command of a professional soldier, Captain Jose Flores, a calm and deliberate man who harbored a deep hatred toward the United States. His second in command, Lieutenant Gomez, despised Americans even more than Flores; he had been wounded at the Alamo and had lost several relatives there, not to mention a lot of dignity and a promotion. He went straight to Captain Flores when he learned that Jamie MacCallister was in town.

"Find him," Flores ordered. "We'll hang him publicly and that will break the spirits of the damned Americans."

But a Californio who knew that Jamie was a fair man who had no hard feelings against people of Spanish descent, learned of the order and slipped up the back steps of the hotel, tapping softly on Jamie's door.

"You must flee," he told Jamie. "The orders are to find you and hang you."

"Gracias," Jamie told the man. "But that's been tried before and I'm still walking around and breathing."

The Mexican shrugged his shoulders and slipped away. Jamie charged all six of his heavy caliber pistols and both rifles and blew out the lamp. Ian was also armed with numerous pistols and two rifles. Together, father and son waited in the darkness for the attackers to come. The streets had turned even more dangerous, for by now, hundreds of armed and angry Californios were roaming the town, looking for Anglos.

Gomez, leading a dozen men, rushed into the lobby of the small hotel and charged up the stairs with several of his men in front of him.

Jamie and Ian were waiting on the second floor landing. Six of Gomez's soldiers were either killed or badly wounded during the first few seconds, turning the landing slick with blood and creating panic among the living.

Gomez was no coward, but neither was he a fool. He ordered his men back and the small hotel set on fire. Jamie and Ian had rushed back to their room and grabbed up their saddlebags before the gunsmoke had cleared and were gone out the back way before the first torch could be lit. They squatted in the alley beside the hotel and watched as the first torch was fired into life.

Jamie lifted a pistol and put a ball into the man's guts. He screamed, doubled over, and dropped the torch, the flames setting another man's britches on fire. Had it not been so tragic, it would have been comical.

Lieutenant Gomez took what men he had left and got the hell out of there.

Jamie, unpredictable as always, reentered the hotel through the back door and set about making coffee and cooking an early breakfast.

The revolution was less than twenty-four hours old, and so far, the Californios had suffered far greater losses than the Anglos, mostly due to the shooting skills of Jamie and Ian MacCallister.

But all that was about to change.

Before dawn broke, Jamie and Ian made the livery and managed to slip out of Los Angeles without getting shot, but they did get shot *at* a couple of times.

"I think those were our people shootin' at us, Pa," Ian said, while the men were resting their horses.

Jamie grinned. "They still missed us."

Back in Los Angeles, Gillespie sent a messenger north to Monterey to seek help from Stockton, who was busy getting his fleet ready to sail to Mexico. But after eluding his pursuers for several days the messenger was captured. On the fifth day of the revolt, Gillespie surrendered his small and badly outnumbered garrison to Captain Flores.

In a rather magnanimous gesture, Captain Flores allowed the Americans to march out to San Pedro, where they boarded a naval vessel. But Gillespie broke his word and instead of sailing out of the harbor stayed put, awaiting rescue from Stockton. He did not know his messenger had been captured.

Jamie and Ian, meanwhile, had taken refuge in an old abandoned church just outside of Los Angeles and were sitting it out.

"These desert jackrabbits are tough," Ian griped, gnawing away at a rabbit they'd caught in a snare.

"Beats no food at all," Jamie told him. "Eat."

"Are we just going to sit here and do *nothing?*" Ian questioned.

Gillespie's messenger had managed to escape from his captors and made a hard and dangerous ride north to Commodore Stockton. The messenger would forever after be known as the Paul Revere of California.

Gillespie and what was left of his garrison were still sitting aboard ship in the harbor of Los Angeles, waiting to be rescued. So far, the entire mess was a debacle, due in no small part to Stockton, who, like Gillespie, despised Californios and treated them abysmally.

Meanwhile, Jamie and Ian had made friends with a Mexican farmer and his family who had no interest whatsoever in who ran the government as long as they were left alone to mind their own business. The spicy food was a damn sight better than what Jamie and son had been living on for the better part of a week, which consisted mostly of rattlesnake meat and an occasional rabbit.

"Who is winning the battle in Los Angeles?" Jamie asked the man.

"Who cares?" the farmer replied, passing the beans and tortillas. "Flores is arrogant and Gomez is a fool."

"And Varela?" Ian asked.

"A thug. Eat, the war is a long way off."

Not really. Only about five miles. It just seemed to be a long way off.

Stockton, aboard his flagship, had ordered the *Savannah* to set sail to rescue Gillespie and his men, still in Los

Angeles harbor aboard the *Vandalia*. When they arrived, some two hundred men, plus Gillespie's small force, went immediately ashore to attempt to recapture the town.

It was to be yet another debacle for the Americans. Most of the men, with the exception of Gillespie's troops, were sailors and had no training in land combat. But Gillespie could not be reasoned with and ordered the troops ashore.

Jamie and Ian had saddled up, over the heated protests of their Mexican friends, and decided to ride into the town to see what was going on.

Captain Flores was an experienced campaigner, a veteran of many battles. He was busy planning a guerrilla war. He ordered all livestock, including chickens and hogs, to be driven or carried by wagon inland. He then ordered all foodstuffs in the town's stores to be seized and carried inland also, thereby depriving the Americans of anything to eat—except what they could carry with them. They had left the ships in such a hurry, they only carried a couple of days' rations.

Another thing that Gillespie, in his rage, did not consider was that his men would be facing not only experienced soldiers, but the expert horsemanship of the Californio Lancers.

When Gillespie and his men got ashore, they found themselves on foot, for every horse had been driven away. Gillespie was, in the words of one of the officers, "Unreasonable with anger."

Jamie and Ian could not get through the steadily growing lines that Captain Flores had thrown around the town and decided to cut north for a day and try to come back south that way. Amazingly, when they got about twenty miles north of Los Angeles, they found the Spanish people to be very friendly and very hospitable. And many that they encountered cared nothing about the war to the south of them.

"We just wish to get along," the leader of one community told the men. "We are so far separated from Mexico, we feel that we have lost touch with them and they with us."

But not all felt that way and Jamie and Ian knew it. Father and son could read it in the dark eyes, and they were careful.

At camp one evening, Jamie asked, "What day of the month is it, son?"

Ian grinned. "Hell, Pa. I don't even know for sure what year it is."

It was October 8, 1846.

Earlier, Stockton had learned of the presence of Jamie and his son and had sent a messenger to find them and tell them they were now in the Army as scouts. They were to report everything back to him. The two men Stockton sent would act as message bearers between Jamie and the Commodore.

"Can they do that?" Ian asked.

"I guess so, son. They just did it!"

The two small armies met on level ground between San Pedro and Los Angeles. The Californios had a single artillery piece, a four pounder, and that single artillery piece was to decide the victor for this day.

The ship's captain and Gillespie marched their men in close column right up the middle of the road, with only a few skirmishes on either side. Flores ordered the cannon to be fired and the ball sailed right over the heads of the advancing Americans. The ship's captain ordered his men to charge, and they charged right into murderous grape-shot from the freshly charged cannon. The Americans charged two more times, and after the last, they quit for the day and retired to the ships. They had suffered ten wounded and four dead.

Jamie turned to a messenger. "Tell your boss that Gillespie doesn't know what he's doing and that the sailors need some army training. They just lost their first battle."

"You think I'm going to tell him that?"

Jamie found paper and pen and wrote it out and signed it. "Now take it," he told the man.

Upon reading the first dispatch from the field, Stockton was highly irritated at the report. So much so that he relieved Jamie and Ian from their scouting duties, which pleased them both to no end.

The war would drag on, with both sides taking limited casualties, for about four months, until early in 1847. The American flag was finally raised over Los Angeles on January 10, 1847.

"What do you want to do, Ian?" Jamie asked.

"How about going home, Pa?"

Jamie thought about that for a moment. "You go home, boy. I got some wandering to do yet."

"But Ma—"

Jamie shook his head. "She doesn't expect me 'til spring, Ian. I've stayed close to hearth and home for two years. She'd probably faint if I came back this soon. 'Sides," he said with a grin, "you might get a real surprise when you push open the door to your cabin."

"What do you mean, Pa?"

"Ride on home and find out, boy. Tell your ma I'll see her come the spring, and you, too, I hope."

Jamie turned Horse and rode off to the north.

Eight

Charleston, South Carolina.

"Miss LeBeau," said the young gentleman from Virginia. "Permit me to say that your performance this evening was simply outstanding. Your talent is surpassed only by your loveliness."

"Why, sir, you are much too kind," Anne said, blushing furiously and hiding the lower half of her face behind a tiny fan.

"Please forgive me for being a bit forward, Miss LeBeau," Cort Woodville said. "But since the play closed here in Charleston this evening, and I could not bear the thought of your leaving without my seeing you, I shamelessly admit I bribed the stage door guard to let me in. Miss LeBeau, would you have dinner with me?"

"Why . . ." Anne was thinking fast. The play was moving west the next day, and she had absolutely no desire to travel west of the Mississippi River. And because of her temperament—which some members of the cast had compared to an enraged grizzly—Anne was having trouble finding directors who would put up with her frequent temper tantrums. Anne knew all about Cort Woodville; she'd been aware for days that the young man was interested in her. Anne had investigated Cort Woodville very carefully and very thoroughly. Now here he was, the goose whose family laid golden eggs—by the bushel basket.

"Mr. Woodville," Anne said, "I would be delighted to have dinner with you."

"Oh, Miss LeBeau," the love-struck Virginia gentleman said. "My heart is so filled with happiness I fear it might burst with joy."

Idiot! Anne thought. "I'll be ready in half an hour, Mr. Woodville."

"I'll count the seconds, Miss LeBeau."

What a ninny! Anne thought.

Her brother was waiting for her in her dressing room. "We've just been fired from the cast, Anne," he told her.

Anne peeled out of her dress and shrugged her pretty shoulders. "No matter. Cort Woodville just took the bait, swallowing hook, line, and sinker."

"The fool that's been in the audience every damn night we've played this town?"

"Yes. He's really quite attractive . . . though somewhat of a simpleton. But his family is one of the wealthiest in all of Virginia—if not the richest."

Roscoe's eyes shone with greed. "This could be our ticket, Anne."

"Don't you think I know that? Why do you think I bribed the guard to let Cort in this evening? Now get out. I have to bathe and dress. I'll see you back at the hotel."

Her brother gone, Anne stripped and inspected herself in the full-length mirror. She knew she was beautiful. Her body was the color of pale ivory, and flawless. Her hair was black and her eyes a dark blue. "Tonight's the night, Anne," she whispered. "Play your cards right, and you're set for life."

Anne put on the finest performance of her life that evening. Thirty minutes after she'd entered Cort's carriage, the young man had taken the bait. Another thirty minutes and she had him hooked forever.

"I can't bear the thought of you leaving," Cort said over dinner in Charleston's finest. "I just can't."

"Well," Anne said, sipping her coffee. "I really don't know what I'm going to do."

"What do you mean . . . dear," Cort was so bold to add, delighted at her smile.

"I have six weeks before I have to leave for New York City. And my brother and I don't have the foggiest idea how or where we want to spend those weeks."

"At Ravenswood!" Cort blurted.

"At where?" Anne asked. She knew all about Ravenswood. It was the largest plantation in all of Virginia. Thousands and thousands of acres and hundreds of slaves.

"The most beautiful plantation in all of Virginia," Cort said. "Oh, we'll have a grand time, Anne. And my parents will love you." He started to add, "As much as I do," but decided that might be rushing things just a bit.

Anne hesitated, frowning. Cort took her soft, perfumed hands in his, which were just about as soft, and said, "It's settled, Anne. I will not take no for an answer." He gazed into her blue eyes. "Anne, it is my fervent hope that once you see Ravenswood, you'll not want to leave."

She smiled at him.

Jamie put the war behind him and headed north. He did not dislike California, but it was too settled for him. Jamie liked the wild country. He liked to go to sleep listening to the wolves howling and the coyotes yipping and yapping. He felt better once he was in northern California and better yet when he crossed over into the territories.

The nights were getting downright cold, the days crisp, and for three days, he had known that someone was dogging his back trail. They—and he was certain it was more than one—were laying well back and had shown no signs of being hostile. But Jamie had a bad feeling about it in his guts. And Jamie had long ago learned to trust his instincts.

He smiled as he recalled talking with his son while camped outside of Los Angeles, after Ian had complained about so many people wanting to see him dead.

"You've got a ways to go to catch me, Ian," Jamie had told him. "Counting all the inlaws and outlaws of those who have sworn to kill me, I figure I've got four or five hundred men wanting my scalp."

"Still, Pa, after all these years?"

"Oh, yes, son." He looked hard at his son. "You knew that Wesley Parsons and Winslow were in Los Angeles, didn't you?"

"They were there, Pa. I got there too late. How'd you find out?"

"Same way you did, boy. I asked around."

"I got no more hate in my heart, Pa. I want to see Ma and the valley again."

"Then do it, boy," Jamie had said softly.

Jamie was so lost in thought he almost missed Horse's ears pricking up. Then he felt the sudden tension of the big animal and Jamie touched his heels to Horse's flanks and jumped him off the trail and into the timber. The shot that was intended for him slammed into a tree.

Jamie left the saddle and let the reins dangle. He grabbed his rifle from the boot and slipped into the brush, heading back in the direction he'd come, for the shot had come from behind him.

Jamie found a good position and bellied down on the cool ground. He could hear not a sound, for at the boom of the shot, the forest critters had fallen silent and tense.

Jamie was almost certain his attackers were not Indians, for the Indians in this area were mostly peaceful fishers and farmers. Coos and Siuslaw and Alsea and Tillamook. Jamie had been hugging the coast for several days, enjoying the smell and sounds of the ocean.

He did not enjoy being shot at.

Jamie's patience, taught him by the Shawnee Indians who had taken him as a small boy, was limitless. He did not move. Somebody down there would make a mistake, sooner or later. But it would not be Jamie.

Finally, he caught a small splash of color that did not fit in with the terrain or the foliage. After a few moments, the color moved and became larger. Now Jamie could make out the chest of a man. He hesitated, then lifted his rifle and sighted in. His rifle boomed and the splash of color was now all mixed with crimson. The man rose up to his full height, swayed there for a moment, and then slowly toppled over backward, to lay in a still sprawl.

The sounds of cursing reached him. Then a voice. "I told you Perry didn't get him."

"Well, he shore got Perry," another voice said. "Now what?"

"We wait. He's just a kid. He'll make a mistake."

They think I'm Ian, Jamie thought. But by now Ian'll be home, or very close to the valley.

Then Jamie caught movement off toward the west, his left from where he was lying in the brush. He had shifted locations immediately after the shot. Somebody was trying to circle around. But they made a mistake, and in stalking, one mistake could be fatal.

Jamie began to stalk his stalker, and Jamie had no equal at man-hunting. For a man of his size, he was soundless in the timber, moving like a ghost.

Jamie often used the Indian method of concealment, simply hiding where there is no cover. Most people look at things, but never really see them.

The man Jamie was stalking was very good, for twice Jamie lost his quarry. Then Jamie made his move, as quick and silent and awesome as a puma's strike. Jamie clubbed the man on the side of his head and the man dropped like a stone. Jamie trussed him up and then slapped him into consciousness. The man opened his eyes to feel the cold steel of Jamie's razor sharp Bowie knife on his throat.

"As any fool can plainly see," Jamie whispered. "I'm the boy's pa. And I don't like people shooting at me. Now I would have to say that you fellows made a really bad mistake. What do you think about it?"

The man was scared but defiant. "Don't make no difference. They's gold on your head, too."

"Howard!" the shout came from below them. "Watch it. The kid's moved. He's after you."

"Wrong!" Jamie shouted. "I've got him. And my name is Jamie. Ian is my son."

There was a few seconds of silence. "Shit!" a man said.

"MacCallister!" another voice was added. "Don't hurt Howard. He's my brother. You hurt him and by God I'll trail you straight into Hell if I have to."

Jamie suddenly rose, picking Howard up as if the man were a child and flinging him down the slope. Howard bounced and slammed into rocks and trees and howled in pain. Jamie quickly shifted positions, back to his original spot.

"Goddamn you, MacCallister!" Howard's brother yelled up the slope, for a moment exposing himself.

Jamie snapped off a shot, the ball whining off the huge rock beside the man, chipping off fragments and lashing the man's face with the tiny bits of stone.

Just as soon as he shot, Jamie raced back to Horse and led the animal a few hundred yards into the brush before mounting up and quietly riding out. If those pursuing him were fool enough to follow, the next time they met, the advantage was going to be all Jamie's.

They followed. An hour later, Jamie sat Horse in the timber and looked with a disgusted expression in his eyes as the men pressed on after him.

For a moment, Jamie debated whether or not to just lose the men and go on about his business. Then he thought of home and Kate and all the kids in the peaceful valley. If he didn't stop the man-hunters here, they'd surely come into the valley, just like those who came after Wiley Harper did.

He slid off Horse and took his rifles. Without even realizing he was doing it, Jamie's eyes had already found the best defensive position. He got down behind the fallen logs and waited. He had made up his mind about something else, too: once this pack of man-hunters was dealt with, he was going to take the pressure off of his son. He was going to lay down the warning and have it spread from one end of the wilderness to the other: End the hunt for my son or face me. One way or the other, Jamie was going to see to it that his son did not have to endure what he had been forced to endure all his life: one seemingly endless fight for survival after the other.

Jamie lifted his rifle and punched a hole in the chest of a man below him. The man threw his rifle into the air and fell backward, rolling down the grade.

"You damned murderin' bastard!" a familiar voice reached him. Howard's brother.

Jamie reloaded and waited.

Then Jamie watched through unbelieving eyes as the bounty hunters came screaming and charging up the hill.

"Idiots," he said, and quickly emptied both rifles, stopping the charge of two of the men. The other men hit the ground and hugged it close.

He shifted positions until he found an upthrusting of rocks. He recharged his rifles and then sat down, settling his broad back against one huge boulder that seemed so secure it must extend all the way down to bedrock. Jamie put his feet against the huge boulder in front of him and began pushing. The rock began to teeter under the strength from Jamie's legs. Jamie grunted and pushed and the rock gave way, slowly leaving its perch and rumbling downhill. As it rolled, it dislodged others and soon a minor avalanche was sending tons of rock down the slope, destroying anything and everything in its path.

Jamie heard men scream and others yell in panic for friends to get out of the way. But the man-hunters had nowhere to go.

The ground-trembling and the roaring went on for several minutes, the larger rocks gathering other rocks and logs and small trees before them, pushing them all toward the bottom.

Jamie sat with his back to the boulder and waited until the awesome slide was over. He chewed on some jerky and listened to the silence while he thought things through.

There must have been ten or twelve men in this bunch.

That meant, to Jamie's mind, that somebody with a lot of money was posting the bounty on his son's head . . .

"Oh, God!" a man called weakly. "Help me, for God's sake."

And that somebody was more than likely the rich man from back east. What was his name? Yeah—Evans. Big man in industry whose son had raped and killed a girl and then had to hit the outlaw trail. His final mistake was coming after Ian.

"Please!" another man called. "My legs is crushed."

Jamie didn't like the idea of traveling back east, but if that was what it was going to take to get the bounty hunters off his son's trail, then so be it!

"You got to help me!" the first man called. "I'm buried from the waist down. You can't leave us here to die."

There was a trading post about a day's ride from the avalanche site. Jamie would go there and start spreading the word to trappers and pilgrims alike. He'd post a letter to Kate, too, give it to someone traveling back east, telling her what he was planning. He felt sure she would approve.

"You rotten son of a bitch!" Howard's brother called. "My back is broke. My kin will avenge me, damn your black heart. You'll not get clear of this."

If he had to stay out in the wilderness for the next two years, he would, by God, reach every bounty hunter after Ian and read some Scriptures to the men. Or over them, didn't make a damn bit of difference to Jamie which one it was . . .

Below him, men were both cursing and praying. It was a very strange mixture.

He was going to end this hunt for his son. And if he had to wade through blood to do it, that was fine with him.

"MacCallister! Is you gonna hep us, or no?"

"No," Jamie called down the slope, then walked back to Horse and rode out.

Nine

Ravenswood was just as lovely as it had been described by Cort. His parents, both elderly, were immediately taken in by Anne and Ross LeBeau . . . why not? They both were skilled actors.

Both the mother and father were glad that some female had finally taken an interest in their only son. Cort was a good boy but a bit on the foppish side. He was not a good horseman, nor did he like blood sports, never going with the other young men on hunts. But Cort was an excellent businessman, having graduated with honors from the University.

A gala ball was planned and held, and naturally Anne and Ross put on a small performance and both sang; both had excellent voices and both were talented with piano, violin, and guitar. The gentry just loved them both.

Two weeks after arriving at Ravenswood, Cort, ever the gentleman and steeped in tradition, got down on one knee and proposed marriage to Anne LeBeau. She blushed and flustered and accepted.

"Oh, Anne!" Cort said. "You've made me the happiest man on earth."

Anne smiled and kissed him gently. But her eyes were as cold as the depths of the sea.

* * *

Ian rode in late, well past midnight and, as was his habit, came into the settlement without being noticed. He was amazed at how much the village had grown. Why, it was a regular town.

Like his father, Ian had a way with nearly any animal, and he was quick to make friends with and silence the barking dogs in the settlement who had come to see about this stranger. He stabled his horse and walked the short distance to the cabin his pa and friends had built for Ian and Linda. But he could not bear to enter it just yet. He walked silently to the cemetery, all the dogs padding quietly along all around him, and stood for a moment at Linda's grave.

He thought about spending the night in the cabin but felt the cabin would be dusty and in need of a good cleaning. He went back to the barn and settled down in the hay loft for a few hours of rest. He was asleep in minutes.

Ian was sitting on the long porch of his parents' cabin when Kate stepped outside for a breath of cold morning air, a mug of coffee in one hand.

Ian turned his head, stood up, and smiled at her. "Hello, Ma."

Kate stood for a moment, staring at her oldest. For a moment, she thought it was Jamie. Before the happy tears blinded her eyes, she set the coffee cup on the railing and opened her arms and the bulk of the man filled them.

Her wandering boy was home.

The Northwest Territories.

Jamie pushed open the door of the huge trading post and stepped inside. He was big and woolly and uncurried and unshaven. He looked mean as hell and he was. For two weeks he had been on the trail of a couple of bounty hunters who had made their brags about Jamie and Ian. Jamie had trailed them here. Now the men were going to back up those brags . . . or die.

The post was filled with men, men who fell silent and turned and looked at the man who had to duck his head to step through the door. Jamie walked to a table and tossed his saddlebags into an empty chair.

"A plate of food and a pot of coffee," he said, then took off his battered hat and hung it on the back of the chair. "And after I've eaten, they'll probably be a killin'. Anybody who don't care to witness that had best leave now."

No one left. But two men sitting at a table across the room suddenly became very uncomfortable.

"Fine," Jamie said, savoring the rich smell of the huge bowl of stew placed before him.

"I ain't seen the old Silver Wolf in a few years, Mac-Callister," an aging trapper said. "How he be?"

"He's dead." Jamie chewed for a moment, then swallowed, washing it all down with a large swig of hot, black coffee, sweetened with generous spoonfuls of sugar. "I buried him up in the high country."

"I'm right sorry to hear that. Mac was a damn good man."

"Yes, he was," Jamie agreed. "A hell of a lot better than the scum who've been sent out looking for me and my boy. As a matter of fact, they're about the lowest sons of bitches to walk the face of the earth."

"Now, look here, MacCallister," one of the men Jamie had been trailing protested, standing up. "Your boy is a wanted man. Legal and all that. Me and my partner here ain't said nothin' about you. But your boy is a killer and the law has papers to back that up."

"No, they don't," Jamie said, after chewing and swallowing another huge mouthful of stew. "And you're a liar. You boasted to Gene Morton what you were going to do to me. Gene thought he was man enough to do it. He wasn't. I killed him last week, down on the McKenzie."

"You're a lyin' bastard!" the man said and reached for the gun in his belt.

Jamie lifted the pistol he'd been holding in his left hand and drilled the man-hunter in the chest, knocking the man backward tangling him up in his own boots as he fell to the floor, dead.

The old trapper who had inquired about Jamie's Grandpa grunted and said, "Clumsy sod, ain't he?"

The recently departed man's partner placed both hands on the rough table. His face was very pale. "I'm out of this, MacCallister! You hear me? I say I'm out of it. Leave me be, man!"

Jamie laid his empty pistol on the table and pulled out a fully charged pistol. Those sitting in the line of fire quickly moved out of the way. The man across the room started shaking and sweating.

"I told you I want no part of this, MacCallister. Good Lord, man. Can't you hear?"

"Who is the western agent for Evans?" Jamie asked. "And don't tell me you know nothing about either man. If you lie to me I'll kill you."

"A lawyer in St. Louis name of Laurin," the badly shaken man blurted. "He's commissioned to handle all of Mr. Evans's holdin's east of the Mississippi. That's all I know about it. I swear to you it is."

Jamie reached inside his jacket and pulled out a small bag. He tossed the bag to the man. It landed on the table with a clink. "That's money. Far more than you're worth. I want you to ride and spread the word."

"What word?"

"As of right now, this hunt for me and my son is over. Stopped. Ended. Finished. Through. I'll give you one month to get the word spread, and if you tell enough people, they'll do the rest. Then you ride to St. Louis and you tell this Laurin person that the hunt is over. I'll give him until springtime to get word to Evans in New York City. That's about five months away. Plenty of time. After that, all bets are off. Any man who comes after me or my son, I kill on sight. Without a word being exchanged. And I'll know, mister. I'll know. The Indians will tell me, trappers will tell me, old mountain men will tell me, and I have friends back east who will tell me. Now you ride, mister. And don't ever let me see you again. If I do, I'll kill you. Ride now. Move, goddamn you!"

The man grabbed up the sack of gold coins and was out of there like the hounds of Hell were nipping at his heels. He didn't even chance a second look at his dead friend or bother to close the door behind him. Within seconds, the sounds of a galloping horse reached the inside of the trading post.

"I know some about Maurice Evans," a man spoke. "He's worth millions. He set some store by that sorry son of hisn. He'll not take kindly to your threats, Jamie MacCallister."

Jamie's smile chilled those hard rough men in the room. It was as if they had been touched by the hand of death. Jamie said, "If he's smart he will."

* * *

Spring, 1847

Jamie Ian and Caroline hit it off right from the first. The entire community noticed it and to a person were pleased. And it was Caroline who told Jamie about the trouble she'd had with her pa. She left nothing out. To Ian's eyes, that made her a bigger person. He told her so and she wept for a time on his shoulder, both of them sitting under a tree in a meadow away from the settlement.

"I put flowers on your wife's grave every week, Ian," Caroline told him. "And on my dead baby's grave. The people think I don't know where the baby is buried, but I do. Tobias Goldman told me one day. He didn't mean to and made me swear to never let on that I knew or that it was him that told me, and I swore I wouldn't."

"It's safe with me."

"I know it is. Ian, when is your pa comin' back home?"

"Only the wind knows that, Caroline." Sparks had stopped by for supplies and had coffee with Kate and Ian. The scout told them both about Jamie's quest and looked at Ian and added, "You stand clear now, boy. This is the way your pa wants it. I heard the words from his own mouth not a month ago up on the North Fork."

"The hunt, Sparks," Kate asked. "What about the hunt?"

"Seems this Maurice Evans is a mighty uppity man. He don't cotton to people tellin' him what to do. He pulled the ante off of Ian's head and laid it all on your man's back."

"Then God have mercy on his soul," Kate said.

"On Jamie, ma'am?" Sparks asked.

"No," Kate said with a thin smile. "On Maurice Evans and any man who comes after Jamie."

After Sparks had provisioned up and pulled out, Ian said, "I ought to go to Pa, Mama."

"No. Absolutely not, Ian. You heard Sparks. This is your Pa's show now. And he'll brook no interference."

"Ma . . . don't you worry about Pa?"

Kate smiled. "Of course, I worry about him. Every day. But I know your pa well. Better than any person alive. He'll be back, Ian. Probably come the spring. You'll see."

"And if he doesn't come in the spring?"

"Then he'll come in the summer or the fall." Kate turned and walked from the porch back into the cabin.

"They're hard after you, lad," Big Jim Williams said to Jamie. "Word I get is that Mister High-Up Muckity-Muck Evans got all pissed off when that lawyer man told him what you said."

Jamie smiled, poured another cup of coffee from the blackened pot, and leaned back against his saddle. "How many men, Jim?"

"Don't know about the regular riff-raff bounty hunters, Jamie. They come and go. But the word I get is that he's hired professional man-hunters."

Jamie's smile widened. "Professional man-hunters from where, Jim?"

Big Jim chuckled. "I see what you mean, lad. But wherever they come from, don't sell them short."

"Oh, I would never do that. Which way you headin', Jim?"

"South. I plan on stoppin' in your valley for some of Kate's good cookin'. You got airy message?"

Jamie handed him a folded piece of paper and Jim tucked it safely away in his parfleche. "I'll see she gets it. Jamie? Me and some boys could end this thing afore it ever gets started good—you know we'd do that, don't you?"

"Yes. But what was it that Preacher told me long ago, back in Arkansas? Yeah. Out here, a man saddles his own horses and stomps on his own snakes."

"Well, that sounds good in the tellin', but if you find yourself knee deep in snakes, only a fool wouldn't give a holler for some help."

"I'll sure keep that in mind, Jim. And that's a promise."

"Oh, they's something else, too. I nearabout forgot. Them two that run off from your settlement some time back, the brother and sister what done good on the stage back east?"

"Yes."

"I read in the papers a couple of months ago that the girl she done married up with the richest man in all of Virginny. Quite a to-do it was, accordin' to the paper. Her brother's done tooken over the opry company there in Richmond and the girl she's settled down to be the wife of gentry. Things do work out for the best, don't they?"

"I hope so, Jim." Just don't have children, Anne.

June, 1847

Jamie squatted down on the ridge, behind scant cover and watched the men ride toward the pass. He had no way of knowing for sure who they were, but he had him a mighty good idea. Trouble was, he didn't want to shoot someone who wasn't out here to shoot him. Come the dark, he'd pay their camp a visit. And they would be reining in for the night before long . . . if they had any sense. Jamie smiled at that thought. If they had any sense they wouldn't be chasing him deep in the heart of Indian country.

Jamie watched the men until the canyon walls had swallowed them and walked back to Horse. He rode to the other side of the ridge and swung down from the saddle, watching the men find the creek with good water and graze all around. He saw what appeared to be the leader raise his arm, military style, and the men slowed, reined up, and dismounted.

Jamie sat high above, chewed on a piece of jerky and watched the crowd of men begin to make camp, again in military fashion—tents all in nice neat rows. There was no danger of sunlight reflecting off glass, so he took his spy glass and brought the camp in closer. Twenty-eight men with lots of pack horses and spare mounts. Their equipment was all new and looked to be the finest money could buy—Maurice Evans's money, he was sure. And he smiled at what else they had—a damn cannon! Looked to be a four pounder from where he sat . . . a cannon. They had really brought a cannon with them.

After watching for a time, Jamie felt sure the men below were all ex-military men, and from the way some sat their saddles, not all were Americans. But he could be wrong about that. Some easterners rode like they had a corn cob stuck up their butt and didn't know how to get it out.

Jamie wished he knew for certain whether they were hunting him.

Jamie faded back from the ridge and saw to Horse and his pack animal's needs, then sat down and ate some cold pan bread, washing it down with water. He had hoped Fancy-Pants Evans would take his warning to heed and stop this foolishness. But he'd known in his heart all along that was not to be. Some rich folks thought that because they had all the money in the world, they could just push other folks around in any direction they wanted them to go. But they usually hired it done, not wanting to get their own lily-white hands dirty.

Jamie waited until full dark and then slipped down the ridge and into the creek that meandered by the camp of the men. He carried four pistols, his rifle, and bow and quiver of arrows. If Jamie was awake he was never without his knife.

He hoped these men were on their way to the northwest territories or maybe out to California to seek their fortunes. Because if they were hunting him, some of them were going to be buried right alongside that pretty little creek.

Ten

Hired thugs, Jamie concluded, after spending the better part of an hour listening to the men talk. But not trash. Some of the men spoke like they had more than their share of education.

But there was no doubt in Jamie's mind now: they were hunting him.

But one of the men was definitely not a warrior. He was a rather timid talking fellow who looked totally out of place among these brigands. Then Jamie got a shock: the man was some kind of photographer, brought along to take pictures of Jamie's dead body when the hunters killed him. As near as Jamie could see, the man didn't even carry a gun.

Incredible! Jamie thought. Then he got mad through and through. That damn Maurice Evans was going to post his tintype all around New York City and boast about the killing.

Jamie fitted an arrow and let it fly. A man doubled over with a grunt and fell to the ground, both hands wrapped around the shaft of the arrow embedded in his stomach.

"Oh, my God!" the photographer hollered. "The red savages are upon us."

Jamie dropped another man with an arrow and then jerked out two double-shotted pistols and let them bang.

Jamie quietly slipped away into the night, making his way back up the high ridge. He left the camp of the man-hunters in confusion and wildly shouted oaths.

As Jamie lay in his blankets that night, the stars winking high above him, one question kept worrying his mind: How did they know where to find him?

Long before dawn cleared the dark night skies, Jamie had moved his location several miles to the north of the man-hunters' camp. And for the first few miles, he had not tried to hide his trail.

Resting now, in a spot where he could see for miles in all directions, Jamie reviewed all that he'd heard in the man-hunters' camp the night before.

Rolly was the leader, and some of the men called him Major. A major in what army, if any? No matter. The war was on and Jamie had no intention of losing it. Other bits of overheard conversation had lifted his spirits. Seems that Maurice Evans had nixed a plan to attack the settlement in the valley. For the settlement was well established and to do so would surely be highly publicized. And since Mr. Fancy-Pants Evans had been foolish enough to make his brags about what he was going to do all over New York City, the finger of guilt would point straight to him if anything happened to the people in the settlement.

But those who hunted Ian and Jamie because of past deeds done to kin would have no such reservations. However, attacking the settlement would be a foolish thing to do, for there were a goodly number of adults there now— it was a regular village—and all the adults, men and women, were skilled with weapons and would not hesitate to use them.

Jamie took his rifle and stretched out on a flat and

waited. Sure enough, they came, riding straight up the pass just as big as brass.

"Stupid," Jamie muttered, sighting in the lead man. He let the ball fly and the man was knocked out of the saddle. He hit the ground and did not move.

Jamie had guessed accurately what was coming next, so as soon as he had made his shot, he was off and running for Horse. About a minute after his shot, the cannon boomed and the cannonball impacted with a loud explosion. But Jamie was safely away and smiling as he rode. The cannon was probably the reason the group of men had not been set upon by Indians . . . more than once. For the Indians in this area had never seen such a weapon, and upon hearing the fearsome roar and seeing the incredible damage it could do, they backed off and let the men pass.

Jamie had counted twenty-six riders before he shot, and a couple of them rode as if in pain. Now there were twenty-five, for his shot had been a killing one.

For a week, Jamie exchanged no shots with his hunters as he led the men deeper and deeper into the rugged mountains of western Montana. Then he cut south. He was going to take them down into the Hole, and there he would make his stand.

Several times Jamie had come up on bands of Indians out hunting for food. He either spoke or signed with them, explaining what was happening and being certain to tell them of the cannon and its enormous power. He wasn't sure they believed him about the cannon, but he managed to convince them to leave the white men alone. This was his fight. The Indians understood and respected that.

He came upon trappers and mountain men who wanted to deal themselves into this game, but Jamie prevailed upon them and they reluctantly agreed to let MacCallister have his way. Besides, everybody knew Ol' Mac was about half crazy and from the looks of things, his grandson wasn't far behind.

Just to the scant west of the Absaroka Range, Jamie made his first hard stand against the man-hunters. He found an ideal ambush spot and there he waited.

By now, the men were tired and saddle-sore, for Jamie had been leading them on a torturous journey through some of the wildest country west of the Mississippi. They would be ready for a hot soak and rest. Jamie led them right to a hot springs, just north of Emigrant Pass and slightly east of the Yellowstone. He was chuckling as he made his plans. This was going to be quite a sight to see, and if all worked out right, he'd have the pictures to back up his story . . . and some mighty embarrassed and pissed-off men.

Cort and Anne had returned from their honeymoon abroad, and Cort was now building Anne the largest, most lavish and beautifully appointed plantation home in all of Virginia. Cort's father and mother had retired from running the huge empire and had turned the entire operation over to Cort . . . and unknowingly, the greedy and hot little hands of Anne.

Ross had been named director of the Opera House and stage company in Richmond and was really turning the city into a bastion for the fine arts. Many women flirted and carried on with Ross, and he treated them all gallantly. However, Ross's sexual appetites lay in a different and darker (in more ways than one) direction. But he was careful to be very, very discreet.

"You goddamn stupid fool!" Anne raged at her brother. "Do you know what will happen if your sexual . . . preferences are ever discovered?"

"Relax, sister dear," Ross told her. "You know me; I'm very careful and highly selective. Besides, I'm not all that different from the man you married."

"What the hell are you talking about?" But Anne knew. Cort was weak when it came to lovemaking. It was almost an effort for him to make love to her. Already, they had separate bedrooms, although that in itself was not unusual among the gentry.

"You keep your hands off my husband!" Anne flared.

"He isn't my type," Ross told her.

Ian MacCallister and Caroline were married shortly after the first warm winds began to blow through the long valley. The entire settlement turned out to see it, including the now aging war chief Black Thunder and several of his tribe. Ian put his reputation behind him and took up the plow.

His father's reputation, already legendary, was in still yet another growing stage.

Jamie watched the man-hunters test the hot springs, then peel out of their stiff and stinking clothes and take to the water with bars of strong soap and much whooping and hollering.

While the men were having a good time in the springs, seemingly without a care, laughing and soaping and ridding themselves of fleas and dirt, Jamie slipped into camp and stole every stitch of clothing they had, right down to their underwear. He left the little photographer's clothes out. Then he quickly helped himself to a goodly amount of their supplies. He waited.

A half dozen Indians had watched the scene and were convulsed with laughter as they headed back to their village. What a grand story this would make.

Jamie waited until the men had emerged from the refreshing waters and then confronted them, both hands filled with double-shotted, heavy caliber pistols. "Come right on up, boys," he called cheerfully.

The naked men complied sullenly. "That's far enough," Jamie told them. He looked at the badly frightened photographer. "Set up your equipment, Mr. Picture Taker. And start doing what you do."

"Goddamn you, MacCallister," Rolly snarled at him.

"Shut up," Jamie told him. "You're in no position to make threats. You take your pictures from all angles, now, Mr. Picture Taker. And be sure and get their faces in there plain. I want these pictures preserved for all time."

"Shit!" one of the man-hunters said, shivering in the cool winds. "This is embarrassin'."

The photographer, whose name was Clarence, took his shots from all angles. Jamie finally called a halt when he noticed the men turning slightly blue. "Pack up your gear, Clarence, all of it. You're coming with me."

"What about our clothes?" Rolly demanded.

"Well, now," Jamie said with a smile. "You might have a problem there. I 'spect you boys will have to make you some clothes out of blankets." He pointed one cocked pistol at a man. "You. Load up that cannon with a double charge of powder."

"Huh?"

"You heard me. Do it."

The four pounder fully charged, Jamie said, "Now pack that barrel full of mud, and pack it in tight. Jam it in full."

"Goddamn you!" Rolly said, resignation in his voice.

"Now run a long fuse to the fire-hole," Jamie said. "You ready to ride, Clarence?"

"Yes, sir."

"Get in the saddle and take up that lead rope to your pack horse and ride down yonder a-ways and wait. And you'd better wait. 'Cause you'll be lost as a goose in about five minutes if you don't."

Jamie set fire to the pile of clothing and waited until he was sure it was blazing. "Run, boys," he told the men, picking up a burning brand and riding over to the cannon. "Run just as fast as you can."

The men took off, stepping gingerly along on bare feet, for their boots and shoes were on fire with the clothes.

Jamie touched the brand to the fuse and got the hell away from there.

When the cannon blew, it sent chunks of metal and mud flying in all directions. When silence once prevailed, Jamie emerged from cover and shouted, "You boys have been warned. I'm giving you your lives. I'll not be so generous if we ever meet again. You boys go on back and tell Mr. Fancy-Pants Evans this game had better be over. Now cover up your nakedness and ride!"

An hour later, Jamie said to Clarence, "You will see that those pictures get circulated, won't you?"

"Friend," Clarence said, still chuckling, "I despised those men back there. I'll distribute these wherever there are people. If I can ever get back to civilization."

"You'll get back," Jamie assured him.

Jamie had left the man-hunters' saddle blankets, not out

of any compassion for them, but to spare the horses getting all gaunted up in the back.

Jamie rode into an Indian village and met with a chief he had known and respected for years, explaining what had happened. The Indians thought it was the funniest thing they had ever heard. And yes, they would escort the frightened little man to a trading post and protect him. In return, Clarence would have some of the finest pictures of the noble red man to ever come out of the west, and those pictures would make him famous, moderately wealthy, and much sought after as a photographer.

Jamie headed back to the valley and Kate, thinking that surely this would be the end of people coming after he and Ian—and that he had accomplished it with a minimum of blood shed.

The news of what happened to the man-hunters quickly spread all over the wilderness, from the Mississippi River to the Pacific coast, with everybody on Jamie's side in the matter. The man-hunters stopped at half a dozen trading posts on their way to Bent's Fort. But the trading posts were quite suddenly and very mysteriously out of shirts and britches and underwear and shoes and boots.

When Rolly and his "professional" man-hunters finally made Bent's Fort, they were a pitiful-looking sight. The blankets they had fashioned ponchos out of were ragged and coming apart, scarcely managing to cover their nakedness. All of the men were so sore from riding without saddles they could hardly do more than hobble about. Their feet were cut and torn. The trappers and mountain men at the fort went down to their knees laughing at the man-hunters. Rolly and his men endured it all in silent and deadly rage. Clarence, of course, had been to the fort and had long left for the east and fame.

One grizzled old mountain man, who looked to be about as old as the country, had some good advice for the men. "Jamie MacCallister let you boys live—this time. This was his way of tellin' you all not to ever come back here after him. You got off good. You're alive. If you come back again, he'll kill every one of you. You been warned. Take the advice and go on back home."

Rolly and men provisioned up—with pants and shirts and boots this time—and headed for St. Louis for a talk with lawyer Laurin.

After they had gotten clear of the fort and Jamie's friends, Rolly said, "If that goddamn MacCallister thinks this is over, he best think again. If it's the last thing I do on this earth, I'm gonna kill him!"

Eleven

"Pa's comin'," Matthew shouted, pointing to the north.

Megan ran out to ring the community bell, and the entire settlement turned out. Sparks had been through and told them what all had happened to the man-hunters, and everybody had a good laugh at what Jamie had done.

All but Kate, although she had managed a smile. She knew that Jamie was tired of the killing, knew he wanted it over. But this time he had made a mistake. Those men would never forgive the humiliation caused them by her husband. Not ever. And they would be back. And Mr. Maurice Evans would not take kindly to this slight against him. He would just outfit the men again, probably hire more men, and send them right back west with orders to kill Jamie MacCallister . . . and anyone who rode or sided with him. *No, husband of mine,* Kate thought, *this time you made a mistake.*

"I never thought about it, Kate," Jamie said later that night, snuggled in the feather tick with Kate. "But you're probably right. I did a foolish thing in the name of humor."

She giggled. "I do want a picture of those man-hunters, though."

"Kate!"

* * *

Those close to Maurice Evans stated later that the man went into a towering, screaming rage when he learned of what had happened to his hand-picked mercenaries. Then he saw the pictures, which had been circulated under the table, so to speak, all around the city and almost succumbed to a fatal bout of apoplexy. But Clarence was already the darling of the literary and fledgling photographic societies and was too popular for Evans to touch.

He arranged a meeting with Rolly Hammond. "I want you to be ready to go early next spring," he told the mercenary. "I want you to find fifty men, good men, outfit them with the most modern of weapons, and get ready to ride. I want you to have your most trusted lieutenant to ride west and find western men who know the country and who hate MacCallister. While MacCallister is out hunting, or fucking Indian squaws, or whatever he does when he is away from the valley, I want you to burn that goddamn settlement to the ground and kill everybody there. Men, women, children, horses, cattle, mules, sheep, goats, dogs. And then bury the bodies so deep they will never be found. Do you have objections to doing any of this?"

"Not if the money is right."

"Money is no object. Name your price."

Rolly did.

Without batting an eye, Evans said, "Done!"

1847 saw more and more settlers continuing the westward push. In April of that year, Brigham Young, prophet of the Church of Jesus Christ of Latter-Day Saints, pushed off from Council Bluffs to the new Zion—a place that would in only three years be proclaimed as Utah Territory.

In June, the Mormons crossed South Pass but then got hopelessly turned around in the Rockies. Toward the last of July 1847, Brigham Young arrived and called the arid expanse "The place." The state of Deseret was born, later to be called Utah.

In September of that year, Stephen Foster performed "Oh, Susanna" in a Pittsburgh saloon. That same month, General Scott's troops broke through the walls surrounding Mexico City and raised the American flag over the "Halls of Montezuma."

Fort Benton was established at the head of the Missouri River, Cyrus McCormick opened a new reaper factory in Chicago, and in November, missionary Marcus Whitman and twelve others were massacred by Cayuse Indians at his missionary station in Oregon.

By the middle of February, Rolly Hammond had quietly recruited his army of mercenaries to ride after Jamie and the settlement come the spring. They gathered all up and down the western Missouri border, waiting word, well-armed, with the very latest in modern weapons. They would start the ride west to the Rockies in one week.

March 1848

"You feel that old urge to roam again, Jamie?" Kate asked, stepping out onto the porch of the cabin and sitting down in the chair beside her husband.

A few minutes after a beautiful early spring dawn in the Rockies, and husband and wife both had huge steaming mugs of coffee.

Jamie smiled and reached over, taking Kate's hand. "No, Kate. I have no such urge. I just want to stay here with you and watch our kids and grandkids grow and be happy. And that is the truth, my love."

"Age might have something to do with that," Kate said with a smile.

They both were thirty-eight years old. Kate looked as though she might be twenty-five at the most, and Jamie was aging just as well. People traveling through the valley were, to a person, astonished to learn that the young-looking couple had been married for over twenty-five years and had grandchildren.

This spring's travel to Bent's Fort had brought a dozen letters to Jamie and Kate, half of them from Andrew and Rosanna. They were planning a trip home in the late spring of that year. Both were enjoying enormous success as musicians and had married musicians, the unions producing four children. The letters contained numerous newspaper clippings hailing their accomplishments as concert pianists. They were due to arrive back in the valley that summer.

The triplets, Matthew, Megan, and Morgan, now sixteen, were all sparking the children of other settlers, and Megan had already announced that she would be getting married that summer. Her beau, a gangling seventeen-year-old named Jim, was hard at work, in his spare time, building their cabin. So far he had managed to fall off the scaffolding once and flatten two fingertips with a hammer. Jim was just a bit nervous about the wedding.

"Good thing he landed on his head," Jamie remarked, after Jim's fall. "Otherwise he might have been hurt."

That got him a very dirty look from Megan.

Joleen, almost fourteen, had announced that she was

going to start seeing a boy named Angus. That lasted until Kate took her out into the barn and with the help of a belt convinced the girl that her attempts at sparking could wait at least another year.

Angus started walking past the cabin so often he was wearing a new path. Jamie finally wearied of the lovestruck lad and told him that he could sit with the family during Sunday worship services, have supper at the MacCallister cabin every other Saturday night, and sit with Joleen out on the front porch for a time and hold hands, adding, "And boy, that by God, better be all you grab hold of."

Falcon, now nine, was already playing gun man. Jamie had fashioned his two pistols and holsters, and the boy was stalking everything and everybody he encountered. He was uncommonly quick in getting those toy pistols out of leather.

The settlement now boasted three stores and a combination barbershop/doctor's office/tavern; it was a strange combination but it worked for them. The "tavern" was actually no more than a half dozen tables and chairs and was more a place for the men to get away after a hard day's work and talk. The settlement had a regular school and a separate church building and a community hall. There was a road of sorts leading out of the valley and over to Bent's Fort. However, Goldman and the other two merchants still had to wagon travel to the fort to pick up ordered supplies.

About the same time that Andrew and Rosanna and their families were landing in St. Louis and making plans to travel to the wilderness, Rolly Hammond and his army of mercenaries were riding into the area in twos and threes. They would not gather until the afternoon before the raid.

Most of the able-bodied Indian men in the region were gone on the spring hunt, so the mercenaries could slip in undetected and quietly gather hours before they were to do their dark deed.

On a bright, warm Sunday morning, the men and women of the settlement were dressing in their best to attend Sunday services. Kate had noticed that Jamie was unusually quiet and seemed to be tense. He had not dressed for church.

"You're not going to church?" Kate asked Jamie.

He shook his head. "Something's come up. You go on. Take Joleen and Falcon. I'm going to need the other kids with me." He cut his eyes to her. "Go on, Kate."

As was Kate's way, she did not question him . . . that usually came later and was sometimes heated. There would be no "later" on this day. She took the kids and went off to church.

Jamie pulled Ian to one side and spoke briefly to him. The son nodded and left the porch. Jamie put Matthew in the barn, armed with several rifles and pistols. He put Megan in the shed, with rifle and pistols. Morgan stayed in the house, in a back bedroom.

Jamie's senses were working overtime. He had gone hunting the day before, planning to stay out for several days. But the game was elusive and the timber silent. He did not know what was wrong, only that something was not right. He had ridden back into the valley late on a Saturday night and surprised Kate with his arrival. He had nothing to say, but she knew something was very wrong.

Jamie talked briefly with the men of the settlement. Swede elected to man a post between two stores. Sam went to the loft of his barn. Juan chose a place by the livery. Wells and Moses and Robert and Titus positioned themselves between cabins. Eb and Daniel and a few other men took up well concealed positions throughout the settlement.

Finally, Jamie walked to the church and broke into a song service. "There might be trouble coming our way. It just may be my imagination, but I don't think so. You all know we have long planned for attack." He stomped the floor with a boot. "There are guns and water and food and blankets stored under here. Get to them and make them ready. Some of you continue singing. Sarah, play the piano—"

"Pa!" Ian shouted. "Riders gathering to the east. A whole damn army, it looks like. You were right."

Jamie reached down and jerked open the trap door leading to the concealed basement of the church. "Get all the younger kids down here. Move quickly, kids. Joleen, Ellen Kathleen, look after them."

Jamie walked to a window that could be easily shuttered, with gun slits in the heavy shutters, and called, "Ian! What are they doing?"

"I can't tell, Pa," the young man called. "They've moved into the timber and appear to be circlin'. My guess is they'll come in from the south."

"Goddamn dirty bastards!" Jamie cussed.

Reverend Haywood did not admonish him for his language in the house of God. The reverend agreed with him and silently added a few unChristian-like phrases of his own as he worked loading up rifles and pistols.

Kate had taken a carbine and several pistols from the cache of weapons under the floor and moved to a window. She was quietly and quickly loading up all the weapons.

This was nothing new to Kate or to many of the other women who were busy loading weapons.

"We'll shutter the windows when they start their charge," Jamie told the men and women in the church. "Hold our fire until they're in the village. Let them think they have the element of surprise on their side."

Ian was looking through a spyglass from his position in a nearby barn loft. "They're all white men, Pa," he called. "All of them ridin' fine stock. And all of them heavily armed. They got pistols hangin' all over them and two rifles in saddle boots."

"You're dead, Mr. Maurice Evans," Jamie muttered. "You are a walking around dead man."

Jamie was standing close to Kate and she heard him. "Make sure this time," she murmured low.

"I will," Jamie said. "Play that piano loud, Sarah," he called. "Really bang it out. Sing, people. Sing!"

The men and women lifted their voices in Christian song and tightened their grip on rifles. The singing reached Rolly and his mercenaries.

"Sing, you sinners!" Rolly said with an evil smirk. "In ten minutes, you'll all be in Heaven."

"Or gettin' fucked," one of his men said.

"That's even better," another man-hunter said. "I like 'em young. Like to hear 'em holler when I give it to 'em."

"Plenty of time for that," Rolly said.

"I like boys," a thick-lipped man said. "Young and tender."

Several others moved away from the man called Fritz.

"Ain't that singin' purty?" another man said sarcastically. "Them fillies down yonder gonna be beggin' and prayin' right shortly."

"I can't hardly wait to lift them petticoats," a man called Macklin said.

"Ain't another livin' soul within a hundred miles," a man called Calvert said. "This here party can last until we wear them gals plumb out."

"Did you see all them young gals?" Bob Dalhart said. "I'm a gittin' me a boner just thinkin' 'bout it."

"Let's do it," Rolly said. "Move out, men. We hit the village from all sides."

Ian had propped his rifle up against the wall. He was slowly sharpening his scalping knife.

"Jamie," Kate whispered.

"Yes, love."

"Kill that damn lawyer in St. Louis, too."

"I'll get him on the way to New York City," Jamie assured her and cocked his rifle.

Twelve

The first ten men to ride into the settlement were blown out of their saddles by the surprise gunfire that came from all around them. Several of the men had their boots caught in the stirrups and were dragged beyond recognition before the galloping and gunfire-spooked animals finally slowed and stopped from exhaustion. A half dozen more charged the church and were cut down by the withering hail of lead coming from the men and women inside.

With more than a third of his force and the element of surprise gone (something that Rolly only thought he had) he signaled his men to retreat.

But the settlement also suffered losses. Two of the men were dead and one woman was badly wounded. The mercenaries had managed to set some buildings on fire, and the settlers forgot about pursuit and concentrated on saving their homes and barns.

Jamie jerked one slightly wounded man to his boots and shoved him toward a barn. "I ain't tellin' you nothin', MacCallister!" the man shouted defiantly.

Jamie smiled the same sort of smile a rattlesnake does before it strikes.

He came out of the barn about fifteen minutes later. "The man's alive," he said to Kate. "I just roughed him up a bit." He looked around him. The fires were all out and had done little real damage. Ian had saddled Thunder and Kate had fixed him a nice bait of food, tucked in the saddlebags. Jamie's bedroll was tied behind the saddle.

"Melinda is missing!" a mother wailed. "My girl's been taken." Her husband grabbed her as she fainted and looked around helplessly.

The man Jamie had roughed up to get information about the gang laughed from the barn. "You'll not see that squatter's bitch no more!" he shouted. "By now Bob Dalhart's done spread them legs and had his way."

Reverend William Haywood gave Jamie a bleak look, got a rope from a porch, and started fashioning a noose. "I'm a God-fearing man," he said, "but trash is trash."

"I agree," Swede said. "Toss the rope over that tree limb yonder." He pointed. "I'll go fetch that brigand." He looked at Jamie. "You have objections?"

"Not at all. We might as well send a strong signal to any who might think of doing the same thing." He touched Ian on the arm. "Go saddle your horse. You'll bring back the girl's body for proper burial."

"Yes, Pa."

Jamie put his arms around Kate and held her close for a moment. "I'll be back when you see me, love."

"I know you will. Take care."

Jamie was in the saddle and riding. Ian could catch up.

Swede picked the mercenary up and threw him into a saddle, then fixed the rope around the man's neck.

"You have anything you would like to say before you meet your Maker?" Reverend Haywood asked.

The man spat at the minister. "Go to hell, you son of a bitch!"

Haywood slapped the horse on the rump and the man swung. He kicked a few times and was dead.

"William," Haywood's wife said. "We forgot to ask his name."

"I personally don't give a damn what it was," the reverend replied.

Jamie found the body of Melinda about five miles from the settlement. The girl had been raped repeatedly and then her neck had been broken.

"That outlaw said the man's name was Bob Dalhart," Ian said, after getting a blanket from his horse.

"I won't forget."

Ian handed him the lead rope to a pack horse "You'll be needin' these supplies. I 'spect you'll be gone for some time."

"I 'spect. Look after things, son."

"I will, Pa."

Jamie swung into the saddle and rode west after the gang. Ian picked up the blanket-covered body of the girl and got into the saddle. He remembered that the girl was ten years old. She'd had a birthday party just a few days back.

Rolly and thirty-three of his men had escaped the killing gunfire in the settlement. To a man, they knew they were in trouble. Men killing men was nothing new. But to attack a peaceful settlement on a Sunday morning and attempt to kill women and kids, plus the taking and raping and murdering of a young girl, that would never be forgiven, not even in the west. Now, to make matters worse, they had Jamie MacCallister on them like a leech. He had already killed nine, all of them either from ambush or after slipping silently into their camp at night. And Jamie had spread the word about the men. No one would lift a finger to help them . . . yet. They were welcome at no trading post. Worse yet, although Rolly and his men did not know it, the residents of New York City were going to be outraged when the news of the attack on the settlement in MacCallister's Valley reached them, and Mr. Maurice Evans was going to be finished in that city. He would be forced to get out and make his headquarters first in St. Louis and then finally in San Francisco.

Some twenty-odd very tired and very frightened men sat their exhausted horses and looked at Rolly Hammond for leadership.

"Split up," Rolly said. "Small groups. It's the only way."

"I ain't believin' this, Rolly," a man called Ned griped. "They's twenty-five of us and we're turnin' tail and runnin' from one man."

Sonny Andrews looked at the man and reminded him, "There was fifty of us when we started."

"I'm done runnin'," Ned stated. "I make my stand right here."

"I'm with you," Lenny said.

"Me, too," a hulking lout called Claude stated. "I ain't runnin' no more."

"Count me in," Peter Hart said.

"I think you're all crazy," an outlaw called Red said wearily. "But I'm damn tarred of runnin'."

"Good luck," Rolly said and lifted the reins, urging his tired horse on. "Let's go."

Four men rode out with Rolly.

"Good luck, boys," Vic Johnson said and rode away, taking four men with him.

"I hope you kill the bastard," Witt Chambers said. "Good luck." Four men left with him.

Soon the men were all alone . . . or so they thought. Had they looked up they would have seen Jamie squatting about a hundred yards away on the side of a rocky timberless ridge. He was using the oldest Indian trick in the world: simply remaining still where there was no cover.

Jamie waited until the men were busy gathering wood for a fire and moving logs and rocks into a crude fort, then he vanished from the ridge, moving behind the men and settling down in a good concealed position about seventy-five yards to the rear of the barricade. He listened to the men talk, and their talk was filled with what might have been back at the settlement if the attack had been successful. It was disgusting and sickening, evil in its perversion. They talked and laughed and made crude jokes about someone named Fritz using young boys in terrible ways, about Bob Dalhart and the young girls he had raped and abused and killed. And they talked about their own past, dark and twisted and filled with debauchery. They spoke highly and with much admiration of a man called Witt Chambers, whose vile acts made their own evil pale in comparison; of Vic Johnson, who had killed his own mother and father and had then raped and murdered his sister back in South Carolina; of a man called George who enjoyed torture. Jamie could finally stand no more. He lifted his rifle and shot Peter Hart through the head.

The man pitched forward and landed against the man called Red, splattering him with gore. Red screamed and tried to push the body away. His hesitation was just enough for Jamie to pull his second rifle to his shoulder and plug Red in the center of the chest.

Jamie quickly changed locations and reloaded. He waited amid rocks and brush.

"MacCallister!" Lenny shouted. "Damn it, MacCallister. Listen to me. It was a job of work, that's all. Just like cleanin' out a nest of red niggers. It's over. We ain't got no hard feelin's agin you. Let's call it even. Let us be and we won't be back."

You damn sure won't, Jamie thought. He shook his head. A job of work. Jamie began slowly working his way above the men, trapped in the crude log and stone fort just off the Indian trail. Then he noticed a small band of war-painted Sioux on the other side of the ridge. A warrior made the sign for Jamie to go. Jamie raised his hand and vanished back into the timber, heading for his horses. He had a good hunch that those remaining mercenaries would not die quickly . . . or well.

Jamie knew Rolly's sign well, having been on it for days, and that was the trail he followed, for he had heard the men back at the makeshift fort say that those with Rolly included Fritz, Calvert, Macklin, Bob Dalhart, and probably a man called Sonny.

These were the worst of the worst including the head of this particular snake pit. The real snake pit lay far to the east: a rich man named Maurice Evans and a lawyer called Laurin. He would get to them. All in good time.

Now that the raiders had broken up into small groups, and since there was no real description of any of them, chances were good that any trading post the small groups stopped in would have no reason to deny them food or supplies. The word was out on a large group of men, not four or five men riding together.

And Jamie knew of a trading post not a day's ride from where he was. He followed a slow, winding creek south. Rolly and those with him had tried to hide their trail by riding in the creek, but that wouldn't work with an experienced tracker. Jamie could easily see the hoof prints in the bottom of the shallow creek, could see where the men rode out of the water and went back in.

He knew exactly where Rolly was heading, for Goose Creek ran right past a trading post and then petered out just a few miles later.

Jamie stopped long enough to bathe and shave and fix something to eat. He was running out of supplies and planned to resupply at the Goose Creek post . . . after he dealt Rolly and the others their last hands in this game. Would he then go after the others? Jamie doubted it. He knew he probably should, for men like those who had attacked the settlement were the type who harbored long smoldering grudges, and they might well return at some later date.

But his original anger and outrage had tempered somewhat. Jamie had learned over the long and brutal years that men of the type who attacked the settlement usually came to no good end.

But what bothered Jamie was how much damage and destruction and misery to other people they would cause before the end came to them.

He tried to tell himself that was no concern of his.

Didn't work.

But Jamie's mind was still puzzling over some of the gunfire he'd heard back at the settlement, coming from a few of the raiders. It had been just too rapid to make any sense. So rapid that it had to have come from one pistol.

But Jamie could not for the life of him figure out what it could be.

And that musing almost cost him his life.

Thunder tensed under him, screamed as only a horse can do, which can be frightening, and jumped to one side, almost throwing Jamie out of the saddle. A rifle crashed and Jamie could feel the hot breath of the ball as it sailed by his head. He kicked out of the saddle and rolled on the ground, still clutching firmly to his rifle.

He came up on one knee just as a man charged out of the brush toward where he'd seen Jamie leave the saddle. Jamie leveled his rifle and shot the man in the chest, stopping the ambusher in mid-stride and throwing him to the ground.

Jamie waited for a moment, watching to see if the man would move. He didn't. Then Jamie could see where his ball had blown all the way through the man, exiting out his back.

Still, Jamie did not move, not wanting to reveal himself in case the man was not alone. After several minutes, Jamie eased up to the dead man and knelt down. The rifle by the man's side was nothing to write home about, but the pistols belted around his waist were like nothing he had ever seen before. Then he realized these were the revolvers he'd heard Sparks talk about before.

Jamie slipped them from their flap holsters and hefted them. To an ordinary man, they would be very heavy, to Jamie they were light.

He didn't know it, but he was looking at a pair of the Walker Colts, .44 caliber, six-shot revolving cylinder, weighing nearly five pounds apiece. Slightly over eleven hundred had been manufactured by Samuel Colt for the Texas Rangers, and each was serial numbered and engraved, starting with the number 1, and then either A, B, C, D, or E for the five companies of Texas Rangers. But these had no such numbers or engraving, for this was part of a shipment that had been stolen from the factory and sold to men traveling to the west.

Jamie went through the man's jacket pocket and found a half dozen fully loaded cylinders for the Colts. There was nothing else except lint to be found. No letters from home, no money, nothing. He rolled the man under an overhang and caved dirt over him. He felt reasonably certain the man had been a part of the gang who had attacked the settlement but could not be sure. So he said a few words over the man and let it go at that.

Then he found the man's horse and discovered two more Walker Colts in the saddlebags with another six full cylinders. He found a sack of brass percussion caps and .44 caliber balls, lead, and a mold to make more.

Jamie turned the horse loose and then rode on for another couple of miles before dismounting and beginning a careful inspection of the weapons. He loved the balance and the feel of the heavy pistols, but he didn't like the flap holsters taken from the dead man. Jamie cut the flaps off, punched a hole through the leather and ran rawhide thongs through the holes that would fit over the hammers and thus secure the Colts in the holsters. Then he started practicing with the pistols.

The thought of seeing how fast he could get the pistols out of the holsters had not occurred to him.

Yet.

Thirteen

Jamie could tell by the way the horses were traveling they would not last much longer unless the men riding them stopped and gave them several days rest. Brigands and trash to a man they might be, but they all knew that without a horse in this country a man vastly increased his chances of getting seriously dead.

Jamie took a chance that they would either stop at the trading post for several days or ride a few miles past it and then stop and continued his working with the Colts. Then the thought of his youngest son Falcon practicing with the toy pistols came to him: why not see how fast *he* could get these revolvers clear of the holsters, cock and accurately fire.

"Pretty quick, Jamie," he muttered after the second day of practice.

He made his supper and sat by the flames, not looking into them, that destroyed night vision and lingered long over a pot of coffee. A friendly band of wandering Crow had stopped by his camp for food and coffee and conversation and they told him of a group of very disagreeable white men who were camped near where Goose Creek vanishes into the earth. The Crow said the white men were loud and talked ugly.

Tomorrow, Jamie thought, some of them would stop talking ugly. They would stop talking altogether.

Andrew and Rosanna and family had arrived in the valley. Their spouses and kids were still somewhat numbed by the vastness of their journey and by the wild behavior of the men they had encountered during the last months of Bent's Fort at its old location. In the middle of 1849, the Army wanted to buy the place, but the government offered such a ridiculously low sum of money that the Bent brothers blew it up and moved to another location some thirty miles away.

Andrew's wife, Liza, was French, and Rosanna's husband, Alfred, English, and they were not at all accustomed to such harsh living conditions or such uncouth behavior from some of the men they had encountered. But with the help of the settlers in the valley, they soon lost most of their stiffness and began to enjoy the wide and wild open spaces, all the while keeping a very close eye on their kids.

In Virginia things were not going nearly so well. Try as she did to prevent it, Anne became pregnant. Cort did not yet know, Ross was amused, and Anne was furious.

"I fail to see the humor in this," Anne snapped at her brother.

"I fail to see anything *except* humor in it," Ross retorted. "I never thought that milquetoast you married was man enough to father a child."

"You're a great one to be talking about manhood!"

Ross laughed. "Now, now, sister. You know I enjoy an occasional dalliance with the ladies."

Anne glowered at her brother. She was not yet showing, thanks to her wearing very loose-fitting dresses, but obvious signs of her pregnancy would be only a few weeks away.

Ross smiled and said, "Have you given any thought to what might happen should you give birth to a natty-headed pickaninny, dear?"

Anne's returning smile was not pleasant. "You'd better think about your own future should that occur, brother dear."

"Why? I'm an innocent in all this. Your husband will simply think you've been sneaking out of the great house to roll about in the hay with a heavy hung field hand. I won't be suspect."

"You son of a bitch!"

"Of course, you could tell him the truth."

"Then you would be ruined as well."

"Oh, I've managed to put back enough money to see me through quite well, sister."

"You mean you've embezzled money from the company."

"What an ugly way to put it."

"But true."

Ross shrugged his shoulders then sat down in a chair in his lavishly appointed home on the outskirts of Richmond. "It's been a good long run, dear. But living in a house of cards is precarious at best. We have to look at it that way."

"Don't be a fool. I plan to abort the child."

"You better do it quickly."

"I've already started. I've been riding and exercising daily. Nothing seems to work."

"Taking our background into consideration, have you thought about voodoo?"

Anne leaned out of her chair and slapped him. Ross was still laughing as she stalked out of the room, slamming the door behind her.

Jamie pushed back the blanket that served as a summer door to the trading post, ducked his head, and stepped inside. The place was empty except for the man behind the counter of the bar and another old man who was obviously a trapper. Both men looked up with interest as Jamie stepped in. They both were taken by the guns strapped around Jamie's waist.

Jamie walked to the bar, his moccasins whispering on the plank floor. "Something to eat?" Jamie asked.

"Got venison and beans," the counterman said. "And a fresh pot of coffee."

"Sounds good." Jamie pointed to a table in the corner where his back would be to the wall. "Over there."

The counterman nodded.

"Ye be a MacCallister, right, laddie?" the old mountain man asked.

"That's right," Jamie said, sitting down. "Silver Wolf was my grandfather."

"Was?"

"He's dead. Three years ago."

"Sorry to hear that. Me and old Mac rode some trails together. I'm MacDuff."

"Heard him speak kindly of you, time to time."

The old mountain man nodded his head and took a sip from his cup of whiskey. "Them no-counts you're trailin' is camped 'bout two miles from here. One or two of 'em comes in ever' day 'bout this time, lad. They're bad ones."

"They won't be for long," Jamie said after chewing on a chunk of venison. It was tender, and that told Jamie the counterman had either pounded the toughness out of it or had a squaw chew it until it was tender and then cook it. Either way it made no difference. He was hungry. The beans had been sweetened with something, probably honey, and they were delicious.

"Six rode in here, then two more joined them. You need some help, you just give me a sign. Otherwise I'll stay out of it. But I owe ol' Mac. I'm ready when you are."

"Thank you."

Jamie had just finished sopping a chunk of bread through the juices left in his plate when he heard horses slowly approaching from the south. He had left Thunder in the stable next to the post on the north side. Jamie watched as the old mountain man loosened the pistol tucked behind his belt. He smiled at Jamie and Jamie returned the smile.

"I'll stand clear unless I see you're in trouble, lad."

"This won't take long," Jamie assured him.

MacDuff chuckled. "Not if'n you got the blood of Mac runnin' through you, and you do. I heared about the attack on your settlement. That's a low thing. Whiskey, John," he said to the counterman. "And get ready to kiss the floor."

"I been ready!" John said, pouring the cup full of whiskey.

"Four of 'em, lad," the mountain man said.

"Just right," Jamie replied, and the old mountain man laughed.

The blanket was jerked back roughly and the men crowded into the room.

"You still here, pops?" one said to MacDuff.

"I don't think I'm anywhere else, kid," the mountain man came right back at him.

"He's shore got a mouth on him, ain't he, Fritz," a man said.

"He shore do, Bob," Fritz said. "If he wasn't so damn old, I'd slap it off him."

"Why don't you try slapping me?" Jamie spoke from the gloom of the corner table. "You goddamn baby-killing scum!"

"MacCallister!" another man yelled and grabbed for the pistols behind his belt.

Jamie exploded into action, both his big hands filled with Colt .44s. The trading post rocked with the enormous reports of the Colts and the low-ceilinged room quickly filled with gray smoke, the cries of the hideously wounded, and the forever lasting silence of the dead.

Bob Dalhart, the man who had raped and then killed Melinda, was leaning up against the bar. His pistols were on the floor and both hands were holding his .44-caliber perforated belly. The other three were either dead or dying on the floor.

"Shit!" John the counterman said, from his position in a corner behind the bar. "I ain't never seen nothin' so quick as that."

"You bastard!" Bob cursed Jamie.

"You'll rape and kill no more children," Jamie said, his eyes holding a terrible light. He lifted his left hand .44 and shot the man in the center of his forehead.

"Hell," MacDuff said. "I didn't even get airy chance to go into action." He looked at Jamie. "You unholy quick with them things, lad. Ungodly quick."

All the men had been carrying Walker Colts, and Jamie

retrieved the pistols, giving one and a sack of caps and balls to the old mountain man.

"Thankee," the man said, hefting the pistol.

"And you can have their horses and equipment, too," Jamie said.

"That is kind of you. Mighty fine stock they is."

Jamie dragged the bodies out to the rear of the post, and the counterman swabbed the place out with buckets of water and a worn mop. Jamie stepped back into the trading post.

"Are you goin' to be leavin' now?" the counterman asked, a hopeful note in his voice.

"No," Jamie said.

"Shit!" the man muttered.

"Their friends will likely come callin' when they don't get back," the mountain man said. "This time, give me a chance to do something." He held up the pistol. "I want to see how this big heavy bastard bangs."

The counterman pointed to the rear of the store. "What about them back yonder? It's warm out, man. They're gonna get ripe real quick."

"I'll dig the holes," Jamie said. "After their friends join them."

"I got a better idee," MacDuff said. "John, you just moved the privy, didn't you?"

"Yeah! I did. Just last week. The old hole is still uncovered."

"I'll drag them over there and shove 'em in," the mountain man said. "That'll save a lot of diggin'. And I can't think of no better restin' place for scum like that."

MacDuff refused any help, so Jamie drank coffee and listened to the sound of bodies splashing and slopping into the old privy pit. The mountain man came back in grinning.

"Worked me up a thirst, I did. Whiskey, John. And make it quick. Two more is comin' up the trail."

The counterman shook his head and picked up a couple of buckets to fill with water so he could sluice down the floor after the shooting was done.

Jamie waited at the table in the corner. The horses of the dead men were still at the hitch rail so their absence would not alarm the other raiders.

The counterman peered out the open window. "I know them two's names. George and Witt, I heard them called."

The pair stepped into the trading post and stood for a moment, confusion on their faces at not finding their fellow brigands there.

"What the hell?" George said.

"That's where they've gone," Jamie said, standing up with both hands filled with .44s.

The pair of raiders clawed for the pistols stuck behind their belts just as the guns in Jamie's hands boomed. George took two in the chest and was knocked out the open doorway, taking the brightly colored blanket with him. Witt was slammed into the bar, gut-shot. He dropped his cocked Colt .44 on the floor as his hand no longer had the strength to hold it. The pistol fired and the ball blew off part of his right foot.

Witt died with a very strange expression on his face.

The outlaw camp was deserted when Jamie reached it. He found the tracks of three horses leading south, he recognized two as Rolly's and the pack horse's. The other was new to him. The pair must have panicked when the others didn't return. The ashes of the campfire still contained live coals, and a lot of blankets and ground sheets and clothing had been left behind.

Jamie started tracking but with caution. Rolly and the second man now knew Jamie was only a few hours behind, and a scared man is a very dangerous man. But as he tracked, Jamie soon realized the men were running hard, without any thought of setting up an ambush. He still kept the thought of an ambush in mind.

Jamie now rode with two .44s belted around his waist, two more in holsters on either side of the saddle, hooked onto the saddle horn, and two more ready to bang in his saddlebags. He had two more packed away to give to Ian. He bedded down with his quarry's campfire in sight, about two miles ahead and below where Jamie had made his cold camp on a ridge overlooking a valley.

Vic Johnson looked up at the mountains and shivered.

"What's wrong with you?" Rolly asked, even though he knew perfectly well what was the matter.

"MacCallister. He's up yonder. I can feel his eyes on me."

"Nonsense."

"You scoff if you like. He's up yonder. Tomorrow's the day we both die."

Rolly Hammond felt a cold shiver of fear run icy fingers up and down his spine. He said nothing.

"My mother don't even know where I am," Vic said.

"Does she care?" Rolly asked sarcastically.

"I reckon not. I left home years ago and ain't never been back."

"Why'd you leave home?" Rolly didn't really give a damn why Vic had left home, but conversation was a comforting thing with MacCallister breathing down their necks.

"I killed my pa with a hay fork."

For a moment, Rolly was speechless. Finally, he asked, "Why'd you do that?"

"I got tired of workin' the fields and of him beatin' on me when I didn't work. So I cornered him in the barn one day and run him through and through. That sure was one surprised man."

"I can imagine," Rolly said dryly. "But very briefly surprised."

"Naw. He lived for days afterward, so I heard. I hope he suffered. I hated that bastard."

Rolly stared at the man for a moment. "Did anybody ever tell you that you were a real prince of a fellow?"

Vic's face brightened. "No. Say, Rolly, thanks!"

Fourteen

When Rolly Hammond and Vic Johnson rolled out of their blankets the next morning, their horses were gone, including the pack horse. They still had their food and their weapons and blankets. But they were afoot.

Rolly thought they were somewhere in Oregon, but he wasn't really sure of that. He didn't know that he'd been running in a near perfect circle, first west, then north, then east, and then south. For days the sun had not shone, and the men had gotten all turned around in the silent wilderness. They were less than three days' ride from the settlement in MacCallister's Valley.

"The son of a bitch stole our horses!" Vic said.

"I don't think so," Rolly said. "I think Injuns took them while we were sleeping. I heard tell that Crow Injuns was the best horse thieves in the world."

Jamie had heard the Crow come close to his camp. He spoke to them in their own language without rising from his blankets. The Crow braves chuckled in the darkness. "We did not come to take your horses, Bear Killer. I only came here to see if I could count coup. I should have known better." He laughed softly. "Go back to sleep. We shall have our fun with those who camp below you."

"Now what?" Vic said, looking warily all around him.

"We got our guns and a lot of firepower with them, Vic. We pack up and walk out." He looked around at the mountains. "Place looks familiar," he muttered.

"Say what, Rolly?"

"Nothing. Look. The damn sun finally came up. Now I know for sure which way to go."

"I hate this place. Goddamn mountains look the same to me," Vic said.

"You'll get used to them after a few hundred years," the voice came from behind the men.

They whirled around.

Jamie stood there, his hands at his sides.

"So you got the rest of my boys, hey, MacCallister?" Rolly asked, his voice calm.

"Yep. Buried them in an old privy pit."

"That ain't decent!" Vic said.

"Who are you to speak of decency?" Jamie challenged. "You ride with scum like Rolly Hammond."

Rolly cursed Jamie and his hand flashed for his pistol. He didn't make it. He saw Jamie's .44 belch smoke and fire and the mercenary sat down hard on his butt, a huge numbness in his belly. He looked down at his shirt. It was all covered with blood. "Laurin said he had it all planned out. Maurice Evans saw to the last detail. It should have worked. It should have . . ."

Vic stared down at the man, dead on the cold ground. He slowly lifted his eyes, ready to face the ball with his name on it. But Jamie was gone.

"MacCallister? MacCallister!" he shouted. "Where are you? Look, finish it. Don't leave me here. I'll never make it out, man. I'm lost. Damn it, MacCallister, this ain't right. MacCallister! MacCallister! Goddamn you, MacCallister! Don't leave me here!"

* * *

Jamie again sat his horse on his favorite ridge overlooking the valley named for him. The damage done by the raiders had been repaired; no trace of the burning remained. But there were new crosses and stones marking new graves in the settlement's growing cemetery. Those were things that only time would erase.

Jamie started Thunder down the trail, and someone started ringing the community bell. The rutted streets soon filled with people. As he drew nearer, Jamie could see Kate with all the kids gathered around her. Andrew and Rosanna had come home.

Ian rode out to greet him. "Mighty fine lookin' pistols you got strapped around you, Pa," he said after shaking hands with his father.

"I got a couple for you in my saddlebags. Everything all right here?"

"It is now. Ma's been missin' you something fierce."

Jamie looked at his son and saw the twinkle in the man's eyes. And he is a man, Jamie thought. And I am growing old. He shook that away. "Don't you be speaking ugly thoughts about me or your ma, boy."

"Me? I was just gonna remind you of what you told me some years back, right back yonder on that very same ridge you just rode acrost."

"Across, boy."

"Right."

"What?"

"Nights sure get lonely, don't they, Pa?"

Jamie laughed and reached over and knocked his son's hat off, then it was a race to the settlement.

Jamie jumped down from Thunder and swept Kate up

in his massive arms and whirled around with her, kissing her soundly as they whirled. Liza and Alfred and their kids looked on with undisguised awe in their eyes at the big, buckskin-clad man, guns and knives belted about him. He was whirling Kate around and around as if she weighed no more than a bouquet of meadow flowers.

Jamie finally lowered Kate to the ground, hugged all his kids, and Kate led him over to meet his new son-in-law and daughter-in-law. Alfred braced himself for one of those bone-crunching handshakes that so many borderline bullies like to use. He got his first real lesson about Jamie MacCallister. The man's handshake was gentle. Alfred could feel the rock-hardness of the huge hand, but it was a gentleman's grip.

Jamie had been careful to bathe and brush off and air his buckskins before riding into the valley, and when he bent his head to gently kiss Liza on the cheek, she could smell only the odor of strong soap and scrubbed leather. Both Alfred and Liza were much taken by the big man, and instantly felt close to him.

Later, when the residents of the community had returned to their homes, the immediate family sat on the long front porch of the cabin enjoying cakes and coffee. Then the talk turned serious.

"Is it over?" Kate asked her husband.

"The hunt for the raiders? Yes. But I still have the lawyer and the rich man to face."

"How many of the raiders did you get, Pa?" Ian asked. He sat on the edge of the porch inspecting the Colts his father had given him.

"Enough," Jamie said, with a finality to his one-word reply that closed the subject. Later, if she asked about it, and he was sure she would, he would tell Kate all about the man-hunt. But it was not the sort of thing one discussed in front of people like Alfred and Liza, who were not accustomed to the violent ways of the American frontier.

But Jamie had underestimated Alfred and Liza. Liza said, "When there is no written law or uniformed authorities to stand up for the people, then the people have to enforce their own laws."

"Quite," Alfred said. "You and your friends have taken a wilderness and carved out a settled community, with a proper school and homes and places of business and a house of worship. This is a pocket of civilization surrounded by savages. It must be defended at all costs."

The talk turned to lighter subjects, and Jamie asked, "Andrew, your mother said that you and your sister were about to start an American tour. Where would you start?"

Jamie had heard of the gold strike in California and how San Francisco was booming, growing by hundreds of people a day, people who were starved for some vestige of culture and willing to pay enormous sums of money for entertainment.

"Why . . . I don't know. We have an agent, of course. But we've had no communication from him since leaving New York City."

Kate cut her blues to her husband. She knew he had something on his mind, and with Jamie it would more than likely be wild. Her son and daughter, in addition to their immediate family, had brought west many of their traveling entourage: musicians and stage hands and dancers and the like. They had been put up in other homes in the settlement and were kept busy with telling of all the places they'd been and all the wonderful sights they'd seen.

"Well," Jamie said, "why don't you ask all the members of your troupe if they'd like a little adventure, something they could tell their grandkids and friends about? Something they would never forget."

"What do you have in mind, Papa?" Rosanna asked.

"Brace yourselves," Kate said.

"Oh, a little trip," Jamie replied. "I took a look at those wagons you came across the great plains in—fine workmanship. And your stock is first rate. I could get some ol' boys to ride along with us for protection and we could have a grand old time. I figure we could make San Francisco in no time at all." He looked at Kate. "You want to see the Pacific Ocean, Kate?"

And suddenly Jamie was covered with females, all laughing and hugging his neck and crawling around on his lap. The chair he was sitting in broke under the added weight and dumped them all on the porch floor.

Jamie sent out Utes to find those he wanted to accompany them to the west coast, and they all agreed to go. Alfred and Liza and their entourage stood in silent shock when the dwarf Audie and his huge sidekick Lobo rode in, followed that afternoon by Preacher and Sparks.

"My dear," Audie said, his head barely coming up to Liza's breasts. "Might you have in your repertoire something by Mozart? Perchance his Allegro maestoso for violin?"

"Ah . . . oui," she replied, flustered at the sight of this savage-looking little man with guns and knives hanging all about him inquiring about Mozart, and momentarily slipped into her native tongue.

"Magnifique!" Audie replied in perfect French, and the two of them walked off, chattering in Liza's native tongue.

"Incredible," Alfred said, when he finally found his voice.

"Ain't my partner a kick in the ass?" Lobo asked the stunned Englishman.

"Ah . . . yes," Alfred said, looking up at the huge bear of a man. "Quite."

"He was a professor back east. Havert, or some goddamn place like that."

"Harvard?" Alfred asked.

"That's what I said, ain't it?"

"Ah . . . certainly."

Sparks rescued the Englishman before Lobo completely boggled his mind.

"We got to make it 'fore the snow flies, Jamie," Preacher said. "It's gonna be close."

"We'll make it. I know a shortcut. Grandpa told me about it and I rode it once. Grandpa took wagons through to the coast long before anybody else even thought about it."

"Yeah, but them was tough settlers, not lily-handed musicianers."

"Piece of cake, Preacher. I've got some drivers coming in from the fort. They'll be here in a few days. Good men. I just want these people to see what wilderness is really like."

"I 'spect they'll manage to do that, all right," Preacher said drily.

Kate thoroughly shocked Liza and Alfred and most of the troupe when she appeared one morning wearing buckskin britches and shirt and moccasins with high top leggings. She shook out a rope and dabbed a loop over a horse's neck, her favorite mare. She saddled the mare and hopped into the saddle, riding astride. Liza felt somewhat faint at the sight and Alfred and the troupe looked on in disbelief.

"My God!" a troupe member from London said. "The woman is wearing a *gun!*"

"That's my mother," Rosanna said, then ran into the cabin and emerged a few minutes later wearing men's britches and one of her brother's shirts. She hopped bareback on a mare and went riding off into the valley with her mother, holding onto the mane.

"Great stars and garters!" Alfred bellowed when he finally found his voice.

Andrew was doubled over with tears in his eyes, laughing at the expression on Alfred's face.

"You're in the country, now," Caroline MacCallister said. "We don't hold with all the stuffy standards that apply east of the Mississippi. Out here, they're just too much fuss and bother."

"Indeed," Alfred said.

Andrew looked around for his wife, but she had disappeared into the cabin. His mouth dropped open in shock when Liza appeared on the porch, wearing men's pants and one of his shirts. Jamie had already saddled up a horse for her and, laughing, scooped her up in his arms and deposited her in the saddle, astride.

She had told Jamie that she was a good rider, and watching her now he had no doubts.

Ian walked to his side and stood silent for a moment. Jamie asked. "You going with us, son?"

"No. Caroline is expectin'. I don't want to take any chances with the baby."

"Good thinking. I'll feel better with you here."

"Pa?"

"Yes?"

"Twins and triplets run on her side of the family, too."

Jamie grinned and clasped his son's shoulder. "The more the merrier, boy. Between you and me, the MacCallister name will never die."

BOOK THREE

You shall judge a man by his foes
as well as by his friends.
—*Joseph Conrad*

One

There were ten sturdy wagons, pulled by mules, big Missouri Reds. The interiors of the living quarter wagons were lavishly appointed, but then, Jamie had reminded himself, these people were used to the finer things, not roughing it.

Jamie would scout ahead most of the time, Audie and Lobo on one side of the wagons, Sparks and Preacher on the other. All of them were armed with the new Colt revolvers, and each man carried on him or near to hand at least six fully loaded pistols. In each wagon there were shotguns and rifles, and rifle and shotgun boots had been added to each driver's box. The men Jamie had recruited from the fort were all good, steady men who wished to go west to find gold. They were willing to drive the wagons in exchange for hearty food, safety, companionship, the constant sight of beautiful women, and the occasional entertainment by professionals.

The entire community had turned out early that morning to see the wagons off. Alfred Wadsworth wrote in his diary, which would become a bestseller in England: "The greatest adventure of my life. A journey through the American wilderness, fraught with danger, each mile filled with wild red savages, ferocious beasts, and other man-eating creatures that science has not yet named."

Really, it wasn't quite that bad. When Sparks and the others saw what Jamie was doing, they were amused: he was taking the wagon train over the Oregon Trail.

"You taking them all the way north?" Lobo asked.

"No. But I won't use the Hastings Cutoff. We'll go to Fort Hall, follow the Snake, and then cut south and take the California Trail."

"They wanted to see some rough country," Preacher said. "By God, they'll see it."

The first few hundred miles was very rough, for there simply was no road. There were trails that the Indians had used for centuries, but nothing that resembled a road. Andrew and Rosanna had grown up in this country, and they knew what to expect, but the others were, for a few days, shocked into silence by the enormity of it all. The daring of their trip finally sank home.

Alfred had at first cast a very dubious eye at the western saddle provided him, having sat nothing but English saddles all his life. But the man soon found that the western saddle was much more comfortable and practical for long journeys. As for the women who chose not to ride in the wagons or walk, as they were forced to do many times, they wore men's britches and rode astride.

The dancers in the troupe soon proved their mettle, for both sexes were tough and strong; when wagons became bogged down crossing creeks or rivers, they were the first at the fore and seemed to enjoy it all.

The women in the company soon cast aside their bonnets and cut the sleeves off of their dresses and let the sun tan their skin and arms, and to hell with the dictates of the times.

"One thing for sure," Sparks said. "They gonna be a healthy bunch when we reach the blue waters."

At the end of the first week, those in the troupe who had been finicky or picky eaters were wolfing down huge portions of venison or buffalo steaks, cowboy stew, baked grouse, beans and potatoes, fried cakes, and dried apple pie, washing it all down with cup after cup of strong black coffee. Everyone was sleeping better than ever before.

At least once a week, when the actors and singers were not too tired, they put on a performance after supper, much to the delight of the hired drivers.

Jamie rode back to the wagons one mid-morning and called, "Sweetwater River just ahead. We'll take a long nooning there and everybody can have a long bath."

They had seen Indians along the way, but most had been curious rather than unfriendly, although Jamie had spotted a few bands that carried trouble in their eyes. For those Indians, Jamie, Lobo, Sparks, Preacher, and Audie put on a little show using their Colt revolvers. When the Indians saw how fast and how long the men could shoot, they decided it would be best to make friends with those in the wagon train. The white man's medicine was just too strong; they had never seen guns like those they named Many-Shoots.

Although by now, hundreds of wagons had rolled over the Oregon Trail, the Indians were still fascinated by the women's long blonde hair.

One chief was particularly taken with Kate and wanted to trade for her. Jamie patiently and with a straight face explained that Kate had a temper that would match that of a grizzly bear, refused to cook, would not make clothes, would not chew venison to make it tender for her man, and would only share his robes once a month. And no matter how often or how hard Jamie beat her, she would not change.

The stunned chief pondered all that for a moment, then said, "Have suggestion."

"What is it?"

"You keep," he said and rode off.

"What was that all about?" Kate asked, riding up.

"You wouldn't believe me if I told you," Jamie said, trying his best to maintain a straight face.

When the wagons reached the Hudson's Bay trading post on the Snake, the delighted trappers, mountain men and local army troops collected a small fortune for the performers to put on a show. And what a show it turned out to be. Healthier now than they had ever been, the actors acted, the singers sang, the musicians played, and the dancers danced until late in the evening, taking encore after encore. It was a show the likes of which would never again be seen at the old post.

And it was there that the old mountain man MacDuff joined the wagons west.

"There be trouble up ahead for ye," Duffy, as he chose to be called, told Jamie. "Somebody who wears a stupid lookin' black stovepipe hat. "You know him?"

"Winslow," Jamie said. "He and his bunch attacked the settlement some years back. I had just about forgotten all about him."

"He ain't forgot about you," Duffy said. "He's got hisself a pretty fair-sized gang and they's been playin' hell all up and down the wagon trail 'tween here and Sacramento. They're gonna hit the wagons, boy." He smiled, exposing a goodly amount of strong teeth for a man his age. "You got airy objections if I tag along with you?"

"Be glad to have you."

Preacher walked up. "Hello, you old coot," he greeted MacDuff.

"Preacher, you big bag of wind," Duffy said. "I ain't seen you in a while. I figured you'd tooken up farmin' and gotten hitched by now."

The two mountain men walked off, trading heated insults and huge lies.

Jamie walked off to find Kate.

"Kate, spread the word among the members that a large gang of outlaws is going to hit us somewhere ahead. Stay close to the wagons and keep your rifle loose in the boot."

"Anybody I know?" Kate asked calmly.

"You heard me talk about Winslow, the leader of the gang who hit us years back?"

She nodded.

"That's the one—Duffy just warned me."

"I like that old man."

"So did Grandpa."

"That says a lot."

"Tells me he's a man with no back-up in him."

After leaving Fort Hall, the wagons followed the Snake River until reaching the California Trail, then cut south and west. This was the route first blazed by the mountain man Joe Walker back in 1833. San Francisco then was called Yerba Buena. The California trail was in many ways just as arduous as the Oregon Trail, winding north of the Great Salt Lake and then along the brackish Humboldt River, across the alkali Nevada Desert, and then across the Sierra Nevada mountains.

"Winslow will hit us before we reach the wastes," Preacher said to Jamie, riding up to the point.

"He'll do it soon," Jamie predicted. "And probably at night."

"Good water and graze up ahead," Preacher said. "You thinkin' tonight might be the time?"

"Yes."

"I'll pass the word."

Jamie put the wagons in a circle with the stock in the center that afternoon, halting the wagons several hours earlier than he usually did. He was not worried about Winslow firing at the wagons, for the outlaw wanted the wagons intact, for resale.

"He sells the women," Duffy said. "Takes them to 'Frisco and sells them to ships' captains for transport to some Godless country where they're sold into slavery as whoors. If the men are good and strong, he sells them, too, into terrible cruel bondage before the mast."

"I thought all that had stopped," Jamie said.

"Put that out of your mind. It's still goin' on. And these fillies with us will bring a pretty penny, believe you me. And don't think you'll be safe when we get to 'Frisco, for you won't. That town's a dangerous wicked place." He grinned. "Of course, I would know naught about the wicked part of it."

Jamie laughed and began walking the circle of wagons. Alfred Wadsworth had loaded up a double-barreled goose gun with nails and shot and was now checking the loads in his pistols.

"We'll be ready to fight," he assured Jamie. "An actor and musician I may be, but it's tradition in my family to do one's time with the Lancers. The sounds of gunfire will not be new to me, Jamie MacCallister."

Jamie smiled and walked on.

The other men in the troupe, while not experienced fighters, were familiar with weapons, most of them having grown up in small towns around the land. They sat eating their supper with their guns close to hand.

Everything was as ready as Jamie could make it. All they could do now was wait.

It wasn't a long wait.

"They're out there," Sparks said to Jamie about an hour after full dark had laid night's blanket over the land.

"I know. They're good but not that good. I heard them slipping up about fifteen minutes ago. I told everyone to act like they're going to bed, then quietly get into position. Nobody fires until my word."

"Got you."

Jamie moved around the circle, talking in low tones. He was letting the fires burn down to coals, and for half an hour he had forbid anyone to look into the dying flames. But outside the circled wagons, Winslow's men were forced to look directly at the wagons and therefore into the flames of cookfires. Their night vision would be somewhat impaired.

The members of the wagon train had slipped under their wagons and were as still as the night, heavily loaded shotguns, rifles, and pistols at the ready. Winslow was going to be in for quite a surprise.

Jamie had listened carefully as the outlaws slipped up in the dark. He guessed their strength at probably thirty. But they would be a desperate thirty, cut-throats and brigands all—men whose limits of cruelty would know no boundaries, men who would do anything.

Jamie waited. Winslow was giving the men and women ample time to fall into a sound sleep. It's easier to cut a sleeping person's throat.

Far off in the distance, a coyote sang his lonely song. Song Dogs, the Indians called them. Then a moment later, another coyote joined in, then another, and the night was suddenly not so lonely or bleak.

Jamie's eyes caught a very slight movement outside the circled wagons. He was instantly alert. He waited for another movement, but none came. Had he imagined it? He didn't think so. He had survived too many attacks such as this one to be imagining things in the dark.

No, there it was again. The outlaws were creeping closer. They obviously had this down to a fine practiced art. Preacher had told him of finding several wagon trains that had been set upon by white brigands, and Jamie himself had personally witnessed one a few years back.

"Sorry bastards," Jamie muttered under his breath.

The gang of cut-throats came in a rush out of the night, silent death and depravity running toward the wagons.

"Fire!" Jamie yelled, lifting his twin Walker Colts and letting them bang.

Several of the women had been holding torches, ready to light, and at the first shot, they lit the torches and flung them outside the circled wagons, catching the outlaws in the flickering flames.

The fire power from inside the wagons was devastating and at close range, killing and maiming those in the first wave. Double-barreled shotguns did the most damage, for at close range a heavily loaded shotgun can very nearly cut a man in two.

Winslow lost half his men within fifteen seconds. The wounded lay on the rocky ground, moaning and writhing in pain, calling out for help, for mercy, and, most disgusting to those in the circle, for God to help them.

"Can you believe it?" a dancer named Nancy said,

breaking the awful silence after the deadly fusillade. "They want God to help them."

"God damn them!" one of the hired drivers said. "I hope they all burn in the Hellfires."

"I'll be back, MacCallister," a shout came out of the night. Jamie recognized Winslow. "You've not seen the last of me."

Jamie did not reply. He had reloaded his pistols and now squatted by a wagon wheel in the darkness.

"It's a long way yet to California," Winslow offered up his final words.

Then the night grew silent after the faint sounds of hooves faded into the distance.

"What about the wounded?" Liza asked, appearing by Jamie's side.

In the faint light from the stars, Liza read the silent answer in her father-in-law's eyes and said no more about it. She turned and walked away.

So many pistol and rifle balls and heavy charges from shotguns had been pumped into the charging men, Jamie felt there was little use in seeing to the wounded. The cries of the hideously mangled men had already tapered off to a few low moans and whispered prayers. The wagons carried medical supplies, including laudanum, but Jamie had no intention of sharing their precious supplies with the crap and crud who rode with the likes of Stovepipe Winslow.

By ten o'clock that evening, the cries of the wounded had all faded.

"They're either dead or unconscious," Audie remarked.

"Good riddance," Sparks said.

At first light, Jamie and MacDuff were prowling among the dead, gathering up weapons and balls and powder.

They found several revolvers, but they were of the type that used a lever under the barrel to turn the cylinder; pull down the lever, the cylinder turned, clamp the level snug against the bottom of the barrel, you were ready to fire . . . hopefully. Several had pepperboxes in their pockets; many men called them "suicide pistols" because they sometimes jammed up and blew your hand off or—several fingers, if you were lucky.

Jamie smashed the pepperboxes, rendering them useless, and then threw them away; he had no use for them but didn't want any Indians to find them.

The dead men were dragged off and buried in a common grave, not out of choice but necessity, for none carried any type of identification. The outlaws had some money, and Jamie gave that to the drivers to divide among themselves. Some took the money, others refused it.

The wagons were moving west by mid-morning.

Jamie spoke briefly with Lobo and the big man nodded his head in agreement. A few minutes later, after whispering to Kate, Jamie rode off with Sparks, Preacher and a few days' supplies, trailing Winslow's outlaw pack.

The trail west was fraught with enough dangers; the three of them were going to remove one of the perils.

"When we come up on this pack of hydrophobee skunks," Preacher said. "How do we play it?"

"We ride in and kill the bastards," Sparks said.

"That sounds simple enough," Preacher said with a smile. "Hell, there ain't but about twenty of 'em."

Two

It was Preacher who pointed out the circling carrion birds just ahead. "One more of them dead," he opined.

Several of the birds had already settled around the dead man and were feeding, tearing at the dead flesh, pecking out his eyes, and going deep into the stomach, making it impossible for the men to see what had killed him. But all could make a pretty good guess.

Buzzards were landing in force now, and the men did not feel like taking the time to drive them away, even if they could—which sometimes proved impossible if the buzzards were hungry enough. They had nothing with which to dig a grave, so they left the outlaw where he lay.

"Even them ugly bastards got to eat," Preacher summed it all up.

A mile further on, they found another man sitting alongside the trail, his back to a rock. He was alive but just barely. He had taken a load of buckshot from a shotgun right in the stomach. He looked up at the men, the hate in his eyes overriding the terrible pain.

"If I had the strength," he gasped, "I'd take my gun and kill you all right now."

"How does a fellow get to be so snake-poison full of hate?" Sparks asked the man.

The man opened his mouth to speak, but his eyes glazed over and his mouth filled with blood, dribbling down his chin. His head slumped to one side and he died along the trail. About a hundred yards away, the carrion birds waited with all the patience of a million years bred in them.

Jamie, Sparks, and Preacher rode on.

The carrion birds moved in to feast.

A few minutes later, they could smell the dust kicked up by Winslow's gang.

"Won't be long now," Sparks said.

"Our horses are a lot fresher," Jamie said. "Let's get ahead of them."

The men spurred their horses and began a short loop. They trotted their animals for a time, then walked for a time. An hour later, the Winslow gang was about two miles behind them and coming on at a slow but steady pace.

"Good place right up yonder," Preacher said. "The horses can graze behind them rocks and we can get siteated amongst 'em."

Jamie cut his eyes at Preacher and hid his smile. He knew that the mountain man was capable of speaking perfect English when he wanted to.

The men did not even consider that the hunt might go on past these upthrustings of rock in the earth. They knew it wouldn't. It was going to end right here. They stripped saddles from the horses and let them roll but not drink; they were too hot for that. They put the picket pins down on about a quarter acre of grass and climbed into the rocks just as Winslow, with his stupid-looking tall stovepipe hat held on by a strap under his chin, came riding up.

The three men silently stood up in the rocks, their

hands filled with Colt .44s and without a word just hauled the hammers back and let the lead fly.

Horses were rearing up and screaming in fright and men were cursing and shouting while their comrades were being knocked out of the saddle to fall onto the ground and be trampled under the hooves of their horses.

The attackers each carried four Colts, all of them loaded up full. When the hammers finally fell on the last loaded cylinder, the scene on the ground below the rocks was carnage.

"Didn't kill nary horse," Preacher said with some satisfaction, for like most good western men, he liked and respected horses.

The men loaded up full before venturing down out of the rocks. Winslow had taken two .44 slugs in the gut and had lost his pistols. He had managed to pull himself into the rocks and was sitting up when Jamie found him. He was still wearing his stovepipe hat.

"You should have gone on back east, Winslow," Jamie told him. "You might have lived a little longer."

Winslow cussed him until he was out of breath.

"Is that all you got to say?" Jamie asked the man just as Sparks and Preacher walked up.

"I reckon it is, Jamie," Sparks said. "He's dead."

It was mid-morning of the next day before the men caught up with the wagons.

"Everything go all right, Pa?" Rosanna asked.

"It did for us," Jamie replied.

His daughter had to ask no more questions. She knew they would never again be bothered by Winslow and his gang.

The wagon train now began the long dry pull to the Sierra Nevada mountains. Some wagon masters led their wagons on the Walker route, but Kit Carson had told Jamie of a better way, crossing near Lake Tahoe, and that was the way Jamie led this now-seasoned group of travelers.

Once they crossed the mountains, the way became infinitely easier and the mood of the travelers lighter. MacDuff rode on ahead to spread the word that entertainers were coming.

The entertainers weren't the only ones coming to California. Thousands were on their way to seek their fortunes. In January of 1848, gold was accidentally discovered at Sutter's Creek by James Marshall, a man who was building a mill for John Sutter. Ironically, although the gold was discovered on his land, John Sutter would see little of it. A few days after the gold was discovered, Mexico ceded California to the United States and Sutter's title to the land was contested. He was unable, legally, to drive off the hundreds of prospectors who suddenly appeared on his land, digging and panning for the precious yellow metal. Within a few years he was bankrupt, and he went back east to petition the U.S. government for the rights to his land. He died broke in 1880.

Gold fever gripped the United States and thousands started on their way to California; many turned back, but many more continued on. One year after gold was discovered, more than one hundred thousand people had moved from the east into California, making it the fastest growing area in North America.

San Francisco became a boom town—It was often referred to as the "Boomtown on the Bay." From mid-1848 until well into the 1850s, San Francisco grew faster than any other American city. Few accurate records were kept, but it was estimated that starting in mid-1848, thirty to forty new houses a day were built along the bay. By the time Jamie and Kate and the troupe arrived, there were more than five hundred bars and nearly twice that many gambling dens. Hotels were grand for the time and restaurants in the growing city featured more on the menu than the fancy eating places of New York City. There were also three to five murders a day and whores walked the streets all hours of the day and night. It was reported that one whore retired after only a year working the streets— she had made over seventy-five thousand dollars in one year from the gold-laden and sex-starved miners and sailors. Fresh eggs were selling for twelve dollars a dozen. Ships crowded the harbor and many a ship's master quickly learned he could make more money by grounding his ship and leasing it out as a store or hotel than he could by sailing the seas.

It was the wildest town in North America, where nearly anything went for anybody who had the stomach to do it, and practically everybody did.

MacDuff settled the problem of no available hotel rooms in the city by stating simply, "No rooms, no shows."

The residents on one entire floor were kicked out, and the rooms were ready for Jamie, Kate and company when they arrived; placards were quickly printed up and a hall rented. In one day, every seat in the hall was sold out for one entire month. One performance a day Monday through Friday, two shows on Saturday.

The gold rush was not the only thing of importance that was taking place that year. The Mexican-American war ended and New Mexico, California, and the Rio Grande border of Texas became part of the United States. Wisconsin joined the Union. The territory of Oregon was formally organized. Zachary Taylor was elected president.

But gold was the dream that gripped the nation, instant wealth sometimes discovered and lost all in the same day.

Gold had no allure for Jamie, for he had already found and cached enough gold to keep his family comfortable for a hundred years. And while the city was filled with some of the roughest men to ever congregate in one spot, most gave Jamie Ian MacCallister a wide berth.

Jamie didn't know that lawyer Laurin was in San Francisco, as was Maurice Evans, both of them there under assumed names, both having been run out of New York City and St. Louis.

"MacCallister," Evans whispered, laying aside the newspaper as the old hate once more filled him. Thoughts of revenge rushed into his brain. "And many of his family." Evans immediately summoned lawyer Laurin and showed him the newspaper.

"I know," Laurin said, taking a seat. He held up a finger. "But a word of caution. We could probably get away with the death of Jamie MacCallister, but to do harm to some of the most popular entertainers in all of America would bring a very swift and thorough investigation. It isn't worth it."

"There must be a way," Evans whispered. Every misfortune that had befallen him since the death of his beloved son, Blake—one of the most worthless bastards to ever walk the face of the earth—Maurice Evans blamed on Jamie MacCallister. He was consumed with hate.

"I just might know a way," Laurin said. "I just might."

"Then get busy on it."

"Maurice, we have to be very, very careful. One more slip-up and we're finished. All avenues will be closed to us."

The look the lawyer received was of unbridled hate. "You think I give a damn about doing business when my son's unavenged body is rotting in some unmarked grave, buried without benefit of the words of God? I want the whole damn MacCallister family dead. Do you hear me? *Dead!*"

Cort had been walking into walls ever since Anne announced her pregnancy. He insisted that she stop all her exercising and immediately take to her bed. Anne complied, since no matter what she did, she could not abort the damn baby. But her doctor nearly did it for her when he said he was sure she was carrying twins.

Anne fell back against the pillows in genuine shock. Twins!

After the doctor left, Anne cut her eyes to her personal maid, Selma. The black woman was arranging a vase of flowers, a smile on her lips.

"I fail to see anything amusing about this, Selma. Get out!"

Selma turned around slowly, then walked to Anne's enormous four poster bed. She stood looking down at her. "You poor stupid bitch!" she said, and Anne's eyes widened in shock. "You really didn't think you could fool your own kind, did you?"

"I . . . don't know what you mean," Anne stammered.

"I knowed you was colored tryin' to pass the second

you walked in the house, *Mistress.*" She slurred the title. "But that's all right. Cain't blame no one for tryin' to break the chains of slavery. Now, you listen to me. My mammy was the plantation midwife and when she died I took her place. When the time comes, we don't call no doctor. Cain't take that chance. One or both of these babies could be a nappy-headed nigger. You want Master Cort or Doctor Monroe to see that?"

Anne could but shake her head.

"Now you beginnin' to be smart. Birthin' babies ain't no big thing. You be fine. You just put that pretty schemin' head of yours to thinkin' 'bout how we gonna get Master Cort away from here when the time comes."

"Selma," Anne spoke, strangely relieved at having someone other than her brother to confide in. "What happens if the babies are black?"

"One of 'em stands a good chance of that, Missy. If that be the case, we give it away right quick. Your time is near and I know a woman done lost her baby. She'll take it. She won't know where it come from. Nobody will 'ceptin' you and me. Relax now. I 'spect you be birthin' 'fore the week is out. Hopefully durin' the night. Better that way. We got to git the master outta here, good and gone a distance. Think on it."

In San Francisco, lawyer Laurin had recruited a half dozen thugs to take care of Jamie. Once Jamie was out of the picture, Kate could be handled easily. Laurin had plans of his own for the blue-eyed Kate. He had wanted the petite lady from the moment he first saw her riding in a carriage. Laurin was determined to have her.

People disappeared all the time in the rough and rowdy

city. Knocked on the head and tossed in the bay for the money in their pockets, sold to ship captains, and worse. What worried him was Evans's insistence that the kids, Rosanna and Andrew, be dealt with, too. That was chancy. The musicians were known world-wide and a massive investigation would be immediately launched unless . . . He smiled. Of course. It occurred all the time in the city. Fire. The hall would catch on fire. He could arrange to have some bully-boys backstage to lay a cosh against the heads of the twins and they would perish in the fire. Yes. Perfect. It would work. He hurried over to Evans's office to tell him the good news.

Anne went into labor two days after she and Selma had talked. Fortunately, Doctor Monroe was clear over on the other side of the county. Unfortunately, Cort was home and pacing the floor.

"You just sit down here in the parlor and relax," Selma told him. "I done this a hundred times. It might help if you had a good strong drink. Here, let me fix it for you. Now you drink this down and relax. Them babies gonna come with or without you worryin' and frettin' yourself into a sickness. I'll call you when it's over."

"I don't know what we'd do without you, Selma," Cort said, taking the bourbon and water.

I don't either, Selma thought. "Yes, sir. I'm goin' upstairs to tend to Miss Anne now. This might take some time, so you just try to relax. When you gets done with that drink, you fix you another. They's soup and hot bread in the kitchen case you gets hongry. I'll call you when it's time for you to come up."

In the foyer, she jerked her husband to one side. "You

come with me. Things don't turn out right, you got to get a baby over to Georgia Washington on the quiet."

He shook his head. "Woman, you completely lost your goddamn mind? Master Cort learns about this he'd have us both stripped nekked and whupped to death."

She glared at her husband. "Now, you listen to me, Tyrone. And you listen good. We do this right, and you and me is treated-good house servants 'til the day we die. No more workin' in the fields for you and no more slavin' over a hot stove for me. Now you go fetch me hot water and clean white cloths. And wash your damn hands 'fore you do that. Move!"

Tyrone walked off, muttering to himself. Thunder rumbled in the distance and a slow rain began to fall. Cort sat in the parlor and got drunk.

The babies came within the hour, in the midst of a violent storm. The day turned dark as night; winds battered the huge plantation home and rain and tiny balls of hail lashed out in fury. Tyrone was busy bringing in clean cloths and toting out pitchers of water. No one saw Cort stagger up the curving stairs and slip into the sitting room. He peeped into the bedroom, a bottle of bourbon in one hand.

"First one is fine, missy," Selma said. "Lily white and pretty. It's a girl." She wiped Anne's sweaty face.

Cort grinned drunkenly. But the grin was wiped from his face at Selma's next words.

"The boy ain't colored like me, Missy. But he ain't white neither. He do have good hair, but he never gonna pass. Ain't no way in Hell for him to do that. Your mammy's side done showed up in him."

"Damn it!" Anne cursed.

"Not to fret, Missy. My man will be back in a few

minutes and he'll take the baby over to the quarters. Georgia's got milk in her tits and the baby will be fine."

"I want to hold him."

"No! Not now, not ever. You had one baby and that's all. Master Cort don't never need to know."

Cort stumbled blindly down the steps and out into the storm. He looked up at the lightning-blazed and thunderstunned sky and screamed, "Heaven help us all. I married a goddamn nigger!"

Three

Jamie always took a walk just after supper, then would return to the hotel and sit on the porch and smoke a cigar. This Monday evening was no different. At Kate's insistence, he had packed away his buckskins and was dressed in a dark suit; Kate had ordered several of them made for her husband. With his sparkling white shirt, string tie, and hand-made boots he was quite a striking figure walking the boardwalks of the city. His long shoulder-length blond hair still showed no sign of gray.

Laurin had hired his thugs, and this evening they were to strike at Jamie while others were to grab Kate from her room and spirit her off to a warehouse, where Laurin would pleasure himself and then kill Kate.

But Laurin and his hired thugs had vastly underestimated Jamie Ian MacCallister and Kate.

Andrew and Rosanna and company were already at the hall, and arsonists and other hired thugs were waiting for the signal to start the fires blazing. Kate was in their room, in a robe, getting ready to take her bath. She stood up and started to remove her robe when she heard footsteps in the hall. Very furtive-sounding footsteps. She picked up one of Jamie's .44 Colts and waited. She did not have to check to see if it was loaded. She knew it was.

She watched the doorknob turn quietly. But she had

locked the door after Jamie had left, at his instructions. She cocked the .44. The door was kicked open and Kate drilled the first man through the shattered doorway right between the eyes. The recoil was hard, but she held on and shot the second man in the chest, knocking him back and over the landing. He fell with a crash to the lobby below and people started shouting. The third man tried to wrest the pistol from her, but Kate put a quick knee into his parts and doubled him over, gagging and coughing. The fourth man turned to flee and Kate split his spine with a .44 ball, and he fell bonelessly to the hall floor. Boots were pounding on the steps as people ran up to investigate.

Kate cocked the .44 and put the muzzle against the downed man's head. His face paled and his eyes widened. "You have ten seconds to tell me who sent you, or by God I'll kill you," Kate said menacingly.

"I don't know, Missy!" the man cried. "I was hired by Tommy yonder. The man you shot 'tween the eyes. I swear to you, that's the truth."

Two men rushed into the room and snatched the brigand up to his boots. "We'll take care of—"

"You'll take this lowlife to the storeroom and tie him up and wait for my husband," Kate interrupted him, steel behind her words and a very large pistol in her hand. "He'll want to talk to him."

"Yes, ma'am," one of the security men said. "As you say, ma'am."

Jamie sensed the attack as he was mid-way across a dark alley and turned to meet it. Dressed to the nines he was, but he still carried one Colt tucked behind a belt and his Bowie knife. He cut the first thug from adam's apple to belly and then whipped the razor-sharp blade across the face of the second man, bringing a scream of fright and pain.

Laurin had sent six men after Jamie. It wasn't enough. Jamie nearly took the head off of the third man with his Bowie while he was drawing his .44 with his left hand. The Colt boomed and the fourth man went down, a hole in his chest. The remaining two men ran for their lives. Jamie took careful aim and fired, the ball breaking the knee of one of the men and sending him hollering and tumbling to the muddy street while the last man managed to run away into the night.

What passed for law in the nearly lawless city by the bay came riding up. "Here now!" the man shouted. "Cease and desist in the name of the law, man!"

"Go to hell," Jamie told him, and tucked his .44 back behind his belt and started walking swiftly back to the hotel. He took the stairs two at a time and rushed into their door-shattered room. He held Kate for a moment while she told him what had happened and he told her his story, and then she pushed away.

"See to the kids," Kate said. "I fear for them."

Jamie buckled his guns around him and went running down the steps, meeting Sparks on the way up. "Stay with Kate!" he shouted, and then was gone into the cool night.

Preacher fell in with him and it was a foot race to the music hall, with Jamie telling the mountain man what had taken place as they ran.

The back door man knew Jamie and asked no questions, just threw open the door to allow them entrance. "It's a rough crowd this night, Mr. MacCallister," he called. "They're mighty raucous and crude, they are."

Lobo and Audie had ridden up, and Preacher told them what had happened.

"Someone is out to get the entire MacCallister clan," Audie said, just as a scream cut the oil-smoke air of backstage. The scream was abruptly cut off.

Jamie ran to the dressing rooms in time to see two men dragging what appeared to be an unconscious Rosanna out of the room. Jamie did not want to risk a shot in the hall for fear of missing and hitting an innocent, so he waded in, big fists swinging.

He downed one man with a blow that broke the thug's jaw and then smashed both fists into the face of the second man. He could suddenly smell smoke.

"Fire!" he shouted and picked up Rosanna just as his son appeared in the hall, dressed for the evening's performance. "Andrew, get the troupe clear of the hall, boy!" He handed Rosanna to Lobo and the big mountain man raced outside with her.

One end of the backstage burst into flames, quickly engulfing the new sap-rich lumber.

"Everything's gone wrong!" a man shouted. "Jamie's here. Run for it, boys!"

The man appeared, still shouting for his cohorts to flee, and he was a huge bull of a man, running up the narrow hall, knocking men and women alike out of the way. When he reached Jamie he tried to knock Jamie out of the way. Bad mistake. Jamie grabbed him by one muscular arm and propelled him out onto the stage. He ran the cursing man up to and then through the closed curtains. The man landed on his belly in the orchestra pit and did not move.

One entire end of the music hall was now a wall of flames, quickly consuming everything it touched.

"Everybody's out back here, Jamie!" Preacher called. "Let's get clear of this!"

Fires were not uncommon in San Francisco, and they were often set by paid arsonists. In one sixteen-month period, between late 1848 and early 1851, the city was nearly destroyed a half dozen times. But it was always rebuilt, bigger and grander and sometimes gaudier than before.

Jamie checked on Rosanna, and she was his daughter all right. She was sitting up cussing like a sailor.

"All our costumes!" Liza wailed.

"Can be replaced," Jamie said. "Get on back to the hotel, your lives are in great danger."

Jamie and Kate were moved to another room while the door to their original room was being replaced. "Who?" Kate asked when they were once more alone.

"Somebody with money enough to hire twelve or fifteen thugs to do their dirty work," Jamie said.

"Evans?"

Jamie shrugged his shoulders. "That would be my guess. But since we received word that Evans had left New York City and Laurin was run out of St. Louis, I inquired here in the city about them. If they're here, they've changed their names. And that's not unusual. Lots of men do that." He smiled at his wife. "How did that .44 handle, Kate?"

"Kicked like a mule. And the butt is too big for my hand. But I got the job done."

"I would certainly say so," Jamie said drily.

Cort never slept with his wife again nor would he allow himself to grow close to his daughter, whom Anne named Page. He never once held the baby. Cort rented an apartment in the city and was spending more and more time there.

"He knows, Selma," Anne said to the colored woman.

"I don't know how he found out, Miss Anne. But I think you right. He shore actin' mighty strange since the baby been birthed. And he takin' a strong interest in the opera house in the city, too."

Anne perked up at that. "Oh?"

"Talk is he got to be big friends with your brother." Selma rolled her eyes and grinned.

"You have *got* to be joking!"

"No'um, I ain't. Sometimes they be with ladies, sometimes by themselves."

"How do you know all this, Selma?"

She shrugged. "You done been passin' so long you forgot how it is to be a slave. Maybe you never knowed. We cain't afford to miss nothin', Miss Anne. We got to stay keen of ever'thing all the time. Mister Cort, he ain't the only fine gentleman to, umm, turn to his own kind, if you know what I mean."

"Only too well," Anne said acidly.

"We got 'em amongst us, too, Miss Anne." She straightened up from arranging the flowers in the sitting room. "What puzzles me is, what 'xactly do they *do?*"

Workmen were clearing away the hot rubble of the music hall before the timbers even stopped smoking, but the fire had dampened the spirits of the troupe and they decided to leave San Francisco and return to New York City—by ship. Jamie and Kate elected to stay in the city until they found out who was behind the attempts on their lives. They saw their kids and the rest of the troupe off and then returned to the hotel, checked out, and moved to a rented home in the hills above the city by the bay. Sparks, Audie, Lobo, and Preacher stayed close by. The mountain men had a hunch that when Jamie did find out who was responsible, all hell was going to break loose, and they wanted a piece of it. Several dozen people had died in the fire at the music hall, but that was not uncommon and not much was made of the deaths. People were just too busy making enormous sums of money and spending it as fast as they could dig or pan the nuggets or dust, get it into town and assayed and weighed, and get paid.

Jamie had been approached to become an officer of the law in the city, a position he quickly turned down. The job would later be handed to a man named Isaiah Lee, who would be instrumental in bringing some sort of order to the raucous city. But before law and order was more or less brought into play, public lynchings by citizens groups were a common sight, and they weren't too particular where they strung up the victims.

Jamie knew something about gold, and after carefully checking out the location, he ended up grubstaking more than a dozen men in return for a portion of their mines. Jamie would leave the city a moderately wealthy man. Kate, meanwhile, at Jamie's suggestion, was making friends with a few of the ladies in the city, who were married to gentry, going shopping with them and attending teas and so forth, always under the watchful eyes of her mountain men bodyguards.

Audie would occasionally give Shakespearean recitals at various halls, usually to a bunch of drunks who didn't have the foggiest idea what in the hell the little man was talking about but were willing to pay to hear him anyway because everybody said they ought to.

Audie was amused by it all.

Maurice Evans and lawyer Laurin kept a very low profile after the abortive attempts on the lives of the Mac-Callister family. But Evans's hate was so great and so blindly unreasonable, all that was about to change.

Before gold was discovered, the population of San Francisco was estimated at slightly less than five hundred souls. Within a year that had mushroomed to more than twenty thousand; a year later, it was twice that, and three times that number had stepped off ships before heading into the hills and engaging in their frantic search for gold.

Jamie got into real estate and bought up a number of lots, then turned right around and sold them for as much as ten times what he had initially paid for them. It was a game for Jamie, since he didn't really need the money and had no intention of spending too many more months in the city by the bay.

He and Kate decided to stay the winter and return by the northern route come the spring.

But Kate wasn't fooled. She knew Jamie was staying solely because he wanted to find out who hated them enough to want them dead.

Meanwhile, the mountain men had been doing a bit of snooping around on their own, frequenting the rougher bars and standing shoulder to shoulder with thugs and foot-padders and brigands, talking and listening. Finally, their vigilance paid off and hit the mother lode.

"Evans is in the city," Sparks told Jamie one afternoon. "He's goin' by the name of Charles Russent. And Laurin is here, too, goin' by the name of Robert Brown. Their offices is in the same buildin'." Sparks took a big swig of fresh coffee Kate had poured him and sighed. "Good. Best coffee in the city."

Jamie waited, figuring that Sparks had more.

"They pretty much stay out of sight 'ceptin' for business, but I heard a thug name of Phil Packer is in their employ. And from what I hear, there ain't no sorrier no-good rascal west of the Mississippi than Phil Packer. He's got him a gang of thugs that'll do anything for money. And Preacher heard it was his boys that busted in on Kate and set the music hall on fire. But no proof that'll stand up in court, even if there was a decent court of law in this city."

Jamie started to say something, and Sparks held up his hand. "They's more. Ain't nobody seen hide nor hair of Phil Packer since the night of the fire, nor none of his boys."

Jamie drummed his blunt fingers on the table for a moment. "Add that all up, and you might get the idea that Packer and his men were responsible for the attacks and for the fire, and are hiding out until everything cools down, so to speak."

"Well now, that very thought did cross my mind," Sparks replied with a smile.

Jamie pulled out a small sack of gold dust and clunked it on the table. "You reckon that much dust would loosen someone's tongue, Sparks?"

Sparks laughed and then held up a big, balled fist. "If it don't, this will!"

Four

Ian had been pondering an idea that he thought his pa would approve of. Since the valley had long been homesteaded and his pa had written word from the government that the land would belong to those who laid claim to it, Ian began marking out sections in the adjacent valley and having those kids old enough to file on it do so. As soon as they did, he promptly bought it. Trappers and mountain men who knew Ian rode through, thought it was a good idea, filed, and then sold to Ian, since none of them had any inclination whatsoever to homestead. Before the fall was over, Ian owned the entire valley that lay east of MacCallister's Valley. He tore down the old cabins and barns and sheds that had been built a few years back—and not built all that well, either. Caroline worked right beside him with the baby close by.

There were more settlers coming in and passing through and many were unwilling to give the Indians a chance to be friendly, adopting a shoot-first-and-ask-questions-later attitude toward any Indian. Black Thunder decided to move most of his band and headed north. "Too many whites," he said sadly. "Too much trouble coming. You tell Bear Killer that my heart is heavy because I do not get to say farewell to my friend."

With the leaving of Black Thunder and most of his people, the valley seemed a little bit less lovely, for Black Thunder had been a good friend to the settlers for over a decade.

During the absence of Jamie and Kate, the late summer of '48 and the spring and early summer of '49 brought several wagon trains near the twin valleys now claimed by the MacCallister clan. Most of the movers took one look at the lushness and wanted to stay, but like his father, Ian was very selective, selling or granting permission to stay to only a very few of the pioneers. Ian had unknowingly set up the first zoning restrictions west of the Mississippi River.

One mover became so irate over Ian's refusal to sell (and all the choice spots had been claimed by Ian) he made the mistake of cursing Ian and then grabbing for a gun. The tiny cemetery on the east side of MacCallister's Valley grew by one.

Another mover saw Moses and his family and kin and wanted to know how come it was that a bunch of goddamn niggers could live there and a decent white man (like himself, presumably) could not. He was shown the way west and wisely took the not-so-subtle hint. MacCallister's Valleys, as the area was now known, became the first spot west of the Mississippi where racial tolerance was practiced. Color or creed meant nothing to the longtime settlers there, only what was in a person's heart. And the settlements grew by a few more families and one more store during the absence of Jamie and Kate. When the population in the valleys hit a hundred and fifty, Ian was approached by Swede, Sam, Moses, and some of the others and asked to become their sheriff.

Ian was amused. "I think not, gentlemen. Talk to my father when he returns."

In California, the mild winter was over and spring was soft in the air. All that past winter Evans and Laurin tried unsuccessfully to locate Phil Packer and his gang, but they were never located. Jamie and the mountain men struck the camp of the outlaws at dawn one fall morning and wiped them out to the last man. They were back in the city two days later with no one the wiser.

Using his wealth to buy information, Jamie had built a solid case against Maurice Evans, known as Charles Russent, and Laurin, known as Robert Brown. But what law there was in the city was so corrupt, and the two men so rich and powerful, they were untouchable by any legal methods.

"Keep an eye on Kate," Jamie said to Sparks and Preacher early one spring evening. "I'm going for my walk."

Neither man thought anything about it, for Jamie always took a stroll that time of day. Nor did they think anything about Jamie tucking a Colt .44 behind his belt. Nearly everyone in the city carried a gun.

Jamie walked straight to Pierre's Restaurant, where he had learned that Maurice Evans ate his dinner every Friday evening.

It was known throughout the city that there was a blood feud between Jamie and an eastern businessman called Maurice Evans. It was not known that Charles Russent was Maurice Evans. The manager of the small and very expensive restaurant was delighted to see Mr. Jamie Ian MacCallister walk in. He rushed up to greet him, smiling.

"Stand clear," Jamie told him.

The manager hit the kitchen at a fast walk and didn't look back.

"Maurice Evans!" Jamie called in a loud clear voice. "Stand up and face me, you son of a bitch!"

The cafe fell silent. Not one click of knife or fork against plate could be heard. Everybody knew who Jamie Ian MacCallister was.

"Now see here!" one of the so-called policemen in the city said, standing up from the table where he was dining with Maurice Evans.

"Shut up and back away from that table or drag iron," Jamie told the man.

The man quickly stepped away from the table. He thought he might be able to sneak a shot at Jamie if the opportunity presented itself.

"There is no one here by the name of Maurice Evans," a nicely dressed man said. "It is my understanding that Evans fled New York City for Europe."

"Wrong," Jamie said. "Maurice Evans sits yonder. Evans, you've sent men to kill my son, my wife, my family, my friends, and me. They've all failed. Now it's over. Your son, Blake Evans, called my son out. I've spent hard money learning the truth, and I've found that you did, too. Still you sent man-hunters out to kill me and mine, knowing that your son caused the trouble and forced the issue. You are directly responsible for the rape and death of a little girl. You're directly responsible for the deaths of good men and women. You're wearing a gun, Evans. You wear one tucked down in a holster on your left side. Stand up and face me and let's finish this once and for all."

"You ignorant savage!" Evans said, throwing his knife and fork onto the plate. "I've killed a dozen men in duels."

"You won't kill this one," Jamie told him.

"My son was good decent boy!" Evans shouted, his face mottled with rage.

"Your son was a bully, a murderer, and a rapist. You bought him out of trouble until society finally said enough. The sad thing is you know all that I say is true. You're a liar and a cheat. You built your empire by bilking good, decent people out of their money. You're nothing more than a blood-sucking leech. Now, stand up, Evans, or I'll kill you where you sit."

Evans smiled and stood up. "You're a damn fool, Mac-Callister!" he said.

Both he and the crooked cop reached for their pistols at the same time. Witnesses said that the nicely dressed big man's draw was so fast it was a blur. The Colt .44 leaped into Jamie's hand, roared twice and two men were down and dying.

Jamie tucked the .44 back behind his belt and walked out of the cafe. He headed straight for lawyer Laurin's home, located just outside the city.

Jamie kicked in the front door and nearly scared the piss out of Laurin. Crossing the room in great strides, Jamie grabbed the lawyer by the shirt collar and flung him against a wall.

"I'm not armed!" the man screamed. "I never carry a gun."

"You're finished," Jamie told him. "You will leave this city and disappear from public life forever. I don't care how you make your living; you can farm, trap, scout, run a store, do whatever you like, as long as it is not the practice of law. The reading of the law should be in the hands of honorable men. You are not an honorable man."

"Maurice will have you killed for this!" Laurin shouted.

"Maurice Evans is dead. I just killed him."

Laurin stood up, a man of better than average size, with good arms and shoulders on him. "You lie!"

"I never lie."

Laurin lifted his hands and balled them into fists. "I know something about fighting, MacCallister."

"Good. I was afraid this might be easy."

"I'll have you arrested and sent to prison for this, you damned backwoods savage!" Laurin screamed.

Jamie advanced toward him. "You don't have to worry about anyone recognizing you when you start your new profession, Laurin, because I'm going to see to it that your own mother won't be able to tell who you are. Commencing right now."

Jamie stepped in, brushed off a quick punch by Laurin, and hit the man flush on the mouth. Blood splattered and teeth flew and the lawyer bounced off a wall, sending books and vases and bric-a-brac tumbling and crashing to the floor.

Across town, in the home in the hills, Kate said to Preacher, "Jamie is taking a bit longer than usual with his walk."

"Yes'um," Preacher said. "I 'spect he found someone who needed a grubstake."

"I'm sure that's it," Kate said and returned to her reading.

Laurin got to his feet and tried to run. Jamie grabbed him by the seat of his tailored britches and spun him around and around in the living room. When he turned loose of the man, the lawyer sailed through a front window and went crashing into the street, rolling ass over elbows in the mud.

"When do you suppose Pa will come home?" Caroline asked of Ian.

Ian looked up from the catalog he'd been reading. The catalog had been brought to him by a trapper who'd gone back east for a visit. It was the most amazing thing Ian had ever seen. Even had ladies' bloomers in it. He had it hidden behind a week-old newspaper. If Caroline saw it, she'd snatch it away from him and toss it in the fire. That is, as soon as she got done looking at it. "Oh, I 'spect they'll be back this summer. Soon as Ma gets her fill of shoppin'."

"You reckon Pa is having a good time?"

Ian smiled. "I bet you that Pa is havin' the time of his life out yonder."

Lawyer Laurin got up from his belly-down position in the mud, stood swaying for a moment, and Jamie knocked him down again. Laurin cussed and got up and kissed the mud again. He ran his tongue over where his front teeth used to be. MacCallister's fist had broken them off at the gum and knocked them clean out of his mouth.

"You sorry son of bitch!" Laurin cussed, struggling to get to his feet.

Jamie's huge right fist exploded against his jaw and the world inside Laurin's head lit up like a skyrocket as his feet flew out from under him. The lawyer landed on his butt in the mud.

Jamie reached down and hauled the man to his feet. He held him there with his left hand and began pounding the man's face with his right fist. Each blow sounded like a watermelon being hit with the flat side of an axe. Jamie was so mad he gave no thought that the man might well be long past feeling anything. That is, until he woke up.

After a few minutes, Jamie cooled down and realized the man was unconscious. He slowly unclenched his fist, let his right hand drop to his side, and looked at the bloody mask that had once been a human face. It was unrecognizable. The nose was flat, the lips pulped, one ear was hanging by a thin bit of skin, both eyes were swollen shut, and the man's jaw was obviously broken, pushed over to one side.

Jamie dragged him over to the side of the wide street and let him drop to the mud, on his back. He didn't want a wagon to run over the man; he wanted lawyer Laurin to live a long, long time. Lawyer Laurin flopped unconscious in the mud and did not move and probably wouldn't move for an hour or so.

"Nighty, night," Jamie said to the man, then turned and walked across the narrow road to the man's house. Laurin's office safe was open and Jamie went through it, finding stack after stack of stocks and certificates and bank notes. Laurin was a rich man, but he wasn't going to be for long. Jamie piled everything in the safe on the floor and tossed a lighted lamp onto the pile. Within seconds, the room was blazing.

Jamie waited until he was certain the house would soon be nothing but smoking rubble, and then he went out the back way, circling the road until the blazing house was far behind him.

He stopped at a horse trough and bathed his hands and face and brushed the drying mud from his clothes. He used an old cloth he found to wipe his boots clean. He smoothed his hair and replaced his hat, then stepped into a bar to have a cold beer. Just as he stepped in through the bat wings, the clanging of the fire bells on the pumpers reached him. Seconds later, the horse-drawn pumpers and ladder wagon raced by, heading up the hill, shouting kids and barking dogs close behind.

"This goddamn city catches on fire nearly ever'time I look up," the barkeep said, shaking his head and wiping the bar. "What'll you have, mister?"

Jamie ordered a beer and stood by the bar, chatting

agreeably with the bartender and the fellows left and right of him. He introduced himself and bought a round so all would remember him and recall that he had been in the bar at the time of the fire and not in the least disheveled or out of breath or muddy. No way did Jamie Ian MacCallister look like he had been in a fight. The law being what it was in the city, Jamie didn't think he would need any type of alibi, but when dealing with a shyster lawyer, one just never knew.

Jamie drank two beers, told a few jokes, and then excused himself, stepping out into the night. He walked back to the hotel, whistling a little tune and doffing his hat to the ladies and speaking to the men he passed.

The fireball that had been lawyer Laurin's house was no longer even a glow in the night behind him.

He and Kate would start back to the valley tomorrow. She had said she wanted to go home, and Jamie couldn't think of a better time to do just that.

For more reasons than one.

Five

The mountain men were hesitant to let Jamie and Kate travel back to the valley by themselves. But Kate merely laughed that off. "I know you boys want to head back east," she told the men. "Jamie and I will be just fine. Just ask Preacher about the time two fourteen-year-old kids crossed from the Kentucky wilderness to the Big Thicket country."

Preacher smiled. "They done that for a fact. How you headin' back, Jamie?"

"We're going up into Canada and ride east for time, then cut south in time to be home by late summer or early fall. I want Kate to see that country."

"You watch them Blackfeet," Lobo warned. "Them ain't the friendliest Injuns on the face of this earth."

"I've encountered them before," Jamie said.

Jamie and Kate rode out of San Francisco the afternoon following the killing of Maurice Evans and the beating of lawyer Laurin. MacDuff had ridden off to the east some weeks before without saying a word.

Horse had terrorized anyone who tried to come near him during the stay in the city and had broken down half a dozen stalls. The liveryman was delighted to see him go.

Preacher and the others were taking Kate's mare back to the valley, and for this long and rugged trip, where endurance and speed might be necessary to save their lives, Jamie had bought her a fine, rugged gelding named Star, who right from the first moment wouldn't take any crap from Horse. After circling each other and exchanging a few bites and kicks, they decided they'd best be friends, at least for this trip.

Jamie had scoured the city and found four Colt Baby Dragoons for Kate. They were .36 caliber, four-inch barrels, and held a five-shot cylinder. Jamie had a man cut down the handles to better fit Kate's hand and a leather worker make them matching holsters. They both carried rifles and both had a revolving shotgun in the boot. They might be set upon by hostiles or outlaws—the probability was high—but those who tried it would pay dearly for their efforts.

Jamie had given a goodly amount of cash to Sparks to take back to the settlement, and the rest was carefully banked or invested by reputable people. For the time, Jamie was a rich man.

All of Kate's shopping, some for herself but most for family and friends, would go to the valley by commissioned wagon train. Jamie had told her to spare no expense, and she hadn't.

Jamie and Kate had an uneventful ride up through northern California and into Oregon. Sometimes they followed established trails, many times they left the trails and blazed their own. This was a real vacation for Kate, the first time she had been away from the kids in twenty-five years.

The Indians they met riding through Oregon and then Washington were friendly and curious about the pair, many times inviting them to their villages to share their food. Settlers had been coming into this arca since the late 1830s, so these Indians were accustomed to the strange ways of the whites and unlike the Indians of the plains, they had seen golden-haired women before. What they had not seen was golden-haired women who could handle a gun the way Kate could. They were impressed and warned Jamie and Kate that there were bad white men up ahead of them, men who robbed and raped and killed for no good reason.

"Do they have names?" Jamie asked.

"Oh, yes," the chief of one tribe said. "We have heard the names of Jack Biggers and John Wilmot. They are very bad men."

"Jack Biggers," Jamie said, when he and Kate were once more on their way. "I had almost forgotten all about him. I dismissed him as being dead years ago."

"That's the one who tried to ride Horse?" Kate asked.

"Tried is right." Jamie patted Horse on the neck. "Ol' Horse here almost killed him. I'm going to put this fellow out to pasture when we get back. He's getting old. He's still got a lot of trails he could ride, but he's earned a rest."

They were in north-central Washington, following an old Indian trail when both Horse and Star became tense, their ears pricked. They kept swinging their heads to look behind them. Jamie quickly left the trail and headed into the timber and brush. He and Kate dismounted, rifles in hand, ground-reined the horses, and slipped through the timber until the trail was in sight. Jamie bellied down and put his ear to the hard ground. He looked up at Kate and held up two fingers, then motioned for her to stay put.

He slipped up to within a few feet of the trail and waited. Soon he could plainly hear the sounds of the horses' hooves coming up the old trail. Then he could hear the men talking.

"I still think we better ride on up ahead and fetch Jack and Wilmot," one said. "If this is MacCallister and his woman, my guts get all tight just thinkin' 'bout the two of us tryin' to take him alone."

"All that talk 'bout how tough MacCallister is ain't nothin' but shit," the second man said. "Jack Biggers whupped him, didn't he?"

"Jack says he did."

"You callin' Jack a liar?"

"I didn't say that. But if he whupped him, why didn't he go on and kill him and take his head for all that reward money that was on him at the time?"

The two men reined up, studying the trail.

"I don't know, Axel. Do seem queer, don't it?"

"Yeah. The damn trail just quit, Clyde. What do you make of that?"

Before Clyde could reply, Jamie flung one of the stones he'd picked up and hit Clyde's horse solidly on the butt. The sharp stone scared the animal and he started buck-jumping on the narrow trail. Jamie flung another stone and the animal really went wild. Clyde was holding on and hollering as the horse started chasing its tail, going round and round on the trail.

Jamie left the brush, grabbed the other man and jerked him off his horse, slamming him on the ground so hard the wind was knocked out of him. Clyde was facing the other way and saw none of it. Jamie dragged the man into the lush timber and quickly trussed him up with lengths of rawhide he always carried on his belt. Kate crept forward and placed the muzzle of her .36 caliber Baby Dragoon against the man's head. He looked up at her through frightened eyes and nodded his head, indicating that he understood perfectly that he was to remain still and quiet.

Clyde finally got his horse calmed down and jumped out of the saddle, holding the reins. He looked around him, a rather confused expression on his face. He could see Axel's horse, but where the hell was Axel?

"Axel? Where you is, boy? You answer me, Axel. This ain't no time for games."

Kate pressed the muzzle harder against Axel's head and the man peed his pants. Kate sniffed and glanced down at him, a disgusted expression in her eyes. Axel blushed under the dirt on his unshaven face.

"Damn it, Axel!" Clyde shouted. "You bes' talk to me, boy. You hear me?"

Jamie stepped out silently and tapped Clyde on the shoulder. When he spun around, his mouth open and his eyes wide with fright, Jamie popped him with a big fist. Clyde's eyes rolled back into his head as he hit the ground hard. He did not move. When Clyde awakened, he was lying on the ground beside Axel, both men trussed up tight.

"Oh, shit!" Clyde whispered. "MacCallister! Axel, we be in big trouble."

"You got that right, Clyde," Jamie told him. He slowly pulled out his big Bowie knife and laid the sharp cold steel against Clyde's cheek.

"Oh, LordyLordyLordy!" Clyde said. "Don't kill me, MacCallister. I didn't do you no harm a'tall."

"Me, neither!" Axel whispered.

"You boys are riding with Biggers and Wilmot. Where are they camped?"

"Northeast of here," Clyde quickly replied. "Over on the Chewack. It's the truth, I swear it."

"How come you boys are such a long way from your friends?"

"We been down to the settlement to drink some," Axel said.

"What settlement?"

"'Bout three days' ride from here, over to the south and west. It ain't been there long. Used to be just a tradin' post."

Jamie stared in silence at the men for so long they both got very nervous. "Where on the Chewack?" he finally asked.

"Down to where it runs into that other river. I don't know the name of it," Clyde said.

"Any unfriendly Indians around here?" Jamie asked.

"Not no more," Axel spoke up. "Unless you run into some Blackfeet, and they can be downright quarrelsome."

"How many members in the gang?"

"Oh . . . near 'bout thirty, I reckon. They come and go."

Jamie took Kate aside and said, "We'll set them afoot with ample food and the guns they have with them."

"And the gang?"

"We avoid them. If there were four or five of them, I'd tangle. But twenty or so." He shook his head. "No."

Jamie returned to the men and stared down at them. They were plenty scared and made no effort to hide that fact. "I'm going to let you boys live," he finally said.

"Oh, thank you, Jesus!" Axel said.

"But I'd think twice about returning to the gang. They're going to come to no good end."

Staring down at the men, Jamie sensed his words had not gotten through to Clyde. Axel was too scared to do anything other than bob his head up and down. Jamie shrugged and walked off. Gathering up the reins to their horses, he led them back into the brush and dropped the men's saddlebags and bedrolls to the ground.

"Thank you kindly, Mr. MacCallister," Clyde said, but Jamie could see the meanness in the man's eyes shining plain. "You're a real gentleman, you are. Is you goin' to loosen these bonds just a mite, kind sir?"

Jamie looked down at the man and decided he might as well get it over with here and now. Clyde wanted to kill him so bad the odor of it very nearly fouled the cool air. Jamie reached down and cut the man's bonds, then stepped back and kicked his saddlebags to him, figuring the man had a couple of guns in the saddlebags. Jamie took a couple of more steps back.

"There is no money on my head anymore, Clyde. Not a penny that I am aware of. And if you're looking to make a reputation, my advice would be to forget it."

Clyde rubbed his wrists and grinned. "Man who kilt Jamie MacCallister could name his own price."

"If that's the kind of business you want to be in, I suppose so," Jamie said softly.

"What kind of a break is you gonna give me, MacCallister?" Clyde asked.

"Clyde!" Axel called. "Don't be a damn fool, man. He's give us our lives, let's take it and get clear of this whole damn dirty business."

"Shut up," Clyde said, slowly crawling to his knees and reaching for the saddlebags. "I axe you, MacCallister. What kind of break is you offerin' me?"

"None," Jamie replied honestly. "When you reach into those saddlebags, you're dead."

"Now that ain't sportin' of you."

"I never said I was a sport."

"Clyde!" Axel yelled. "Don't do it, man."

"I knowed all along you was yeller, Axel," Clyde said. "Shut up your trap. There ain't no way he can haul them big heavy pistols out of them holsters afore I can jerk and fire. He's a fool, he is."

"You be the fool, Clyde," Axel said.

"You been runnin' your trap for months 'bout wantin' to go back to Maryland and farm the old homestead, Axel. When I see MacCallister dead on the ground, I'll cut you loose and you can get gone to the farm. Me, I'll take me a taste of that there woman of his'n."

Kate laughed at him. "Not you or ten like you," she told him.

Clyde reached into his jacket pocket and came out with a pocket knife. He cut Axel's bonds. "You got a hide-out gun they didn't see, Axel. When I kill MacCallister, you knock a leg out from under the bitch. I'll pleasure myself whilst she's bleedin' to death."

"I ain't a-gonna do it, Clyde. And that's that."

"Then we ain't pards no more, Axel."

"Good," Axel said from his position on the ground.

Jamie's hands were by his side, and he appeared to be totally relaxed as he waited for Clyde to make his move.

Clyde slid the leather straps out of their buckles and slowly opened the flap to one of the saddlebags. "I reckon your woman is gonna shoot me after I shoot you, huh, MacCallister?"

"What do you think?" Jamie asked him, sensing that Clyde was having a lot of second thoughts.

"Well, hell! This ain't a bit fair."

"What it is," Axel said, "is stupid."

"I agree," Kate said.

"This is getting ridiculous," Jamie said, and quickly

stepped forward. He popped Clyde on the side of the jaw and the man dropped like a stone.

"I hate to say this," Axel said. "But you should have shot him, Mr. MacCallister. "He's gonna come after you for doin' this."

"Then he's a fool."

"I can't argue that."

Jamie cut Axel loose and pointed to the man's horse. "You want to go back to your farm in Maryland?"

"More'n anything else in this world."

"Then ride."

Axel was gone in under a minute, heading south.

"Jamie?" Kate said.

"I have an idea."

"What is it?"

"Let's go home."

The wagon train from San Francisco with all the presents arrived in the valley just a few days before Jamie and Kate rode in. The crates and boxes were stacked unopened in a barn, awaiting the arrival of Jamie and Kate. The four mountain men had ridden in with the money Jamie had sent to Ian along with Kate's mare and told the settlers that Jamie and Kate would be along sometime in late summer or early fall.

The man and wife topped the ridge trail overlooking the western valley late one summer afternoon and stopped.

"Prettiest valley in all the world," Jamie said.

"I don't care to leave again, Jamie," Kate said softly. "I had a grand time in the city, but this is my home. I've seen the sights now, and those wonderful memories will last me for the rest of my life. It was a grand adventure going to San Francisco." She pointed to the valley below, her eyes on their cabin. The largest one in the valley. With most of the kids gone, she and Jamie rattled around in the large home like peas in a pod. "That's where I want to stay. Right down there with family and friends and familiar things."

"Then we'll stay here together," Jamie said.

Kate laughed at the words and cut her blues to Jamie. "Don't you be making promises to me that you won't be able to keep, Jamie Ian MacCallister. You're a wanderer, husband of mine; you always will be, and I love you for that. You'll stay for a time, then the wild trails will start singing their soft songs to you, and you'll saddle up and go. I saw that in you when we were just children."

"Then why did you marry me?"

She looked at him with a woman's patience and said, "Because I love you, you ninny!"

"Oh," Jamie said. "Well, I love you too, Kate."

She laughed at the expression on his face and lifted the reins. "Let's go see how the kids and grandkids have grown. My goodness, it feels like we've been gone for years. I want to sleep in our own warm feather bed this night."

"Just sleep?" Jamie asked with a smile.

"You have anything else in mind?"

"I could probably think of something."

"My goodness!" Kate said with mock seriousness. "I just can't imagine what it might be!"

Six

Spring 1851

The westward movement was on and there was no stopping the pioneers. The tide of humanity surged forward, toward new lands, new hopes, new opportunities, new beginnings. They came in wagons, on horseback, and on foot. Men, women, and children. Thousands of them, like lemmings to the sea and ants on a march, invading, overrunning, seizing, slaughtering, and fouling what the Indians had called theirs for centuries. Many killed game for sport, something the Indian did not and never would understand. The Indian was one with Mother Earth; the white man scorned that and ruined whatever he touched. The white man put up wooden houses that could not be moved and built fences around land and called it his. The Indian could understand that, sort of. Many whites tried to make friends and live in peace with the Indians, many more did not.

With thousands of people on the move west, leaving wagon wheel ruts in the earth that would last for hundreds of years, game began to disappear along the Oregon Trail and many Indian tribes met in council and decided to fight. That decision was to mark the inevitable end of the Indian way of life. The Indian simply could not change a way of life that had been practiced for only God knew how many hundreds of years, and the white man demanded that he must change. The irresistible force met the immoveable object.

In late 1849 and during 1850, the nation changed rapidly, with much of that change taking place west of the Mississippi River. The army bought the fur trading post of Fort Laramie and turned it into a military post. Mormon Station was settled in Nevada. It was the first white settlement in the state. A stagecoach line was formed to carry mail between Missouri and Santa Fe, New Mexico. Mail service was established between Missouri and Utah. Millard Fillmore became the thirteenth president of the United States. Gold was discovered in Oregon. California was admitted as the thirty-first state of the Union. Portland, Oregon, now had a newspaper, the *Weekly Oregonian. The Deseret News* began publication in Utah, that state's first newspaper, and the University of Deseret opened in Salt Lake City.

In the late spring of '51, a treaty was signed called the Traverse des Sioux, calling for the Dakotas—better known as the Sioux—to give up their land in Iowa and most of Minnesota.

But in MacCallister's Valleys, crops were planted and babies were born and life was good.

All that was about to change.

Kate had been wrong about Jamie and his urge to wander, but being a tactful person, her husband didn't mention it. Jamie and Kate were both forty-one years old—although neither of them looked it—and as for Jamie, he was content to farm the land, raise horses and cattle, trap and hunt, and be with Kate.

Jamie Ian and Ellen Kathleen were both twenty-four and each had a houseful of kids.

Andrew and Rosanna now made their homes in New York when they weren't touring in Europe.

Of the triplets, Matthew and Megan had married and were busy with families of their own. Morgan had become a scout for the army and was building a reputation as a damn bad man to mess with. He was fast as lightning with a six-gun and not a bit slow to use it. He was, also, like all the boys except for Andrew, approximately the same size and temperament as his father, and looked enough like him to be his brother.

Joleen was seventeen and looked exactly like her mother, and the boys from both valleys were buzzing around her like bees to honey.

"Goddamn it!" Jamie said, after hauling his youngest daughter and a neighbor boy out of the hay loft, both of them panting and red-faced. Kate, holding onto Joleen's right ear with all the strength of an angry badger, marched her into the house and sat her down for a mother-to-daughter talk about the birds and the bees.

"Pat," Jamie said to the boy. "I've about had all of this gropin' and pawin' I'm gonna tolerate."

"Mr. Jamie," the boy stood his ground. "I've been court-in' Joleen proper for two years now. I got me a piece of ground and I've proved it up. I'll have me a good crop and I got some cows and pigs. I been buildin' a right nice cabin, and—"

"Will you get to the goddamn point!" Jamie roared, rattling the rafters of the still-steamed-up barn.

"I want to marry Joleen!" the frightened young man stammered.

"Well, Jesus Christ, Pat! Why didn't you say so? You want my permission to marry her? Hell, yes. Please do!"

Falcon MacCallister was twelve and looked and acted several years older. When he was twelve, he said he wasn't goin' to go to school no more and that was that. If his pa and ma didn't like it, then they could just take turns whuppin' him all they liked—wasn't goin' to change nothin'.

"Go to your room!" Kate told him. "And you get no supper this night."

"I don't care," Falcon said. "I got enough jerky and pemmican up there to last for months. I'll see you both next year." He walked up the stairs, his moccasins barely whispering on the wood, and closed the door.

Kate was so mad she could spit. She sputtered for a moment while Jamie braced himself for what he knew was coming out of her mouth, and hoping he could contain his amusement. Kate stamped her little foot and said, *"Shit!"*

Then she got madder still when she looked at Jamie and he was just barely able to control his laughter.

"You think this is *funny?"* she demanded, standing in front of him, hands on hips.

Jamie was choking on suppressed laughter; he could but nod his head.

Kate pointed to the upstairs. "That's *your* son, Jamie Ian MacCallister. *You* made him what he is. You've rough-housed with that boy and taught him how to fight and shoot and quick-draw when you should have been helping him with his studies. Fine! Well, that's just dandy."

"What do we have for supper?" Jamie asked, wiping his eyes on a bandanna.

A very dangerous look came into Kate's eyes. Jamie recognized it and stood up, moving toward the front door as Kate walked swiftly into the kitchen and picked up a pie, returning to the large family room.

"Well, Jamie Ian MacCallister!" she shouted. "I fixed this jist pie* for dessert. But I think you can have it right now!"

Jamie almost made it but not quite. The jist pie caught him on the back of the head and neck just as he was pickin' 'em up an puttin' 'em down leaving the room. Kate had a pretty good throwing arm on her, too. The pie splattered and the pie pan bonged off his head and fell with a clatter to the porch floor. Jamie reached around and got a mess of pie on his fingers and ate it.

"Good pie, too," he said, heading for the small saloon until Kate cooled down.

Jamie came back home after an hour, cautiously opening the door. Kate was sitting in her rocker, a shawl over her

---

*"Jist pie" was called that for years. It is better known now as "chess pie." Legend has it that in Illinois in the early 1840s, a weary settler came in from working his fields one evening and after supper, asked about dessert. His wife had no apples or peaches or berries in the cabin but she did have plenty of flour, sugar, cream, fresh eggs, and spices.

When she replied that she had pie, her husband asked, "What kind of pie?"

She replied, "Oh, jist pie."

JIST PIE: 3 egg yolks, 2/3 cup sugar, 1 tbsp. flour, 1/2 tsp. salt, 1 1/3 cups whipping cream, 1 tsp. vanilla.

Beat together yolks, sugar, flour, salt. Then fold in whipping cream and vanilla. Bake at 350° until top is golden brown, usually about fifty minutes.

knees, reading by lamplight from Hawthorne's The May-
pole of Merrymount. She pointed to the kitchen. "Your
supper's in there. And I just took another pie out of the
oven."

"What I had of the first one was delicious," he said.

She ducked her head to hide her grin.

While Jamie ate, Kate drank coffee at the table with
him. Finally, she said, "About our son—"

"He'll be out of here and gone in two years, Kate. I see
it in him. He's a wild one. He takes after Grandpa and me."

"But he's just a child, Jamie!"

"So were we when we left Kentucky, Kate. The boy is
tough and he's smart. He reads and figures well. But he's
had enough of it. I've seen this coming for months. You
and Sarah and the others have had him for almost seven
years of schooling. Now it's my turn to teach him what
he *really* needs to know to survive."

"He's going to turn out to be a gun man, Jamie."

"Maybe. Yes, you're probably right. But he will always
be on the side that he believes is right."

"He's too good with a gun, Jamie."

"He's near'bouts as quick as I am, for a fact. Faster
when he uses those Baby Dragoons of yours," he added
with a smile. "Besides, Morgan hasn't done too badly, so
I hear."

Both of them looked up at the sounds of a fast galloping horse.

"At this hour?" Kate asked.

"I'm friendly!" came the shout, after someone in the
village hailed the rider. "Lookin' for the father of Morgan
MacCallister."

"Yonder's his cabin," Dan Noble said.

Jamie flung open the door. "I'm Jamie MacCallister. Morgan is my son."

"I be a friend of Preacher's, Jamie MacCallister. Name is Pete Bristol."

"I've heard Preacher speak of you."

"Morgan's down in New Mexico, Jamie. Little town just south of Taos. So little it ain't even got airy name. But it's run by a rancher name of Barlow—"

"Light and sit," Jamie called from the porch. "Have some food while you tell the rest of it. Is Morgan in trouble?"

"Shootin' trouble, Jamie. He needs help bad."

"Falcon!" Jamie roared, and the door to the boy's bedroom was flung open. "Go get your brother, Ian. Move, boy. Now!"

Jamie and Ian listened to Pete's story while the exhausted man wolfed down two plates of food and a pot of coffee. It was obvious that he had ridden hard to get there.

Matthew had slipped into the room, listening.

When Pete had finished, the man was almost asleep in his chair. Jamie put him in a spare bedroom—they had plenty now that all but one of the kids were gone—and turned to Ian. "Saddle us up two horses apiece, son—"

"And two for me," Matthew said softly.

Jamie turned to look at the young man. Matthew was not a fast gun, but he was steady and puma-mean when angered. Jamie nodded his head. "All right, Matt. Ian, saddle up stock we can trade along the way." He looked at Falcon. "You're the man of this house while I'm gone, boy. You look after your ma and do it right, you hear me?"

"Yes, Pa. You can count on me."

"Boys, have your wives fix some pokes of food. We're riding tonight and we'll sleep in the saddle. Move!"

Kate grabbed hold of one arm. Her blue eyes were flashing fire. "You get my boy out of trouble, Jamie, you understand?"

Jamie smiled. "Yes, ma'am!"

Jamie kissed Kate and held her close for a moment, then gently pushed her away and stepped out onto the porch.

Swede, Sam, Moses, Wells, and the others had gathered outside, all of them armed and ready and willing to go. "You need some help, Jamie?" Sam asked.

Jamie looked at all his friends, good, solid steady men all. He smiled and shook his head. "I'd feel better if you all stayed here and took care of this valley. Pete could have unknowingly been duped into bringing a false alarm." Jamie didn't believe that at all, he just didn't want his friends to get hurt or killed in this mini-war.

"Hadn't thought of that," Swede said. "You're right, Jamie. By golly, you are."

Jamie stepped into the saddle and picked up the lead rope to his spare mount. "Let's ride, boys."

Father and sons rode south into the night. Each carried two Colt revolvers belted around his waist, two more in holsters specially made to fit over the saddle horn, left and right, and two more in the saddlebags. They each carried two full cylinders for each pistol, plus a rifle.

They rode until dawn, changing mounts whenever the ones they were riding began to tire. At dawn, they stopped at a small ranch many miles south of the valley and explained their situation. The rancher yelled for his wife and kids to make coffee and put some food on while he took the tired horses and swapped them for fresh ones from his corral.

The men wolfed down food, swallowed huge gulps of hot, black coffee, and were once more in the saddle.

The rancher had warned them, "Injun trouble south of here, MacCallister. Jicarilla 'Paches are on the prod. Be careful."

Jamie thanked the man and pointed his horse's nose south.

They stopped at noon to once more swap horses and eat and sleep for a couple of hours, then they were on their way.

The hours seemed to melt into one long ride, day or night, it made no difference. The boys learned then why their father was held in such respect and awe. He never seemed to tire. Never complained. Never once did they see the big man slump in the saddle. When they stopped for rest, Jamie stretched out on the ground and was asleep in a dozen heartbeats, awake in two hours and ready to go.

"The man's indestructible," Matt whispered to his brother, during a time they were walking their horses along to save them. "He's twice our age and ridin' us both into the ground."

Ian grinned through the strain on his face. "That's why half the country is scared to death of him," he returned the whisper. "And Falcon's gonna be just like him."

"Falcon?"

"You bet. For a time I thought I'd be the one to step into Pa's boots." He shook his head. "I'm fast enough and mean enough, I reckon, but I'm lackin' something that Pa's got. But Falcon's got it, and it scares ma."

"I just never noticed."

Ian smiled. "Hell, brother, you're still honeymoonin'! You ain't come up for air yet."

Seven

Taos, named San Geronimo de Taos, was settled first in 1621 by a Spanish priest. For well into the middle and late 1870s, the town was wild and free-wheeling. It was that way when Jamie and sons rode in. It was mid-morning. That day and night and part of the of next day would be the stuff of legends. It was also the day that the Bar-B, its owner, his sons, and many of the toughs who rode for the brand would cease to exist.

The three men had camped the night before along the Rio Grande bathed, shaved, and changed into clean clothing.

"You boys sit out here and relax," Jamie said, reining up in front of the marshal's office. "Watch my back. I'm going to have a little chat with the marshal and see if I can find out about Morgan."

Kit Carson had called Taos his home for many years, but even though he married a local woman, he was gone most of the time.

Jamie pushed open the door and stepped in. A man Jamie assumed to be the marshal was at his desk and two of his men were lounging about the office. They looked up at Jamie's entrance and immediately cut their eyes to one another as the MacCallister family resemblance sank in.

"Morgan MacCallister," Jamie said, blunt and right straight to the point. "Where is he?"

"How the hell should I know?" the man behind the desk said. "I'm actin' marshal. Who are you?"

"Jamie MacCallister. Morgan is my son."

"Well, well," the man said, leaning back in his chair. "Another big-shot MacCallister come to town. I'll say this, if you ain't no more than your son, that means you ain't jack-shit, mister. Now get out of my office."

Jamie took two steps, jerked the acting marshal out of his chair, and threw him out the front window. He turned and drew at the same time and blew a hole in one of the two men who was just clearing leather. The man fell back against the potbellied stove, knocking it over, soot flying in all directions, sighed once, and was dead.

"I'm out of this!" the third man screamed, holding his hands wide. "I'm clean out of this."

"My son. Where is he?"

"Back yonder in a cell. He's been hit but the doc says he'll live. I didn't rough him up, MacCallister. The marshal yonder did. Big Ben Barlow railroaded your boy. Morgan was takin' the side of some homesteaders who made the mistake of squattin' on land that Barlow claims is his."

"Is it?"

"No, sir. It's free land."

"Did the marshal rough my son up before or after he was hit?"

The man hesitated, then blurted, "After."

"Pa?" a weak call came from the rear of the jail. "Is that you, Pa?"

"I'm here, boy. Hang on." Jamie didn't just open the front door to the marshal's office, he tore it off the hinges and threw it out into the street. "Ian, Matt, see to your brother." Jamie stepped out onto the boardwalk just as a crowd was gathering across the street and the acting marshal was getting to his feet.

He didn't stay on his feet long.

Jamie walked up to the man and slapped him, knocking the man clean off his boots and into the dust of the street. "You like to rough up wounded men, you bastard. Try roughing me up."

The marshal got to his feet and Jamie then proceeded to stomp him. Three times he knocked the man unconscious and three times Jamie dunked him in a horse trough and brought him back to very painful awareness. Finally, Jamie let the man slump to the street.

During the decidedly one-sided fight, Jamie had seen Morgan being led out of the jail by Ian and Matt and across the street to a doctor's office. If his son was up and walking, he would be all right.

"That's Ben Barlow's man," a citizen said, pointing to the bleeding and unconscious acting marshal.

"Big deal," Jamie said.

"He'll be comin' in here with all his toughs, rippin' and stompin', mister. You got no right to get innocent people hurt."

Jamie then proceeded to tell the citizen what he thought about people who kowtowed to tin-horn tyrants . . . among other things, many of which were extremely profane and would be quite painful to the citizen's rear-end if actually attempted.

The citizen's face turned chalk-white and he went flapping his arms and squawking like a goose back into his store. He slammed the door and hung a "CLOSED" sign in the window.

Jamie slapped the acting marshal awake and threw him on a horse. "You go tell Barlow I'm here. Tell him to come foggin' if that's his intention. This town's graveyard ain't half-filled yet. Now ride, you two-bit bastard!"

Then Jamie went into the doc's office to get the full story from Morgan.

"After Barlow and his men and that actin' marshal shot and roughed me up, they killed that whole family, Pa. Just rode up and shot them down. Killed everything. Horses, cows, dogs—everything that was alive. It was senseless."

"What was Barlow going to do with you, son?"

"Bust me out of jail and hang me. It was all planned. I heard them talkin' about it."

Jamie looked at the doctor. "How bad is he?"

"He'll live. Bullet went clean through the fleshy part of his shoulder and out the back. Another bullet went through the upper part of the back of his thigh without doing much damage. Mister MacCallister, Ben Barlow has anywhere from fifty to seventy-five tough hands out at the Bar-B, and that's not counting his foreman Nick Geer or his top hand Miles Swift. Or his sons Ben, Jr., Royal, Chris, Guy, Hugh, and Andy. Big Ben came in here about twenty-five years ago, married a Mex woman of money and prestige and a lot of political influence. She died shortly after Andy was born. He actually owns about two hundred thousand acres. He claims God only knows how much more. He owns the next town down, that's about twenty miles south of here, and claims everything around it as far as the eye can see in any direction—and that's standing on top of the highest mountain in four counties. Are you going to take on the whole damn bunch of them?"

"Why not?" Jamie replied.

* * *

Jamie and his sons, except for Morgan, went to the general store and bought double-barreled 12-gauge shotguns, then sawed the barrels down to about fifteen inches from the breech. They stuffed their pockets full of shotgun shells and then ordered food sent over to the doctor's office so they could eat and talk to Morgan.

"Ben Barlow's ranch house is halfway between here and that little no-name town where they held me for a time," Morgan said. "So he should be here in about an hour. Ian, you stack mattresses and such over this front window to soak up the lead. Leave me a place to shoot from. That's my revolving shotgun over yonder in the corner. Matt, fetch me my Colts and my rifle. Thank you."

Morgan eased himself into a more comfortable position. "Now, then, I can probably tell you how Big Ben will ride in. He's a man who places a lot of importance on being king of the hill. So he might gather all his hands in a bunch and ride in like some fancy general, showin' off all his strength. Then they'll all go over yonder to the saloon and drink for a time, waitin' to see what you and the boys will do. If you don't do nothin', when they all get their snoots full of Who Hit John, they'll come out shootin' at anything that moves. He *might* do it that way."

"Describe Ben Barlow," Jamie said.

"Big as you are, Pa. Ain't no fat on him, 'ceptin' for his big mouth. He loves to hear himself talk. I 'spect he's in his late forties or early fifties. I was sent in here by the army to do some snoopin' on Ben. The government is just about to move in on him but they can't get around some powerful politician in Washington that Barlow's got in his pocket. Some sleazy bastard name of Olmstead."

"Olmstead!" Jamie almost shouted the word.

"Yeah. What's wrong, Pa?"

"That was your mother's maiden name, boy. Have you forgotten? This Olmstead got a first name?"

"Jubal."

"Damn! That's your ma's brother."

Matt called from the door. "Couple of hardcases driftin' in from the south, Pa."

"I'm going out," Jamie said. "When it starts, you boys be careful. Anything happen to any of you and your ma would skin me."

Jamie stepped outside onto the street and eyeballed the two riders. They were riding Bar-B horses and both men looked capable. Very capable. They dismounted, being careful to dismount with their eyes on Jamie.

Jamie felt the Warrior's Way take possession of him as he wondered whether these were part of the Bar-B group who shot his son and then stood by while the acting marshal and several other members of Barlow's bunch beat him.

Jamie stepped out into the wide street.

The two Bar-B hands stopped their walking into the saloon and turned around.

"You Bar-B trash looking for me?" Jamie called.

Jamie could see the flush on their faces from where he stood.

"Trash?" one of the hands called. "Us?"

"You ride for Ben Barlow and the Bar-B, then that makes you lower than snake shit," Jamie said. "Especially if you had anything to do with the shooting and the beating of my son."

"We ride for the brand, MacCallister," one called. "And your son had no call comin' in here and snoopin' around."

"Every right," Jamie contradicted. "Morgan works for the government, the government sent him in here, and unless you two are as ignorant as you look, most of the land Barlow claims as his belongs to the government." Jamie didn't know who the land belonged to, but he was mad clear through and pushing hard.

"Something pulled Pa's temper-trigger," Morgan said.

"He's damn sure on the prod," Matt said.

"I ain't never seen Pa hook and draw," Ian said. "I think I'm quicker, but Pa never liked to show off, so I don't know."

"Get on your horses and ride out of here," Jamie told the two Bar-B hands. "That's the only warning you're getting from me. Do it if you want to live."

"Falcon says he's quicker than Pa," Ian said. "But I got me a little hunch that Pa's been lettin' him win."

"We'll soon know," Morgan said.

"MacCallister," one of the hands said, "you ain't gonna be nothin' but dog meat in about half a hour. You and them goddamn sons of yourn that rode in here with you, stickin' their damn noses in things that don't concern 'em. But if you don't want to live no longer, just insult me again."

Jamie smiled.

"Pa's smilin'," Matt said.

"Won't be long now," Morgan said.

"Whut the hell you grinnin' at?" the second Bar-B hand shouted.

"Two yellow-bellied rabid coyotes," Jamie said.

Both Bar-B men grabbed for their guns. Jamie's Colts roared and the men went down. Neither one had cleared leather.

"Jesus!" Ian gasped. "I ain't nowheres near Pa's class."

"I didn't even see the draw!" Morgan said.

"I seen a blur," Matt said.

"Shot them both in the center of the chest," Ian said. "Hooked and drawed with both hands and was dead on the mark."

Several men came rushing out of their stores and more men came running out of the saloon. "Leave them where they lay!" Jamie shouted. "I want Big Mouth Barlow to see what he's up against."

The street suddenly cleared.

Jamie stepped out of the sun and under the overhang of a store that had suddenly closed. He reloaded and waited. It was not a long wait. A half dozen riders appeared at the end of the street, took one look at the dead Bar-B hands sprawled in the street, their guns still in leather, and high-tailed it out of town, heading south at a gallop.

"Take your positions, boys," Jamie called. "It's down to the nut-cuttin' now."

Jamie waited until he heard the ground beneath his feet begin to tremble with the pounding of many hooves. He pulled both Colts from leather and waited. The Bar-B men came galloping up the street, shouting and yelling and firing indiscriminately. Jamie and sons opened up from both sides of the street and a dozen saddles were suddenly empty. The street was littered with the dead and the dying and the wounded.

Jamie reloaded, wanting to save his other cylinders until the fighting got red-hot, as he suspected it would very shortly. He watched as a man with a shattered shoulder tried to pull himself out of the street. Jamie walked out and helped the man to his feet, half carrying him out of the street.

"Thank you," the wounded rider said. "You're all right.

I didn't have nothin' to do with the shootin' or the beatin' of your son."

"I believe you. Get fixed up and ride out of here, partner," Jamie told him. "Your boss is finished."

"I'll take your advice and give you some, MacCallister. Barlow's got a damn army ready to throw at you."

"Then the undertakers are going to be very busy for a couple of days, aren't they?"

Another doctor came out and helped the man into a saloon, where he had made ready two tables to use for operations.

"You can help the wounded," Jamie told the town's doctors, who had gathered at the saloon. "Just take their guns away from them."

"How about the dead?" a shallow-faced man dressed all in black said.

"Leave them where they lay."

"Yes, sir, Mr. MacCallister. Whatever you say, sir."

Those Bar-B riders who managed to escape the raid on the south part of the town made their report to an astonished Big Ben Barlow.

"You mean MacCallister is just standin' out on the street and you men can't bring him down?" he demanded.

"Well, he ain't exactly standin' out in the street, boss," one gunhand said.

"Where is he?"

"Standin' in front of the saloon."

"He's still out in the damn open, ain't he?" Barlow yelled.

"Yeah."

"Jesus Christ!" Barlow walked around in circles for a moment, muttering to himself. "Get into town two and three at a time. Don't ride in, *walk* in. Leave your horses at the edge of town. I want two or three of you in the Mustang Saloon, two or three in Sal's Cafe, two or three in the gun shop. Do I have to spell it all out for you?"

Spoiled brats were the same in 1851 as they were in 1651 and would be a hundred years in the future: over-bearing, insufferable, pampered, petted, let's-do-whatever-we-want-to-do-to-anybody-'cause-daddy-will-get-us-out-of-any-trouble loudmouth punks. And Big Ben's brats fit the mold to a T.

Royal puffed out his chest and said, "This MacCallister bunch ain't nothin' but ignorant white trash, Daddy. Let me and the rest of the boys go in and take them."

Big Ben looked at the six bright candles in his life. Such good boys. All of them smart as a whip, handsome, hard-working, and obedient. That all of his sons were just about as worthless as turds in the street would have come as a complete shock to the man. Oh, he knew they'd all been in a little trouble now and then—just boyish stuff like rape and assault and murder, that's all. Nothing that his power and money couldn't fix. When a good boy rolled in the hay with some Mex slut or some squatter's bitch, even if some people did call it rape, well, that really didn't count for nothing. Class will always tell. He looked at his sons and smiled.

"You boys just stay back here with me and let the hired hands handle this," Big Ben told his sons. "If any Mac-Callisters is taken alive, I'll let you boys horsewhip 'em 'fore we hang 'em. How's that?"

That was fine with the boys.

Real nice boys.

Jamie waited in front of the saloon and drank coffee. Morgan had told him all about the Barlow clan, and none of it had been good. Big Ben and his boys had been having their way with folks in this area for years. Not so much with the people of Taos, for men like Kit Carson and some of the other mountain men who had made Taos their home wouldn't have put up with that for five minutes. But in the tiny villages and the lonely farms and ranches outside of town, people seemed to be open game for the Barlow boys. When the Barlow boys saw a woman they wanted, they took her by force, sometimes in front of the girl's parents. In other cases, they beat the husband senseless and then took turns raping the man's wife and/or daughters, and the age of the girls seemed to make no difference to them. The boys all alibied for the other or Big Ben bought the accusers off or killed them, whichever was the easier at the time. And it didn't make a damn bit of difference to Big Ben.

Then the Barlows tangled with a MacCallister. They would have been better off shaking hands with the devil.

Big Ben didn't know it, but his empire was about twenty-four hours away from total collapse.

Jamie held his cup out and a man limped out of the saloon, quickly grabbed it, and had it refilled.

"Thank you," Jamie said.

"You're sure welcome, Mr. MacCallister. I hope you kill all them damn Barlows," he added.

"They done a hurt to you?" Jamie asked.

"Killed my boy, stole my cattle, trampled my garden, shot my wife down like a rabid dog, and then took sticks of wood and broke both my legs so's I couldn't work no more."

"He is telling you the truth, Señor MacCallister," one of the town's Mexican doctors said from the saloon entrance. "And he is only one of many the Barlows have destroyed."

"I reckon me and my boys will have to change all that," Jamie said after taking a sip of coffee.

"You are a man of supreme confidence, Señor," the doctor said.

Jamie shook his head. "No, sir. I just know right from wrong, that's all."

Eight

Jamie watched as two men did their best to act normally as they tried to slip into the south part of town. Ian leaned out of a doorway and busted one on the side of the head with a rifle butt. He dropped like a stone. The second man whirled around and Matt conked him on the head with a piece of wood. The Bar-B hands were dragged out of sight and trussed up. Another Bar-B hand, after seeing what had happened rushed out into the street, his hands filled with guns. Morgan nearly cut him in two with a shotgun blast from his bed in the doctor's office.

Jamie watched it all as he leaned against an awning support porch in the shade and sipped his coffee.

A half dozen Bar-B hands, who possessed more than a modicum of common sense, met in the livery and had a very brief discussion concerning what they figured would be the fate of Big Ben and his sorry-assed sons . . . and anybody who rode with the Barlow clan. The last time the six of them were seen they were riding north and not looking back.

"Dennis and half a dozen more just rode out," a hand reported to Barlow.

"The rest of the men?"

"They're stayin'. They like it on the Bar-B."

They should, they were all drawing top wages, had good

living conditions, and were well-fed. And up to this point, a Bar-B brand meant they could ride rough-shod over anyone they chose and could expect no trouble from the law.

"It's time the people in that damn town learned who's the boss hoss around here," Big Ben said, settling his hat firmly on his big square head. "Let's ride in an' take it."

A young boy, probably about the same age as Falcon, came running up the side of the street to a sliding breathless halt by Jamie's side. "They're coming, Mr. MacCallister!" he panted the words. "All of 'em. Looks like a whole army riding into town."

"Thank you. Now get out of the street, son."

Jamie picked up his sawed-off shotgun just as the first wildly tossed pistol shot from the Bar-B riders reached him.

"That's my horse you shot, you son of a bitch!" a citizen shouted at the mob of riders.

Hugh Barlow laughed and shot the citizen in the belly. The man's wife started screaming that her husband was shot and one of the town's doctors left the saloon on the run, his little black bag in his hand.

The Mexican doctor stepped out of the saloon to take a break from patching up the wounded Bar-B riders. "Nice people aren't they, Señor MacCallister."

"Wonderful," Jamie said, cocking both hammers of the sawed-off shotgun. "Now get back inside. The lead is about to fly."

"And you are invincible, I suppose?" the doctor asked.

"No. I'm just a warrior."

"Someday you must explain that to me," the doctor said just as the Bar-B riders rounded the corner. The doctor stepped back inside.

Jamie lifted the 12-gauge and pulled both triggers,

clearing four saddles. Across the street, Morgan let his Colts bang, as did Ian and Matt. Twelve men lay dead and mangled and wounded in the street.

The Bar-B riders, including the boss and his sons, wheeled their horses and got the hell gone from that part of town.

Outside of town, Big Ben assessed the situation and found it not to his liking. He had ten men dead, about fifteen wounded, and two captured. He stomped around in a circle kicking and cussing for a moment, then turned to a rider. "Get back to the ranch. I want every hand we have here with me. Strip the range. We can round up the cattle later. Ride!"

"Drag the wounded out of the street," Jamie told a group of citizens standing under the awning, looking in awe at the carnage the MacCallister family had just wrought in Taos. "But leave the dead."

One citizen looked up at the clear blue sky. "It ain't gonna take 'em long to get ripe in this weather, mister."

"They'll cool down come the night," Jamie said, picking out the empty shells and shoving fresh ones into the tubes of the sawed-off.

There was a reason Jamie wanted the street littered with the dead. No matter how tough and hard the men Barlow had working for him, very few would deliberately ride their horses over the bodies of men they had worked with and fought with and with whom they had endured all sorts of hardships.

While the crowd was working to drag in the wounded, Jamie told his reasons to Dr. Medina.

The man shook his head. "Perhaps I see now a bit of what you meant by being a warrior."

"Perhaps," Jamie replied and walked across the street

to see about his sons. Few men other than mountain men knew what the Warrior's Way meant, unless they had been seized as children and adopted by Indians as Jamie had been.

"You all right?" Jamie asked Morgan.

"Fine as frog hair," Morgan replied. "You mind pourin' me another cup of coffee, Pa? It's kind of hard for me to get around on this bum leg."

His son's cup refilled, Jamie checked on Ian and Matt, who had barricaded themselves in shops. He told both of them the same thing. "Get out of these stores. It's going to be in the streets from here on in and you don't want to get yourselves hemmed in."

"What about Morgan?" Ian asked.

"Let him finish his coffee and then we'll move him. He's too vulnerable where he is. Right now, let's get us something to eat. We might not get another chance for hours." The Indian philosophy: eat when you can, drink when you can, rest when you can, for you might not get another chance for a long time.

"Where are we movin' Morgan, Pa?" Matt asked.

Jamie grinned. "To the second floor of the saloon."

"Now see here!" the owner of the saloon blustered as Morgan limped in on the arm of Ian. "It's bad enough having my place turned into a damn hospital. But this is—"

"Shut up," Jamie told him. He flipped him a hard-boiled egg from the free lunch counter. "Use your mouth on that."

The owner looked at the egg, then shrugged his shoulders and began to peel it.

Morgan safely installed in an upstairs room with plenty

of water and sandwiches and good protection from stray bullets, Jamie and sons stepped out into the waning light of late afternoon.

"We'll each catch a few hours' sleep," Jamie said. "You boys go on and get some rest. I'll wake you in a couple of hours. There isn't going to be much sleeping this night."

Taos, usually a wild and woolly place when the sun went down, was strangely silent when night spread her cloak over New Mexico.

Ben Barlow, for the first time since the MacCallisters rode into the town, was finally showing some fighting sense. Under cover of darkness, he began sending men into the town in small groups. The men threw a circle around the block housing the saloon and several other businesses. But there was no sign of any MacCallister.

Jamie had left his position in front of the saloon and was now standing in an alley between a saddle shop and a Mexican apothecary. He saw two men with rifles step out of an alley across the street and called, "Here I am, boys." Then instantly dropped belly down on the ground.

The quiet night was shattered by heavy caliber rifle fire. From across the street, Jamie's Colts barked and the two men went down and did not move.

A Bar-B rider got separated from his partner and ran right into Ian. Ian's knife flashed in the dim light and Big Ben Barlow was minus one more man drawing fighting wages.

Jamie could hear boots scuffing the ground behind him and knew then that Barlow had ordered his men to circle the block. He took the sawed-off twelve-gauge and crawled on his belly to the rear of the alley. He saw several dark shapes slipping along and fired both barrels waist high. He immediately rolled to his right, but no returning fire came his way.

Matt was standing by the side of a dress shop in the darkness of the alley when two men suddenly appeared at the rear. Matt's Colts flashed fire and smoke and lead and Big Ben's payroll was further reduced.

Nick Geer, Ben's foreman, walked up to his boss on the south end of town. "This ain't worth a damn, boss," the foreman said bluntly. "At last count we got about sixteen dead, fifteen or more wounded, six who rode away, and two captured. At this rate, we won't have nobody come daylight."

"There ain't but four goddamn MacCallisters in that town," Ben Barlow raged. "That means that a lot of the townspeople have joined them against us."

The foreman shook his head. "No, sir. It don't mean that a'tall. There ain't nobody in that town fightin' us 'ceptin' Jamie MacCallister and his sons."

Big Ben Barlow went into another of his rages, stomping around, kicking, and cussing. It was inconceivable to him, a man who had been the undisputed Bull of the Woods for years, that only four men could do so much damage. "They got help from somewheres," he said, finally calming down enough to speak.

The foreman said nothing in rebuttal. He knew there was no point in it. Nick also knew that there was no good way to tell the boss that about half the men left were talking of quitting and pulling out. There was also no way to tell Big Ben that all the right was on the side of the MacCallisters and all the wrong on the side of the Bar-B. The foreman walked away into the night without saying another word.

All through the night there were brief flare-ups of fighting in the south part of the town. Jamie's face was cut by flying splinters, Matt took a bullet burn on the upper part of his left arm, Ian got creased on the right leg, high up on the outer thigh. But Barlow suffered four more dead and six wounded during the night. That brought the total to twenty dead, twenty-one wounded, two captured, and six gone.

Big Ben Barlow was very nearly out of men willing to fight and die for him.

In the grayness of pre-dawn, Ben looked at his top hand, Miles Swift. "How many men are left, Miles?"

"Eight. The rest pulled out about twenty minutes ago."

"Where's Nick?"

"Gone. He left with them others. He give me a message for you." Miles hesitated, not looking forward to this a bit.

"Well, say it, goddamn it!"

Miles took a deep breath and plunged ahead into the unknown. "Nick said we was all wrong and the community and the MacCallisters was right. Said he wasn't havin' no more to do with lyin' for them goddamn worthless sons of yourn and wasn't takin' no more part in hurtin' innocent folks who just was tryin' to make a go of things. He also told me something else. He told me to tell you to take your boys and to go right straight to hell with them."

Miles braced himself for the blow-up, but it did not come. Ben was silent for a moment. He took several deep breaths and clenched and unclenched his big fists. "You know he's been filin' on land that I claim, don't you, Miles?"

"Yes, sir, I do."

"Some of the boys who left with Nick, they goin' to work for him, eh?"

"Probably."

"What do you think about this situation, Miles?"

"I ride for the brand, Big Ben."

"Come hell or high water?"

"That's about it, I reckon."

"You think that I've been wrong in some of the things I've done, Miles?"

Miles gave that some thought. "I think we could have backed off some, yeah."

"You ever had any children, Miles?"

"None that I know of."

"Then you wouldn't understand about a man and his sons. Besides, there are two kinds of people in this world, Miles. Just two kinds, and that's all. Big dogs and little dogs. Call it leaders and followers. I'm a big dog and I damn well intend to stay that way."

Miles almost told the man that big dogs get buried in the same ground as little dogs but thought better of it.

"At first good light we go into town and call the Mac-Callisters out, Miles. Pass the word. Hell, it's sixteen to four, man. We use our heads, we can't lose."

"Right," Miles said, with about as much enthusiasm as a man about to stick his hand into a den of rattlesnakes.

Nine

Jamie and his sons had each caught a few hours of good sleep and several additional cat-naps, and all felt refreshed. They met with Morgan on the second floor, and over many strong objections from Jamie, Morgan's leg was rebandaged by Dr. Medina and Morgan limped down the steps and over to a table. During the night, four of the wounded Bar-B men had died and the rest of the wounded had been taken to another location where they could receive better care. The saloon floor had been mopped and the tables put back in some sort of order.

Jamie had breakfast sent over from a nearby cafe, and he and the boys ate well and drank two pots of coffee. Then they checked their guns and stood up. A local rushed into the saloon and said, "Most of the men Big Ben had left done pulled out, Mr. MacCallister! But they's still fourteen or fifteen of them ridin' in right now. They'll be puttin' their horses up at the south livery. Least that's what they usually do."

"Thanks," Jamie said. "Have a beer on me."

"Don't mind if I do."

Another citizen rushed in. "Ben and his boys and some of his hands is comin'. On both sides of the street, huggin' the buildin's close."

Jamie tossed money on the bar on his way out. "Give him a beer, too," he told the bartender.

As soon as he had pushed open the batwings and stepped outside, Jamie pulled his Colts and drilled the first two men he saw coming his way with rifles. Morgan threw a chair through one of the front windows and dropped two more, just as Ian and Matt, who had gone out the back way, reached the front of the alley and opened up.

Miles Swift caught a .44 ball in the hip that turned him around and sent him crashing into a dress shop. He got all tangled up in bolts of cloth and spools of thread and ladies bloomers and other unmentionables and was fighting and cussing to get clear when the owner of the shop bopped him on the head with a flatiron and Miles was out of it. The only thing that prevented him from suffering a fractured skull was his hat.

Jamie took aim and plugged Andy Barlow in the belly. Andy sat down hard in the middle of the street and started squalling. Hugh ran over to help his baby brother and Ian drilled him through and through. Ben, Jr. screamed his outrage and ran toward Matt, who lifted a .44 and dropped him gut shot in the street. Jamie put two .44 caliber balls in Royal at the same time Morgan turned his shotgun loose on Chris and almost blew him in two. Guy lifted his guns and Jamie brought the last of the Barlow boys down just as a shotgun boomed off to his left. He turned to see Big Ben Barlow's face disintegrate from the blast. He fell back headless onto the street. The farmer whose family had been killed and whose legs had been broken by Ben and his boys had shot the big man at nearly point-blank range with a goose gun, using both barrels.

"The son of a bitch finally got what was due him!" the crippled man said.

It was over.

Jamie did a little fast work (call it cold intimidation) at the land office and arranged for the survivors of those who had been run off their land to receive about a thousand acres each of what had been the Bar-B. Since there were no heirs, that was easily done, once Jamie got his point across to the man at the land office. Then Bar-B cattle started disappearing. Within a week, the range was bare of cattle. No one seemed to know what in the world happened to all those cattle.

Then the great house that Big Ben Barlow had built caught fire one night, and the next morning, only the rock walls remained. When the army came in to investigate, no one in the town seemed to know just what had happened to Big Ben and his sons, or where they were buried. Since few people liked Ben Barlow anyway, the army investigating team closed the book on the incident and forgot about it.

But for years afterward, in homes and quiet corners of saloons, people spoke of and chuckled about the MacCallisters and the Battle of Taos.

Jamie and his sons waited until Morgan was able to ride then headed back to their valley. Kate immediately put Morgan to bed in his old bedroom and fussed over him for a time, even though Morgan was ninety-nine percent healed by the time he arrived back in the valley.

Morgan pulled out in the middle of the summer, heading back to his job with the army, after a long visit with family and friends. Wagon trains continued to roll westward, with a few angling south off the Oregon Trail to settle in MacCallister's Valleys. And the twin towns of Valley, Colorado, were officially established. During the summer of 1852, an election was held and Matthew was voted in as sheriff. The trail between the two valleys was widened and became a road. In 1853, Indian wars flared all over the west as more and more settlers poured westward. But the wars were hardly noticed in Valley. Indians came into the twin towns to trade, and there was never any trouble, due in no small part to the fact that both sides respected the other's way of life and made no attempts to change it. Valley was one of the few areas in the west that never experienced a single Indian attack in all the years of its existence.

In 1854, Jamie and Kate MacCallister would celebrate their thirtieth wedding anniversary. They were both forty-four years old and still looked fifteen years younger. Early that same year Morgan was named Chief of Scouts for the Army. In the spring of 1854, just after his fifteenth birthday, Falcon MacCallister killed four men in a stand-up shoot-out in Wyoming.

Falcon was born in the high country and was as much at home in the mountains as a puma or an eagle. True to his word, shortly after his twelfth birthday, he never went back to school, but he still loved reading and always carried a couple of books in his saddlebags wherever he roamed, which was all over the new territory. Like all his brothers, except for Andrew, Falcon was well over six feet with a heavy musculature. His eyes were a cold pale blue.

He wore his blonde hair long and favored buckskins. He carried two Colt Navy revolvers, .36 caliber, around his waist, two more on specially made holsters on his saddle, left and right of the horn, butt to him for a quick grab, and two more in his saddlebags. Falcon roamed at will and got along with most Indians, adopting their ways and learning the languages. Falcon was heading home to see his folks for the first time in over a year when he paused at Fort Laramie in Wyoming to buy supplies and catch up on news.

He paid a courtesy call on the commanding officer to inquire about his brother Morgan.

The commanding officer smiled at Falcon as he sized him up. He pegged Falcon at about twenty or so. "You're a MacCallister, all right, lad," he said. "The family resemblance is uncanny. But you missed Morgan by a week. He's out on an expedition." The commanding officer's smile faded. "You going to stay long around here?"

"Just long enough to buy supplies and rest for a time and eat food I didn't cook. Why, sir?"

"You ever hear your dad tell the story about a man named Jack Biggers?"

Falcon laughed. "Oh, yes, sir. That's the fool who tried to ride Horse."

"He and some of his men are in this area. They frequent the trading post about three miles south of here, on the river."

"I thought Biggers was a known outlaw."

"Oh, he is. But I have no warrants on him. He's a slick one, Falcon. He's smartened up considerably since his early days out here. Claims he has a gold mine and is just a law-abiding, hard-working man."

"You believe that, sir?"

"Hell, no. But I can't prove otherwise. Jack Biggers hates your father, Falcon. So do yourself a favor and stay away from that trading post."

"No disrespect meant, sir, but I go where I please."

The officer smiled and leaned back in his chair. "Somehow, that doesn't surprise me. You see, I knew your father when I was in Texas years ago. No, that is exactly what I thought you would say."

Falcon rode up to the trading post on the Laramie River and loosened his guns in leather. Falcon, like Morgan, didn't exactly look for trouble, but he wouldn't back away from it, either. He knew that Jack Biggers and his brothers hated his father and had sworn to kill him. Falcon just figured he might be able to take some of the strain off his dad's back, that's all.

He stepped inside the log building and let his eyes adjust to the dimness before moving toward the bar. He ordered coffee and a plate of food.

The man behind the counter narrowed his eyes as he stared at Falcon. "Boy," he whispered. "You be a Mac-Callister for shore. That's Jack Biggers and some of his gang over yonder at the far table."

"I thought I smelled something rank in here," Falcon said, deliberately raising his voice.

"Shit!" the man behind the counter said.

"That's the odor, all right. Seems to be coming from over yonder." He pointed toward the four men at the far table, who by now were looking at him.

The counterman moved swiftly to one side, out of the line of fire.

"Got to be another one of them goddamn MacCallisters," Jack Biggers said, standing up. "That whore you call a mother drops you whelps like the bitch dog she is."

Falcon shot him twice, one ball taking Biggers in the chest and the next one tearing out a large part of his throat. The three men with him grabbed for their pistols and the old trading post rocked with the heavy reports of gunfire.

The counterman would later say, "That there young feller, he just stood there, both hands filled with them Colts of his'n and he didn't bat airy eye. He just quick as lightnin' hooked and drawed and 'fore I knowed it, all four of them men was dead on the floor. And I'd just swamped out the place 'bout an hour 'fore the shootin'. I thought I never would get all the blood up."

Falcon walked over to the mess in the corner and looked down at the bodies. He stood there for a moment and calmly reloaded. Then he turned and walked to the counter.

"Bacon and beans and coffee and flour," he told the badly shaken counterman.

The counterman, who had spent the better part of twenty years in the wilderness and had survived Indian attacks and had witnessed the acts of both the best and the worst of men, later told the commanding officer of the fort, "I never seen nothin' like that young man. Cold as ice, he was. I'd not like to have that young man as an enemy."

Falcon paid for his goods, walked out of the store, mounted up, and rode away without looking back.

After listening to the man's comments about the shooting, the commanding officer of the post looked south for a time. "And another legend begins," he muttered.

Sitting with his dad on the front porch of his parents'

home, Falcon told his father what had happened up in Wyoming. Falcon was not aware that his mother was standing in the doorway listening. Jamie did not immediately reply. He finished his coffee and set the cup on the floor.

"Jack Biggers has brothers and other kin. They'll be coming after you, son."

"I reckon so," the boy replied.

"What are you going to do?"

The young man looked at his father. "You mean will I run? You know better than that, Pa."

"Maybe I'll take a ride with you, Falcon. Would you like that?"

"Sure would, Pa."

"That's settled then. You stick around here for a couple of weeks, and if the wind is blowing wrong, word will get to us. Then we'll decide what to do."

"Leave Ian and Matt out of it, Pa. They've got kids to raise."

"All right. Falcon, How did you feel after you shot those men?"

"Truthful, Pa?"

"Yes."

Falcon gave that a long moment's thought. "I guess satisfied, Pa."

Jamie expected any one of a whole host of replies, but certainly not that one. It took him aback for a moment. "Satisfied, son?"

"They were murderers and outlaws." Then he told Jamie what Jack Biggers had said about Kate.

Jamie sat in silence for a moment longer. "He really said that about your mother?"

"Yes, sir. And he was right ugly-soundin' when he said it, too."

"Then I reckon satisfied is a good way to feel about it, son."

Ten

Even Cort had to admit that Page was a beautiful child. But he would never permit himself to touch her, which suited Anne just fine, especially since she had caught her brother and her husband naked in the same bed in Ross's home. There had been no big screaming scene. Anne had known for several years that Cort and Ross were having a homosexual affair, and during those years, she had planned and schemed and done it very well indeed.

While Cort had been busy scrambling for his clothes and her brother laughing at the whole situation, Anne had told her husband how it was going to be and would brook no argument unless Cort wanted his reputation ruined.

The upshot of it was Anne was now probably the richest woman in all of Virginia . . . and it was all going to be in writing. With Cort's parents now deceased, the entire plantation, the small town not far from the plantation, the saw mills, grist mills, horses, cattle, everything now was split right down the middle. Anne and Page would never want for anything.

Cort had, unbeknownst to Anne, seen to it that the second baby, adopted by Georgia and named Ben Franklin Washington, was cared for . . . and cared for well. He had quietly shifted Georgia and her husband Rufus to easier work and better quarters. The boy might well be a nigger, but to Cort's fair mind, he was *his* nigger . . . the phraseology something only a Southerner of the time would understand.

It scared Georgia and Rufus half to death to know that Master Cort knew the boy was his own, but Cort, in his gentle way, quickly put them at ease. Cort also felt that war was looming in the not too distant future, and he was realistic enough to know that when it erupted, the south would lose. Cort had traveled extensively in the north and was awed by the population, the factories, and the spirit of those above the Mason/Dixon line.

Cort had matured much since the death of his parents and the shock of knowing he had married a half-breed. But he also knew what he was and had accepted his sexuality. Anne's brother had not done so and because of his indecision was in no small degree of constant torment.

"You watch my sister, Cort," Ross had warned him. "She's a viper. If you're not careful, she'll strip you bare and leave you without a penny."

"I am well aware of that, Ross. More than you realize."

"What about your quarter-breed son?"

Cort looked at his friend and lover. "He'll be taken care of."

"Would you like him on the railroad?"

"Beg pardon?"

"The underground railroad to freedom up north."

Cort sat down on the edge of the bed. "What do you know about that, Ross?"

"Oh, a bit."

"I couldn't have anything to do with it."

"You wouldn't even know when it happened."

"Then do it."

"You'll never see the boy again," Ross said.

"That would probably be a blessing for all concerned."

"Then consider it done."

Sparks had not visited Valley for almost a year, and Jamie was beginning to wonder if anything had happened to the man when early one morning he rode in. He was tired and so was his horse. He swung down from the saddle and gratefully took the cup of coffee Kate handed him.

"I'll bring out a plate of biscuits and a bowl of gravy," she told him.

"Obliged, Kate." Sparks took a swallow of coffee and said, "We been riding relays to get here, Jamie. What do you know about a man named Louis Layton?"

Jamie shook his head. "I never heard of the man."

"He's a lawyer."

"Lawrence Laurin," Jamie said.

"Beg pardon?"

"That's the true name of the lawyer who was all tied in with that big shot rich man from New York, Maurice Evans, the one I killed in San Francisco. Lawrence Laurin, Louis Layton. If I had to take a guess, I'd guess it was the same man. Why?"

"Well, word I get is that he's now a wealthy and powerful man in Washington, D.C. He's in cahoots with some fancy-pants politician out of Louisiana name of Jubal Olmstead. They've contested your right to claim these valleys. The fellers I talked to who just come out here from Washington say that Layton and Olmstead don't have a leg to stand on, but it's going to cost you a lot of money to defend your claims. They aim to bankrupt you and ruin you that way. And if they can't do it that way, they've bankrolled a gang to try to kill you—again."

Jamie smiled and then chuckled. Sparks looked up from his biscuits and gravy. He wiped his mouth with the back of his hand and asked, "You know something I don't?"

"They'll never bankrupt me, Sparks. I could probably buy and sell the both of them and damn sure wouldn't miss the money. What gang?"

"John Wilmot and his bunch."

"Names from the past, honey," Kate said, taking a chair on the porch.

"Yes. I thought we'd seen the last of that crew. Which way you heading, Sparks?"

"East. Over to the army post on the Arkansas."

"Take a message to be posted to St. Louis?"

"You bet."

"What do you know about this gang?"

"It's big. Wilmot brung together a lot of small outlaw bands operatin' out of the wilderness, usually preyin' on small wagon trains and the like. I know some names. The Biggers Brothers, Buford Sanders, Pete Thompson, Rodman, Barney Saxon and some kin of his, and a big thug called Tiny. You know them boys?"

"Every one of them," Jamie said with a sigh. "Well, this time I end it. Once and for all time it's going to be over. Once I do this, Kate and I will live in peace and never leave these valleys."

Sparks smiled. "Don't bet on that, Jamie."

Jamie cut his eyes. "Now it's my turn to ask if you know something I don't."

"War."

"War? Out here. Who's going to be fighting?"

"There's gonna be a war 'tween the states, Jamie—north against south."

"Slavery?"

"That's part of it. States' rights, mostly, 'way I hear it."

"States' rights?" Jamie said softly. "What the hell is that, Sparks?"

"Durned if I know. But a lot of folks in the southern part of the country is right upset about it."

"What does it have to do with Jamie?" Kate asked.

"Well, there was a big shot officer come out to Fort Laramie a couple of months back. I disremember his name right off. Plant or Gant or Grant or something like that. He wants Jamie to be a part of the United States Army . . . in case the States go to war agin each other."

"I'm not interested," Jamie said quickly.

"That's what Morgan told him. But this officer said you'd hear the call of freedom when and if all this happens and come flyin' to hep on wings of eagles. He was a right poetic feller, when he wasn't drinkin' whiskey or smoking the most terriblest smellin' cigars that ever stunk up a room."

"I'm still not interested. I don't hold with slavery, but the federal government's got no right to tell states what they can or can't do. You let that happen and in a hundred years this nation won't be fit for a decent man to live in. Besides, slavery won't last much longer. Fifteen, twenty years at the most and it'll be gone. The government doesn't need to start a war over it. That's the problem with government. You let it get too big, and before you know it, it'll be in everybody's lives."

Kate patted Jamie on the arm and smiled. "I have an idea. Perhaps you should be in politics, honey. You do turn a nice phrase."

"Good God, no, Kate. I'm too honest and too blunt to be a politician. Well, if a war comes, it won't touch us out here. Now then, Sparks, let's talk about this gang."

It had to be one of the most disreputable gatherings of the dredges of humanity to ever congregate west of the Mississippi River. There was not one spark of decency in the whole bunch. John Wilmot felt he had chosen well. He looked over his motley crew and smiled; there were the Saxon boys, and kin of Jack Biggers, Buford Sanders and Pete Thompson had brought their gangs in, Tiny Bates, the huge oaf who cursed the name of Jamie MacCallister daily was there with his sinister-looking band of brigands and cut-throats. When the call went out along the hoot-owl trail, a man named Rodman had answered it, bringing with him a half dozen thoroughly disgusting bits of jetsam and flotsam of what might pass for humanity.

All in all, John thought with pleasure, it was quite a nice gathering.

"I didn't think we was leavin' so soon, Pa," Falcon said, watching his dad snug down the ropes on the pack frame.

"We're not leaving," Jamie replied. "I want you here with your mother. You know Morgan can't come home. He's up in the Dakotas for the Army. Ian's got his hands full with nursin' that busted leg of his. He can't even get out of bed. Matt's got to tend his fields and his cattle and horses. That leaves you to take care of your mother. And I'll brook no argument, Falcon."

"You won't get none, Pa. I'll take care of Ma right and proper."

"Your Ma and me said our goodbyes, boy," Jamie said, sticking out a big hand. Falcon shook it. Jamie swung into the saddle and picked up the reins. "I'll see you when I get back." He rode off toward the northwest without a glance back.

Kate stepped out on the porch to watch him ride away. Falcon turned to look at his mother. She was still beautiful, although there was a touch of gray now among the gold and maybe a line or two in her face. But her figure would still match that of any woman in the village, of any age. "Don't you ever worry about him, Ma?"

She smiled. "Of course, I do. Just like I worry about you and Ian and Morgan and all the rest of my children. That goes with having a family. Someday you'll see. But for you, I think, that's years in the future."

Kate studied her youngest chick. Falcon looked so much like Jamie at that age it was scary. Strong as a grizzly and not an ounce of back-up in him. And like his dad, Falcon wore his pistols like they were a natural part of him.

For awhile, she was afraid that it would be Ian who would turn out to be a gun man, or "gunfighter" as some eastern writers were now fond of. But Ian had settled right down after marrying Caroline. Matthew had never taken to the high lonesome like his pa or his brother Falcon.

Falcon caught his mother looking at him. "You go on about your business, Ma. There ain't nobody goin' to bother you long as I'm here."

Kate turned quickly, hiding her smile. How to tell her youngest that long before he was born, back on the trail in Arkansas and many times in the Big Thicket country of Texas, she had stood alone or beside Jamie with rifle and pistol and defended hearth and home? Chuckling, she walked into the house and into her kitchen and put on water for fresh coffee.

"What's Ma laughing about?" Ellen Kathleen asked, walking up holding her latest in her arms.

"Durned if I know," Falcon replied. "I just told her that she could go on about her business. That nothing was goin' to happen to her as long as I was here."

Ellen Kathleen stared at her younger brother for a moment and then burst out laughing. Ellen was twenty-nine years old and had vivid memories of how fierce her mother could be in a fight. She had personally witnessed her mother chase off curious bears with a broom and had seen her back down a swamp panther. She had also seen her mother kill several men. She was still laughing as she climbed the steps and entered her parents' cabin.

Falcon stared in disgust at his sister. "Damned if I'll ever understand women!" he said.

Eleven

"Once and for all," Jamie repeated several times a day as he headed toward the spot where the gangs were supposed to have gathered, awaiting word from Layton and Olmstead. "I'll settle this once and for all."

But he really didn't believe his own words. The feud between Jamie and Kate's father and brothers and kin, as well as the Newbys and the Saxons had been going on for far too long. It would only end when one side or the other—all of them—were in the grave. And Jamie had to smile at that. It would take some doing to kill off all the MacCallisters and their kin. It seemed like Jamie and Kate had more grandkids running around the twin towns of Valley than nuts on a pecan tree . . . with more on the way.

Jamie had to give lawyer Layton his due. He had chosen men who knew the west and knew it well, for the area where they had chosen to gather, while not that many miles from the twin valleys as the crow flies, was a tough three-day ride for a man on horseback. It was also perfect ambush country.

For them, as well as for me, Jamie had to keep reminding himself.

As he rode, he tried to pull up into his memory the faces of some of the names Sparks had told him. He could remember with some amusement the face of Barney

Saxon, the man who had accused him of stealing money and who had suffered a busted mouth for that remark. He could recall some of the others but not all.

For a short time, he toyed with the idea of calling John Wilmot out and trying to reason with him. But he soon gave that up as a very bad idea. He had tried to persuade other men to give up the hunt for him and always failed with the leaders.

The letter he had given Sparks would reach his attorney in St. Louis, and the lawyer would handle matters on that end, quickly putting a stop to Olmstead's attempts to seize the twin valleys. Olmstead was going to be in for quite a shock when he came face to face with Jamie's lawyer, one of, if not the, most powerful men in the state and well-connected in Washington.

The ride took longer than Jamie anticipated and it was mid-morning of the fourth day before he began to smell the cook-fires of the gang. He immediately began searching for a place to picket his horses and found one after an hour's searching.

He let the horses roll for a time, and when they had cooled down, he let them drink and then they settled down to graze. Jamie picketed them on a long rope, with plenty of room to walk to water, and shouldered his heavy pack. He figured it was about a two-hour walk to the gang's campsite.

"Once and for all," Jamie muttered, as he took the first step on foot to the smoky little valley where the men who had gathered to kill him were camped. "I end it today, Kate. And that's a promise. After today, we start living the remainder of our lives in peace."

* * *

Bob Sutter looked up from his plate of beans and venison and stared at the end of the clearing for a moment. He could have sworn he saw the figure of a man standing there. A man dressed all in buckskins. "Impossible," he muttered and returned to his eating.

Joe Ed Williams was pouring a cup of coffee from the big pot when he paused for a few seconds. He stared at the timber for a moment and then shook his head. "Not likely," he muttered.

One of Buford Sanders's gang thought he heard one of the horses whinny. He raised his head from the blanket he was using as a pillow and listened hard. Nothing. Must have been his imagination. He laid back down and dozed off.

Jamie had cut the horses' halter ropes from the picket line and was slipping around the camp, listening to the men talk. He wanted to be absolutely certain. When he saw Tiny Bates he knew he'd found the gang.

"I want that honey-haired wife of MacCallister's," Tiny said. "And by God I'm stakin' my claim for her right now. Anybody got anything to say about that?"

No one did. They were, to a man, thinking and talking about all the other women in the twin towns of Valley and of all the booty that would be theirs for the taking once the raid was over and done with. They were quite vocal about what they were going to do with the women and the men, and none of it was pleasant to the ears.

When Jamie had satisfied himself that this was indeed the nest of vipers he had come to destroy, he did not hesitate in starting the job at hand. With fully-loaded pistols hanging all over him, Jamie stepped out to the edge of the clearing, a Colt in each hand, and started cocking and firing. It was a rolling thunder of death in the beautiful wilderness of northwest Colorado. Jamie would empty one brace of Colts, holster the empties, hook and draw, step out of the thick whirl of gunsmoke that hung around him, and continue the deadly fire and thunder into the knotted up camp of raiders.

When he had emptied eight Colts, Jamie ran back into the timber and quickly began the job of inserting freshly charged and fully loaded cylinders into all his pistols. Behind him, he had left a camp of death and pain. But he wasn't nearly through just yet.

He still had some snakes to stomp on.

Jamie had poured forty-eight .44 caliber balls into the camp and had personally witnessed two dozen men go down in the first fusillade. The cut-loose horses had panicked and bolted during the attack and by now were a good mile away and still running hard. A dozen had run right through the camp, destroying supplies and doing no small amount of damage to any man who happened to be in their way.

From where he knelt behind a small rise, Jamie could hear the crying and moaning of the wounded in the ruins of their camp . . . and the hard cussing of others.

Jamie flitted through the brush and timber until he had circled the camp, coming to rest on the opposite side of where he had launched the first attack.

"The goddamn hosses is gone!" a man yelled.

Jamie lifted a .44 and drilled the man about three inches above his belt. Without hesitation, he emptied both pistols into the still startled and confused camp and then changed positions again.

Jamie's philosophy of warfare was simple for this day: just attack until you defeat the enemy. He watched as several of the would-be raiders grabbed up blankets and a few supplies and hit the timber, running in the opposite direction of the gunfire. He let them go. It was the leaders he wanted.

"Rally around me, men!" a man shouted, a pistol in each hand.

"Go to hell, Thompson!" another man shouted, and ran for the timber.

"Coward!" Thompson shouted and shot the running man in the back.

Jamie leveled a Colt and plugged who he assumed to be Pete Thompson in the belly. Pete sat down hard and tried to lift his pistols. He gave up that idea after a few seconds and toppled over on his face.

A few of the men had found their horses, or somebody's horse, and were hightailing it out of that area. When the sounds of hooves pounding the earth had faded, Jamie lay in brush and listened to the sounds of what remained of the camp.

"Yeller-bellied, red-nigger-coward!" Tiny Bates shouted. "You ain't got the balls to fight lak a man, goddamn you, Jamie MacCallister!"

Jamie lay motionless and silent in the brush.

"He's gone," a man said.

"Don't you believe that," Rodman said.

The moans and cries of the wounded were fading as the badly hit died and most of the less seriously wounded kept quiet, not wanting to draw Jamie's fire.

"Oh, dear sweet baby Jesus, help me!" a gut-shot man screamed.

"Somebody shoot him," Wilmot said.

"Damn you, John Wilmot!" the wounded man cried.

Jamie heard the sound of gunfire coming from south

of where he lay and couldn't figure out what was happening.

"Jamie MacCallister!" came the shout, and Jamie recognized the voice of Lobo. "We got this camp circled, friend. We found your camp and left fresh venison. Get on back to your hosses and put on some coffee and get them steaks a-cookin'. We'll take care of the rest of these hyenas."

"You didn't think we was gonna let you have all the fun, did you?" Preacher shouted.

Big Jim Williams yelled, "They's a dozen of us out here, Jamie. You done your part, now let us take care of the rest of it."

"Can we deal?" John Wilmot shouted.

"At the end of a rope, you damned worthless ne'er-do-well," Audie yelled.

"Have to it, boys!" Jamie shouted. "I'll have coffee on when you finish." Jamie headed for his horses, glad that his part was over.

"Wait a minute!" Tiny Bates hollered. "You ain't hangin' me, you bastards!"

"Then we'll just shoot you," Preacher said. "That's faster, anyways."

"I protest this!" Buford Sanders squalled. "This ain't right!"

"Take it up with the Lord," Lobo yelled. "'Cause you ain't far from comin' eyeball to eyeball with Him."

Jamie found several of the raiders' horses and led them back to his camp. He had sliced the venison, started it broiling, and was just dumping in cold water to settle the coffee grounds when the last shot rang out.

Preacher rode in out of the silence and swung down. "It's over, Jamie. You and Kate can rest easy for a time."

"Where are the rest of the men?"

"They ain't civilized like me. They're takin' scalps."

"What's that hangin' on your belt?"

"Well, hell, I only took *one!*"

Twelve

The next five years were peaceful ones for those who called Valley, Colorado, their home. But turbulence rolled and rumbled all around them. The United States congress began setting spending precedents that all future congresses would follow: in 1855 they appropriated thirty thousand dollars to import 30 camels from Egypt to settle them in the western deserts. One hundred and thirty-five years later, congress would spend nineteen million dollars of taxpayer money to study cow farts.

In 1856, the first bridge across the Mississippi River was built, running from Rock Island, Illinois, to Davenport, Iowa. The first real blood-letting of what would in a few years become an all-out civil war between the states erupted in Kansas Territory as Missouri pro-slavery forces—including the Kickapoo Rangers of Colonel Buford—attacked and burned Lawrence, Kansas. Later that same year, John Brown, along with his sons and a few other men, murdered five pro-slavery men at Pottawatomie Creek in Kansas. John Brown was later hanged for that. In July of 1856, Fort Lookout was built on the Missouri River in what would someday become South Dakota. By November, when Buchanan defeated John Fremont in presidential elections, the nation had begun to tear apart along pro-

and anti-slavery issues and talk of war was strong. In the south, uniforms were secretly being manufactured.

In 1857, the U.S. Supreme Court, in ruling on the Dred Scott decision, declared that Congress had no right to deprive people of their property without due process of the law. The Butterfield Overland Mail Company was awarded a contract to provide mail and passenger service from St. Louis to San Francisco.

"Imagine that," Kate said, laying down her weeks-old newspaper. "Just get on a coach and ride all the way from St. Louis to San Francisco."

"How long will it take?" Jamie asked.

"About a month. The coach goes from St. Louis to Memphis then down to Texas then over to Los Angeles and San Francisco."

"I want to ride the steam cars," Jamie said. "Preacher said they were fearsome things. He said they can roll along faster than a puma can run and do it all day long and all night long without ever stopping."

"Preacher tells big wackers, too," Kate said, adjusting her reading glasses.

"He swears it's the truth."

Kate laid aside the newspaper and picked up a catalog, staring disbelieving at a full page ad of ladies modeling the latest in corsets and bustles. "That's *disgraceful!*" she said.

Jamie leaned over for a peek. "Looks pretty good to me."

Kate hit him in the head with the catalog and knocked him clean off the porch.

* * *

In 1857, the last mile of track was laid connecting New York City with St. Louis, Missouri.

In May of 1858, Minnesota was admitted to the Union. A modern mowing machine was patented, as was a machine that could bundle grain.

In 1859, Oregon entered the Union, the thirty-third state and the eighteenth non-slave state. Nearly everyone east of the Mississippi River now sensed that a terrible war between the states was inevitable. *"Pikes Peak or Bust"* became the new slogan as gold was discovered in Colorado. Jamie found that mildly amusing; for the past four years he had been steadily mining his claims and caching the gold. Using just a fraction of his wealth, he bought up all the twin valley that had not been staked out and much of that which had been claimed. At the opening of the National Women's Rights Movement in New York City, Susan B. Anthony, in her address, stated, "Where, under our Declaration of Independence, does the white Saxon man get his power to deprive all women and negroes of their inalienable rights?" Sam Houston became governor of Texas.

The *Rocky Mountain News* began publication at Cherry Creek, later to be called Denver. The *Weekly Arizonian* began publication in Arizona.

In 1860, the Pony Express was started and Abraham Lincoln was elected president of the United States.

In the spring of 1860, Morgan rode into the valley for a visit. After his brothers and sisters and all their kids left the homestead, Morgan said to his mother and father, "Falcon's gettin' quite a name for himself."

"As what?" Kate asked.

"A gambler and a mighty slick gunhand. Killed two men during a card game up at Cherry Cheek. They accused him of cheatin'."

"Was he?" Jamie asked.

"No. He don't need to cheat. He's that good with a deck of cards."

"Did he take any lead?"

Morgan laughed shortly. "Hell, Pa, them ol' boys didn't even clear leather. He's swift, mighty swift." He fell silent, staring out into the night.

"Say it all, Morgan," Kate told him.

"I don't know what you mean, Ma."

"You want me to slap you?"

Morgan chuckled. "No, ma'am. I shore don't. You always could read me like a good book. It's Falcon. He's says when war comes, he's fightin' for the Gray."

"The Gray?" Kate asked.

"That's the color of their uniforms, Kate," Jamie told her.

"The Blue and the Gray," Kate whispered the words. "But Falcon never expressed any dislike for negroes."

"Oh, he doesn't dislike negroes, Ma. How could he, him growin' up here? He just says the federal government don't have the right to tell states what to do, that's all."

"I agree with Falcon," Jamie said, after a moment's pause.

Morgan stirred uneasily in his chair at his father's words. The exploits of Jamie Ian MacCallister were already the stuff of legend. Books had been written about him and songs had been sung. A play about his life was still running on stages all over the country. Morgan knew that the Union Army wanted his father to join their ranks as a scout.

"But I'll not fight against the Stars and Stripes," Jamie finished it. "I'll just not fight at all."

Morgan relaxed somewhat.

"That's a very wise choice," Kate said, patting her husband's arm. "You're getting entirely too old to be traipsing around the nation fighting." Jamie and Kate were both fifty. "Is Falcon going to come home for a visit before he goes off to join the southern army?" Kate asked.

"No, ma'am," Morgan told her. "By now he's in Texas. He said to tell you both that he'd come home after the war."

"Too *old?*" Jamie questioned.

Morgan smiled and Kate ignored her husband. Except for some gray in Jamie's hair, he had not aged much in twenty years. There still was not an ounce of excess fat on him and he could still work men half his age right into the ground and then some.

"I'm too *old?*" Jamie repeated.

"Hush, dear," Kate said. "The war will be over and done with before the first news of it reaches Valley."

How wrong she was about that.

"You're a damn fool!" Anne Woodville told her husband. "I can't believe you're actually doing this."

Cort stood before her, resplendent in his tailored uniform of gray and gold. He had been commissioned a captain in the Army of Virginia.

"It's something I had to do," Cort defended his actions. "Besides, the war will be over and done with in no time. The Yankees can't whip us."

"What about Ravenwood?"

"What about it? You're doing a fine job of running the plantation. You're a good businesswoman, Anne."

"Thank you for that, Cort. Would you like to see your daughter?"

Cort hesitated. "No. I think not. I just stopped in to see you and to say goodbye. I've received word that we are being mobilized. Texas has seceded from the Union. Virginia can't be long in following." He stepped forward and took her hands in his. "Goodbye, Anne."

"Goodbye, Cort. Cort? Be careful. And take your scarf, please. You know how easily you catch cold."

Cort nodded and turned away, walking out the front door of the grandest plantation house in all of Virginia.

On March 31, 1861, a contingent of Texas troops, with Falcon MacCallister as scout, attacked Fort Bliss, and after a brief battle, the federal troops surrendered.

On the 12th of April, Confederate troops opened fire on Fort Sumter, South Carolina. The Civil War, as it was called in the North, begins. In the South, it was known as the War Between the States.

Less than a month later, Sparks rode into the valley with a message for Jamie.

Jamie looked at the sealed envelope. It was from the White House. He carefully broke the seal and read the letter twice. He handed the letter to Kate. She read it, then nodded her head and stood up.

"I'll go pack some things for you."

"I reckon so, honey," Jamie said.

Neither one of them knew quite how to refuse a request from Abraham Lincoln, the president of the United States.

WILLIAM W. JOHNSTONE
THE ASHES SERIES

FICTION BY WILLIAM W. JOHNSTONE

BREAKDOWN   (0-7860-0367-7, $5.99)

HUNTED   (0-7860-0194-1, $5.99)

THE LAST OF THE DOG TEAM   (0-7860-0427-4, $4.99)

PREY   (0-7860-0312-X, $5.99)

TALONS OF EAGLES   (0-7860-0249-2, $5.99)

DREAMS OF EAGLES   (0-8217-4619-7, $4.99)

EYES OF EAGLES   (0-8217-4285-X, $4.99)